HEX, LOVE, AND ROCK & ROLL

KAT TURNER

Hope that you love the story!

Kt♡

CITY OWL
PRESS

HEX, LOVE, AND ROCK & ROLL
Coven Daughters, Book 1

CITY OWL PRESS
www.cityowlpress.com

Cover Design by Mibl Art. All stock photos licensed appropriately.

Edited by Tee Tate.

For information on subsidiary rights, please contact the publisher at info@cityowlpress.com.

Print Edition ISBN: 978-1-64898-010-7

Digital Edition ISBN: 978-1-64898-009-1

Printed in the United States of America

PRAISE FOR KAT TURNER

"A fledgling witch finds love with a mature rock star in the midst of occult danger in Turner's magic-heavy debut and series launch. Turner sets up a promising world that readers will be pleased to return to in subsequent installments. Paranormal fans should check this out."

– Publisher's Weekly

"Hex, Love, and Rock & Roll is clever, witty, and captivating from chapter one. Helen and Brian pull you into their world and refuse to let you go. It is utterly a bewitching love story that has it all: chemistry, mystery, *love*, but most of all– rock and roll."

– Jaqueline Snowe, Contemporary Romance Author

"Fantastic, vivid writing and great characters make for a fun, sexy, emotional paranormal riff! Get Hex, Love, and Rock & Roll as soon as you can!"

– Celia Juliano, Sexy, Heartfelt Romance Author

To all of my teachers

ONE

HELEN SCHRADER HATED WITCHES. AFTER ALL, THEY'D GOTTEN HER thrown into foster care. But as her thirtieth birthday approached, she sat across from a supposed witch named Nerissa and worked up the nerve to ask her for a spell. Funny how the past refused to die.

Pentagram knickknacks and a crystal ball collection decorated the old lady's living room, along with vintage furniture and a framed art print of three women mixing brew in a cauldron. A bookshelf full of texts on witchcraft, world religions, and philosophy completed vivid testimony to authenticity.

People all over Minneapolis swore the crone could conjure fast cash. The pagans who took classes at Helen's yoga studio spoke of Nerissa in the reverent tones of worshipers.

Perhaps the universe began orchestrating the current turn of events when one of Helen's students walked in on her crying over unpaid bills and handed her Nerissa's business card. Unless her visions from years ago kicked some grand plan into motion.

Did everything happen for a reason?

Though the hardened cynic in Helen scoffed at bullshit magical thinking, an atrophied, softer side not yet demolished by life's cruelty yearned to believe in synchronicity and magic.

Sweat glued her jeans to the backs of her thighs as she adjusted her weight on the sofa cushion. She could stand to do some Zen breathing to calm her nerves. Besides, she'd run out of options to save her business. Her credit was shot, so no more loans. But Light and Enlightened would not become Dark and Forgotten without a final, radical attempt at salvation. Time to take one last shot at rescuing the only permanent home she'd ever known. Throw a Hail Mary pass. She met Nerissa's keen blue eyes and managed a smile.

The universe has a plan. Everything happens for a reason. You've got this.

You are fucking idiot and a loser who is destined to fail.

"You have an impressive book collection." Helen picked a chip in her nail polish as if repetitive motion would banish negative thoughts. "I'm not sure if you got my email about your fee for today. Does twenty dollars work? I'm so sorry I can't offer more."

A lopsided smirk deepened the wrinkles in Nerissa's cheeks. She petted the arm of the leather recliner she sat in and uncrossed her legs beneath a maxi skirt. A knowing tone smoothed the kinks in her low timbre as she said, "Is that why you made an appointment? To discuss literature? Or did you mention the books as a way of confirming my legitimacy?"

Helen drew in a deep inhale and willed the room's sage scent and mellow lighting to relax her before she blundered another attempt at small talk. "Just curious. I've read some of those books. Not the witchy ones, but the Sartre and Nietzsche. 'That which does not kill me makes me stronger' was my motto for awhile. I have an undergrad degree in philosophy. Sorry. I'm rambling."

Yikes, she was a hot and simmering mess. Intelligent aliens were welcome to zap her with a space laser and implant competence into her brain.

Without a word, Nerissa rose. She walked across the living room to the bookcase and ran her finger across spines. "Don't sell yourself short. You have more than an undergrad degree, you started a doctorate. You're smarter than you think, and I can assure you that failure is not in your destiny. Let's have a peek at my favorite book. It's one of the *witchy* ones."

Helen's heart seemed to jump to her throat, and an icy ribbon threaded up her spine. Nerissa must've figured out the facts about her education through research. The other part? Mere coincidence. A nervous laugh bubbled out with her next words. "Is my aura that strong? You practically read my mind."

Nerissa's gray braid swished back and forth as she turned her head over her shoulder. A twinkle in her eye caught slices of afternoon light streaming in through gaps in the drapes.

"There's no *practically* about it. My ability to access your surface thoughts is a sign of our spirit-born connection. I see magic swirled into those beautiful amber irises of yours, too. You are gifted, but we can't step into our deepest truth until we believe in ourselves."

Helen snorted when her stomach went sour. She'd been called a lot of things over the years, but gifted wasn't one of them. Mind reading amounted to an easier sell. This woman was patronizing her due to some ulterior motive. Everybody had one.

"Oh, please. If I was gifted, I'd have more to show for myself by now. Behold, my impressive roster of accomplishments: a pit of debt, a retired stripping career, and a useless degree. Not exactly ticking off boxes on those 'things every woman should have by thirty' checklists."

The self-flagellation lashed Helen to the bone, and her trusty armor of sarcasm didn't protect her from those whip stings. She covered her face and trained her gaze on an area rug, not looking up until the floorboards creaked.

A massive tome in her hands, Nerissa ambled back to her chair and sat. "There will be bigger birthdays if you're lucky. I still remember the sixties. Woodstock. I was the girl in a famous picture, twirling and twirling. I slept with *all* of those rock stars and enjoyed free love."

Heat spread under Helen's breastbone, tightness squeezing her midsection. Was the 'rock stars' comment a sly knock on Helen for falling for the musician ex who cheated on her with every available groupie? A catty little mind-reading trick of Nerissa's?

Whatever. With her life circling the drain, she could not endure head games. Lisa still refused to speak to her. Bad news for a business partner or best friend, let alone both. She had major problems to solve and not a minute to squander.

"Cool. Sounds like fun. I'd like to talk about your services now. My business goes in to foreclosure next week, and my closest friend blames me. I need money. You can do wealth spells, right?"

A grating guffaw rolled out of Nerissa's throat. She opened her volume and leafed. Pages warped from water damage and crowded with words offered coy peeks at possible solutions.

"Patience isn't among your virtues. Hence your tendency to act before thinking and leave projects unfinished. But your drive is noble, and your will is strong. You dare to chase success by any means necessary, which I admire. Takes gumption to sell the spectacle of one's naked flesh to keep the lights on, and don't beat yourself up about the studio. There's a yoga place on every block these days. Lots of entrepreneurial young women such as yourself are losing their shirts teaching Downward Dog."

Helen clamped her teeth down on the tip of her tongue and swallowed a snarky comeback. Not wise to risk alienating the witch. Better to summon tact and diplomacy.

Nerissa hummed a tune while reading.

Helen tapped her foot. She needed to hit the road before traffic became a zoo, and the final notice of foreclosure stuffed in the bottom of her purse wasn't about to dematerialize.

"Finding any good abundance spells?" The fake-casual lilt in Helen's tone prompted her to roll her eyes at herself. She sucked at tact and diplomacy.

"I want to try an experiment." The gray-haired woman flipped to the front of her book and touched a circle inked on the inside of the cover.

"Alright. Sure." Helen snuck a peek at her watch and squirmed.

"This grimoire was an inheritance from my foremothers. My coven daughter will inherit my sacred text from me to learn the spirit witch's craft and begin the work of the six-fold sisterhood. The spirit element is the most cerebral of the six circles."

God, enough with the pointless anecdotes. Nerissa might have all day to meander, but Helen did not. "Whoever she is will be lucky. Like I said, I'm broke as a joke—"

Another laugh from the old witch made for a jarring interruption. "You may be the *she* in question. Here's a free lesson. Your defeatist tendencies stem from fear of finding your true power, so you self-sabotage in an effort to make yourself less threatening. I understand. We wise women have been taught by the patriarchy to hate our gifts."

Helen ground her molars. Aggravation shot through her in a frying jolt. Cash, not a feminist lecture, would solve her problems. She grabbed her purse off the couch and jumped to her feet. "This was a mistake. I assumed—"

Nerissa muttered in some throaty, incomprehensible language. The old woman's eyes rolled back in her head. Blank slates of white remained.

Breath vanished from Helen's lungs. The bizarre sight and sounds boggled her imagination until skepticism intervened. Nerissa's eyeball move could be a trick, a result of training ocular muscles.

"A trick? I don't deal in cheap parlor tricks, dear. Now let's see if you are the one."

A pop sounded in Helen's ears. She blinked a few times as a dazed, sleepy sensation disoriented her. Lost to pleasurable mugginess and an odd feeling of time slowing to a crawl, she didn't snap back to lucidity until she noticed the cauldron painting again.

The painting was upside down. No. Correction. *She* was upside down, hanging in midair.

Blood roared in Helen's ears while she scrabbled unsuccessfully to reclaim control of her faculties. A scream tore its way up her throat but somehow died before erupting. Electric with panic, she flailed, spinning in a dizzy circle. A few chaotic seconds later, she recovered some semblance of her bearings and managed to stay still despite waves of queasiness.

The room returned to focus as blurs of color reformed into bookshelves, furniture, and other familiar shapes. *Almost* familiar. Her perception was weird.

Helen gaped when she figured out was was wrong with her surroundings. The furnishings and Nerissa were below her. She was stuck to the damn ceiling. To make matters weirder, another woman now stood in the spot she'd occupied, someone in jeans identical to Helen's.

Shock slammed into her as a realization dawned. She wasn't looking at a third person. She looked down at herself, her own body, while her consciousness floated above. Brunette waves streaked with blonde highlights tumbled over her shoulders. At least she was having a good hair day, because the out-of-body experience blew her mind. Separation from her physical form had been the last thing she'd been expecting during the visit.

A coil of phosphorescent light spiraled upward from the middle of the open book while the witch chanted, "Coven daughter, come to me. Show us truth and clarity."

Discombobulated, Helen squinted against a glare. The beam bent and twisted into a hoop. The space in the middle of the illuminated circle glimmered. Images appeared. A highlight reel of her life played while she gawked.

Nerissa pulled from Helen's memories and projected them at her. *Now* her mind was blown. What else could this be besides hardcore magic?

"I can help you, Helen, but you need to listen. Can you?"

She ought to get in line and embrace the insanity, or she'd soon be begging Dreamgirls to let her hump their germ-infested pole again. Hard pass on the humping. "Yes."

Helen crashed back into her physical form with a boom, knees weak and mind spinning. Reeling from the loss of control, she plopped her butt on the couch and shook herself out of a daze.

"Did your mother and grandmother have the gift?" The witch's eyes returned to normal.

Mother. The sound of the word was profane, like the filthiest curses flung at her.

What should have carried a connotation of loving nurturance dredged up a memory of the time the mother in question shrieked about original sin while she forced Helen to eat the pages of her diary. Recollections of the incident still scraped her raw with phantom pain. She should have learned to stop talking about her visions after that day. Or after the next morning, spent whimpering on the toilet.

"I didn't know my grandmother. My mother had major issues."

"You never had a mother figure who embraced your gift. Tragic." A soft tremble rounded the edges of Nerissa's words. "The visions began at the onset of your menses and lasted for years, didn't they? Trances? Seizures? Mine showed up at menarche and didn't leave until I mastered my craft."

Wow. One other person on the planet could relate to her secret.

"One foster family returned me because my episodes scared their pet rats. Yep. I ranked below rats." She spoke the words in a jesting tone, but the long ago rejection still made Helen's chest ache with old hurt.

"Rats are inherently nervous creatures. Let your pain go and describe the episodes."

"Speaking in tongues, chattering teeth, muscle spasms. Visions of spinning out of my body and flying through the air, seeing women burning at the stake. Wild times. Of course none of my temp families believed me." Helen shrugged, over-affecting nonchalance as the uncomfortable topic poked at her insecurities. Too weird and too spacey. Dissociative. Broken. Bad girl, crazy bitch.

"Flying through the air. Oh, yes. You are spirit born."

For the first time, Helen settled back in her seat, her muscles loosening, curious to know more. "Okay, so I'm spirit born. What should I do to save my studio?"

"You must choose a path to proceed on your actualization."

"Excuse me?"

"To actualize means to coax your abilities to the surface, where you may direct and control them. The power you possess is dormant and churning in your subconscious, so you endured episodes. When witches repress what we do best, we suffer."

Helen put her hands up, palms facing out. She could accept the idea of having some psychic abilities, but being a witch...the notion stretched the limits of plausibility. "Hold up. I don't think I'm a witch."

A shadow passed across Nerissa's eyes. She leaned forward in her chair, close enough for Helen to smell her rosy perfume. "Are you calling me a liar?"

"No. It's difficult to take in, though."

"Why? You came to me for help, and I'm showing you how to get what you want. But if you've changed your mind about needing money, this can end right here." Nerissa closed the book with a definitive snap.

"I'm not quite convinced is all. What's in this for you?"

"When witches practice, our powers enhance each other. Mine will grow in relation to yours. So while I wish to help you because I care about the spiritual health of my coven daughter and want to see the sisterhood come to fruition, I'm also being a teeny bit selfish."

Outlandish, but what if Nerissa was right? God, the possibilities for turning her life around. She hadn't taken a chance coming to the witch's home only to run out when things got strange. No more quitting, no more failure. Time to nut up or shut up.

"Fine. I'm all in. You were saying. Initiation. Spirit element. Smash the patriarchy with our broomsticks. How do I choose a path?"

"Your choices are Right Hand or Left Hand path. The Right Hand path draws from your internal strengths and abilities, in your case latent color magic. Astral projection and remote viewing would also come from marshalling the Right."

"How does color magic work?"

"The expression is unique to the witch. You'd call out to meaningful colors in your life and weave emotional union with them to perform spells."

"Such as visualizing the color green for money."

Nerissa shrugged. "If you're thinking long-term, sure."

The words "long-term" bounced around in a series of bothersome echoes. Long-term might not suffice. "What's up with the Left?"

"Left Hand powers originate from outside. Think transferring energy into objects in order to manipulate them, or splitting your psyche so as to exist in two places at once. The Left is potent and capable of producing immediate results, but also volatile and dark."

A surge of curiosity charged through Helen. She scooted to the edge of her seat. Potent power and speedy results could save L&E before the bank snatched it away and Helen and Lisa trudged out carrying boxes.

Helen had slunk out of many front doors with tears in her eyes. Never again.

She pursed her lips, though, wavering at what volatile and dark might mean. In all likelihood, something bad. Yet depending on inner strengths didn't seem like the right move, not when one of Helen's dumb mistakes all but catapulted the studio into the abyss.

"Have you chosen?" Nerissa drummed her fingers on the book's cover.

Bottom line, she could not afford to wait. "I choose the Left Hand path."

"There will be a cost." Nerissa rose and offered Helen the grimoire.

"What is it?" Helen accepted, her arms straining under the book's weight.

Nerissa walked to a credenza. Jars filled with liquids in a variety of colors cluttered the top. Helen watched with interest as the old lady rummaged in a drawer.

The elder witch returned with a small sack made of black velvet and a jar half full of clear fluid. She handed over the pouch. "Depends on one's constitution. Could be as trivial as a stomachache."

Helen took the bag, taking a moment to stroke the silky material. She loosened a string and peered in. Crystals in a rainbow of colors sparkled one after the other as if they communicated. "But it could be worse."

"Oh, yes."

"What's the worst case scenario?"

"If the universe decides the darkness wasn't yours to take, it might generate a hex as punishment for selecting the wrong magic. Think karma, but magnified tenfold."

Helen's insides dropped. "Hold up. I don't need more trouble. How would I deal with a hex?"

"Read your book. That's the answer to all of your questions. But first, deploy the crystals. They are sentient and absorbent, and the clear ones are the most pliable and receptive to their witch's will. Give both clear stones away to good people before you undertake your study, as cultivating others' energies will refine your powers. Make sure to set a mental intention before gifting this pair of crystals. Done correctly, this means giving each one precise directions. Otherwise, the hex might begin with dark entities latching on to one or both stones. Once demons establish communion, they can possess crystals."

Yawning, Nerissa thrust the jar at Helen. "Drink this and leave. The Reveal spell I did drained my energy. If I don't get my nap in, my weakened state could compromise you."

Though her pulse accelerated, Helen took the container and unscrewed its lid. She chugged, gag reflex lurching as she downed the sour glop. Her eyes watered, and nausea roiled her insides, but she finished the nasty potion. Go big or go home. "So twenty bucks is okay?"

"We'll settle up down the road." The old woman's eyelids fluttered closed as she sagged in her chair. "Study now."

A rush of pride prompted Helen to straighten her spine. She could be a decent student. Armed with a big book of witchiness and the crystals, she placed her empty jar on a coffee table and sauntered to the front door of the bungalow with her head held high.

The plan: give away two crystals, figure out magic, get L&E solvent, and save her dearest friendship. Doable? Helen smiled and hugged the grimoire to her chest. Hell yeah.

"*Sacrificium.*" A calm, male voice spoke inside of Helen's head. An itchy surge of adrenaline shot to her toes. Though she'd never taken Latin, she sure got the gist—sacrifice.

Her hand tensed on the doorknob, and she glanced at Nerissa. "Did you hear that?"

"No!" Nerissa bolted upright. Her mouth dropped, and her eyes stretched wide, but the show of fear in her expression fled as fast as it came.

Helen's mouth dried. Talk about a bad omen double whammy. "Are you okay?"

Rubbing her temples, the elder looked around the room. "I'm fine. Take care."

Helen jetted to her Mini Cooper. As she fumbled for her keys, a plume of milky smoke erupted in the recesses of her consciousness, vanishing a second after it arrived. She tried to disregard the inexplicable intrusion. Probably just her magic settling in.

She drove to the Minnesota State Fair, but by the time she squeezed between two cars in a dusty makeshift lot, she hadn't managed to forget the creepy voice and smoke.

A definitive slam of her door shoved the unsettling events out of her mind, and she strode to the flapping banner marking the entrance to the fairgrounds.

Today belonged in the win column, damn it.

TWO

AS SHE APPROACHED THE ROW OF TICKET BOOTHS, HELEN NABBED Lisa's number from her contacts and pushed the green phone receiver icon. The fantastic surprise in store would kick off reconciliation. Let the healing commence.

After three rings, Lisa answered with a sigh. "This better be an emergency."

Helen swiped the foreclosure notice from her purse and crumpled it into a ball, the crunch making a big grin split her face. She chucked the wadded paper into a recycling bin, nailing the shot from five feet away. Boo-yah, three points for the Hel-ster. "Even better. Dontcha know it, I'm a decent businesswoman after all."

Lisa laughed without mirth. "I don't want the details."

"Yes, you do. Meet me at the fair as soon as you can. I'll be near the grandstand."

Helen crossed her fingers. She and Lisa had hung out at the fair every year since the one where they'd bonded over deep-fried chocolate chip cookies while cheating on the austere vegan diet prescribed in yoga teacher training. With any luck, the setting would put Lisa in a mindset conducive to repairing their bond. Convincing her partner to believe the witch news? A bigger challenge. Helen would tackle the whopper when it arose.

"Whatever, fine, I'll be there in thirty minutes." Lisa hung up.

High on victory, Helen stepped to a cashier's window.

An employee with a mullet took her money and pointed back and forth between them. He wore a T-shirt identical to hers. "We're fan twins. You must be here for the show."

Hell, yes. She'd put on her Chariotz of Fyre concert shirt, honoring classic hard rock at its finest. Fyre's biggest-band-in-the-world status had downshifted to encompass the state fair circuit, but Helen and Lisa still adored them without a trace of irony. Long live the New Wave of British heavy metal. "You betcha. Rock and roll completes the state fair experience."

"I know one of their roadies. Find a girl with pink dreadlocks. Name's Marley, and tell her Buster said she'd hook you up with backstage passes."

The universe was showering her with positivity. Even her surroundings radiated optimism. Notes of cotton candy and ride grease perfumed the air. A late August sun relaxed into a long-shadowed afternoon, kissing St. Paul with golden blush. People laughed. Upbeat music blared. Angels in heaven sang the Hallelujah chorus. Best day ever.

Helen gave Buster a giant grin. How long since she'd smiled like this? Weeks? Not since she'd thrown a sleepover potluck at the studio and the community had turned up with blankets, laughter, and scrumptious dishes to share. "I'll do that, Buster. Thank you."

He winked. "What can I say? I hook up my peeps."

Helen set off into the fairgrounds. Squealing children catapulted down an inflatable yellow slide the size of a house, and shrieks belted from a nearby roller coaster looping upside-down.

She wove through packs of people schlepping stuffed animals and enormous cups of fountain pop, making a beeline for the grandstand's empty bowl of bleacher seats. The crowd thinned, booths giving way to littered grass. As she picked up a plastic bottle and shoved it in an overflowing recycling can, Helen spied three black buses and a semi-tractor trailer behind a row of porta potties.

A young woman, pink dreads swinging, lugged black cases down the big rig's ramp. Helen rubbed her hands together. Hello, Marley.

One of the bus doors opened with an airy hiss. Two men walked down the steps, and the sight of the taller one caused Helen to freeze.

Holy shit. None other than Brian Shepherd, Fyre front man and legendary silver fox. A ball cap covered his short hair, and aviator sunglasses hid his eyes, but she recognized his chiseled, clean-cut jaw from television.

Another guy, balding and with fuzzy caterpillars of sideburns crawling down the sides of his face, handed Brian a small bronze envelope.

Brian stuck the paper square in the pocket of a black leather jacket well-worn enough to look cool.

Damn. Brian was a sight, glowing with the greatness suited to a rock icon. Helen changed course and walked to him. Hey, she was a witch now. Might as well own her inner ferocity. She had to open with a decent line.

"If you are taking requests tonight, I'd love to hear 'A Thousand Suns.'"

Brian turned to Helen and slid impenetrably dark glasses down his nose. She looked up into turquoise eyes as inviting and enveloping as a dip in the Caribbean Sea. A friendly smile curved his lips, emphasizing deep dimples and high cheekbones belonging on a male model.

"That experimental B-side? I'm impressed, love. Didn't think anyone but me cared for the track." He spoke in a velvety English voice quickened with what she swore was relief.

The other man scowled.

Huh. Maybe Brian was relieved to have someone else to talk to besides Mr. Sideburns. In that case, Helen was happy to volunteer as a tribute.

"Are you kidding? Your guitar solo was fit to charm maidens in a mythical forest. The Zeppelin influence was strong. 'Suns' got me though final exams." No lies detected. Rocking out to Fyre saved her broke ass big money in therapy bills during college.

Brian chuckled and pocketed his shades. "You've gone and exposed yourself as too young for me, darlin'."

Eh, whatever. His handsome face bore the lines of a traveling musician's life and aligned with his age. Probably late forties. He sported the attractive kind of wrinkles, though. Webs at the edges of his eyes, smile brackets highlighting full, sensual lips.

"Are you fishing for a compliment? You rock onstage, and I'm sure fan girls still swoon hard for you. There you go. You're welcome, Brian Shepherd's ego. FYI, I've been out of college for seven years."

"Noted. Shall I sign your shirt, or do you have a ticket stub?" Brian pulled a marker from the back pocket of his faded jeans, dropping a quick gaze to her natural double-Ds before reclaiming eye contact.

Tingles glimmered below her waistband. It didn't bug her when desirable guys noticed her boobs and yoga-sculpted body. Besides, she'd be remiss not to enjoy the rock god's attentions. Today called for whimsy and fun.

"Sure, but I was actually hoping for a couple of backstage passes."

Brian yanked the pen cap off with his teeth and lobbed a playful wink her way. His eyes gleamed, evidence of some naughty thought dancing through his head.

She caught his scent, spicy cloves and citrus laced with musky maleness. Whew. Anyone have a personal fan?

"Are you always this assertive, asking for what you want?" He drew the words out, playing up a rumbling baritone somehow made even sexier by the cap impeding his speech. This man was a flirting ninja.

Before she could reply with a resounding yes, the other dude scoffed. "Don't toy with the groupies like this, Shepherd. Fair Floozies will stick to the tour like dog shit on your heel if you string them along." Contempt oozed from his nasal, Midwestern cadence.

Helen turned to the mean troll in their midst. Jeez, she was playing. Not like she'd go full groupie and offer to blow Brian for the passes.

She planted her hands on her hips and scowled at Mr. Sideburns, spoiler of fun and wearer of ugly facial hair. "Slut-shaming is rude. And speaking of shit, you mixed too much of it into your metaphor. Epic fail."

In a lightning-fast move, Brian capped the end of his marker and jabbed a finger in Mr. Sideburns's chest, towering over him and getting in his face. "I've had it with you today. Quit hassling my fans and go make me some money."

Unable to help herself, Helen stuck her tongue out at the balding jerk. A teeny, kittenish peep.

His face reddened. "Fine. I'm heading to the Wyoming ranch later to square away some details for the Bronze Phase party. Don't dismiss this, Shepherd. These guys have unorthodox methods, but their results are solid. As you know, you need them more than ever." Mr. Sideburns stalked off, frowning.

Brian took off his hat and ran a hand through short, chestnut hair highlighted silver. Silver, not gray. A distinction that made perfect sense. But a vibe heavier than sex appeal shaped her impression of the rock star. Sadness lurked in his distant gaze. Her heart swelled with a compulsion to erase the distress from his stare and make him smile again.

"Hey, I hope I didn't get you in trouble. I meant what I said. I'm a huge fan of yours. Nobody toggles a whammy bar like Brian Shepherd, in my humble opinion."

He smiled, this one less flirty. But it crinkled the corners of his eyes, so win.

"Thank you. And no worries, I'm the boss around here. I do apologize for Joe. I'm sick of him, but I need his connections. Anyway, yes, of course you are invited backstage. Who should I tell my people to put on the guest list?" Tone crisper than before, he replaced his hat, slid the marker behind his ear, and pulled a cell phone from inside of his jacket.

Though bummed to lose their flash of chemistry, she dug this personable, relatable side of Brian. His affable manner put her at ease. No small feat.

"Thank you. Helen Schrader and Lisa Shimizu, please."

"Which one are you?" A sickle-shaped wrinkle split the left side of his face when he spoke, running from the corner of his eye to the middle of his cheek like a tributary carved by a tear.

"I'm Helen." The softness in her tone startled her. Tough to play the part of Ms. Jaded around such a nice and disarming guy. Swept up in a budding sense of affection for Brian, she reached in her purse and scooped up the velvet bag of crystals. She took out one of the clear minerals. As the charm caught bits of setting sun, the plated sides glittered. "This is for positive energy. Have a fantastic show, and I hope tension with your staff blows over."

Brian accepted Helen's offering, stroking her index finger with his. He slipped the charm in the front pocket of his pants. "Beautiful gift from a beautiful person."

She laughed and scratched the back of her neck. "You don't know me."

Brian pinned Helen with a laser beam stare. "A fact I'd love to change. Find me after the show."

"I guess this would be the time to tell you I don't hook up."

While trying to act the part of the badass stripper chick, Helen had convinced herself she could enjoy casual sex and gotten her heart broken. Hence her policy of informing men right off the bat that one-nighters didn't work for her.

He tucked a piece of hair behind her ear, ghosting a callused fingertip over a sensitive spot near her throat. Tickles of pleasure raced over her skin, making their way between her legs. Warmth pooled in her core. Damn Brian and his rock star superpowers, tempting her neglected body and making her rethink a hookup.

"Neither do I," Brian said in his posh, buttercream voice.

Puh-lease. Everyone knew what happened on tour. And in *her* car. Ugh.

"Sure you don't." Though she laid the sarcasm on thick, Helen kept her tone teasing.

"Come round later and learn what I'm all about."

"In case we miss each other, will you sign my shirt now?" Because come on, Brian no doubt met zillions of women on the road. He'd forget her the second a more willing lady offered him no-strings release.

Brian clucked his tongue. "I need to work for your trust, eh?"

Fair statement, B-man.

He pulled the cloth of her shirt taut with one hand and signed a patch of fabric near her shoulder with the other. Brian pulled away, leaving a pleasant recollection of his touch.

"Can I get a selfie?" Helen asked.

Brian threw his arm around Helen and urged her to his body, smooth leather stroking her bare forearm. Helen surrendered her phone, and Brian held his free hand high and snapped a few pictures.

With a crooked smile, Brian broke the hold. "See you later, Helen Schrader."

"After a while, crocodile. And you got lucky that my name rhymes with the first part of the saying." She missed him already. Double-damn this guy.

He handed her the phone. "Hope to see you later this evening."

Returning cell to purse, she forced herself not to giggle or grin like an idiot. What a player. Best to forget him. She didn't pine over men or even date anymore. Narcissists and others of the asshole persuasion flocked to Helen. They smelled her damage and manipulated her accordingly. No worries, though. Single life suited her. More to the point, she had to circle back to her goal of breaking the good news to Lisa and convincing her to accept the more outlandish aspects of it.

"I'll try," Helen said.

"Brilliant. Do that." He took off, moving in a proud, long-legged stride, and ducked around the front of a bus.

A series of sharp pains needled a spot beneath Helen's shoulder, discomfort akin to when she got a tattoo on her foot. The sensation radiated to her clavicle in a succession of pricks.

Helen pulled her shirt forward and looked down at the affected area. Brian's signature, rendered in tidy cursive, bled through the cloth and on to her skin. But the ink wasn't black. It was as red as the blood from a cut.

Before her stunned eyes, his autograph faded to pale pink, then vanished.

"*Sacrificium*." Following the familiar murmur, a cramp clenched her lower belly. She doubled over and gripped her midsection. Spasms gave way to peculiar energy, swirling like a whirlpool in her abdomen. The puff of vapor she'd seen after leaving Nerissa's reemerged in her mind's eye.

Several rhythmic surges rushed from Helen's toes to her scalp. An arch of smoke shot out in front of her face and twisted serpentine curves in the air. It tore a line between the two buses, retracing Brian's steps.

Pieces drifted together. Hands trembling, she got out her phone and checked the selfie. Her insides shriveled and froze. A tentacle the color and consistency of fog crawled out of her navel area and into the pocket where Brian placed the crystal. Like the autograph, the foggy curl faded away.

Shit. Fuck. A grim darkness swirled to the surface, an epiphany of sorts. She'd messed up the intention. It needed to be mental, not verbal, and given to the crystal as an order. The day's intensity must've caused details to slip her mind.

How would she figure out what was happening and how to stop it? No clue. But she always kept a few life hacks and some moxie stashed up her sleeve.

She clawed in her bag, excavated the second clear crystal, and stared at the twinkling rock until a kaleidoscope of multicolored glimmers filled her headspace. *Hi, crystal, this is Helen. I'm your new witch, nice to meet you. Please keep Brian safe and protected from any bad vibes and fog tentacle demons. Be a beacon of positivity. Cancel out bad mojo with good. Thank you.*

Step two: connect with Brian after the show, get the possessed crystal away from him, and give him the new talisman. Next, she'd have to figure out how to exorcize the curse.

Nobody saved her, but she could save someone who needed help. Somehow. Jesus Christ, she'd made a big mistake by failing to set the first intention. A deadly mistake?

Your fault, devil child. Helen's birth mother screeched in her head, the same old hysterical, unstable banshee. She managed to silence the tirade. Her father's suicide had *not* been her little six-year-old self's fault. She could fix this. Brian must not suffer because of her. She was no devil. She was a good person. For real.

A text blooped on Helen's phone.

Lisa: *Hey. I'm at the animal barns. Petting a goat, LOL.*

Her friend's cute message was an obvious olive branch, so she'd better act positive.

H: *Yay! Be right there.*

L: *Looking forward to the good news. Sorry I was a bitch earlier.*

Was the news still good? Complicated at best, because by bungling a supernatural directive, she'd put an innocent person in danger and unleashed a demon.

Shaking her head, Helen walked in the direction of the livestock. How would she reverse the damage caused by her reckless actions?

THREE

BRIAN PULLED THE STRAP OF HIS STRATOCASTER, SLIDING HIS LUCKY guitar to rest against his back.

Grumbling, he shoved a hand in the pocket of his trousers and felt around for the hundredth time. The smooth plastic of his guitar pick grazed his skin, but no stone. He checked his other three pockets, fingers brushing the muscles of his thighs and backside through cloth. No holes through which the charm could have slipped.

Where had Helen's crystal gone? He hadn't taken his pants down or off since meeting her, not even unzipping them to take a slash. How on earth could it have disappeared?

Shifting on his feet at the side of the stage, he retraced his steps. The crew hustled about, tuning guitars and tweaking knobs on towering stacks of amplifiers as they completed last-minute prep. The wardrobe woman passed, wheels of her cart squeaking.

Among an assortment of clothing hung the leather jacket he'd changed in favor of his performance uniform, a white button-down shirt with the top two buttons undone.

A gust of hope lifted his spirit, and he followed the cart.

"Excuse me, love, I need to have a gander at that jacket," Brian said.

He jogged over and rifled through the pockets, coming up empty handed with a sigh. What in bloody hell? How had he managed to lose the good luck token given to him by the first woman in ages with whom he'd cared to spend time? Brian never lost or misplaced things, let alone important keepsakes. Stellar organization preserved his sanity, especially on tour.

Stupid, stupid. Must've been fatigue setting in as the tour reached its final leg, leaving him knackered and prone to making mistakes.

"What are you missing, Brian?" The blond designer looked on with concern while he cursed his uncharacteristic bout of absent-mindedness.

"A crystal. Clear. About the size of a quarter. I *swore* I had it in my pocket." He dove in his jeans again, scooped out the guitar pick, and strummed a few tense chords.

"Huh." She wrinkled her forehead.

"Huh what? Have you seen it?"

"I ran into Joe earlier, and he was acting odd. He was staring at an object in his hand. I thought it was a piece of glass, but I didn't ask because I didn't want to talk to him any more than I had to. He's a sketchy guy, man. Gives the whole crew the creeps."

The wardrobe lady spoke the truth about Fyre's new manager. Brian would tolerate the unpleasant fellow long enough to use Joe's supposed high-powered connections to secure a position in the executive ranks of the music industry. Joe was ace at hustling big shots, and following the humiliating rejection of his proposal earlier in the year, Brian learned the hard way that he needed to *pay his dues* with the label by keeping their favorite minion, Joe Clyde, employed. But why would Joe have swiped the crystal?

"Find him and tell him I need to speak to him straight away. Please."

"You got it, boss." She pushed her rack past a cluster of speakers and behind a lighting grid.

The crew made final adjustments and dashed offstage.

Brian moved stage left, toward the wings, and drew in a centering breath. Barbecue and cut grass smells mingled with electronic smoke, familiar state fair scents returning him to the present moment. The show had to go on.

He walked a few feet to the edge of the curtain, giving himself a view of the crowd.

Despite an unfortunate smattering of empty seats, thousands of people packed the stadium, an army of tan and brown ants spread across the standing rows and curving upward into seats. Golden sunset spilled over bodies, bringing the sheer number of people into relief. They still came out in droves to pour their energy and love into his band, and for that Brian swelled with gratitude. He was a blessed, fortunate man.

His left hand throbbed, fingers stiffening. Sliding the guitar pick between his teeth, he rubbed a persistent ache with his other hand. Despite the many joys road life still afforded—visiting cities, soaking up the excitement of devoted fans, reconnecting with old friends and making new ones—he had to keep in focus his goal of dialing back on touring.

His daughter, Tilly, needed her father present if she was to veer away from her party lifestyle and have any shot at finishing high school and getting into university. He owed her the guidance of a devoted parent. She deserved at least one.

Wincing against pain as he flexed and released his fingers, Brian shored up his determination. His body needed a break. Transferring into the business side of the music industry would stabilize him in Los Angeles and provide physical rest while keeping him close to the rock and roll he lived and breathed. If he had to deal with Joe to achieve his goal, so be it.

A solid smack thumped his shoulder. "You all right, mate?" Jonnie, Fyre's rhythm guitarist, spoke in a measured tone. He turned a dial on his low-slung Fender. The instrument's spiky angles and electric blue hue enhanced its owner's edgy, leather-pants-and-dark-features appeal.

Brian turned to face his closest band brother, catching concern in the man's keen brown eyes. He forced the corners of his mouth to turn upward into a practiced smile. Even his inner circle wouldn't catch the inauthenticity. Not fair to drag Jonnie into his mess. Brian solved his own problems.

"Yeah. Things are a bit cocked up with Joe at the moment. It'll pass."

Jonnie drew his pierced eyebrows together into a frown, silver hoops glinting in the waning daylight. "Heard the latest kooky rumor about our lovely new manager?" His voice dripped with sarcasm.

Brian's stomach flipped. He rolled up his sleeves, adding the

finishing touch to his casual-stylish uniform. News of this Bronze
Phase hobnobbing party and the bizarre invitation the manager handed
him earlier was all of the Joe-related strangeness he could handle for
a day.

Speaking of Joe, the zeal and professionalism he'd shown in the early
stages of their partnership had been in decline for a while now, with the
ugliness he'd unleashed around Helen marking a new low.

He needed the manager on his team and couldn't afford to poison
their allegiance, however. Joe wrangled many clients and no doubt had
problems of his own. Maybe the man was having a bad month, and his
life outside of managing Fyre wasn't Brian's business.

"No, and I have no desire to hear whatever rubbish you're on about."

"I'm not sure you need his help as much as he lets you believe. Really,
it's the other way around. *He* needs *you*." Jonnie's sharp stare suited the
man's preference for brutal honesty. Brian loved that about his
bandmate. No lies, no false flattery, no ego strokes.

"Well, I need the right industry connections for the label to take me
seriously as a candidate for an executive position. Joe has those. Not like
I can launch a solo project and chase my musical dreams." Frustration
lanced through him as he allowed himself a moment to mourn his lost
inspiration.

"Yes, you can. You'll get your mojo back, mate. I'd love to write with
you sometime. Maybe a collaborative effort would rouse the muse from
hibernation."

"I don't think I'm a songwriter anymore. And that's how it is. It's
fine." He swallowed a lump of pain.

Years of blocked creativity had driven him to the brink of madness,
but what to do about it? The words wouldn't flow from pen to page no
matter how he tried to loosen the logjam in his mind and heart. The few
times he'd looked into hiring songwriters, the prospect of outsourcing
what was once his greatest source of fulfilment made him feel like a
failure and a fraud.

Across the floor, a crew lad held up five fingers, giving the countdown
cue. When the last digit fell, Brian and Jonnie strode to their spots in the
middle of the stage. Matching their rock star struts, Thom walked on
from the opposite flank, bass guitar slung low. Jonas peacocked at his

side, twirling drumsticks between his fingers while dreadlocks the color of octopus ink swished from side to side.

A breeze caressed Brian's bare arms, the first flirtation of a fall evening making goosebumps bloom. Three fireflies blinked, a triangle of ethereal green winks enriching middle America twilight. On heady summer nights outdoors, he remembered how much he loved performing live. Despite the loss of his lucky charm, he flowed into the zone.

From the sea of fans, chatter increased in pitch and volume, climbing until it reached a singular, roaring scream. Feet stomped. Men hoisted women on their shoulders. A group raised a banner.

His heart thumped. Becoming a funnel, Brian took in the fans' energy until their love filled his chest. Electricity shot from Brian's center to his extremities as the crowd poured forth their adulation.

Angst drained away as external validation filled him. Worship from admirers would soon leak out of the holes in his soul, but for now it would do. And he'd enjoy this time to the fullest.

He leaned deep into his microphone stand. "Good evening, Minneapolis."

His voice echoed in godlike reverberations that buoyed him with temporary pride. For the next couple of hours, he would play God.

The sight of a certain someone in the third row made his heart skip. Amidst the legion, Helen drew his stare. She hadn't hidden her face behind a cell phone, one of maybe five people in the front rows unobscured by a rectangular object and the ice-white flashes from its cyborg eye. An intriguing glimpse into her personality, how she'd chosen to appreciate the show unmediated.

What a face she had, inquisitive eyes the color of a fine bourbon and smooth skin undamaged by tanning. Her thick, tousled hair and sexy body also pleased his gaze, but qualities more profound than her physical features compelled him.

Qualities more profound, even, than her intelligence and affinity for the exact sort of repartee and banter that kept his mind limber inspired his interest in her. Her personality traits, though, were a definite bonus. Fun, witty people fired him up and made him laugh.

Her assessment of "A Thousand Suns" laid him flat, but he'd managed not to lose his cool and blather this to her like some infatuated fool.

Decades ago, Brian wrote that song in a scrappy wooded area on the outskirts of London, imagining the handful of acres as a secret forest inhabited by elves and magic. He'd stolen every spare moment he could to indulge his sweet escape, descriptions from his favorite boyhood fantasy novels spinning circles in his mind as he daydreamed about composing the next "Stairway to Heaven."

The polished, final version of his imaginative experiment became the Fyre mega-hit "Deep Dark Woods," but its messy prototype, "A Thousand Suns," would live forever as Brian's creative baby.

In other words, Helen had nailed it. Somehow, the woman saw to his depths. She *got* him, even if she didn't fully know or understand the extent.

Though Brian didn't believe in such sappy bollocks as love at first sight, he couldn't deny the significance of the force meeting her had shaken loose. From the moment Helen stepped up to him, she treated him like the person he wanted to be. Authentic. Creative. Thoughtful. Playful.

She reminded him of the man who got lost in the shuffle of touring and recording and staying alive in the cutthroat entertainment industry. The man who lived in full color instead of existing in a dull gray of drudgery. Brian waved at Helen, and she waved back, wearing a demure ghost of a smile.

As he faced this enchanting stranger who sauntered off some Midwestern fairground, the first layer of his outer shell cracked.

Thom tapped his microphone. An electronic squeal punctured hushed, heavy air. A peal of nervous laughter ripped through the crowd, slicing tension.

Pulled from his inspirational reverie, Brian laughed back, hearty and not awkward. Time to play some fuckin' music.

The noise of fans died down into hushed expectation.

The perfect song for Helen arose from his depths. When they'd stood at kissing distance, he'd noticed shards of emerald in her light brown irises. Four in each, symmetrical, like the leaves of a four-leaf clover. In the crimson remnants of sunlight, the golden streaks in her hair sparkled like gemstones. She herself had blessed him. He didn't even need her crystal gift.

He moaned the opening note of an old favorite, playing the accompanying chords.

Jonnie and Thom caught on and supplied the layering riffs. A wave of uproar rushed from the back of the crowd to the front, blasting Brian with unparalleled energetic impact.

Brian grinned at the masses. His mind dissolved as he lost himself in a tune he'd always loved. One he'd long dreamed of singing to a woman. He broke into song, delivering a full-throated, whole-hearted cover of "Crimson and Clover," which he sang directly to Helen.

Women swooned. More people cheered. "Fyre, Fyre, Fyre."

Brian increased the volume of his vocals, grooves in his callused fingers locking in with thick brass guitar strings as he struck chords. Though that chant normally gave him the willies, classic cry-wolf situation, today he cherished the devotion behind it. As his hands moved over the fretboard, a change in his thought pattern pleased him. Perhaps the crevices in his skin didn't symbolize unshakable ruts in his life after all.

A spike of pain stabbed the inside of his right palm, almost causing him to drop his guitar pick. He powered through it, managing not to strike a sour note. Though his joints and knuckles gave him hell on a regular basis, he'd never experienced such discomfort in the meaty part of his hand.

The unpleasant sensation passed with an aftershock, and Fyre rounded out their set of chart-toppers and beloved radio anthems. For the first encore, they brought a performance of "Deep Dark Woods" that drew a standing ovation. He sang "A Thousand Suns" to end the set.

Brian pressed three fingertips to his lips and blew Helen a kiss before bounding offstage to the soundtrack of whoops and cheers. Euphoria streaked across his skin in shivers, livening his nerves and sharpening his senses. Sweat poured off his body and sluiced down his face, stinging his eyes and hitting his lips with a salty tang.

Every detail, from droplets of perspiration and strands of hair catching the glow cast by the overhead lighting grid to the black cords snaking across the floor, popped into sharp relief.

He stuck two fingers in his mouth and whistled at the first crew member he saw. "Bring me a journal and pencil, please."

Why not try a bit of writing? It would take Helen and her friend a few minutes to cut through the clutter and migrate backstage, and with any luck he could scribble some prose in the interim. He handed his guitar to the roadie.

Jonnie swaggered by, unloading his instrument into the hands of his tech. "'Crimson and Clover,' eh?" The twinkle in his eyes betrayed savvy awareness.

Some temporary staff lad reappeared with a spiral-bound notebook and two pens. Weight of the items perfect and comforting as he accepted them, Brian tendered the young man a nod of thanks. In under a minute, he'd filled half a page. "I'm feeling inspired today. Finally. Figured I'd have a go. We'll see if any productivity comes of it."

Brian paused to shake out a cramp in his hand before writing more. God, he was more obvious than he wanted to be. Though he enjoyed flirting with groupies and fans to keep his skills sharp, he was rather picky about who he dated or slept with. If he connected with a woman on the road, everyone knew right away.

Had he made a lasting connection with Helen? Tough to say, but Brian knew one thing: hadn't felt like this since before he'd become famous. By coincidence, also at a fair. A little fair, close to his dorm, where he'd held hands with a girl named Suzy and won her an ugly teddy bear after their first-year classes at Cambridge dismissed. It'd started pissing rain, and they'd run for cover and hid under an awning behind one of the game stalls. He'd been too chicken to kiss her, she being an elite girl and he a gawky and overly tall boy from too close to Scotland, who somehow stumbled into the prestigious university.

Jonnie played with the barbell spearing his left ear cartilage. "What's her name?"

"Someone I met earlier. She's called Helen. If all goes well, I'll bring her round for an introduction later."

"Nice. I'm happy for you." Jonnie patted Brian on the back.

"Thanks." Brian soaked in the warmth of brotherly love, though he hurt for his friend. Jonnie's fiancée, a fellow guitarist, had left him and shredded the bloke's tender heart.

Jonnie's entourage stormed the side stage, a jovial bunch bearing champagne and thirsty for attention, and the rhythm guitarist went to hold court for his followers. Hangers-on wouldn't fill the void inside, but it wasn't Brian's place to lecture anyone.

"Hey." Helen's charming Minnesotan twang ripped Brian from his musings.

The sight of her sent a surge of excitement through his system. At the same time, her calm, earnest presence grounded him. "Hi. You having a good time?"

"Yes. Awesome show, as always." She spoke words of assurance, though heaviness weighed on her tone.

"Are you okay? Where's your friend Lisa?" Had Joe bothered Helen again? If so, the sod could expect an earful.

She moved her jaw back and forth and glanced to the side. "She had to leave. I'm not sure if I'm okay. Can we go somewhere private?"

Concern and confusion twisted through him. "Yes, of course."

Guiding Helen by the elbow with his free hand, he led her down a short set of metal stairs, ignoring the backstage bustle. They crossed the patchy, trampled grass behind the grandstand and passed a cluster of crew members taking a cigarette break.

Helen tossed a glance over her shoulder, walking a few more paces and stopping. A Ferris wheel spun in the distance behind her, illuminated aqua and purple spokes bringing attention to her furrowed brow, the methodical way she attacked a hangnail. She covered her face.

Suspicion crowded out Brian's positive emotions. Why was she acting downright furtive? "What's going on?"

"This is going to sound weird, but I need that crystal. I shouldn't have given it to you."

A mess of embarrassment for losing a meaningful item and resentment that an element of Helen's behavior had to be sketchy tangled his feelings into a knot. "I don't have your crystal any more. It just disappeared. I looked through all of my pockets. I'm so sorry."

Her eyes bugged. "What? You lost it? Shit." Scowling, she picked her fingernail.

This encounter was off in a big way. Why was this crystal so important, such a big deal? Was the stone not hers to give?

"Pardon, I didn't know it came with a two-hour repossession policy, executable at a moment's notice." Though he tried for tart English banter, the comeback came out a bit sharper than intended. Why couldn't he enjoy a relaxed, uncomplicated evening with a woman without the entire thing going all to pot?

"I wish I could explain in a way that made more sense. But things are happening that could harm you. Things outside of my control." Lazy wind made her locks flutter, though her pretty face drooped.

"What are you talking about?" His arms twitched, but he fought a desire to lay hands on her shoulders and ease her duress through comforting touch.

He had a daughter to protect, and some bad news waves rolled off Helen with her odd, garbled warning. Best to keep physical and emotional distance from questionable people. He had plenty of untrustworthiness in his life with Joe's scheming and duplicity.

"I'm not sure." She rummaged in her purse, pulled out the same black pouch as before, and plucked out another crystal. "Please take this. To absorb negative energy. I think the first one has an evil spirit attached to it."

Evil spirit? Brian's chest calcified into a cast of familiar cynicism. A harmless belief in lucky charms was one thing, but evil spirit talk crossed a line. Helen was some manner of New Age kook swept up in her own personal theatre of delusion. She'd seemed too good to be true for a reason, and now he knew why.

He put up his hands, holding the notebook high as he backed away. "No, thank you. Thanks for stopping by the show. Goodnight."

"Please take this. Something terrible is happening. Please believe me when I say I'm doing what I can to help. This crystal is blessed in the correct way. If you find the old one, text or call me before you leave town." In her palm sat a hunk of what looked like glass with a waxy sheen. With her other hand, she thrust a violet business card at him. Cobalt cursive and a drawing of a golden lotus flower decorated glossy paper stock.

Some shameful corner of his companionship-starved self made him accept the paper rectangle and token with curiosity. Helen wasn't like anyone else he'd ever met, he had to grant.

"All right, Helen. I'll search for it and let you know what I find. Enjoy the rest of your evening." Before another glimpse of her beauty or distress stoked his protective instinct, Brian turned on his heel and made haste for his tour bus.

The second he opened the door, a creepy feeling of having unwanted company settled over him. A rotten egg stench fouled the air. Grimacing, he set his writing supplies and the items from Helen on the dashboard. After pawing the spare key from the glove box, he fired up the ignition. Two rows of runner lights flanking the floor walkway came to life, marking the cabin's main path with a soft white glow.

Making his way down the aisle separating a leather sectional couch from a wall-mounted plasma screen television, Brian scanned for evidence of the inconsiderate wanker who'd broken a cardinal rule of touring by taking a dump on the bus instead of using the porta potties.

He found no signs of disruption. No cigarette butts, used cups, or discarded clothing. In the nook making up the bus's lounge, a few shelves of liquor bottles remained untouched.

Following a yank on the accordion door, he peered into the back bedroom. Empty save for the double bed, dresser, and half-bath with a toilet and sink.

The sole object on the granite bar was the metallic envelope from Joe, Brian's invitation to the pretentious Hollywood party.

As post-show fatigue clouded his mind, he walked back down the slim carpet and to the driver's seat and retrieved his notebook and pen. But his inspiration had fled.

After forcing out a few labored sentences, he gave up and set the implements down in favor of staring out the window. A hundred or so feet in the distance, carnival lights spun dark skies into a high-voltage color palette of whirling neon. Had rejecting Helen blocked his flow? No. He'd done the right thing and was simply worn out and tired.

Faint Diesel fumes reminded him Fyre would leave early in the morning, play another city, followed by another. Bleakly, he reflected on how he was a mere windup toy. Entertainment for the masses, playing fairs and arenas named after office supply stores. Delivered from city to city by plane or bus. And the number of state fair gigs crept upward every year. Twice as many this year as last.

A low-grade cousin of dread nipped at his heels. State fairs. Next came casinos. Then what, bowling alleys? Dive bars?

He'd indulged in wishful thinking about the rediscovery of his muse. If he veered off track from his goal of breaking into the executive side of music, a humiliating has-been's trajectory of low-status appearances and dwindling crowds awaited him. Brian refused to court that chasm, that pit of nothing hovering on the other side of his fame and celebrity.

Unwilling to face his inevitable decline, he pulled his mobile from his back pocket and scrolled through dozens of missed calls and texts from hotshots and famous people, willing the outpouring of attention to fill his cracked and leaking bucket. To make him forget the fleeting, teasing taste of artistic inspiration he'd lost. To banish fantasies of romance.

It was for the best that Helen turned out to be a flake. This way he could focus on his career without emotional investments muddling his focus.

Besides, he didn't have time to date, and certainly didn't need a relationship to feel whole. Brian scanned numbers and messages. Though the deluge of external validation should have done its time-tested job of making him feel warm and loved, hollow numbness and dull pain warred for control of his insides.

In the bedroom at the back of the bus, someone grunted. So the interloper hadn't fled. But who on the crew would act so damn dodgy and hide? One way to find out. Brian strode to the origin of the sound and went back inside the back room.

Joe stood in the middle of the bedroom, a blank, glazed expression sagging his face. He stammered unintelligible gibberish, looking through Brian, not at him. Half-moons of sweat darkened the underarms of his tan T-shirt.

"What the fuck, man? Were you hiding under the bed? Loo emergency you were too ashamed to admit?"

Making a scrunched face like he'd eaten something foul, Joe licked his lips with a smacking sound. "I'm in this for you, we're all in this for you. These guys are for real. Gonna keep your band crackling with magic until you're eighty years old. Make sure you're remembered as bigger than the Stones ever were." He spoke in robotic monotone, as if delivering a memorized speech. Perspiration made his balding head gleam, though the bus's temperature reflected the cooling climate outside.

Listening to the man's disjointed rambling sent an ominous feeling slithering over Brian's skin. Between this and the rudeness he unleashed on Helen, Joe was worse than ever.

Sketchiness aside, though, Brian couldn't argue with the legacy piece of Joe's comment. Still. This scene was beyond irregular, even for conniving, eccentric Joe. "You feeling okay? Please tell me you aren't on drugs."

Joe scrubbed a hand over his pallid face. "No. Ate too much fried food and yeah, sorry about the smell."

A pin of doubt stuck Brian. "What happened to your trip to the Wyoming ranch?"

Even if Joe left for the Aries Records executive retreat location at once, he wouldn't arrive until midnight at the earliest.

"Gonna hop a flight now. Like you said, emergency shitter stop. All of the outdoor johns were taken. Won't happen again." Joe hustled past Brian and off the bus, leaving a cloud of sour body odor in his wake.

What a night. Time to ring the bus driver and get to the hotel, Skype Tilly, and relax with a movie and a bottle of wine before calling upon sleep to blot out the last few hours.

A clanking, metal-on-metal noise sabotaged Brian's effort to calm down. He whipped his head in the direction of the offending sound. In the kitchenette sink, a black handle jutted from the working garbage disposal.

He shut off the switch and pulled out the object, coming face to face with a ten-inch chef's blade with something stuck to it. Brian plucked the errant bit magnetized to the metal, blinking as his rational mind struggled to categorize the finding. A bottle cap? An earring? No. He stroked the smooth contours of a familiar charm between his thumb and forefinger.

He held the crystal Helen gave him moments ago. No mistaking the thing, glimmering like a diamond even in minimal light. What in bollocks? No way this trinket could have travelled to the kitchen from the dashboard. He set down the knife and plopped the rock in his palm, leaning down for a closer look. A hot poke of pain impaled the middle of his hand in the exact spot that bothered him on stage. The stone fell from his grasp when he jerked, clattering against the ground.

Brian glanced askance at the crystal on the floor. Wasn't time to head back to the hotel yet. Not before he confronted Helen and figured out the real story with her.

FOUR

AS CREW TORE DOWN THE STAGE WITH THE CHOREOGRAPHED precision of NASCAR pit mechanics, Helen blazed a path through the dispersing crowd. Skies darkened to a denim jacket shade of indigo, draping packs of jean-clad teens goofily flirting over funnel cake and popcorn.

A musical chair ride whizzed through the air, its tilted ellipses casting off cones of hot pink light. Riders swung dangling legs as screeches rocketed toward webs of stars, but the exciting atmosphere slid right over Helen.

With any luck, the new crystal would keep Brian safe. She turned beleaguered thoughts to the Lisa problem.

Though a rainbow of megawatt colors brought the after-dark fair alive, Helen's spirit dragged through littered dirt. She didn't blame her best friend for passing on the backstage visit.

Lisa had lacked the patience to tolerate Helen's hemming and hawing about the nature of the good news, but how was she supposed to deliver it?

Guess what. Today I found out I'm a witch, and I'm going to use my powers to save us. Except I hexed someone by mistake, so that's an issue. But still, yay me. Right? No? Oh, okay. Bye.

Would she ever stop making catastrophic mistakes? A red plastic cup crunched underfoot. While Helen stooped and collected the litter, a familiar voice nabbed her attention.

"Hear me out. I know it sounds nuts. But I think I can get Shepherd on board. It's all in the pitch." Mr. Sideburns spoke in a hushed, secretive tone, a mouthful of food gumming up his words.

Helen rose to stand and crept in the direction of the Fyre staffer's voice. The sound of his speech drifted from behind a pea-green food trailer.

"I hear you, I hear you, and I don't blame you for not wanting to mess with those forces. Try not to freak out. I'll have more details after the summoning ritual in Wyoming. Come on, man. Led Zeppelin did it. I want Fyre to become the biggest rock band in history, don't you? We all win in that scenario." He belched.

Mess with what forces? Advancing, she settled at the rounded end of the vehicle on wheels. Puffs of smoke billowed from the service window, dragon's breath carrying the aroma of grilled meat.

The employee singing along to a crackling radio didn't seem to notice her presence. Good, he was occupied with cooking and music. Routing her attention back to the task at hand, Helen crept closer.

"Look, I can't say for sure it's a demon. The book describes it as an energy, a force, desire distilled. But if I can get Shepherd to join with it? Jackpot. I found a vessel that looks like it will work for the sympathetic magic."

Her insides flipped. A sinking sensation pulled her center of gravity to her knees, and the edges of her vision blurred. Mr. Sideburns's menacing comment about a vessel might tie in with the hex, the thing in the picture. But there was a distinct positive. Sideburns talked with arrogant bluster, but fear trembled below the surface of a tinny voice pitched low for maximum manly impact.

Helen could pinpoint insecurity quivering under cockiness, having lived behind a similar shield for most of her teenage and adult life. Couldn't let those foster homes pick up on her weaknesses, though no matter how hard she tried to project confidence and assurance that the current home would be The One, she got sent packing.

She corralled meandering thoughts. No time to mope over the lost years. She dove deep into her brain. Joe mentioned a book. He might know Nerissa or practice witchcraft. And this vessel for sympathetic magic? She had a good idea.

Sucking in one of the centering, full-belly inhales she'd learned in yoga teacher training, Helen found strength in the tattoo on her foot. Frida Kahlo's quote, "I paint my own reality," decorated her arch in looping, whimsical font. No better way to create one's own reality than by taking control of a situation.

Helen might have enough flaws to fill a clown car, but she was nothing if not assertive. Brian noticed one of her positive traits, too, picked up on it with incisiveness. His acknowledgment of one of her good qualities became fuel.

She walked around the back of the vehicular food stand. Sure enough, there stood Mr. Sideburns, stuffing a soft taco in his face and hunched over his phone like a shifty ghoul.

Though nervous energy sprinted through her body in spurts, Helen stood tall. The best course of action involved exploiting the anxiety Mr. Sideburns had done a subpar job of masking.

She took a chance on a big bluff, "Excuse me. You stole something of mine. A clear crystal."

He yelped, jumping and coughing. "Fucking hell, don't sneak up on me." Mr. Sideburns hung up and stuck his phone in a holster clipped to his belt. He curled one corner of his upper lip and slid a beady-eyed leer over Helen's figure, gaze settling on her breasts. "You again. Shouldn't you be on your knees somewhere, keeping my roadies happy?"

Helen groaned. Like she hadn't weathered far worse harassment and abuse working as a stripper. "Weak. As you know, I'm immune to slut-shaming, so you'll need to broaden your repertoire. Now hand over my stuff."

Mr. Sideburns threw away his trash and unclipped his phone. Smirking, he used a single finger to punch a key in slow-motion.

"Congratulations. You can use speed dial like a big boy. Cough up my property." She stuck out an open palm, balling her other hand into a fist with her thumb on the outside. If threatened, she could bust out her self-defense skills on this douche. Rough him up a bit and search his pockets.

He snorted and scratched his stomach. "Coupla yellow jackets are gonna be here any second, so you have two choices. Leave with what remains of your dignity intact, or hang around and wait for my boys to toss you out on your fat ass."

Oh, hell no. He did *not* just insult her bootylicious curves. Celebrities paid big bucks for a superbutt like Helen's. This freaking guy and his issues with women could get bent. "Fuck off—"

"We have a problem here, Mr. Clyde?" a man with a voice like a peach pit in the garbage disposal interrupted.

Two hulks, the word "security" written on neon yellow shirts stretched across barrel chests, joined Helen and Mr. Sideburns. Equipment belts slung low on their hips showed off handcuffs and Tasers. Ah, right. Yellow jackets, right down to their stingers.

The snidest of smug victory smirks bent Mr. Sideburns's lips. "Nah. Some psycho slut of Shepherd's, begging to do everything under the sun for a shot at getting to him. Swear to God, man, the girls get crazier every year."

"We good, miss? Moving along?" Speaking in a thick Russian accent, the other security man patted his baton. Three bruise-blue teardrops tattooed on the outer corner of one eye bragged of murders committed.

Helen mad-dogged Joe. "I'm not dropping this."

"We better get to the airport, Mr. Clyde. Last flight to Cheyenne leaves soon." The graying Sasquatch with the ruined voice led Sideburns away. The Russian followed.

"I'm not dropping this. Watch me. I'll get my crystal back and stop whatever the hell—"

"Quiet, honey. Men are speaking." Mr. Sideburns delivered the parting shot over his shoulder while bodyguards whisked him to a nondescript sedan in the parking lot.

Epic fail. Helen was racking up a fair number of those. She resumed casing the fairgrounds for Lisa. Her best friend wasn't mad enough to ditch.

After ten or so minutes of navigating a moving tide of people, she spotted her friend's black bob of hair and cat-eye glasses the color of jade. Picking at a taco wrapped in paper, Lisa sat on a bench by a prize booth and watched a trio of teenage girls blast rubber ducks with plastic water rifles.

The ever-present kaleidoscope of carnival lights ignited blue-black darkness, a frenzy of canary and magenta excitement flickering over Lisa's unsmiling mouth and vacant gaze in burst after incongruous burst.

Helen sat beside Lisa on the bench, internally cringing at the sight of Lisa's frown and distracted, unenthusiastic eating.

"Sorry to leave you hanging. I thought you'd be up for meeting the Fyre guys. Miscalculation on my part." Before Helen could squash it, an awkward laugh bubbled out of her. A cruddy, spreading feeling followed, thick and greasy as motor oil. This was not going to go well.

Lisa tore off a sliver of soft tortilla and fed it to a loitering sparrow. "Yeah, well, there have been quite a few misfires lately, huh?"

The ambitious bird struggled to gulp down its outsized meal. Helen entertained the notion of making a joke about it and nixed the idea. The friends weren't good yet, not by a long shot, and clowning wouldn't solve the problem. It almost never did. No choice but to adult up and show accountability.

"I'm aware that we're living this nightmare because of me. And I'm asking you to believe and trust me when I say I'm taking steps to fix the damage."

Lisa scowled like the mere sight of Helen hurt her eyes. She gave a slight shake of her head and set her meal on the bench. "Then why did you dangle that bait about good news and not deliver? I'm mostly exhausted, though now I'm kind of worried."

Enough stalling. Lisa would react to the truth however she'd react, and Helen couldn't do jack to control her friend's response. "You know the lady who all the pagans love?"

"The wicked fake witch of the upper Midwest? What's she got to do with us?"

A bearish impulse, unusual in its maternal nature, surged in Helen. Nerissa was the only person with faith in her at the moment, and she didn't deserve to be made into the butt of jokes.

"Don't make fun of her."

Lisa sent a frosty appraisal over Helen's face and parted her lips. She smacked her forehead. "You got conned into another scam, didn't you? Unbelievable. Unreal."

The words were shards of glass in Helen's ears, sharp and cutting, though brittle in their fragility. Lisa was hurting, too, and when wounded she lashed out. This common, shared trait added a complicated dimension to their kinship.

"I didn't get conned."

Not this time, though Lisa's evocation of the blunder made heat rise up Helen's neck. She touched her cheek and turned away from an incriminating look she wished carried more shock and disbelief. But no, Lisa *expected* a second imbroglio.

At the women's sandaled feet, the happy little bird fluttered in dust, chirping as brown feathers puffed and flapped. Helen envied the bird's lightness and unfettered joy.

"Whatever. At the very least, please don't tell me you paid her with what remains of our money." Lisa's tone quaked while she tossed more scraps to the sparrow.

"I didn't pay her a cent. If that's what you care about, you can stop worrying." Helen swallowed a dose of shame, though she couldn't blame Lisa.

Her friend managed to escape a dead-end, trailer park life and get into college thanks to genius playing of the stock market. And now Lisa had to watch as the money that brought her salvation, the money she'd invested in yoga teacher training and later her half of L&E, vanished into the belly of an insatiable beast they called "bills."

"But you went to her, right? Saw her for some kind of spiritual consultation?" Lisa put quotes around the word spiritual, doing zilch to couch her disdain.

Helen peeled off a sizable sheet of nail polish. Lisa's sarcasm hadn't helped lessen her grief and humiliation one damn bit. Not that Lisa had any obligation to ease Helen's feelings.

And following the original disaster, no wonder Lisa had an ax to grind with all things esoteric or spiritual.

"Yes. I met with her. But it's not like before, I swear. This is real, Lisa. She is real. An authentic witch. I saw things with my own eyes. Heard them. I tapped into forces over there. Ancient and powerful energies. Magic. I'm asking you to try one more time. One more chance."

Lisa stroked Helen's upper arm. "I'm trying to be empathetic and open minded and reasonable. On your behalf. I love you, but you need to start using critical thinking. You have this beautiful, pure thing inside of you, this part of you that wants to believe in things like magic. But it makes you susceptible. Vulnerable. I wonder if you're so anxious to secure stability that you think you have to do these over-the-top things to get security. Gurus. Witches. But you don't have to cast a magic spell to make a lasting home, Helen. You just have to figure out how to build that environment through love. You aren't fighting your way through the foster system anymore."

Bracing her elbows on her thighs, Helen slumped forward so far her hair fell in her face. She shrugged off her friend's patronizing touch.

"I'm aware." The words ejected from Helen's lips like bad food, some ugliness she didn't care to examine festering under her skin.

"I'm not sure you are. Because I don't feel like you learned a lesson."

"Message received. You think I'm stupid." A whole-body hurt overcame Helen. After hearing "stupid" shrieked in her ears for years, even uttering the insult herself stepped on a trigger.

Civilizations rose and fell in the crushing pause that followed. Wobbling water pooled in Helen's eyes. Searing ripples of scarlet fury scorched away her heartache. Fuck this. Fuck Lisa and L&E and the crystals and Joe.

Helen forced herself to breathe mindful, meditative breaths. Her anger could be toxic and destructive, and she didn't plan to burn her life to the ground yet.

"No, I don't think you are stupid." Lisa's careful inflection cut even deeper than if she'd replied in the affirmative. She'd considered her answer, figured out how to package and hazard a palatable response. Bully for her and her adroit skills of diplomacy.

"But? Say what you mean. Say it to my face."

"Fine. All of this talk of witches and magic does make you look naïve, and you have potential to see through this crap. Granted, the charlatan stuff was understandable, given what you went through. But it's a fool-me-once kind of thing. And now it sounds like it's happening again, and

I wonder why. I wonder if you've got this notion in your head that the world is senseless, so you need to do senseless things for survival."

Lisa danced near some truths. The swindler who'd stolen their bank account numbers and cleaned them out before falling off of the grid bore a striking resemblance to Helen's dead father.

But to Helen's credit, before hiring the supposed guru to lead workshops designed to take already-struggling L&E to the next level of spiritual and financial success, she'd subjected him to what she thought was rigorous vetting. Not rigorous enough. Never good enough.

Perhaps she'd succumbed to some self-defeating tendency to get duped by a powerful, charismatic man promising her the safety she craved.

"You're right, as always. I was an idiot to trust him."

"You have more than a modicum of awareness. Great. So why are you falling for another snake oil scam?"

"I told you. This time is different."

Another painful moment of silence stretched the space between the friends.

"What age did your mother have her first psychotic break?" Lisa used a clinical voice, a new voice, and Helen detested it.

Helen snorted, though Lisa's points came off intelligent and sane and scientifically ordered. Like pinned, categorized, and labeled butterflies.

Scrabbling for the shreds of her pride, Helen sat up straight instead of slinking back in shamefaced retreat. All she could do was own her new identity. "My mom's issues don't matter. I'm not stupid or crazy, I'm a witch. And I'm going to prove to you that magic is real. I'll show you I can use witchcraft to help us."

Two passing fair patrons, encumbered by behemoths of inflatable pink bunnies, swiveled their necks to stare. Helen ignored them. She needed to stay on track and yank out all weeds of doubt. Plus, she had Brian to think about now. Nobody saved her from the foster system, but she could use her gifts to save someone in need.

"At what age did your mom have her first psychotic break?" It came in that goddamn medical tone again, detached and superior.

The age I am right now. "It doesn't matter."

"Come on, sweetie. Facts do matter."

"Stop. I'm not a child or a fool."

"So quit acting like both."

"You're being cynical, even for you."

Lisa scratched her head and huffed, like the entire conversation was some burdensome drag far beneath her great big brain. "I'm not cynical, I'm right. The nice thing about facts is they stay real whether you believe in them or not."

Unable to meet Lisa's condescending face, Helen trained her gaze on a random target, in this case a toddler eating popcorn off the ground when his parents weren't looking. She was done. Done feeling dismissed, unheard.

Somebody needed to give her a shot, some encouragement.

"You know what, Lis? Spare me the quotes from your Neil deGrasse Tyson meme collection. I believe in what I experienced. I know my experiences don't align with your worldview, but that doesn't mean they're wrong."

"It's like I'm trying to show you two plus two equals four, and you're insisting the equation adds up to potato."

"Yeah, well, maybe you should open your mind to the possibility that realities exist outside of the scientific method. Potato, po-*tah*-to."

"Nope. I'm out. Don't call or text me again until you're ready to listen to reason. I'm going to go home and rest so I can face our bankruptcy lawyer with some degree of dignity tomorrow." Lisa sprang to her feet, snatched up her leftovers, and stalked off into the masses of people.

"I can go with you to talk to the lawyer. Don't play the martyr. It's a bad look."

Lisa said nothing and blended into the crowd.

Talk about best laid plans going splat. Before she could degenerate into self-pity, Helen got out her bag of crystals and shook the contents into her palm. Lisa would come around or she wouldn't, but in the mean time Helen had to figure out a solution to the supernatural debacle.

With an index finger, she sifted through the colorful chunks in her cupped hand. Fourteen total, two for each color of the rainbow.

Interesting, how the even number of tokens divided into two sets. Did the balance have to do with the Right Hand and Left Hand paths? What did the clear ones represent? The colors of the crystals aligned with the colors of the chakra wheels, energetic disks that yogis believed ran up the spine. An opportunity to explore color magic, maybe.

Lots of uncertainty in the mix right now, but one witchy person in particular could offer answers. Helen re-bagged the minerals and rose from the bench.

"We need to talk." The stern, English male timbre snapped Helen out of her thoughts. "I'm hoping you'll be able to offer an explanation for what I found on my tour bus."

FIVE

ALONE ON THE BUS'S GRANITE ISLAND, THE SECOND CRYSTAL resembled a several-carat cubic zirconia on a black sand beach. The rest of the tour bus lobby, from a leather couch to the subtle scents of lemon and bleach, projected order and tidiness in lieu of rocker debauchery.

Helen treated herself to a taste of enjoyment in the violation of her expectations. Not a bong or a groupie bra in sight.

Brian turned to her, eyes a touch hooded and one corner of his mouth quirked in a curious expression. "What?"

"I didn't say a word."

He took a step closer, tapping an index finger twice on the island. The gesture stirred excitement in her, the deliberate manner of his touch a subtle act of flirtation the weird context failed to repress or squash. The air flexed as unseen but potent masculine power insisted its way out out Brian. Awareness flickered under her bra cups.

Details of him rose to her perceptual surface. Jeans worn to a comfy, faded blue hugged the sculpted planes of his thighs. On a more intangible level, he carried himself in a way that was neither casual nor tense. Brian moved with grace suited to a dancer. Self-aware without being self-conscious. Dignified. Regal. Artistic.

"You giggled." His rumbling cadence lilted as he delivered the faux accusation.

"I did not." Okay, she'd made a slight peep that could be interpreted as edging into the vicinity of a chortle.

"What's on your mind? Tell me." He dashed a look over her face in a hesitant flick, like a lost part of him reached for a forgotten memory of how to desire.

Helen ran fingertips over the cool, smooth surface speckled like a robin's egg, aware that Brian was watching her hands and enjoying the feel of his gaze. "Your bus is so clean and neat. I guessed I've watched too many trashy documentaries, because I assumed a rock band's tour bus would be all cocaine and blowjobs."

In a moment as sudden as it was inappropriate, Helen became aware that Brian was a man with biology like any other. He got hard and shot his seed. Did he swear or moan while he came? A hazy fantasy of his stiffness in her mouth drifted through her mind. In her scenario, he tasted as pleasing as he smelled, healthy and clean.

A big part of his allure involved how much he left to the imagination. An aura of propriety swirled around him, a primness that begged her imagination to picture him reduced to a grunting mess of lust.

Oddly enough, nothing about his upright personality was incongruous with his life station. Brian was no oversexed party animal who got lucky, shoving a groupie off of him in time to run on stage and stagger through a show drunk with a needle hanging from his arm.

Nope, she'd wager he conquered the music industry by sheer force of will, achieving his meteoric rise thanks to peerless focus, determination, and drive to succeed. What was going on with her all of a sudden? Male power had never worked on her as an aphrodisiac before, quite the opposite until now.

She forced her attention back to the crystal. Twin strands of beaded light flowed upward from rows attached to the floor, altering the hue of the rock into a prism of milk and butter tones.

Brian cleared his throat, the gesture neutralizing whatever sensual current wove through the lounge seconds ago. "Yes, well, I don't do drugs, and my nonexistent sex life is the farthest thing from my mind at the moment."

Nonexistent? Why wasn't Brian—hot, classy, rich, talented, legendary —enjoying warm and willing job perks on a nightly basis? None of her business was why. And she had to play things cool, because he might be able to help her locate and recover the first clear crystal. "What did you want to talk to me about?"

Brian backed away from the counter and collapsed on the couch, resting both hands on the top of his head. His body slackened into the cushions, a physical language that both stirred her empathy and pleased in her in some forbidden way. Brian's becoming unguarded in her presence, allowing her to see his search for physical comfort, did not go uncatalogued.

Helen took a seat beside him. His legs parted, enough to assert ownership over the space but not enough to convey macho disrespect in the form of the dreaded manspreading. He extended his arms over the top of the furniture. She scooted a few inches closer to his hip as if a magnet pulled her.

He cocked his head and tilted it to one side, surveying her out of the corner of one lidded eye. In that moment, Helen saw Brian's X factor, the essence of his cool.

Brian didn't need to flaunt his status to show off, which magnified his potency by a factor of a million. He was stately, composed, polite and kind though not quite warm. And stretched out on the couch, he communicated his prowess without uttering a word. He was the king of rock, unchallenged and free with nothing to prove.

He had a few miles on him, his lightly tanned skin was creased and a bit weathered, but that made his attractiveness that much more poignant. Model hot in his youth, present-day Brian had a mourning angel's beauty, the look of a rock god past his prime and in full awareness of his age. A portrait of a man, not a denial-filled boy in an older body.

A puff of air, the smallest of audible gasps, broke from her lips. She sat in the presence of a god.

In an imperceptible atmospheric shift, intangible mystique fled through a crack in reality. Brian sighed, shape-shifting to a person once again. "I want to talk to you about these stones. What they are, where you got them, and why you gave two of them to me."

Comporting herself made for a borderline laughable challenge given the circumstances, but she managed. "A situation with my business kicked the whole thing into motion."

He lifted one eyebrow in a supreme gesture of British dryness. "What on earth do you do?" Cautious curiosity lifted his speech.

"I'm a yoga teacher. I own a studio with Lisa, the woman I asked you to put on the guest list." Helen played with her hair, staving off the compulsion to slouch. "Owned, maybe. Not sure if we're in past or present tense."

"What happened?" he asked with petal softness, fingers twitching as his eyes roamed from her face to the piece of hair in her hand.

Helen let herself smile in response to his considerate question, though her heart clenched. "I did something stupid."

"Ouch. I doubt that."

"Why?" Unintended, her question flew out as a barb. She wrapped her arms over her midsection as if the dart would boomerang back and lodge in her underbelly.

He leaned in an inch closer. "You seem too thoughtful to be stupid."

Her rogue smile spread. The air thickened to a pleasant perfume, supportive and cocooning. Easy on the eyes, Brian was easy to be around, to talk to. He knew how to listen and wasn't one of those guys trying to mess with her mind, manipulate, or take advantage. He'd proven his goodness. The spikes on her armor retracted.

"Thank you. I made a mistake, for which I take full responsibility. And then in trying to fix the mistake, I seem to have made another one."

A rumble stirred in his throat. His Adam's apple bobbed. A traitorous flush spread between her legs at the sight of his neck captured in movement. How effortless it would be to kiss that inviting column of flesh, kiss her way up to his cut jaw, brush her mouth against masculine lips just plush enough to invite sensual thoughts.

"Which is why you asked me to return that clear crystal."

The mere mention nullified her lust. "Yes."

"Tell me they aren't stolen or trafficked."

"No. I'm no jewel thief."

"What's the gist?"

If he booted her out for the truth, he booted her out for the truth. "I visited a local mystic for help saving my business. Rumor has it she's a witch, and she gave me a book and told me to drink a potion. She also gave me the crystals to give away to others and, I guess in a moment of impulsiveness, I saw you standing there with Joe and I thought you needed some positive energy."

Helen masked her wince, waiting for Brian to stand up and show her to the door. Instead, his movement seeming to slow time, he slid the piece of hair she'd toyed with between two of his fingers. Her scalp throbbed with pleasurable awareness, registering his gentle tug.

Particles seemed to vibrate in the inches of space separating his hand from her neck. The promise of his touch on her skin, the absolute slightest of sensory thrills, proved enough to ignite her sex. She was more attracted to him than she'd been to anyone in years. Not that it mattered. Seducing him would escalate a problem into an utter fiasco.

"Your gift worked. I've been in a bad way for awhile now, unable to write or make new music. But I don't know if the power of suggestion kicked in or if I awakened again after realizing someone else cared, or what, but when I was up on that stage tonight, I felt my potential returning. My passion, my breath, my reason. And I'm so sorry I lost your crystal. I looked everywhere, because I wanted that reminder of you up there with me. Wanted to feel it in my hand, to touch it while I sang." His eyes revealed oceanic depths true to their rich color and reflected his poetic, complex intensity.

She played with her hands, grappling with an emotional mix of humility, validation, attraction, and fear. The crystal was powerful. Where was it? There was an evil force with a vested interest. How to stop the demon? Was this monster doing something messed up as they spoke?

"I wanted you to have it for that exact reason. We don't know each other, obviously, but in the moment I was compelled to give something special to you. And my intentions were good and pure, if spontaneous. But those stones can carry a charge, otherworldly powers that act like a magnet, sucking in dark forces."

The hex loomed large, unseen and unspoken.

"Not too long ago I'd have dismissed such talk as utter rubbish." Brian toed off his loafers. Good. Meant he was adjusting to her presence. Still, best to proceeded with caution.

"What changed?"

Slapping his thighs, Brian rocked to his feet. "That subject calls for a bit of social lubrication. Fancy a drink? I'm having one."

"Sounds great." Alcohol could lessen awkwardness and facilitate conversation.

"What would you like? There's red and white wine, beer, whiskey. Soda and sparkling water, too."

"I'll have what you're having." Her core softened. In some different scenario, she'd be all about getting this older, dignified, more than a little guarded and enigmatic rock god into bed.

Alas, sexual escapades didn't align with the purpose of her visit.

Brian walked to a minibar and got down two lowball glasses and a bottle of whisky with a brand label she didn't recognize. He pulled a plastic bucket from a freezer and used metal tongs to grab ice balls. He dropped an icy sphere in a cup, ball meeting glass with a soft clack. After depositing the second orb, he whisked back his tongs like a magic wand. A meticulous quality colored Brian's mannerisms.

Helen held back a clap of appreciation. Brian Shepherd, always performing.

He kept up the performance, or she noticed new dimensions his mini-show. His movements, the way he held the liquor bottle high to make an elegant arch pour from a long-nosed spigot capping the bottle, added a touch of elegant flair to otherwise mundane action without crossing the line into cheesiness. Brian rocked top-notch style, an aesthetic of living that he executed with unique panache. Her knees drifted apart as he mixed their drinks with cocktail straws.

Brian handed her a glass and eased back into his seat, clinking his cup into hers with a melodious note that cut still air with intrigue and promise. They were allowing the tiniest steps of a mating dance to happen. Chemistry would emerge despite or because of their fighting it, so no point in denying their feelings space to breathe. This needed to go unsaid, imbuing their flirtation with an intoxicating charge.

"Cheers." Brian lifted his glass and brought the rim to his lips.

"Cheers." Her first drink delivered notes of oak and ink followed by an ethanol bite.

Flavors mingled with her desire, spurred by Brian's dignified air, his

British-isms, and the shape of the peculiar night. Contours tapered into points, spiky reminders of danger. The form of the evening, those knife edges, made their rendezvous sexy in an unspeakable, impossible way reserved for the two of them. "As you were saying."

He winked, the look smart and tart and white-hot. "Right down to business."

"I think something terrible is happening, and I need information to figure out how to stop it."

Brian's nonverbal reply spoke volumes. A strong chin tipped upward in a dry show of detachment, a courtly parry. His eyes glistened with the effect of a stormy sea at night. Suspicious, aroused, or both?

In one of his exacting movements fit for an observer of the world, a born storyteller, Brian fingered a miniscule chip on his glass. Her breath snagged. Did thoughts of fingering a small spot on her body teem in his head?

Helen had never met a man as opaque as Brian before. Most were obvious, in the puppyish, endearing and uninspired way men were. But not this one. He had the whole puzzle wrapped in an enigma thing down pat, and holy hell his gamesmanship got her motor running.

"Can I trust you?" His posture didn't shift from the statuesque, careful arrangement he'd cultivated. But a quiver in his posh speech unmasked vulnerability, albeit a small peek. The first show of openness slipped through Brian's shell, a secret she was privileged to see.

Perhaps he wore armor like she did, a brittle veneer covering skin bruised by letdowns and betrayals.

She organized her thoughts before gushing out an emphatic "yes," so as not to come off short sighted, too thirsty to prove herself.

"I'm going to be one-hundred percent honest with you. I mean you no harm. I was trying to help. But with the first crystal I did something without meaning to. So I want to say yes, you can trust me, but I hesitate to say so because I'm not positive I trust myself at the moment."

"Let's take it from the top. Why did the witch give them to you to give away? What's that got to do with saving your business?" Brian sliced a stare from Helen to his drink. He prodded his ice sphere with the straw, sending frozen water bumping into the sides of the glass. The effect was one of an aloof deity moving a planet, a presentation of self that drew her in while keeping her at an emotional distance.

"She said I was a witch and gave them to me during my initiation. I was supposed to give two clear crystals away to good people before starting my study of spell craft. But I missed a crucial step before giving you the first one."

Brian sipped his beverage. Liquid glistened on his bottom lip, bringing attention to its kissable fullness in proportion to the top one. Ugh, why did he have to be so alluring? She had to concentrate.

"You're also a witch?"

"Yeah." She shifted in her seat, running the pad of a forefinger along the rim of her cup. In the painful silence that followed, she wished the movement of flesh against glass made noise, a warbling tone to create parlor trick distraction.

"Where's your cauldron and broomstick?" He winked again, diffusing some tension while stirring a different sort between her legs.

"Who knows? When it comes to domesticity, I'm pretty much trash." A well-timed joke had its place, such as strategic application of self-deprecation used to lighten an encounter.

He chuckled, tipping a finger at her. "You can take the piss. I like you. Do you believe her claims?"

"About being a witch?"

Brian nodded, slipping back into his practiced countenance of neutrality.

"Yes. I've had visions for most of my life. The woman I saw seemed to know about them and proved she could read my mind. She convinced me."

Brian set his cup down and ran the tip of his tongue back and forth over his top teeth. "What do you see in the visions?"

"The ancient past, like the European witch hunts. I've flown through air and seen what seems like different parts of the country or world. It's hard to explain. Like an out-of-body experience, I guess."

"Flying through the air. So you're familiar with remote viewing I take it?" His question was pointed.

She'd heard of the phenomenon but hadn't studied remote viewing with any sort of intention or dedication, which he seemed to insinuate.

And more to the point, why did the subject of remote viewing pique Brian's interest? "Somewhat. Why?"

"What's about to happen that's so terrible?" His syllables crisped. Brian searched behind her eyes. She didn't blame the man for his directness, straightforward questions, or hesitance.

Others would have laughed and dismissed her as a nut. Still others would have reacted with fear and told her to get lost. Brian, on the other hand, sought facts and information from a level-headed, calm place. Suited him, or what she knew of his personality. He'd steered the conversation away from remote viewing for a reason. She ought not to press the issue and risk alienating him. They already treaded tricky ground, maneuvered around land mines.

"After I gave you that first clear crystal, I saw a cloud of smoke I'd seen before. I think there might be a force attached, an entity without the best of intentions." She didn't need to spill every single detail. Not yet, at least. Best to keep Brian close, and an excess of alarming information about hexes and voices in her head could backfire.

He knocked back what remained of his drink, walked the glass to the kitchen, and set it down. Bracing his hands on the counter, Brian sighed. "The thing I don't understand is why, as you say, you gave me the stone for positive energy and a good show, but then a bad entity shows up."

"I don't fully understand either." Fully was such a weasel word. She was holding back big chunks of the truth. But what would unfiltered honesty accomplish? If she freaked Brian out, odds were she'd never see him again. He had to be a difficult man to get to, and she wasn't tight with his staff by any means. "Do you have any idea where the first one might have gone?"

"Do you?" he fired back in less than a second, his reply not aggressive but toeing the border of an accusation. Brian wasn't dumb. He knew she was hiding things.

Sensing she'd been moved to some category designated for suspicious people, Helen loosened the reins on a bit more of the story and proceeded with caution. "I think so. Earlier at the fair I overheard Joe on the phone. He mentioned summoning and forces, energies, and Wyoming. A book and a vessel came up as well. I think the vessel in question might be the original crystal."

"You just so happened to stumble across Joe saying all of this?" Dragging out the syllables of his dry speech, he rinsed his glass and set the tumbler in a rack.

"Yes. I did."

Brian stood still, his stare distracted. The effect was uncanny and sad, like his outward expression resulted from inner labor to spackle over whatever machinations went on in his head.

Watching Brian Shepherd locked in a struggle with whether to open or close, whether to lower his wall or buttress his defenses, she connected with how weird, how squirmy in the most existential of ways, being famous must feel.

Plenty of creeps angled and leveraged and schemed to exploit the celebrity of others for personal gain. In her estimation, having to forsake the ability to let one's guard down would be crazymaking. Especially with someone like Joe having breached Brian's inner circle.

She took her peace and relative invisibility for granted and wouldn't trade it for all of the Yogi Tea in Whole Foods. "What are you thinking about?"

"I don't buy it." His response popped out in a snap, though his voice trembled. "You want him out of the picture for some reason. Why? To assume his place at my right hand? Easy access to whisper influence in my ear? Put spells on me?"

Shit. He was degenerating into paranoia, some self-defense mechanism. Concern for Brian trumped any impulse to get annoyed or offended by his implications, though. Over the course of his life in the spotlight of fame, he'd no doubt been burned by many a malicious goblin.

She joined him behind the kitchen island and offered an assuring touch above his elbow. "No, I'm not gunning for leverage over you. I'm going to figure out more, but if I had to guess, I'd say he knows the same witch I went to. Or he's a member of a coven with a big tent, one that's connected to her. I know it's hard, I know I sound like a lunatic, but please believe me when I say I care and want to help. And to do so, I need that first clear crystal. Can you work with me to help us recover it from Joe?"

Brian lobbed a dark look at her. He cut his gaze to the stone on the table. "Pick it up. Please."

Helen made eye contact with him and scooped the object into her palm.

He blinked, a muscle in his jaw feathering. "No response?"

"No. What were you looking for?"

"No pain, discomfort, or burning?" Putting his drinking glass in a cupboard, Brian snorted a laugh bereft of good humor. "Christ, I'm proper gobsmacked at what I'm saying aloud today."

"No pain. Why does my reaction matter?" She set the rock back on the counter, showing her palm as proof. Sure, she could pocket the stone, get the thing away from him, but rash behavior might make him balk.

Brian backed away a foot, a curtain of blankness falling over his face. He gathered her tumbler and blasted the inside with a stream of water. A shrunken ice ball dissolved under the tap, ending their camaraderie in an unceremonious trickle down the drain. "I need to get back to my hotel room now. I'll call you a car so you don't have to walk across the grounds to the car park."

As she registered Brian's expressionless visage in profile, his physical and emotional shutoff as he turned his back to her and fussed at the sink, an irrational wallop of pain and anger sucker punched Helen in the middle of the chest. She should be in sleuth mode. But his rejection hit too hard.

She tamped down her hurt. "You need to listen to me. Because there are people plotting to harm you with witchcraft."

"Is that a threat?" He slammed the cabinet door, the sound as harsh as the question he fired.

"Of course not. Like I said, I overheard Joe breaking down the plot with someone else."

"I'm sorry, Helen, I'm not buying this story. Shall I call you a car, or not?"

She stepped closer, trapping him with the most intense look she could muster. "Pushing me away won't help. Rejecting me will do the opposite."

"I can't do this right now. I need to talk to my daughter and get some sleep."

Persisting undeterred, she grabbed his hand and squeezed assurance into his warm, dry palm. "You mentioned the past. A while ago, you would have dismissed all of this supernatural talk as mumbo jumbo, but not now. Meaning facts changed. What? If I know, I might be able to work with the information. Put new details in context with the things I heard."

Brian pulled his hand away. "Who are you? What's your angle?"

He'd entered full retreat mode, stabbed some celebrity panic button and shut down. And in his shoes, she would have done the exact same thing. No wonder so many famous people lost their minds, turning into recluses while babbling about microchips in their heads.

"I don't have an angle beyond trying to repair damage. If you knew me, you'd know I'm the least duplicitous person on the planet. I think I'm physically incapable of guile."

Brian offered a ragged exhale, evidence of weariness that kept his humanity in the foreground despite his guardedness. "I played a two-hour show on three hours of sleep, and I'm repeating the process tomorrow and the next day. I'm sorry, Helen. Not now. I can't. I'll hang on to your card. I sent a text alert to one of the band's drivers. A ride will be here in one minute."

Game over. For a second, she thought she'd broken through. Teased herself into thinking she and Brian shared a special connection. But nah. Helen didn't connect with people.

Her shell, a spiny exoskeleton forged in defeat, fury, and an indefatigable drive to guard her soft bits, closed over her body. A blast of air tore through a ceiling vent, making her hair squirm like cockroach feelers to round out her buglike sense of alienation. She'd empathized hard with poor Gregor Samsa ever since reading Kafka in her Existentialism seminar.

"Whatever, Brian. Your choice I suppose. I drove, so no thanks on the car."

Helen left. But she didn't march off into the night lacking direction. No way.

Crossing the sparsely populated lot on route to her car, she dialed Nerissa's number. Time to get some information and get cracking casting spells, because she had a hex to reverse and a business to save.

SIX

A TRIO OF JOURNALISTS STRODE INTO THE DRESSING ROOM, CHATTING
as they lugged tripods, cameras, and black cases. Seated in a director's
style chair with taut fabric supporting him, Brian brushed a thumb
against the hard bump of the crystal impressing into the material of his
jeans. Of course he'd saved Helen's gift. Chances were, "out of sight, out
of mind" didn't apply.

Whether Helen was spying or conspiring against him, he couldn't say.
But after Tilly had confessed to him what she'd seen at some Hollywood
Hills party, he couldn't dismiss or laugh off subjects like witchcraft.
Though now he wondered if he ought to have trusted Helen enough to
tell her the entire horrific story of Tilly's witnessing.

Brian glanced at Jonnie, who sat beside him in an identical chair. On
the rhythm guitarist's mobile phone screen, a social media feed blew
past. "What was the rumor you heard about Joe?"

Jonnie set the device on his lap. "You really want to know?"

"I wouldn't have asked if I didn't."

"Just making sure, because before you said you didn't want to hear
the gossip."

That was before he needed to rule out the possibility that the kind,
intelligent, and witty woman he'd met was embroiled with the manager

in question for God knows what reason. He'd been a world-class arsehole to Helen, closing down and sending her away. But if she was party to some supernatural plot, he could not abide. Not when he had a child.

"Now I do."

Jonnie leaned in, close enough that Brian could smell the sandalwood scent of the gel the man used to spike his shaggy black hair. "They say he's into witchcraft. That he's a witch himself, or a warlock or whatever."

A sizzle of dismay skated across Brian's breastbone as a link between Helen and Joe clicked into place. A tenuous and vague one, though, rooted in hearsay. Starved hope trembled inside of him, hope that he didn't need to write Helen off yet.

"Who's 'they?' If such a thing is even true, so what?"

"Right behind ya." The voice came from one of the interview crew, a lad of perhaps twenty with a black cord looped over his shoulder and a mop head of beach bum blond hair.

The bloke shoved a cardboard bookcase into an empty spot behind Brian and Jonnie, leaving a cloud of patchouli fragrance in his wake. He pulled items from a messenger bag and stuck a cheap vase and a neglected bonsai tree into one of the empty shelves.

Adding a romance paperback with a rip across the cover that tore Fabio's body in half, the guy nodded in triumph. "Spruce up the joint a little bit."

"It's a spitting image of my living room." Jonnie's deadpan response startled a chuckle out of Brian. The rhythm guitarist winked, his usual cheekiness on point.

Brian treasured his closest band brother. A commitment to professionalism shone through in how Jonnie curated and maintained his image. Plus, the man had shared his mum's secret curry recipe with Brian. All around good people, Jon was, someone who'd earned the gift of Brian's tested trust.

The interviewer rejoined his colleagues in affixing cameras to tripods and fiddling with wireless microphones.

"As you were saying." Brian matched Jonnie's conspiratorial lean, coming close to laughing at his own furtive behavior.

"I went out on a few dates with a bird who said she'd escaped some weird cult. Long story short, around two weeks ago her cult sponsor, or recruiter, or whatever the fuck they call them drives her to a West Hollywood mansion for some kind of leveling up ritual. This person puts a hood or mask over her face and leads her into a room. When nobody's looking, she peeks, right? Claims she saw your boy Joe standing in the middle of a pentagram chalked on the floor, chanting with a book in his hand. According to her, there was an A-list actress levitating in the pentagram with him. Someone you've definitely heard of." After dropping his bombshell in a rapid whisper, Jonnie sucked in a loud breath. "A being floated in there, too. An inhuman creature."

Air fled the room, leaving Brian's lungs tight. A chill threaded up his spine. His rational mind grasped for purchase, though Jonnie's piece of gossip came too close to Tilly's account for logic to gain much traction. "What did Joe do with the actress and this inhuman thing?"

Jonnie's olive complexion paled to the color of putty. He splayed a hand over his flat belly. "According to my date, Joe cut...he took out organs...removed parts of her to make space for this entity. The entity went inside her body cavity."

A dark, empty feeling settled in Brian's lower belly and seeped outward, leaving him with an upset stomach. Tilly had reported chanting and cutting, but minus Joe. Brian was the record label's most dependable ATM machine and bankable cross-platform product, though, meaning hurting him didn't align with Joe's best interests.

He didn't like or trust the man, but at the very least he wanted to believe that the two of them existed in some semblance of a symbiotic relationship where Joe got to enrich his brand by attaching himself to a top act, and Brian got nods of approval from the big shots over Joe's head.

Plus, Jonnie's piece of tabloid gossip made no sense. For all of his foibles, Joe wasn't capable of murder.

When Brian's rationalizations failed to soothe him, he asked, "Who was she?"

Jonnie named the woman. Brian's jaw fell at the mention of the award-winner. The actress was alive and well, and if the ritual in question actually happened, no way would she survive it.

The dressing room's four walls, cinderblocks painted a drab eggshell hue, advanced in a claustrophobic squeeze. Grimacing as he pictured this ghastly scene Jonnie had painted, he bit a knuckle and ran through his memory log. Jonnie's date could have lied, but to what end?

"I said hello to the actress at a fashion show the other day, and we made small talk."

"I don't know, mate. I'm repeating what I heard. Take it for what it's worth."

Many questions remained. Chief among them in Brian's mind: who the fuck was Helen Schrader?

His heart jumped in with answers.

Someone caring and tender and disengaged from the fake celebrity rat race, whom he could appreciate every second of getting to know.

Someone with a network of freckles dotting flawless skin he longed to kiss and touch.

Someone who inspired him to create again. Someone he could be his best self around—who *saw* his best self.

Or so he thought. He shut off his heart's wishful thinking.

Jonnie returned to phone land. "I know that was outrageous and utterly bizarre. The source was a classic unreliable narrator, in any event. Dragged me to a Kaballah meeting *after* she told the whole weird story. I stopped seeing her when she tried to recruit me to join her latest multi-level marketing obsession."

Brian managed a limp nod, sickening imagery still branded on his brain.

A purple-haired, heavily pierced girl of perhaps twenty dashed into the room. "Woot, woot. Who's ready to get the old stallion ready for the auction block? Spoiler: me. Now sit back and let Miss Teagan work her totes awesome sorcery."

She unfolded a wheeled table, slapped it, and unrolled a soft makeup palate the size of a computer keyboard. Using tweezers, Teagan attacked Brian's brows.

"Nobody's looking at my bloody eyebrows." Brian rubbed his stinging forehead, but he couldn't patch the holes burned into his stinging heart.

"Gotta keep those fangirls swooning for as long as possible. I'd say you got five years, but maybe ten. Technology's magic these days. For example, this we can fix in post-production, since you refuse to get work done." Smacking red lips, Teagan traced the line down his face, her fingernail scratching his cheek.

She returned to pruning and dusting and daubing. The stranger's clammy, presumptuous, unwanted touch made his skin crawl. He'd grown rather tired of people pawing him.

Helen's memory invaded his weary mind, everything about it offering solace and respite from the present. The gentle yet intelligent way she'd talked with him, how she'd listened to him, soothed his battered soul. Everything about her did. Her throaty laugh and folksy Minnesota upswing. The freckles dotting her nose and arms like miniature constellations of stars.

He'd never forget those *eyes*. Forest fire eyes. Inquisitive and catlike, golden with sparks of jungle green, they glinted with brilliant mischief. Danced, like lush leaves in the warm heart of summer. Looked at him with such sweetness.

Helen hadn't seen him as a sex object past his prime. Nor had she seen the entertainment product: Brian Shepherd© Aries Records, LLC. She'd seen him as a person. A man.

Or so he thought.

Hurt and panic stormed the gates. Brian tried to shut down. He hit the reset button, seeking his numbed-out mode. Emptying himself out and filling the cavity with the blankness he needed to cope worked, so he did it.

Except now, a torch blazed in the cave. A certain brunette held it, someone who inspired in him a raft of giddy fantasies of things he assumed he'd forsaken. Picnics on the ocean. Laughter and kisses on the couch. Movies and conversation and drives up the coast. He'd give back all of his platinum records to experience a taste of normalcy. Of genuine human affection.

Too bad he couldn't trust the woman who'd awoken that side of him from torpor.

Teagan dabbed a damp sponge triangle on his face. Surfer Lad fumbled with a boom mic. Another reporter, a voluptuous woman in a suit, stalked up to Surfer Lad, and they argued.

Brian tensed, bunching his shoulders as the kerfuffle escalated to raised voices. What was wrong with these journalists?

He fixed his posture. Like the reporters, Helen was a wild card he couldn't predict or control. But his persona he could control. He'd put on a damn good interview. Act polite and professional, as expected, showcase his likeable, relatable, down-to-earth reputation for any label executives or television producers who might be watching. He'd embody his image with as much authenticity as he could muster until he drew his final breath. His goal in the moment was to remain on brand, and he could accomplish it.

A rotten urge spiked his blood. He clenched a fist. What would it feel like to trash the room? Upend chairs. Break cameras and stomp on mobile phones. Wreck the entire sodding place like the tantrum-prone manboy of a rock star he wasn't. He saw, though, why they melted down. To feel alive. To counteract the ennui. The freak-outs amounted to resistance. Refusal to pay the price of celebrity, rejection of the bum deal.

Tears nipped his ducts, and he screwed his lids shut, sucked in air, and opened them once the threat passed.

"Sneezing is bad luck." Teagan tapped his nose and finished up her makeup application.

"I've never heard that wives' tale," Jonnie said. "Do I need a touch up, love?"

"Nah. You're good. You could pass for thirty-two. You a vamp, with your whole eternal youth vibe? Drink the blood of groupies, only the ones on their periods get backstage?" She threw her makeup kit in a patch-covered backpack.

Following an odd beat of silence that Brian lacked the energy to analyze, Jonnie laughed and shook his head. "No, but I do avoid the sun, and I use quality moisturizer. You get points for creativity though. You come up with that on the fly, sweetheart?"

Teagan flicked her eyes from one man to the other, handing each a pink business card.

She advertised herself with a multitude of artsy titles from graphic designer to jewelry maker and looked to be on every social media platform in existence. Everyone was hustling, trying to get famous. No. Not everyone. Not Helen.

"Yeah. I have a screenplay I'm seeking representation for, so keep me in mind next time you mingle with film industry people. Can I pitch?"

Jonnie shrugged as he flipped the card over and looked to Brian. The others deferred to him when matters veered into business territory, a protocol which fed him a dose of pride.

"Sure." Brian widened his legs. Like a good dancing monkey, he reviewed the interview statement from Aries.

The crew arranged their cameras in a circle. A trio of dead black eyes stared Brian down. Cords lay across the floor, writhing as the reporters pushed their mounted camcorders. Someone said "test, test" into a clip on microphone, and the device emitted an obnoxious electronic whine.

"In the midst of a zombie apocalypse, a campus Republican and a radical feminist activist fight to destroy the undead—and their growing feeling for each other. Yeah. That's it." Grinning, Teagan whipped out her mobile and tapped.

"I'd go with radical feminist or activist. You don't need both to convey her values and how they conflict with those of the opposing lead." Brian stuck a finger in his ear and rubbed out the lingering pain left by the static squeal. These interviewers couldn't quite get their technological shite together, and it set his teeth on edge.

"Thanks, man." Teagan dashed off.

Surfer Lad and a female reporter set up three folding chairs.

The third, the brunette whose pinstripe suit was tailored to hug every curve on her lush figure, strode over.

"Christine Durlinger, *Currently Amplified* magazine." She extended her hand to Brian. Christine's firm, confident handshake matched the attractive and successful woman.

"Brian Shepherd, good afternoon." His voice came out authoritative, booming, and he escaped to the respite of his own sense of power.

Currently Amplified threatened to usurp *Rolling Stone* as *the* music magazine, and the publication's finger caught the scene's pulse. Brian squared his shoulders, locking her molten chocolate eyes and shoring up perspective. Fyre still sold out most shows, sold millions of records. This. Was. Him. He forced thoughts of Helen from his mind, forced himself to stay on task.

"Better now." Christine leaned down, offering him a peek of ample cleavage beneath her the scooped neck of her blouse. She clipped the mic to his collar, her hand brushing his jaw as notes of sweet, floral scent she wore shimmied to his nose. Christine smelled a bit like Helen and had a similar body type.

His cock twitched. Her mink-colored hair wasn't far off, either.

"Is that so?" He did his signature wink, excitement blooming below his belt. He was a man, after all, a man with needs. Why not enjoy, now and again, some of the countless women who made themselves available? Christine was offering herself. Flirtatious foreplay games were as clear to him as checkers.

"Yeah," she whispered in his ear, threading the slim black cord under his shirt, treating herself to a feel of his chest. Long nails gave a bit of scratch, offering a preview of wildness. A stew of arousal, shame, and loneliness churned in his lower belly. "That's so. Hyatt Regency, room eight-sixteen. Come by later and tell me in that hot accent of yours all of the filthy fucking things you want me to do."

She patted his arm and sauntered back to her interview chair, swinging her hips and presenting her full, round bottom to his gaze.

The air grew oppressive with gamy odors of human bodies doused in grooming products, the stench of too many people in a room. He squinted at her backside, biting his cheek, her crudeness having diluted his interest. She'd sat in pink chewing gum, the poor thing. A big glob, right in the middle, puckered her skirt like an external arsehole.

Christine whipped her glossy mane and flashed Brian a smoldering look, sitting down and crossing her legs high on the thigh.

He mustered a polite smile. Had she walked around all day like that?

Jonnie leaned close and laid a palm over his microphone. "Really mate? When was the last time you did a stranger?"

Brian covered his own mic. He couldn't remember the last time he'd had some meaningless encounter with a woman he hadn't cared about. No wait, he remembered. Right after Janet died and left him a single dad. "I need to forget Helen. Get her out of my system. I feel like I'm going barking mad."

"Perhaps what you need is the opposite of getting her out of your system—"

"Okay, we're rolling in five, four, three." The upbeat reporter who'd staged the bookcase spoke.

Never more than a few moments of privacy, stolen snatches of time to have meaningful conversations. Brian slapped on his winning smile for the cameras.

"Two, one." Electronic clicks followed.

"We're honored to be here with the Brian Shepherd and Jonnie Tollens of the classic, veteran rock band Chariotz of Fyre."

Classic *and* veteran? Ouch.

"The honor is ours." Brian's fake grin hardened to stoniness fit for a statue.

The interview kicked off with some inane chit chat. Brian went through the motions, staying in character.

"How do you see yourselves staying relevant in a changing music industry defined by youth culture?" Surfer Lad leaned forward, hands on his knees.

The question's subtext stung. You old boys washed up yet? Perhaps wiped vigorously, with a damp cloth?

Jonnie tipped his chin at Brian.

Brian returned the gesture, thanking his bandmate, a shared understanding passing between them. Brian could field these loaded questions with acumen. He pushed aside his insecurity and handled the issue.

"Our approach has always been fairly intuitive. We make the music we want to make, we create what inspires us. I do think, though, the key to staying fresh in these times is innovation. We have a changing sound that remains true to our roots yet reflects the energy of the current moment. Wouldn't you say, Jon?"

"I think that's true, but also willingness to honor the fan base matters a lot. Recognize and respect what they want. If they want the hits, play the hits. Strike a balance between the expected and the unexpected. Keep listeners guessing, but not too much."

Brian hummed an agreement. "We've always had a blues influence. And the New Wave of British heavy metal, of course, shaped our music significantly. Zeppelin and Sabbath, followed by Def Leppard and Iron Maiden and The Cult, all the rest of the bands associated with the movement. You get that, even in songs like "What's Your Sign?" The wordplay, the free association. London rhyming slang. In my opinion, lyric fluidity absolutely captures the English hard rock tradition. We'll always embody that and always have."

Christine licked her lips. "What are you working on now?"

Brian looked at his lap, tactile memory of Helen's silky hand tingling from wrist to fingertips. He stroked the crystal through his jeans. Wouldn't be the worst thing, to drift a bit and discuss what she'd inspired. "I've got an idea for a new song, about wholeness. The theme is synecdoche—part to whole, whole to part. There are rare times when you see a luminous element in a person, and her shine resonates with you on a cosmic level. A woman's body can symbolize her soul, and her soul touches universality. Even in something as tiny as a freckle."

An epiphany broke, clear as the crystal he'd lost. He couldn't give up on Helen. After this interview, he'd ring her with an apology for his skittish, reactive behavior on the bus.

Brian's face warmed. He rubbed the chronic soreness out of his hands. Decades of guitar playing caused the pain, but he'd grown accustomed to the ache. His pain was part of him now.

He flicked his gaze up to the reporters. Opening up freed awareness and peace in him.

Jonnie slapped Brian's back, two strong and supportive pats. Brian squeezed his bandmate—his brother's—shoulder.

"That's gorgeous, Brian." Christine laid a hand over her cleavage, big dark eyes going to liquid. "You express your thoughts with such poetic depth. No wonder you're a songwriter."

His stare fell to the floor, the blush seeping to the roots of his hair. He was a songwriter at heart, now wasn't he? Perhaps he could scrap this executive goal and ditch Joe along with it. Even the idea felt liberating, thrilling. Dumping his cumbersome shed load of baggage would free up time and mental space to write. Then he could focus his energies on his art.

A cracking sound, followed by a sizzle like oil in a hot pan, injected urgency into the room. Reporters swore and shouted. A chair hit the ground with a clash of metal against metal.

Brian snapped his focus to the source of the noise. Stress hormones zapped his extremities. On the floor, resting against the leg of the chair in which he sat, a frayed cord jerked.

In the throes of spasms, the live wire belched luminous white sparks.

The petroleum reek of electronic smoke and melting plastic gassed him. Brian fanned the space under his nose. How had the team failed to notice such severe equipment damage?

"Sorry, sorry." Surfer Lad, his hand wrapped in a towel, yanked a plug out of the wall. The offending cable flopped dead.

The incident put a damper on the interview, which wrapped up in short order. Everyone shook hands and exchanged polite thanks.

Christine undid Brian's mic, silky hair brushing his cheek and feminine touch ghosting his collarbone. "So you're the sensitive, thoughtful, artistic type, eh? A musician, not a rock star."

"I suppose." Still rattled from the sparking incident, Brian attempted without success to steer his thoughts back to writing. Drama and chaos sure snuffed creativity. But as his mind meandered to Helen, and the song she'd inspired, tranquility filled his chest once more.

"I bet there's a caveman in there, though, begging to come out and play." Not to be deterred, Christine waited, wrapping the skinny microphone cord around her fingers.

She pushed her full lips out, though her latest attempts did nothing for Brian.

He knew who he wanted. "I met someone I can't forget. I'd be using you."

"So use me. Pretend I'm your someone."

But he didn't want to pretend with a woman fixated on some illusory fantasy of him. She craved an image, whatever false and shallow idea of him ran through her mind.

With her talk of pretending, Christine sealed the non-deal. "No thank you, sweetheart."

The journalist pouted. "Someone's a lucky lady."

Yet he felt lucky, having met a woman who saw through to the real him. He could at least hear Helen out, allow her more space to explain while he listened with an open mind.

"Thank you. And it appears you have something stuck to the bottom of your skirt. Thought you might want to know."

"Oh, you have got to be fucking kidding me." Christine left in a huff, picking at the gunk in her clothing.

Why waste another second? Brian pulled his phone from his jacket pocket and fished in his trousers for Helen's business card. Her crystal came loose and fell to the ground, skipping across linoleum in a clacking rhythm. He pushed out of his chair, stooped, and picked up the rock. Touching the stone hadn't hurt his hand since the knife handle debacle. So he'd imagined the sensation. Or perhaps someone had put the charm in the bus's toaster as a prank. Who knew?

Brian rose.

"Duck, man," Jonnie shouted, a hard shove to Brian's upper back sending him sprawling forward.

Brian swiveled his neck in time to see the vase sail over his head, smack the opposite wall, and shatter into pieces.

Surfer Lad, mouth agape, pointed to the bookcase. "It flew across the room. Fucking flew on its own, nobody touched it."

Jonnie's grim expression tendered agreement. "It launched the second you picked up that stone."

Alternating a withering look between the wreckage and the malevolent trinket, Brian put the Helen issue on the back burner and pulled up Joe's number instead. The bloke had some major explaining to do, and Brian would pull the truth out of his shifty manager.

SEVEN

"You have reached Nerissa Ivanhoe, purveyor of strange. I'm indisposed at the moment, but leave a message and I will get back to you. If you have an appointment for a consultation, please come to my home office in Uptown Minneapolis, but do not park in my designated space. Violators will be *toad*, hehe." A tone beeped.

Helen adjusted the straps of the messenger and yoga mat bags digging into her shoulder and continued her stride down the sidewalk.

A spreading yolk of sun dipped below the horizon, giving way to the purple bleed of sunset. The first notes of frost perked up end-of-summer warmth, adding an autumnal zing to the air. Perfect atmosphere for getting proactive.

"Hey, it's me, Helen Schrader, again. I was hoping I could come over today and touch base with you about spells. Or talking on the phone is fine if that's more convenient. I also text, and I'm on social media. Anyway, I'm finished teaching for the day, and I'll have my phone on for another thirty minutes. Please call me back."

With an impatient sigh, she hung up and tucked the phone in the front compartment of her messenger bag. Helen supposed she lacked grounds for irritation. The old witch wasn't home when Helen called or dropped by at lunch, either, but Nerissa was locally famous. She had to be on the move a lot, booked and busy.

Regardless, Helen didn't have an eternity to wait around for Nerissa's schedule to open, not with the clock ticking on L&E and Brian being stalked by a mist monster. Nope, she needed to level up, and pronto.

Helen patted her bag, brushing the bulge made by the crystal pouch. Nerissa's guidance or no, it was witch o'clock. She breezed though her condo lobby and opened the elevator with her key fob. The silver door closed, reflecting Helen's flushed face and sweaty ponytail.

"Wait, wait. Sorry." A young woman pushed the door open and stepped inside, her fingers capped with French-tipped acrylic nails. Platinum-blond hair, dip-dyed black, cascaded down her back, ending at a plaid miniskirt. Shy smile serving as thanks, she poked the button to her floor. "Sorry, sorry."

"No need to be sorry. It's fine." Helen had been there, apologizing for existing. The other woman's concert T-shirt, jagged-font logo the color of flames, advertised an all-too-familiar band. "You go to the Fyre show at the fair?"

The blonde's hair fell in her face as she looked at her strappy sandals. Her pedicure matched her manicure, those chalky ends with the pink base. The elevator dinged up a couple of floors.

"Yeah. It was kind of a fucked up night, or morning I should say. I've been seeing their bass player for a few years now. We hook up when they come to town or nearby, but there's more to what we have than sex. He met my mom last year."

The woman referred to Thom James, Fyre's notorious playboy bassist. Hm. If the dejected groupie had been backstage or on the buses, she might have seen or heard something related to Joe or the hex. "Fucked up how?"

Thom's lover snorted and flipped long locks to one side. Silver hoops and barbells competed for limited real estate on her ear.

"I really thought we were moving toward exclusivity, you know? He went down on me until I came, which the other girls say he *never* does. After we had sex, he got out some weed, and we smoked while I read him a few poems I'd written. But in the morning? Poof. He goes all cold and distant, telling me he doesn't think we're compatible anymore.

Bullshit, you know? Like he'd studied *Sex and the City* for lame breakup lines. I'd rather he said 'your voice is ugly and your vagina stinks.'"

Helen laughed. She liked this chick and her salty attitude. "Can I ask you a weird question?"

The blonde sliced Helen a sly look. "Ask whatever you want. I've got the gossip on everything from dick sizes to drug preferences."

Bubbles blinked from white to pale yellow in numeric succession, the elevator moving up floors. She didn't have the luxury of easing in, not when she couldn't be sure if she'd see this person again.

"Did you or Thom see or hear anything strange? People acting off, this manager guy named Joe doing weird stuff? Or even ghostly whispers, clouds of white smoke?"

The young woman dropped her stare to Helen's forearm. "Are those prayer beads? You mediate?"

Helen ran a finger along the pearlescent strand of mala beads circling her wrist. "Yeah. I teach yoga, meditation, and chakra and energetic cleansing in Uptown. And I think there might be some bad energy following Fyre. Brian in particular."

The blonde swayed back and forth and made a wailing sound fit for a wandering haunt. "You're a trip, dude. And no. All I saw that night was an aging rock star with an ego the size of Antarctica. Sorry."

Blind alley, dead end. "Never mind."

"Naw, naw, it's cool. I like that kind of stuff. *The Secret* knocked me on my ass. Law of attraction. You think I'd like yoga?" The elevator door opened, and the blonde pushed the button to hold it. The squeaky and girlish way she asked the yoga question changed the game.

A gentle sister of sadness nudged Helen. The blonde sounded lost, like she lacked a sense of self and a toehold on her personality. And damn, had Helen been in a similar place. She rummaged in her bag and gave out a card for one free class.

Brian situation not withstanding, she had a life to lead and a business to save. And attracting new students served that goal. Plus, this woman might remember helpful details about the fair down the line, so it made sense to stir her into the mix.

"Yeah. I think you'd love yoga. You should come sometime. Light &

Enlightened is on Calhoun Street, between that organic ice cream shop for dogs and the haberdashery."

Thom's ex-conquest read the card and slipped it into her bra. "Cool. I'll see you around hipster central, Helen. I'm Stacy, by the way."

"Nice to meet you."

Stacy exited the metal box, and the elevator continued to Helen's floor.

Helen unlocked her condo with a tinkle of keys and swung open the front door to a dark living room. She walked to the floor-to-ceiling window and looked out over the view that had sold her on the place four years ago.

Near the border of the sculpture garden, where grass met sidewalk, a pond reflected glinting winks of starlight. The famous cherry spoon statue stretched across the water in an illusion of flotation, garnet dollop poised at the oval tip of an outsized piece of cutlery.

On the wall perpendicular to the window hung the magazine she'd framed, featuring her and Lisa on the cover of their special issue about local women entrepreneurs under thirty. Nostalgia threaded a needle through her heart.

Four years ago, Helen was high on herself. Her business was gangbusters. She'd finally achieved success. Come a helluva long way from the bitter, anxious, unloved little bitch who'd aged out of the foster care system with zero life skills and owning nothing except the pieces of meat almost any woman can sell.

L&E had thrived in a squished, ultra-competitive market, no less. Though her ego had ballooned to bloated proportions, the largess of arrogance never managed to fix the low self-esteem underneath.

Enough reflection. She had work to do.

After a shower and change of clothes, Helen turned on every light in the house. She tugged the grimoire free from a bookshelf, sat on the floor, and leafed through the tome.

God, where to even begin. Translucent, whisper-thin page after page brushed by, making soft flutters. Drawings, runes, and script inked in Latin and German, as well as arcane languages she didn't recognize, filled ancient parchment. Too much foreign writing for Google Translate to handle in a timely manner, and her high school Spanish would not offer jack.

So much esoteric, pagan symbolism. Helen's neck hairs stood at attention. A creak in the building's foundation prompted her to look over her shoulder before returning to squinting at symbols for which she lacked a frame of reference.

The occult material was overwhelming, charged with a frightening, unpredictable obscurity. This stuff was real. Why did Nerissa think Helen would be qualified?

She glimpsed at her phone. No green light signaling a call or text.

Flips through the pages growing aimless, Helen streamlined her thoughts in hopes of gaining direction. She had two goals: neutralize the hex and get L&E solvent. Meaning her best bet was to find a spell that could promise both.

Starting at the beginning of the book made sense, so she shut the volume with a thud, dust tickling her nose, and re-opened the cover.

After passing a few blank pages, she settled on the first viable page one, a table of contents broken up by six symbol headings. She tapped a finger on the one matching the spirit circle on the inside cover and opened to the first page attributed to that section.

At first, she skimmed more unreadable script, a mix of handwritten notes and inked calligraphy. Upon coming across a peculiar graphic, Helen stopped and studied. Crude stick figure etchings of bodies lying spread-eagle in the middle of circles filled a sheet. Additional sketches showed X's and pentagrams overlaying identical human forms.

The sixth in a series depicted a double image—the splayed body in one circle next to an identical, empty one. Scribbled beside the drawing, the words "curse" and "transfer" loomed large on the page. Six drawings like this. Huh. Nerissa brought up the number six and said the book would answer all questions. So she had to be doing the right thing, researching.

Drowning in a sea of words beyond her capacity to decipher, she ferreted out a paragraph in English. Excellent. Progress at last.

Helen ran a short red nail down the page and read:

Curses of the flesh spring from requests made from a space of desire, and all crave a referent. These parasitic forces seek a host body to use as a vehicle or puppet, for they strive to move through the physical world with ease. Exorcism has proved unsuccessful or deadly for the practitioner, but transference spells may achieve success, esp. when used in accordance with personal talismans or charms.

A list of page numbers followed the directions, and Helen flipped to the first one. In Roman Numerals, it offered steps.

First, arrange charms or talismans into a circle of protection.

Alright. Helen shook the crystals onto the carpet and laid them in a circle around her body.

Next, practitioner utilizes personal charms to drop self into trance state. Once altered state of consciousness is achieved, practitioner travels astral highway and visits alternate dimensions in search of new host.

Recruitment and retention may entail visiting and manipulating dream states of others, bewitching target via hypnosis, seduction of a male, or psyche splitting. All require craft proficiency to execute.

Pinching her bottom lip, Helen eyed her circle of crystals. Though she'd chosen the Left Hand path, Nerissa had talked about astral travel as associated with the Right. Maybe she could mix Left and Right.

She sure as hell didn't want to "recruit" any poor, unwitting person to be the patsy for this hex by infiltrating their dreams like some creepy succubus. Brian deserved to be saved, yes, but as good of a person as he was, his life didn't warrant the sacrifice of another.

Helen pressed a palm into her forehead in hopes of calming messy thoughts. Her classes in ethical and utilitarian philosophy never covered conundrums of the magical persuasion.

Maybe once the spell got underway, answers would unfold. No way to gain craft proficiency unless she practiced. Helen pinned her stare on a crystal the color of rouge and speckled with garnet spots, allowing her mind to melt into its waxy surface and jagged edges.

She drew in a long, mindful breaths and took a crack at color magic.

Starting with a chakra meditation would lower her brain waves to a state necessary for meditative calm, so she focused on the lowest chakra, the red wheel of incandescent energy spinning at the base of the spine. Yogis associated this energy channel with safety, grounding, and security, so with any luck those traits would protect her and Brian from fallout while she hunted for answers.

Helen counted off seven seconds on the inhale and eight on the exhale. Soon, her head grew fuzzy and light, a floating balloon. Warmth enveloped her scalp, body melting into a weightless state. Her mind blanked. She was nothing but breath, in and out, moving through her energetic nodes and animating the whirling disc near her tailbone.

A shade of red so saturated the hue surpassed maraschino cherry flooded her mind's eye.

She didn't realize that her lids had closed until they opened to mysterious surroundings.

Though some facets of Helen's condo remained the same—the full bookshelves, her patchwork couch made from upcycled clothing—others morphed. Walls bent and shifted, stretching into shadowy corridors. Her living room expanded, tripling in square footage as cream-colored carpet changed to tile flooring patterned like a chessboard. To her right, a wide staircase, marble steps crumbling and banister carved into ornate swirls, curled to a second floor.

She was aware but spacey, like living in a dream, and electricity buzzed up and down her spine as her activated root chakra engaged energetically.

This had to be some kind of astral shadow realm, so she might as well explore the alternate dimension. Her barefoot steps silent against the ground, she walked down a narrow passageway, tile cool against her soles and the foreign smells of dampness and musk in her nostrils. She went on for another ten or so feet until distraught moans and a mechanical screech like a dentist's drill floated down the hall.

She ran in the direction of the commotion, opened a door, and stifled a squawk. Images bombarded her eyeballs in stabbing assaults. Concrete floor, stained a monstrous, sanguine shade. Runes and symbols painted walls black. In the corner, a temple stood erect. The chamber smelled of sweet smoke, a bit like incense and fittingly occult.

Some statue, a frightening mystery of loops and arrows and crosses forged in iron, served as a scary altar. Lodged in a circular depression near the apex of the shrine, the lost clear crystal glittered with diamond majesty.

At the base of the idol lay a staircase descending into a pit that ate light. Tile drenched in ruby gloss embellished the fucking hole in the ground with unmistakable ceremonial flair.

The scene in the middle of the room was so horrific her brain melted into a puddle of incomprehensibility.

Three figures, robed in black with mirrored slabs shielding their faces, chanted. In the middle of them, a lifeless body lay on a cot. The masked men pulled entrails from their victim, tossing them to the dirty ground where they landed in coils like shell-pink snakes. She clutched her belly, empathetic agony gutting her midsection.

Helen forced herself to look at the face of the sacrifice. And yes. Brian on the cot. A growl murmured in the pit, animalistic yet terrifyingly other. The crystal pulsed in spurts of phosphorescent light, peppering the grim surroundings with a jumble of wavering pastels.

"Do you forsake all other masters, both worldly and beyond, giving yourself in joy and supplication to the joining?" Joe said, flinging a handful of Brian's guts to the floor.

Brian croaked nonsense.

"Do you forsake all other masters, both worldly and beyond, giving yourself in joy and supplication to the joining?" A different man spoke, frustration sharpening his query.

The noises in the pit grew louder, snaps and snarls of pure evil. A cone of brightness streaked in the corner of Helen's eye.

She looked, oh God, she looked. Sinewy hands the size of dinner plates and capped by scissors of claws raked the floor above the top step.

An aberration crawled out of the depression and came into view, lithe and terrible. A cool, pyramid-shaped glow cast off by the crystal illuminated what slunk forward on hands and knees. Hunched shoulders, bald head, nude flesh the graying color of decomposed hamburger.

The face was a skull. Smoke like cumulus clouds floated around the fiend's outline.

"It's coming, it's ready," Joe hissed. "Do you forsake all other masters, both worldly and beyond, giving yourself in joy and supplication to the joining?"

"No." Brian slurred like molasses filled his mouth. "No, no, no."

"No use. We need to find the hex generator and bring them into the fold, like the spell said. I keep telling you." The man who wasn't Joe wiped his hands on his robe.

Posture stiffening with alertness as he seemed to notice something,

Joe swiveled his head in Helen's direction. In his mask, her own horrified, grimacing expression stared back at her as a reflection.

Joe advanced, left palm raised. He chanted. Frigid water invaded her veins.

"Come here," Joe whispered, reaching for her. "Join us on our Left Hand journey, coven daughter. One of six, a sacred order, we welcome you to the helm of our practice."

"Yeah, that's a hard no." She broke into a run, weaving down hallways.

Catching her breath, Helen stopped and took stock. No Joe. She'd lost him. Helen found herself in a square room about the size of L&E's yoga practice floor. Four mirror walls populated the unfurnished space with images of her.

Helen felt for a door, but her hands brushed smooth glass. One reflection moved on her own, squishing the side of her face in an absurd distortion of features. Yelping as shock jolted her system, Helen jumped backward.

"Let me out." The other Helen knocked on the glass, wild eyes matching the frantic plea of her voice. "Save me, help me."

Helen shook her head and fumbled shaking hands along the wall until she found a latch hidden between two panes of glass. She wouldn't be freeing anyone or anything until she touched base with Nerissa, thank you very much.

"Please. I can bear the load of your curse. I volunteer."

Helen pulled her fingers away from the handle, meeting her own desperate, undignified face. She recognized that expression, having pulled it while begging foster families to allow her to stay. Pity wrenched her. "Why would you do that? What's in it for you?"

Clone Helen hung her head, brown hair blanketing her features. "I ferry curses back here and feed them to my master, and he rewards me with peace."

This mirror-her worked as some kind of hex mule for her overlord?

"What are you? An aspect of me who lives in another dimension?"

Clone Helen lifted her face to view, a pitiful smile crossing her lips. "I'm your castoff parts. Those broken pieces your psyche can't integrate. Your weaknesses, fears, envy, and hate. Your subconscious sends those elements into me, and as penance for accepting them, I must toil in the inferno until my master deems me worthy of absolution."

Heavy guilt piled upon Helen's shoulders. She'd created some kind of psychic scapegoat. Unconscionable, and shot through with somber irony.

She'd been slotted into the fall guy role time and again in her foster homes, taken the blame when some other kid broke a glass or came home from school in a foul mood. Though she assumed she'd gotten over her resentment, had she instead poured the poison on some version of herself locked in a dimension of suffering and grief?

"So *if* I agree to do this, if I hand the curse to you and you feed the hex to your hell overlord or whatever, we both get a break?"

The double nodded. "Do you know the spell for psyche splitting?" Hope pitched her tone to a squeak. Helen's own sad eyes stared back at her.

Helen rubbed her thighs in fast motions. "No. Tell you what, I'll wake myself up and study Psyche Splitting in the grimoire. Then I'll come back here and help."

Shrugging, the clone tapped her toe into the edge of the mirror. "If you managed to get yourself here, you probably have enough skill to try. Psyche Splitting is a lower-level spell."

Though her intuition requested she slow down and proceed with caution, urgency pushed back against the sensible inner voice. Time marched on, with Brian facing a gruesome fate. She'd come this far, and reluctance could result in death.

"Okay. I'll try—I'll do it." Hey, in the immortal words of Yoda, do or do not. She'd act with boldness, striking that impotent word "try" from her vocab.

The clone pressed hands together in prayer. "Thank you."

Helen concentrated on the orange crystal on her floor until a tangerine orb appeared between her brows, figuring that her best bet was to move up the chakra chain to the next highest level. She drew upon the power of the sacral chakra, site of fluidity, creativity, and flow.

The mineral glowed like a crackling fireplace, moving down and taking a seat right below her navel. She pictured the graphs in the book, those sketches of bodies with lines overlaying them, doing her best to remember relevant text.

Psyche splitting, psyche splitting, psyche splitting. She repeated the mantra until coherent words blurred into meaningless sounds, the chant dropping her mind into a strange frequency where fur covered her thoughts. Ripples undulated across the mirror, wobbling from center to end in concentric circles as they invited Helen to infer what to do next.

She stuck her hand through the pliant glass, her fingers making quicksilver flutters as they sank into liquid. Flesh met flesh when a warm, strong hand gripped Helen's. The mirror yielded, a quivering hole gaping in the middle. The clone stepped out, the look on her face unsettlingly smug.

"Are we done?" Helen asked.

The clone smirked and blinked into nothing.

Well, great. In trying to solve her problems, she may have created a new one. Helen concentrated on the mundane details of her living room until she woke up in the fetal position. She snatched her phone, gritting her teeth when she brought up three missed calls from Nerissa. The witch couldn't have reached out a wee bit sooner?

An orange digit indicated a single text. From an unfamiliar number: *I found what you're looking for.*

Helen Googled the area code. Los Angeles. Brian.

She texted: *Good. I'll come to where you are. Until then, stay away from Joe. Rule number one: don't let him lead you anywhere. I'll explain in person ASAP.*

EIGHT

ON THE HOTEL TELLY, A BRUNETTE REPORTER SPOKE WITH GRAVE
certainty, "Something in your kitchen wants to kill your children. Details
at ten."

The ad for the evening news cut to a different commercial, some
inane animated gimmick to sell potato chips.

Alone on a plush bed shrouded in pristine sheets the color of snow,
Brian yanked one of the pillows out from behind his head and pressed
cloth against his face, growling his frustrations into marshmallow
softness. Speaking of reporters, he could be getting his cock sucked by
one right about now. But alas, his pesky conscience and aversion to using
women for sex got in the way of quick release, like always.

So instead of exploiting Christine like the chauvinistic sociopath he
wasn't, he hung around a generic, posh hotel room somewhere in
Wyoming with bugger all to do while he waited for his dodgy manager to
take him to a party where he'd mingle with a bunch of aging men in ties.

Ah, to live the crazy, hedonistic life of rock star Brian Shepherd.
Born to be mild.

He threw the pillow across the room and grabbed the remote,
shutting up some onscreen clown with the push of a button. On the
night stand, his mobile beeped. Brian scooted to the end of the bed and

checked the latest notification. At the sight of Helen's name, a blend of giddiness and dismay battled for control of his emotions.

Recalling the havoc in the dressing room reminded him that he couldn't let his guard down and trust the witch who'd given him the stones. Not yet.

Brian typed. *Hi. Thanks for thinking of me, but it was all a misunderstanding. Turns out I put it somewhere and forgot about it. Can u send me your address so I can mail it?*

So what, she was an attractive, interesting, alluring woman. Didn't mean anything, except perhaps that his libido wanted attention. But not from her. She was too eccentric, and in all likelihood disingenuous. Hiding things, withholding. Nope. He could not give in, no matter how deep she'd burrowed into his marrow.

Helen: *Can u text me a pic first?*

Sliding off the bed, he crouched and unzipped the inner pocket of his suitcase. The original stone from the fair rested against the second one, twins reunited. Brian caressed the first stone, the little piece of Helen he'd stuck in his luggage in some forgotten moment.

Warm pulses radiated from the rock and into his fingertips, and for a fleeting instant he imagined the nub he massaged between his thumb and forefinger was the sensitive pleasure center situated an inch above the entrance to her body.

What types of strokes did she prefer? Hard and fast, or soft and slow?

His cock swelled, balls tensing. Pressure gathered in his lower abdomen as the fantasy took over. In his mind, he rubbed her and rubbed her, making her moan and spread her legs wide.

He bet she was flexible, able to make those long legs span the width of a king-sized bed. His eager dick ached, begging for a kiss or caress.

Brian dragged himself out of the lust haze. Doing his best to ignore the tightening of his trousers, he balanced the crystal on his thigh and positioned his phone camera. He maneuvered his leg, angling it so that his raging erection didn't sneak into the frame. Even if he never saw Helen again, he'd hate to offend her by sending a dick pic on accident.

After a few tries, he got a focused shot of the stone and texted it to her.

Helen: *It's a fake. Someone wants to lull you into a false sense of security. Do you have the second one still?*

Brian: *Yes.*

Helen: *Let's see it. Please.*

He repeated the photographing process with the second stone, taking a picture of the two side by side for good measure.

Helen: *They're both different than the ones I gave you. Bogus. So someone stole both clear crystals and replaced them with these duds.*

Brian: *None of this makes a shred of sense.*

Well, that wasn't entirely true. An expansive cast of staff including Joe and the security guards he liked to boss around had access to Brian's personal effects and could have switched out the stones.

To what end, he couldn't say, but he could say with certainty that Joe would not blab what he knew unless offered an incentive or given no choice. Which was the purpose of the party, to back Joe into a corner and get him confessing.

Helen: *I know. Can I come see you? I have some explanations. I think we should go over the situation in person.*

A numbing sensation marked Brian's emotional retreat, blotting his nerves in an anesthetizing current. Perhaps he ought to cut ties with Helen and block her number. He had enough on his plate with Joe and didn't need another problematic person in his life, strength of the pull he felt toward her be damned.

But three bouncing white dots on his screen, the signal of an incoming text alert, prompted him to keep looking in anticipation of what she'd say next.

Helen: *The original crystal is being used for nefarious purposes. Demonic stuff to hurt you. I'm guessing they think they can use the second one to enrich their power. I already told you who's in charge. I might be able to stop the plot, but you need to listen and be in this with me.*

A shudder swept over Brian. He held his phone at arm's length, shaking his head though his conviction wavered. Tilly had seen things of a sinister persuasion. So had Jonnie's ex.

Made minimal sense, though, why Joe would want to harm him. Even if a murderous plot *was* afoot, Helen could have fingered the wrong antagonist. Or, acting on some unknown motive, she might be blowing a smokescreen to confuse him.

At worst, she was spinning a yarn to distract him from his goal, prodding him to cut Joe loose and renounce his mission to get his foot in the doorway of the entertainment industry's executive ranks. Anyone's guess why. People jonesing to get at celebrities schemed for all sorts of selfish reasons, most of them boiling down to greed.

Brian held off on messaging back. Helen was a black box. He didn't know who she worked for, what master she served, what hidden agendas or vested interests cooked beneath her surface. Joe, at least, was a devil he knew and could, quite literally, manage.

Brian: *I don't think so, Helen.*

Yet he watched the screen for a few moments, setting the device back down with a palpable sense of defeat when she didn't respond. Brian stripped to his boxers, folded his jeans and shirt into neat piles, and tucked them into dresser drawers.

He went to the closet and pulled out the rented suit for the evening's networking soiree, plastic dry cleaning sheath crinkling as he tossed the bag onto the bed with a rather startling degree of force.

Ripping off the protective cover filled him with destructive joy. He didn't want to go, would rather veg out to the news than attend some tiresome function and endure Joe's company.

But he must. He must, must, must. After using this gathering to his advantage, he'd interrogate Joe and figure out what he knew about cults and sacrifices and switched talismans of a crystalline sort.

For now, at least, he needed Joe's contacts. Brian wasn't established or connected enough yet to make the jump from stage to suite, a fact borne out by experience.

Remaining relegated to performing while he continued to age, however, was untenable. The show Fyre had played a couple of hours ago confirmed Brian's rising suspicions about the band's downward slide. He slipped the dress shirt over his arms, tailored material sheathing his skin.

It was a perfectly respectable venue. They'd performed in a retro theatre with an old marquee out front. Inside, gilt balcony seats and a musty aroma of grandmother's attic added to the place's vintage cool. The set was stripped, the band's showy prop forgone.

He swallowed, pulling on the trousers one leg at a time and tucking in the ends of his shirt. Abandoning making music would leave a sucking void inside of him. Perhaps he could continue to churn out the hits from years past, even if he wasn't creating anymore.

Nagging thoughts about the earlier show undermined his rationalizations while he did up his zipper and buckled his belt. Lots of irritating irony filled the crowd. He couldn't deny or downplay the self-aware scene: over-affected rock and roll horns, handlebar mustaches, T-shirts bearing the logos of other *classic, veteran* bands.

Hipster money was as good as any, Jonnie and the others insisted, but the inauthenticity of Fyre's emerging fan base made Brian squeamish. He craved the undiluted, unfiltered adoration of pure fandom. If that made him an egomaniac or narcissist, fine.

An executive job wouldn't give him fans, but it would bestow fresh prestige upon him, which beat retiring. Fame was all he had and all he'd known. Did anything even exist on the other side of celebrity?

Brian's clothes no longer fit. A starched collar strangled him, and blended synthetic fabrics chafed his torso and legs. He cut a glance to the mirror above his bed, looking into his own eyes as he knotted a cobalt tie. Though his body boasted the lean, conditioned results of his daily running regimen, his face looked tired. Women still responded to his natural handsomeness, his good bone structure and facial symmetry, but feminine attention hadn't filled him up for quite some time.

He loved to fuck women as much as any other straight man with a sex drive, but not in shallow, soulless encounters. Relationships, though, caused anguish. So that pretty much ruled out all options except celibacy, undertaken with begrudging resignation.

In any event, his needs eclipsed those of the flesh. His work demanded the majority of him, the bulk of his libidinous passion, and he wasn't about to squander that by wiling away aimless days in his mansion like some eccentric recluse. So no, nothing of merit existed on the other side of fame. Nothing in terms of his identity.

Throwing his shoulders back, he imagined himself wearing the outfit he had on while sitting in a corner suite. Signing new acts. Producing television. Putting his mark on the world, albeit from behind a polished desk as opposed to on a stage.

Brian inserted his curated fantasy of success into his mind and ordered the scenario to stay there, but it refused to drop down and fill his heart.

A watery, impressionistic image of Helen's face trespassed into his boardroom dream, mingling with the vision of his future in a welcoming way that didn't make sense. Because nothing about her, about *them*, made sense.

But that didn't mean he could forget her. How she made him laugh for the first time in months, with her charming and unpretentious humor. Helen made him see the artist, the creative man with whom he'd lost touch.

How had he made her feel? He knew how he'd *like* to make her feel, if he got her alone on this bed. The sound of his name, moaned in orgasmic delight in her voice, charged through his bloodstream like lighter fluid. His prick stiffened to full size. Speaking of size, did Helen care about length and girth? If so, she'd be in luck. The stubborn thing got even harder.

Enough thoughts of sex. No more daydreaming of a woman who would make his life more stressful, who would complicate him. Brian palmed his mobile off of the end table and rang Joe, thoughts of the man's doughy face killing his hard-on right and proper.

The manager answered after many rings, right as Brian anticipated the click to voice mail. Odd. Joe was always so eager to talk, made a habit of being at Brian's command like a good little Hollywood arse-kisser.

"Hey, man, great to hear from you. I was just about to call. Got, eh, tied up in a meeting." Joe gasped out his words in a struggle for breath. Rhythmic sounds, like choral music, hummed in the background.

Brian cocked his head. "Is that chanting I hear?"

Joe laughed, so loud and forced, Brian had to hold the phone away from his ear. "Yeah, man. I'm stepping out of a screener for this insane— and I mean fucking bananas—horror movie. Good news for you, though. Producers might want Fyre to supply the music."

"At first you said you were in a meeting."

"Right, yeah, they screened the film during the meeting. Like I said, doing the sound would be a great opportunity for Fyre."

Skepticism coiled around Brian's heart. "Sounds like the score's already been produced."

On Joe's end, a door closed. "They're gonna redo the sound. But you let me take care of minutiae and stupid details, man."

"Ready to head to the gathering?" Once he got this party over with, he could assure himself that he'd leveraged the final leg of the tour to take proactive steps on behalf of his future.

"Uh huh. I'll be there in ten." Joe's voice came out greedy and soured him with the sound of unchecked zeal. What an obsequious runt of a man.

Brian hung up and channel surfed, stupefying his brain in lieu of thinking about the upcoming party.

* * *

SPARSE CITY LIGHTS FADED TO BLACKNESS. RURAL SCENERY DRAPED the sleek white Lexus as the car coasted down endless stretches of lost highway. A deer crossing sign riddled with bullet holes flew past, giving way to a wasteland of nothing. At the horizon's edge, an abyss of dark swallowed the headlights of the vehicle chauffeuring Brian and Joe to the party.

Brian stuck a finger in the basin of his collar and pulled, the new car's chemical odor sickening him. "If I bought a second or third home, I sure as hell wouldn't pick one all the way out here."

"The name of the game is discretion." Joe glanced at his phone, then looked out the window. He wouldn't make eye contact. Brian could smell the manager's sweat, reeking like onion soup mixed with musky deodorant, from the neighboring back seat.

"I thought the name of the game was self-promotion. Why else would they give their event such a horrendously pretentious title?"

Bronze Phase. Good grief. Worse, the series of three parties counted upward to gold, like Olympic medals. Sometimes Brian could not suffer the industry. Perhaps he could fake his own death and fall off the grid with nothing but his voice and an acoustic guitar, see if a truly radical move unlocked his inspiration and got the music flowing with consistency.

"Let me handle this, okay?" Joe spoke in a clipped tone.

The car hung a sharp right and bumped over an unpaved road. Seatbelt locking with straightjacket tightness, Brian clutched the bar above his door. In every direction, the staggering and utter absence of light closed in on their vehicle. The driver switched on his high beams, but twin halogen columns illuminated nothing but lumpy dirt.

"What's there to handle about a party? It's work the room and promote what I can do for the Aries brand in a managerial role, not brain surgery."

Joe teethed on a cuticle. "Gonna level with you. You're on thin ice. Aries is concerned with your behavior."

Brian scoffed. By musician standards, he was a monk. How in the world had he managed to ping some Aries Records executive's naughty boy radar? "I think they have the wrong man in mind."

"Quit being glib and willfully obtuse," Joe snapped, a hardness in his gaze as he met Brian's stare. "It was that fucking interview where you rambled about a side project. Aries doesn't want to see you spread thin. They want to know that you're one hundred percent invested in the project, not acting out your midlife crisis with solo shit."

Brian narrowed his eyes at his manager, turbulence jostling him. "What do you mean *the* project? I wasn't aware that there was a specific plan in mind beyond currying favor with the hotshots."

"You're off the rails and off message. For your information, I talked Aries out of cutting you loose and managed to salvage your invitation to this party."

Brian's guts hardened. Foul tastes filled his mouth. A flailing sensation, like the floor had dissolved beneath his feet, destabilized him. The manager's tone, an undiluted reprimand, threw Brian for a loop. He hadn't felt so in trouble since Grandmother had shrieked at him, years and years ago, for failing to put down the bloody guitar and clean her flat before dinner. But he gathered his wits.

"That's ludicrous. Fyre is Aries' top act. You think they're keen to break their best performing cash machine? I think not."

"Your ego is standing in your own way. Aries has new acts signed, a floppy haired, lip-synching club boy they pulled out of Florida. Some singing, dancing little morsel from Iowa. These guys are looking to the future, and I don't have to be the one to tell you that over-the-hill English rockers ain't it. And if you've got some indie fantasy swirling through your outsized head, good luck getting that off the ground after alienating the biggest label in the biz. You'll be blackballed all over Los Angeles. Aries has powerful people in their back pocket, and they will sabotage you at every conceivable turn."

The warning should have made Brian angry or defensive, but instead he found himself confused and a bit afraid. "Why are you telling me all of this? Why now?"

The bumpy ride smoothed, and the car pulled onto pavement leading them under a canopy of trees. Faint lights gleamed in the distance.

Joe blew out a massive gust of air, his flabby body deflating like a balloon. "I apologize for getting short with you. I just want this party to go well."

"And you think I don't?" Though he had to admit, his apprehensions kept mounting. He checked his phone. A black X crossed out pale signal bars. He couldn't leave. At the end of the tree tunnel, a gated mansion came into partial view.

"It's, well, what I'm trying to say." Joe slashed a hand through what remained of his hair, resetting greasy strands into some semblance of a comb over. "What I'm trying to say is try to keep an open mind, okay? Things work differently at these upper levels. Trust me."

Brian said nothing, though sweat made the fabric of his shirt sticky. The slick way Joe requested trust didn't inspire any faith. The car approached a fortress wall of an iron gate, and the driver hopped out and punched a code into a box. Bars spread open with a groan. The driver got back in. The car resumed a creep.

Invisible bugs crawled over Brian's skin as the Lexus advanced upon a Victorian-style estate at the end of a mile-long driveway and manicured lawn. A few lights, too few, lit a smattering of windows on the first story.

Total isolation. Desolation. No neighbors in sight. The kind of place one dumps a body.

Damn Joe for putting him on edge, whipping his unease into a lather.

The Lexus pulled into a roundabout and stopped. There were no other cars. An internal sensation of a ball rolling downhill careened through Brian. He and Joe got out, slamming their doors in unison.

Joe rang the doorbell, rocking on his heels. His cheeks puffed.

"Nervous?" Brian drew out the word. Though Joe had always thought far outside of the box in pursuit of ambitions, Brian had acted in error when assigning a positive value to those traits.

The manager shook his head like he had a lit cigarette on his scalp.

"Hold up." This from the driver, jogging from the idling car. In each hand, he held an item about the size of a Frisbee.

Brian dropped his gaze to the driver's offerings. Time slowed to a drag. Two masks. Joe accepted one, an eerie mirrored thing the color of bronze, and slid the costume over his face.

"You're kidding." Brian eyed the one meant for him, latex molded to look like a skull. The driver thrust the mask forward, its plastic flesh trembling. They had to be pranking him, having him on. "Nice one, really."

"You've never been to a masquerade ball? I told you, these guys like to maintain their discretion when brokering big deals." Joe's voice came out muffled behind the shiny shield concealing his face. Brian almost laughed at the absurdity. Almost.

"Makes no sense."

"Fine. Have it your way. Get in that car and head back into town. I'll tell these guys that the deal is off. Good luck getting even a Vegas gig after tonight."

Cheap, sleazy Vegas imagery invaded Brian's head, obnoxious bachelor parties and bored non-fans standing on tacky, frayed carpet while they took a break from losing money to slot machines to halfheartedly watch Brian's show.

What was wrong with him? He could handle some stupid, off-season Halloween party. He accepted the mask and tugged flimsy latex over his head, breath muggy against the material. Its sickly-sweet odor overpowered him, befitting the overwhelming nature of the bizarre event.

From inside, footsteps advanced. Behind Brian, the car engine grew fainter and fainter and vanished. He swallowed a lump of dread. Nothing to do now but roll with things.

The door opened, and there stood a lanky fellow in a mask like Joe's.

A silver platter rested in his hands, the effect rendered dreamy and faraway through the narrow slits of Brian's eye holes.

"Wallets, keys, phones." The doorman spoke in robot monotone.

Joe acquiesced, diving in his pockets and forking over the aforementioned things. Brian plunked his items on the tray. The butler walked to some sort of cubby underneath a carpeted staircase, ducked inside, and came out with an empty tray. Good to know where they stashed the personal effects, in case a quick getaway was warranted.

With a scoop of his hand, Joe moved in front of Brian and beckoned him to follow.

Brian stepped inside. Masked, suited-up men and unmasked women in skimpy dresses and sexy heels filled an opulent parlor room.

The space dripped with accoutrements of wealth: velvet furniture, artifacts from around the world. Turkish rugs. A crystal chandelier burdened the ceiling, and oil portraits of monarchial subjects hung on the walls. Mellow classical music played, complemented by a soft din of polite chat from guests.

But neither the décor nor the setting disturbed him. No, that dubious honor was reserved for the costuming. Every single man wore a mask like Joe's. Every single one.

Why was Brian's different? Why was it a fucking *skull*?

"I'll facilitate some initial introductions." Walking a foot ahead of Brian, Joe moved with determination, though his voice shook.

Mirrored faces reflected Brian's death mask as men watched him and the manager cross the floor of the main room. This wasn't right. All eyes were on him, and not in a good way. He was a person of interest, a curiosity, a player in a game whose rules nobody taught him. An outsider. The other.

Brian caught up to Joe. "I need to use the restroom first." By that he meant steal a private moment to gather his thoughts and plan how the hell to proceed.

"What?" Joe paused, knocked on a door. When nobody answered, he resumed his stride.

Leaned against rose and black damask wallpaper glossed with an ivory shine, a masked man and his date halted their conversation the second

Joe and Brian approached. They stared, and Brian caught a disconcerting flicker in the woman's dark eyes. Recognition, trauma, empathy. Vestigial memories of humanity lurking behind an otherwise dead gaze.

His intuition flashed the truth in a red light. Something was wrong with the woman, with this party. Plain wrong.

"You heard me. Have to take a slash."

Joe grunted. "It's two doors back that way." He bent his thumb in the direction of where they came.

Brian did an about face and hustled to the spot in question, ducking into a washroom frosted with marble and gold accents. He sat on the closed loo. If he could find a land line, he could call a ride service and leverage his celebrity to insist they venture out into these bleak parts.

The doorknob rattled, a feminine voice giggling on the other side. Shite. In his distracted state, he'd forgotten to lock.

"Occupied." Brian hopped up from his perch, but he was too late.

A blond bird in a sheer dress leaving little to the imagination backed in to the bathroom, pulling a masked man behind her. They froze when they spotted Brian, the guy undoing his pants as the woman slid the mask to the top of her man's head.

Time to seize an opportunity.

Brian pushed up his sleeve, revealing the high-tech watch Tilly had bought him for his fiftieth birthday the other week. His cheeky daughter had meant it as a gag gift, because surely her stogy old man couldn't wield the latest technology. Lucky for him, his precious baby got this one wrong.

He scrolled through apps, found the one he needed, and snapped a photo of the stunned couple, flash reflecting off the bloke's mirror mask. While the woman cursed, Brian dashed to the door, turned a lock, and stood in front.

"Is this your wife?" Brian asked the man, pointing to the blonde.

The man stammered sheepish nonsense. His date folded slim arms over a chest augmented to cartoonish proportions.

When she moved, Brian caught a glimpse of a vertical scar beneath the see-through fabric of her clothing. The mark began below the dip of her collarbone and stopped at what looked like a brand right above her bikini line. Some kind of sigil or rune, a cluster of swirls and triangles rendered in puffy, raised flesh.

He needed to escape, pronto. This place was not safe, not alright. Brian hung on to his cool. "I'm sure your wife's divorce lawyer or private detective would love to see this photo. The settlement and alimony payments you'd have to cough up would make a whole lot of people rich and you poor. Mask, please."

A string of expletives flew from the man's mouth, but he handed his mask to Brian.

"Thanks." Brian tugged off his skull mask and slid malleable plastic under his suit jacket, tucking the wad of material beneath his arm. He donned the other man's disguise. "You lost your costume, and you never saw me. If I find out you tattled, I leak the picture. Now both of you stay in here until half-past."

The couple nodded in unison.

Brian left the restroom in a casual stroll. Stationed at the entrance, the doorman fumbled to remove a woman's bulky coat. Brian whisked to the cubbyhole and fished his things from a woven basket.

While the butler slid a fur off an Internet model's shoulders, her masked escort looking on, Brian passed the trio and slapped the servant on the arm. "Great party, but I have an emergency."

He left the house and ducked into the shadows flanking the property, calling upon a keen sense of direction earned from distance running to find his way back to the dirt trail leading to the main highway.

Walking along the side of a road, Brian removed his mask and checked his phone. Two signal bars. He powered through reluctance and fired off a text to Helen.

You're right. We need to talk. Can you meet me in Denver in two days? I'll cover airfare.

NINE

DENVER'S SKYLINE, JAGGED GRAY TEETH STUCK IN A PALE MAW OF morning sunlight, loomed on the horizon. Even the drab buildings took on a veneer of menace, like the inside of a monster's mouth. While her taxi closed in on the city, Helen shook a restless leg. Jitters flew through her system, her sense of responsibility as heavy as lead.

She had to untangle Brian from the hex during her weekend visit. And armed with the grimoire, her crystals, and whatever new info he could offer, she would fight like a boss to get him out from underneath this curse.

During their brief phone call, Nerissa confirmed Helen's suspicion. The old witch couldn't diagnose the problem or offer assistance on how to solve it until she saw the stones up close and performed an energy assessment.

Meaning the name of the Denver game was get the transparent talisman into her hot little hands ASAP and ferry the crystal back to Minneapolis. Nabbing the cursed one would be better.

Helen's ride pulled up behind a black Humvee limo idling out front of the Ritz Carlton hotel. On the sidewalk, a wedding party, the bride an exuberant poof of white frosting, posed for photos. Through her backseat window pane, Helen observed their happiness with clinical detachment. Romance was the furthest thing from her addled mind.

She texted Lisa: *Wish me luck.*

Her phone dinged a second later. Lisa: *Good luck. What are you going to tell Brian?*

The pair still stood on shaky ground friendship-wise, but at least they were speaking.

Mainlining the positivity gleaned from Lisa's text, Helen paid the driver and hopped out of a backseat perfumed with saccharine strawberry air freshener. Wind nipped her nose, dashing hair in her face along with misty blasts of drizzle. But the dreary day couldn't dampen her rising spirits.

Thanks to Stacy, her mom, and a bunch of people the rocker chick brought to L&E from her bartending job, the studio was doing better. Much better. If the influx of new students hung on to their memberships for a few months, Helen and Lisa could get the mortgage current by Christmas. Despite the brisk breezes penetrating her fleece jacket, Helen warmed. She'd done something right for a change, and through the use of smarts and legitimate business savvy for that matter. Maybe Nerissa had the right idea with her talk of Helen using inner strengths.

She sucked in a breath of frigid air and typed a reply. No time to soul search or get ahead of herself.

Helen: *Try to convince him that the vision was real, and that he needs to get away from this Joe dude and find that crystal.*

Lisa: *You got this. Gotta run, off to sub your classes! Wish I could do all of those arm balances as well as you. Hope I don't splat on the floor and break my nose, LOL.*

Helen: *Go forth and kick ass. And thank you for understanding.*

Lisa hadn't climbed aboard the witch, magic, and vision train, not yet, but she was humoring Helen and being a good sport. So progress.

The driver plopped her suitcase on the curb, slammed the door, and took off with a squeal of tires. Okay. Go time. Head up, shoulders back.

Wheels of her rolling bag squeaking behind her, she strode through the hotel's sleek, minimalist lobby while calling upon every ounce of confidence in her arsenal. Real strength came from a place of integrity, personal conviction, and honesty. And honesty was her best bet for getting Brian to open up and to help them undo the hex.

A quick elevator ride deposited her on his floor, fancy as the rest of the hotel with sumptuous carpet in a rich shade of burnt sienna and impressionistic landscape paintings beautifying the walls. She rechecked her text for his room number and made haste to his door.

He'd agreed to see her, and she needed to take this shot. Do right by him.

Helen knocked, and the sound of his footsteps ignited a rush of nerves. Brian had put her up in a different room in his hotel so she wouldn't have to run around. A small act of consideration rich with kindness. Though the devil allegedly resided in the details, Helen found an angel in the nuances of Brian's actions.

He swung the door wide, greeting her with a businesslike nod. In a black hoodie and worn jeans ending at bare feet, he emitted a downplayed sort of eroticism. Must have been the subtle intimacy of bare feet. Long, high arches tapered into graceful toes. Made her wonder if the rest of him was like his feet. Well-proportioned, nice length.

She coughed a fake cough, blasting the fantasy out of her mind. This was a serious work visit, not a social call or hookup. "Good to see you."

"You too. Come in." Caution in his tone put distance between them. He touched her waist as she walked past, pulling away like he had to guard himself against more contact. She killed the urge to hug Brian. They weren't on comfy-cozy terms.

Helen propped her bag in a corner, taking the initiative of putting the luggage somewhere in order to bypass mention of a bedroom.

With a panoramic glance, she took in a swank suite more akin to a penthouse apartment than a hotel room. A plush sofa, glass table set with a vase of black calla lilies, and overstuffed chairs dressed a living room overlooking downtown Denver. A few guitar cases and small amps sat piled in a corner. Dang. She had to admit the fancy digs and sprawling view caused her chest to swell with excitement.

"Nice place," she said.

Had he already brought a woman to his sexy, anonymous, tour-stop bachelor pad? Called upon the services of a random groupie to sate his male urges? The thought lit a flare of envy. But she didn't smell perfume or other residual traces of femininity, neutralizing the baseless jealously. Yeesh. Why did she even care?

Brian cracked a smile, dimples denting both cheeks. "Thanks. You can help me trash it later, but I get to throw the television out the window."

Helen twiddled her fingers like a cartoon villain. She had to admit, a man who could deploy observational humor with aplomb took her down like kryptonite. "Is TV defenestration the apex of the rock star hotel room freak-out?"

Brian shook his head and stepped closer. His sea eyes drowned her, mesmerizing in their searching desire. The look in his stare heightened her awareness of his scent, musk blended with shower freshness.

"Oh. No. That's beginning of the night shenanigans. When I hit my peak I'm driving a Mercedes into the pool and snorting kitty litter mixed with what's left of the blow."

"I see. What happens after two a.m.? Gluing the furniture to the ceiling? Stealing a groupie's pet monkey and lighting its tail on fire?" She eyed his fit, lean body. Good thing she had willpower in spades. Yeah. She did. She had lots, tons.

Helen was here to work on a supernatural conundrum, not to seduce or be seduced. She repeated the reminder twice in her mind.

His gaze fell to her lips. "Who knows. By then I'm rolling so hard on my bath salts that I'm a proper disaster."

"Busted." Wetness flowed from her core and into her panties. She couldn't remember the last man with whom she'd enjoyed witty repartee. The sparkly pleasure of sparring with a guy she liked was as refreshing as an oasis in a desert. "If you were a true bath salts zombie, you'd know that one geeks out or tweaks out on bath salts."

The point of his tongue poking from the corner of his mouth, he looked her up and down.

"Ah, well, perhaps it was meow-meow I was hooked on." His voice came out hoarse, a sandpaper scratch roughing up that polished accent.

A current of desire flowed from her nipples to her clit as if a wire connected her sensitive parts. Did he talk dirty during sex? Moan words or phrases in that voice of his?

Helen barked an awkward monster of a cough-laugh before her lust took over and she did something dumb, like vault to her tiptoes and plant a kiss on his lips. "We should debrief."

Did Brian wear boxers or briefs? She'd like to slide either type of underwear down his narrow hips and sculpted legs. Ack, even her attempt to change the subject to buzzkill matters came out sounding like an innuendo and got her hot.

"Yes, well." Brian chuckled. The apples of his cheeks pinked. "I suppose so."

Masking her urges with a no-nonsense façade, Helen dragged her suitcase over to the couch and sat. She pulled out the grimoire and velvet bag of crystals.

Brian settled on the cushion next to her, close enough that his proximity caused butterflies to take flight in her belly. But no way would she let stubborn attraction lead her astray, or heaven forbid fall into bed with the man. Sex was too complicated. But what would sex be like with Brian? Methodical? Romantic? Filthy? Would he make her come?

Before she could quash naughty thoughts, the cloud of hex smoke burst in Helen's core.

Tendrils coiled through her midsection, forming a tempest. Dread clomping in like the horsemen of the apocalypse, she laid a hand over her stomach and tried to guess what awakened the bad energy.

"Are you alright?" Brian touched her knee, withdrawing his hand seconds later. "Ouch. Shite."

"What?" Muzzy fog filled Helen's head. The pressure in her center loosened, pushing out of the front of her head in an ashy white plume. Bending the air with wobbles like heat waves, the emission slithered to the front of the room, flattened itself, and slipped through the crack separating door and floor.

Brian clenched his wrist, flexing his fingers. "I've been getting these pains. I assumed carpal tunnel at first, degenerative issues from playing guitar for so long, but I had a flare when I touched your crystal on the bus. And again just now."

Five and five made ten. "The curse feeds off something in me, charges up and then goes off seeking the crystal. Whoever has the crystal is working this to their advantage. This entity is getting more powerful."

Brian scowled, his gaze sliding to her big book of esoteric weirdness. "Entity? Curse?"

She sighed and geared up to barf out the truth. "Yeah. I accidentally cast a curse."

"What? Why? What type of curse?"

"It was a byproduct of choosing my path as a witch. I wasn't suited to the type of power I took, and the universe generated a hex to punish me."

Brian fluttered his eyelashes, face bending into a grimace. "Why is this curse after me? You see how bolloxed up this is?"

"I do. Could be the curse needed someone to attach to, and you were the first person I paid sustained attention to that day. But now I think it's more. I think whatever entity this curse is associated with, you're already on the radar. Primed. Someone in your inner circle is messing around with the same type of magic I have, which helped the curse to identify you. There are people controlling the entity, encouraging demonic manifestation. So you made an easy target."

Brian looked through Helen, not at her, his mind seeming to drift to a memory or thought horrible in nature. "They're cutting people and taking out their organs."

Shock came at her so hard that she got heartburn and saw double. "Who's cutting people?"

He dug a thumb and a forefinger into the inner corners of his eyes. "Some secret society, I don't know. But there's multiple witnesses. The victims should die from the procedures, but they don't. Which makes me wonder what they're doing besides cutting and surgery."

"On your bus, you alluded to other odd happenings. Tell me anything you can." She could cross-reference Brian's account with the grimoire and consult Nerissa. The incident with the clone in the mirror was a loose end, a weak flank, but telling Brian wouldn't help.

Before casting a spell to undo damage, she ought to do her best to make sure she was as powerful as possible. In control of her magic.

"Joe got into mysticism a few weeks ago. I dismissed it at first as Hollywood nonsense, another pyramid scheme to separate fools from their money. But then he tells me about some ritual he went to, a workshop where he learned remote viewing. And you know what? He described, in perfect detail, what I was doing the other day on a different side of town. The implication, the implicit *threat*, was that he's using this newfound power to spy on me. That'll make you paranoid, right? That's when I started suspecting him, but I tried my best to disregard my feelings. And shame on me. I wanted to use him for my own selfish gain. So I downplayed his dealings and went on like normal."

"I get why you went into denial. This stuff isn't easy to accept at first, and we're hardwired to rationalize. Do you know of anyone besides Joe who might be in this cabal?"

Brian laughed, a dry grunt. "Oh yes. An entire nest of them. Got dragged to this weird party the other day. I was leaving when I texted you. They held a gathering in the middle of nowhere. Joe led me there, of course, and he seemed more piqued and wired than usual. But also scared and furtive. So I'm already unsettled, and when we arrive all of the men are wearing masks."

Vertigo sucked Helen's perception in and out in blurry contractions. The content of her vision bombarded her memory. She couldn't pinpoint how her clone fit in, but now she had evidence verifying the significance of masks.

"What did the masks look like?" She supposed she asked out of some sense of false hope, denial. Because she knew what he'd say, like she sometimes knew what song would play on the radio a moment before a tune started.

"Mirrored slabs." He drew the syllables out it a flat cadence laced with bitterness. "Except mine. Mine was a skull. There was a woman there with a long scar and a brand on her body, too. I left before I saw anything more disturbing. Got the hell out of that box of rabies."

Poor Brian, having to endure such hell. She rested a palm over his knuckles, squeezing support into him. "That's horrible. And you did the right thing by leaving."

He gave a wan smile. Puffy red pads lined the undersides of his lids, the physical evidence of his distress slicing through her. The incident clearly upset him. Apt response.

"There was a time, around a year ago, where I thought I could trust Joe. He was so, so good at pretending to be my friend, my advocate, a rare champion among the social climbers. He'd talk me up, praise me, and I always felt proper chuffed when he was around. A manipulation tactic, but my ego didn't let me see it for what it was."

She nodded, listening, a bath toy adrift in the ocean of Brian's confession. And she needed to channel Poseidon's strength and stop these assholes before they made their next move. "But then he showed you who he really was."

Pain shone behind Brian's eyes in a stark gleam. "Yeah. I'm grateful for all I have, but there's this cost. I'm careful, I'm cautious, I act smart. And then I feel safe, okay, and I let my guard down. I go, 'this one's good people. A friend, not a ghoul. I'm not alone.' And that's the second they strike. They plunge the knife in every time. And you're back at square one. Alone in the darkness. Where nobody cares." He pursed his lips.

Deep inside Helen, a balloon burst and filled her chest with compassion. She placed her hand over Brian's sternum. His heart thumped beneath soft cotton and the press of her palm.

"I care." She slid the hand from his chest to his cheek, finding his lived-in skin firm but not baby-soft. A single bead of warm water slipped from his eye and wetted her finger pad. Right then, her heart shattered into a billion shards. "I'll protect you."

Bemusement brought a knitted element to Brian's gentle face. "I appreciate the gesture, but how? You're in exquisite shape, but you don't strike me as the bodyguard sort."

Helen lifted her bottom off of the couch, leaned up, and pressed her mouth to Brian's. She massaged and nibbled his top and bottom lips, treating each to equal attention.

Lavishing, she willed magic into the union of their flesh, pretending she could bless a kiss with the power to cure his pain.

A moan left his throat, and he kissed her back. He deepened their contact, moving a hand to rub the back of her head, his skilled lips sucking hers. His taste, minty fresh, its uniqueness woody-sweet, spun her into a cloud of arousal.

She slid her tongue in to take his inviting, warm and wet cave. At her invasion, a startled little growl, a sound male and animal and so damn *raw*, leapt from Brian.

Tongues nudged, stroked, savored. She licked his teeth, diving deeper, and allowed her hand to rove to his trim abdomen. Helen sent her wandering and shameless hand to his waistband.

Brian's tongue stiffened against hers. His probes grew faster and deeper, became sublimated fucking. Oral thrusts claimed her. The grip in her hair tightened. She matched him plunge for plunge, her tongue as bold and curious as his. Her hand, equally so, ventured down and touched his full erection over his jeans. The hard length of him, so long and wide, pushed stiffness into cloth. She stroked his bulge and landed at a wide crown close to his waistband.

He groaned into her mouth, a pained sound of need, crushing their lips into urgent congress.

Helen rubbed Brian's swollen tip, the pads of her index and middle fingers gathering hot friction against denim. His heart sounds merged with hers. The musky scent of his excitement drifted up. She fumbled with the snap on his jeans, ready to kneel before him and make him feel incredible. Because this man deserved a great blowjob, and so much more. More than she could give, but she'd damn sure offer whatever she could.

Brian broke the kiss. Lips swollen and wet, he looked at her like she was a scrumptious meal he wanted to devour. "Not the best idea."

"Right. Need to stay on track. Research."

"Research mode requires cold shower. Be right back." Brian brushed a kiss to her cheek, rose, and walked down the hallway. Water ran.

Helen lost her grip to a bizarre, uncanny relative of déjà vu. She blinked, spacey. A misty whirlpool coiled below her navel, whipping in frantic circles, gathering steam. This sensation marked the onset of curse activity, a type of clarion call.

While she awaited the energy's rushing from her body and darting in the direction of the crystal, Helen reached for her bag. From now on, she'd track nefarious behavior in her journal and search for patterns.

A whoosh, as deafening as a howling gust in a wind tunnel, blew into Helen's skull. She fell to her side, equilibrium gone and mind empty. But the hurricane inside kept churning when the force should have zipped out of her by now.

"Lift your right arm." The slick male voice from Nerissa's house and the fair paralyzed her with fright.

Though she'd all but forgotten about him, he hadn't disappeared. He'd been dormant, lying in wait. Plotting.

"No," she whispered, clamping a hand over the arm in question for good measure.

A string of words in an unknown language followed. Helen's fingers and toes numbed, becoming as dead and heavy as rubber. A rumble quaked inside of her, and black horror bobbed to her surface.

"Lift your right arm."

"No."

A flash of movement and the outline of a person attracted Helen's attention to the window overlooking the city. Fear zipped around her system, making her surroundings crystal clear and sharp as sizzling tingles piqued her nerves.

The petals of the lilies, tips as pointed as forked tongues, popped into ominous relief.

Rain beaded glass, slashing diagonal splatters. Watery streaks painted an apparition in the window. The double of Helen stood there, smiling like a maniac.

This was no simple reflection. Though she wore an identical outfit of jeans and a T-shirt, she stood while Helen sat.

The male voice grunted more of the spooky language. "Raise your right arm."

The double in the window complied, bringing her limb to hover at hip's length in a creepy, zombielike pose.

Clicks, snorts, and harsh syllables lacking the harmonious curvature of vowels bombarded Helen's ears. "Lift. Your. Right. Arm."

Unable to look away from the clone, Helen lost a battle to hold on to her faculties. Zoned out, she watched in shock as her arm shot up into the air.

"Excellent, excellent, excellent. Now we find something sharp to put in our hand."

Hysterical laughter followed the male voice's declaration. The clone joined in, adding to a cackling frenzy, and dematerialized.

Helen snapped back to clarity. Her arm flopped to her side.

"You alright?" Brian walked into the living room.

Nope, but no point in alarming him. She'd spoken too soon when allowing herself to slide into fantasies about beating this thing with her wits and moxie. No, an opponent of this magnitude called for heavy-duty witchcraft. Big-ass spells.

As soon as she got back to Minneapolis, she'd get to work on levelling up her skills, but for now she'd have to wing it. In the meantime, she could team up with Brian on the hunt for clues—anything they could dredge up that could lead her to a stopgap.

"Fine. Let's find some ammo to help us beat this thing."

TEN

Brian thumbed through a few pages of Helen's arcane book, pausing on a fascinating yet foreign illustrated portion before moving on. The research session reached a lull, the sort of comfortable silence he hadn't enjoyed with another person in ages.

Typing on her laptop with soft clacks, she lay on her stomach, stretched across the floor of his penthouse suite with her legs bent in the air and crossed at the ankles. Her posture of comfort and ease mellowed him.

His back resting against the couch as he sat on the floor, he watched with respect as she worked. Outside, rain tapped a calming drumbeat. A realization hit. In this moment, he didn't need to move or hustle or plan. Didn't need to order anyone around. Didn't need to worry. He could unplug from the fame circus and be, if only until they spoke of their problem again.

His thoughts drifted to his past, before everything went sideways and barking mad with the soon-to-be-fired Joe. His mind open, the sensation serene and thoughtful, he considered new possibilities. Not everyone who was into esoteric things was like Joe and his goons. His mum certainly wasn't.

And now, cozied up with the mysterious woman who'd taken control of his emotions with her passionate kiss, Brian craved understanding about what made her tick as much, if not more than, he wanted a solution to his predicament.

Helen rolled to her side and stretched. The mermaid pose highlighted her voluptuous curves, and craving stirred below his belt. Where was his restraint? On most days he possessed sexual continence in droves, but on this one his hormones wrestled control out of his erstwhile iron grip.

When they'd kissed, he'd felt more than lust, though he'd felt plenty of that. But their kiss left an impression on him, one that transcended the ranks of sex.

He'd escaped with her to someplace he'd never been. Not with any other woman, even his wives. With her, he escaped from himself, from a certain cold inaccessibility he projected to keep other people at a safe distance. When Helen melted his defenses with her kiss, his heart grew.

And for that, despite whatever she'd done or thought she'd done, he would remain in her debt. Whether they—or, rather, she—needed to talk about the kiss or forget, he couldn't say. For now, the pleasure of her company sufficed.

"How long have known you were different? In possession of these abilities?" he asked.

"Since I was a teenager. But back then I didn't have a name for it. I thought I was a mess, broken in some fundamental way, and so did the families. Therapists said I had episodes of disassociation and depersonalization related to Complex Post Traumatic Stress Disorder, but that never felt like a complete explanation. I'm sure trauma was a factor, but I suspected more."

Interest in her history took the place of an urge to get her naked. "Families?"

Her posture stiffened. She flipped back to her belly-down position.

"Foster families," she muttered, fingers clacking over keys like she wanted the sound to muffle her words. Her shoulders cranked up to her ears.

"Sore subject? I don't mean to pry." And he didn't. She'd open up when, and if, she felt ready. The woman didn't owe him her life story.

"Ugh, it's fine. Yeah, it's sore, but that's on me. I really need to let that wound heal." She typed, poking a key a bit too hard.

He slid along the front of the couch, bringing himself within touching distance. "Why is it sore, if you don't mind me asking? If you do mind, feel free to respond with 'piss off, Brian' or similar."

She humored him with a quick chuckle. "No, I'm not that volatile or reactionary anymore, thank goodness. But I suppose there's a part of me that blames myself for the fact that I never got adopted. Before that, my life was one intense thing after another. My father's suicide, my mom's psychotic break, Child Protective Services getting involved. There's this part of me that's always wondered if I was some kind of cursed person from the get-go, flawed to the core, attracting bad things."

"You aren't flawed to the core. I think you're wonderful. You endured a bout of bad luck and walked away from it with poise and strength. I admire your tenacity. You're a fighter."

"Yeah, well, it gets hard to believe you have worth when your mother is tying you up in the basement, shaving your head and doing exorcisms on you. And then you go to school with rope burns and no hair, and all of the teachers assume you're a stupid girl acting out for attention. And then it gets worse. Yay you." A shaky undercurrent jostled her hardened words.

Her hands shook as if her body was mirroring the cracking of fault lines beneath her rocky surface.

Brian sure could relate to such an aggressive effort to block pain, the act one enacts due to lack of trust, a skittish fear of others. He squeezed the arch of her foot and massaged the sole with his thumb. "I'm sorry that happened to you. Sounds awful, like something I wouldn't wish upon my worst enemy. You deserved a stable life and a proper head start."

With a definitive jerk, Helen pulled her foot out of his grip. His heart sank. What had he done?

"It's fine. Ignore my self-pitying bullshit. The past is gone. Over. You find anything useful in that book?"

"I apologize. Did I hurt you? Touch you wrong?"

"No. I said it's fine. Anything of value turn up in the big book of weird?"

Though Brian reeled from her retreat, he heeded her call to switch subjects and returned to reading pages full of various languages and eerie drawings. Avoiding difficult emotions by way of productivity was his forte, so he could respect Helen's move.

Her apparent tendency to repress via labor also evidenced traits in common, albeit a sad alignment of broken pieces. Maybe he'd found the right woman at long last, someone whose cluster of pathologies mirrored his own.

A bizarre, unintended noise, steeped in a muddle of ironic amusement and childlike delight, sneaked out of Brian's mouth.

She flipped her hair, shooting him a side-eye that betrayed the faintest flutter of vulnerability. "What the fuck was that, you swallow a whoopee cushion?"

He flinched, but not at the sound of her curse. She'd called him out, something he never experienced from the disingenuous flunkies who hung around the perimeter of his world.

"You remind me of myself sometimes is all."

"Um, huh? I'm neither rich, nor famous, nor talented."

"I meant your defense mechanisms. And of course you're talented. I don't see why you downplay your many positive traits with self-deprecation."

"I feel so seen." She fixed him in the crosshairs of her askance look. But now the corner of her mouth curved and a twinkle shone in her eye.

Moving a piece on his mental chessboard, Brian allowed a pause to linger. Just a few seconds, enough time for her to process the fact that he was thinking of her. "I do see you."

The look passing between them drew intrigue, trepidation, and a hell of a lot of attraction into a strong field. Brian ran a single finger over the bottom of Helen's foot, watching with delight as her sole curled like a caterpillar. He sucked his bottom lip. He'd love to make her toes curl from a different kind of stimulation.

"You're a total player." In one swift, fluid motion suited to a person gifted with superior balance and equilibrium, she scooped up her laptop and vaulted her body to sit beside him.

The teasing way she'd called him a player, combined with how she moved to get closer to him, betrayed the inviting nature of her retort.

Helen's fragrance, smoky and floral, drifted from the lazy coils of her brown hair.

"Why would you call me that?" Though he tried to mask the sultry ache in his inflection with a cloak of neutrality, his speech insisted on coming out all low and rumbling.

She quirked her lips like she knew where treasure was hidden. He longed to see the riches inside her guarded, compelling mind as much as he craved the sight of her sexy body naked.

"You're disarming. I'm sure you have quite the effect on women."

"Do I have an effect on you?"

"Casting aspersions on you asking a question you already know the answer to, ego man."

Helen pretended to read a webpage, scrolling down a wall of text though the waxy gloss over her eyes unveiled disinterest in the content. But her body heat, and the instinctual way she angled herself toward him, radiated sexual chemistry.

Brian neglected his sexual and emotional needs, sure, but that didn't mean he couldn't read women. "Is that why you kissed me? To cast your aspersions?"

One of her shoulders bent, the gesture an overblown attempt to convey nonchalance. "I kissed you because I'm attracted to you."

The harder he worked to assemble her behaviors into some semblance of a coherent whole, the more insecurity emerged in the big picture of Helen. And he didn't blame her, after surviving severe neglect and navigating the emotional wasteland.

She slackened beside him but still pretended to read.

The woman dared him to get close to her, offering tiny concessions. It struck Brian that, perhaps, she lacked the lexicon of social skills or vocabulary required to approach him with authentic assertiveness. Yet she'd been so assertive at the fair.

Which factors pushed her in one direction or the other, swung her pendulum to the brash or meek extremes? Did an in-between exist, a resting state of balance?

Instead of delving into her psyche more than he already had, he chose to open a bit of his own malfunctioning prototype of a heart. "My mum saw a palm reader—or psychic, I can't remember which—a couple of months ago. She called me up in tears, ecstatic, saying how the woman delivered information about my sister who died. How she was at peace. Happy. In a good place. Mum's been doing a lot better since then. So I'm not opposed to the idea that there's more out there. And that whatever that more is, that it can be good. In some sense I welcome the idea. Adds mystery to life. Comfort. Meaning."

Helen closed her laptop. Matching his stare with a searching look, she rubbed a circle on the closed notebook. "I'm sorry about your sister. What happened?"

"She was a baby. Got sick with the croup. We lived on a farm, middle of nowhere near the Scottish border, and health care wasn't great. My mum always blamed herself, no matter how much we reassured her. But now she's stopped."

Brian couldn't quite list all of the reasons he chose to tell Helen this. But seated beside her in an anonymous hotel room, listening to the rain, he took pleasure in talking with her.

He liked her. She was prickly yet compassionate, genuine but aloof in a way that heightened his interest. A beautiful knot of harmonious contradictions, she interested him on mental and physical levels. Her layers stirred him to song.

Human connection, even if an illusion of the connection he was loathe to admit he yearned for, provided solace.

As a younger and more reckless man with endless access to women, he'd found false bonding in fleeting road relationships, temporary partners held close for a couple of nights. He now understood that confusing love with sex was a mistake, but he could enjoy emotional intimacy with Helen if they steered clear of physical coupling and its tendency to create attachment. *His* tendency to form attachments. Brian knew himself by now and avoided casual sex for distinct, clear reasons.

"Are you close with your family? I love hearing stories about happy families. They give me hope," she said.

Noted. He'd have to censor the uglier parts of his filial saga, which suited him fine. He could talk about Mum and Dad and Alan without having to fib. "I call my parents every couple of weeks, my brother a few times a year. Visit yearly. Our lives are as different as can be, but we take comfort in each other. I enjoy hearing about day-to-day life on the farm, how the animals are faring. Keeps me grounded."

"When did you move to London? Didn't the band meet in London and break into the music scene fairly young? I thought I remembered hearing that in an interview."

Empty pain unspooled beneath his ribs. He rubbed his knuckles, easing a bit of the ever-present soreness out of his joints and bidding adieu to the concept of self-censoring. "I moved there when I was thirteen, to live with my grandmother. My parents thought I needed more opportunities to hone and pursue my musical talent."

"It paid off in spades. I want to say 'good call, Mum and Dad,' but I sense from your tone that the whole thing was a mixed bag at best?"

In an efficient show of self-preservation, Brian's defenses kicked in and stashed unpleasant memories into their lock box. He didn't need to subject Helen to his past woes, for she had enough on her docket without having to deal with his baggage about spending his teen years feeling unloved.

Besides, he was doing well now. He had a healthy, thriving child. No addictions or fights or other drama plagued his band. Brian lived a great life, wealthy and successful and full of travel and music. He had no right to complain. No right.

"I suppose," he said.

She answered with no words and a small smirk made enormous by the wisdom it held.

Their little push and pull, their dance of advance and retreat, ended in a tie. And in that draw was parity, equanimity, and respect. Her Mona Lisa smile rendered their feelings into a touché they could share like an appetizer over candlelight.

He pointed to her computer and patted the hefty text splayed over his lap. Reminiscing time had ended. Helen and he communicated well on the unspoken plane. "Shall we review what we have so far?"

"Yes. So, based on what you've told me, we've got your manager Joe, a mystical neophyte who's into remote viewing and nightmare fuel parties involving masks. You've heard rumors of a secret society cutting people open and saw a woman with the evidence of such an atrocity branded on her body. On my end, I dabbled in witchcraft in a desperate attempt to save my business and unleashed something bad. The clear crystal I gave you went missing the day we met, and this implicates Joe."

"Apt summary."

"We have a lot of dots, but we need through lines to connect them. I can't get to a definitive reason why Joe wants the crystal, what he's doing, and how his agenda ties in to what I did. I'm hoping once I get back home on Sunday I can clear some of that up, but for now do you have anything else we might be able to use? Any more dots?"

It embarrassed Brian that he fixated, with disappointment, on her comment about leaving.

A relevant memory, though, saved him from sinking into a brooding and unproductive crush on her. He took off his watch and brought up the photo of the party guest unmasked.

"Okay, good. Do you know who this is?" Her pretty eyes sparkled with engagement.

A ridiculous amount of pride in his accomplishment buoyed him. He'd found a solution she sought. He'd pleased her.

"I think he's a record executive. Aries, probably, though I can't be certain." Brian squinted at the photo. Despite a film of blurriness clouding the image, a few of the man's features jumped out. His long nose, sallow complexion, and a cluster of moles beneath one eye all dinged bells. He'd seen this bloke around Los Angeles in recent months, working the scene.

"It's a start." Helen unfolded her computer and plugged keywords into the search engine. After a few tries, she landed on a sleek page of thumbnail photos arranged in symmetrical rows and pointed at a headshot of an unsmiling middle-aged man. "That's him, right?"

Brian compared his picture to the one onscreen, getting distracted by the shape of Helen's full lips. "Look at you, Lois Lane."

"Well, I didn't have to sleuth too hard. The executive ranks of Hollywood are small. They don't refer to the elites, the one-percent, because their legions are many." She scrolled to the top of the page, paused and mouthed a few words, then backtracked to the search results and clicked on a link. "So our guy is James Elwell, the new chief financial officer of a record label who merged with yours a few years ago."

The most significant takeaway from this was a connection to Aries. All roads led there. "We have a name. Let's see what else he's in to."

"I have a guess." Stretching out her response in a dry drawl, Helen keyed in the man's name alongside "dark cult" and pressed enter.

Dozens of links to Elwell populated the screen. Hovering a finger over the track pad, Helen cringed. He didn't want to know the gory details either, but they needed them.

With a lift of his chin, he signaled her to go on.

Helen selected pages. Brian's breath hitched every time a site loaded. She surfed, and they read, words and meaning sucking oxygen out of the room and filling the hole with awfulness.

Brian wrapped a hand around his throat like an invisible devil stood poised to rip out his jugular. "It's all in the realm of conspiracy theory and speculation. So we can't be sure what's real." Yet he croaked the words out as if he spoke through a mouthful of sand, relinquishing any remaining claim to skepticism.

"It checks out, though. With our preexisting suspicions." Helen used the zoom tool, and text swelled when the page magnified.

Plain as day, in lurid yellow font against black background, allegations from an amateur webpage hurtled at Brian's eyeballs. He forced himself to read and reread, though the words pierced like arrows. And Helen was correct, it all lined up. A secret society of Hollywood elites supposedly dealt in demonology and human sacrifice. Projects included turning celebrities into vampires in efforts to create cash machines of eternal youth and hollowing people out as part of a demonic possession ritual.

Talismans and other types of magical objects facilitated the transfer of energy, allowing the summoned entity to slide into and inhabit the host body. In the lower left-hand corner of the page sat a symbol. The sigil matched the brand etched on the party guest's stomach.

Brian rubbed his face. "I suppose the end game has to be mind control, or appeasing the whims of their demon master in hopes it will bring them money and power. Christ, this all sounds so preposterous."

"It's insane. And scary. Insanely scary."

"How are you implicated in this?" he asked without expecting much.

If she hid anything, she wouldn't say. And though Helen didn't wear everything about herself on the surface, he'd ceased suspecting her.

A theory of her as a spy or crony for this cult didn't make sense. Not one shred of evidence pointed to Helen having aligned goals with Joe. Except the near-universal motive of money. At one point, Helen faced bankruptcy. He ought to keep all options on the table.

She tapped the cursor, bookmarking pages. "They must be casting energy transfer spells to move the crystals. Look, I have to get home and touch base with this witch. I'll call you when I have more."

A flurry of taps, and Hotwire appeared on the screen. A rock formed in Brian's gut. He touched her busy fingers, halting her motions before she selected a late flight from Denver to Minneapolis. "Stay. Please. Just for the night. We'll figure out more in the morning."

She turned away from the screen, forehead bunched in puzzlement. "Why? I'm no use to you here."

He let his hand stay on hers for longer than he should have, stroking silken skin over delicate veins. "You mentioned desire, in a roundabout way."

What was he doing? Brian hadn't felt this awkward around a woman since his teen years, spent strumming his guitar behind the prestigious secondary school in another ill-fated, pathetic effort to show off to the girls.

Those bored, elegant, London society princesses had tendered a clear verdict. Brian the imposter would never be enough. Never rich enough, refined enough, posh enough, princely enough. Still he'd tried, as hard as he could, to prove them wrong. Prove to them his worth, his talent, his merit. He'd never ceased his quest to prove himself.

Though Helen pulled a face, she rubbed the inside of his index finger in two playful strokes. "I guess I did, yes. I thought for a minute that the curse fed on something inside of me, maybe my emotions. But again, I'm not sure how that links in with your manager and this demon cult agenda or stolen crystals. But, like I said, I'm hoping the witch in Minneapolis might be able to help."

Brian swallowed, stuffing down his old stuttering habit with a gulp. Good grief. Get him around a woman he liked, and he regressed to a gawky schoolboy. "You brought up being a fan of my music, so I had an idea. Sort of like a test, or an experiment if you prefer."

"Yes, I am a fan. True statement. But I'm not sure I get what you're driving at here."

Bringing a closed fist to his face, Brian cleared his throat, noticing after the fact how overloud and comical the gesture sounded. A meteor was welcome to plummet from outer space and strike him dead.

"I thought if I played you some songs we could monitor your reactions and responses. Watch for curse activity and chart progress. Kind of like testing your hypothesis. About desire. Or emotions. Or things inside of you."

Things inside of you? What a sodding idiot he was. Where was his rock-star cool when he needed it?

Helen pressed her lips together, a muffled, airy giggle slipping from her sealed mouth. "An appeal to my scientific side? Bold move there, Brian."

He figured himself to be the color of tourmaline, or perhaps even persimmon, at the moment. "Never mind. At least let me buy your ticket home."

"I'm joking. Sorry, I have a bad habit of using humor and sarcasm to mask emotions. You had a good idea, made a sound point. And a private show from Brian Shepherd? Amazing. Count me in."

He managed to stop himself from grinning like a besotted fool.

An odd silence passed. They looked at each other for a little to long. Helen played with her hair, batted her eyelashes. Another second dragged. She rubbed her thighs with many vigorous strokes.

Brian couldn't read her signals, the confounding way they collided, so he doubled back to an area where he'd achieved success. Being straightforward, no games, was proven a strategy when faced with uncertainty.

"Fantastic. I'll get the equipment and bring it out here. My best guitars and amplifiers are in the bedroom."

Helen's eyes darkened to the hue of the chocolate that spilled from a lava cake. She closed the space between them and kissed him until the focus of all thought narrowed to his greedy dick and her luscious, supple curves and pockets of wet heat.

Breaking the kiss with a nip to his bottom lip, Helen whispered in hot, minty breath, "Show me this bedroom of which you speak, Brian Shepherd."

ELEVEN

"WHAT HYPOTHESIS ARE WE TESTING AGAIN?" THOUGH SHE ASKED AN earnest question, Helen ached for a break from curse talk. She could lose herself in the body and attentions of a sexy, smart man and forget the things in her life that sucked. Selfish? Sure. Heavenly? Hell yes.

And Brian was making it damn easy to forget the suckage. She arched beneath him, pressing their smooth bellies together. Her back sank into the firm mattress, scents of detergent and his personal fragrance swirling through the room.

His erection pressed into the juncture of her spread legs, his hot breath quick against the side of her neck. "The effects of desire, I think. Except you're so fucking sexy I can't think."

The first f-bomb Brian uttered, a roughness taboo in his sleek, polished accent, shot a dose of lighter fluid through her system. Her sex clenched, hungry to be filled, every nerve in her body awakening.

She wrapped her legs around his waist, pulling him closer and urging the hem of his T-shirt to the middle of his back. "Checks out."

With an eager, two-handed pull, he tugged his shirt over the back of his head and threw the garment to the floor, a gesture of assuredness steeped in erotic potency.

She ran her hands up and down his torso, making a tactile study of chest muscles and firm biceps, those strong male arms caging her in their sensual fort.

An epic black tattoo painted a path of swirling Celtic knots from hip to pectoral to collarbone, covering the majority of his left side. "Stunning. There a story here?"

"Yes." He trailed a row of kisses down her neck and peeled off her top. She pushed her chest up, affording him access to her bra. He undid the clasp in a single, one-handed maneuver.

No bumbling or fumbling in his experienced, practiced fingers. This distilled sip of arousal, fine as wine, warmed her inner spaces.

She danced her fingertips through the maze of his ink latticework, stroking his lightly tanned skin. His warm flesh brushed her bare breasts, skin-on-skin intimacy for both of them.

In an unhurried, claiming motion, she traced a trimmed nail through the black pathways. His nipple stiffened beneath her touch. "That feel good?"

"Quite." He cupped the sides of her breasts and curved slow hands down the sides of her waist. Under his nimble motions, the button and zipper of her jeans yielded.

"So what's the story with your tattoo?" Matching her actions to his, keeping up, she attacked the fastener of his pants until the fly opened.

Tandem wiggles of synchronized bodies shed two pairs of jeans. She smiled, nibbling his earlobe. Their sexual compatibility so far was stellar. A good sign. Egad. She shouldn't be watching for signs. This was a one-time thing. At least she figured.

Toeing his socks over ankles and feet, Brian pushed up on his palms and gazed into her eyes. Though primal lust darkened his irises, soft affection offset that hard glare of male desire.

"I wanted to make my body into a living diary of sorts. Every swirl and line in the gathering of knots represents something meaningful that happened on a tour. Someone I met, a landmark, an experience. It's my reminder to appreciate my life in all of the peaks and valleys, to live in gratitude for the journey."

Right then, Helen's surroundings overpowered her. She slipped beside herself, awash in strangeness. Strange city, aiming a glitter blast of skyline lights through the chic window of a swank penthouse bedroom.

A man, mega-famous and all over television, on top of her. Someone adored by everyone was hers for a bit, telling her a personal story about his tattoo.

For a sweet, eternal second of surrender, she forgot the malevolent thread uniting them.

With nothing to say, awareness of her maleficent connection to Brian returning in a loathsome creep, she looped her arms around his shoulders and let his sea-candy eyes spirit her to a distant universe far away from the self-created prison of her own meddling.

He kissed her forehead. "Are you alright, Helen? You got a little tense there. Did you want to stop?"

"No, I'm just thinking."

"About what?" He skated the pad of his thumb over her cheek in a reassuring touch.

"The circumstances that brought us together." How her existence, hell, her proximity in and of itself, threatened to ruin him. How little sense it made to deepen their entanglement, yet how right and good it felt.

"Perhaps this is how we help each other, and we don't know it yet." Honeyed wisdom floated his comment, a magical river she longed to drift down on an unhurried voyage.

Tenderness swelled to high tide, filling her dark crevices with gold. For that alone, she cherished Brian. The words he spoke enhanced his tragic aura and artistic allure.

"You said help each other, and here I was thinking I was the one helping you," she said.

His eye contact, fiery with passion and conviction, held her steady. "The energy here isn't going in one direction, and I believe you know that as much as I do."

She nuzzled his shoulder. The busted disaster of gory clumps making up what remained of her heart gathered together, fusing into one center mass. A lost memory of wholeness, nostalgia for a place that perhaps never was, made her hurt with a yearning ache.

"What are we doing?" She swallowed the threat of more words before they tumbled from her in inappropriate declarations of feelings or expressions of gratitude involving the repair of her ruined heart. Not okay to feel big emotions for Brian. Even less okay to heap them at his feet.

Brian searched behind her eyes. A precision in his look let her know he'd found what he was looking for. And the scariest part? She should have been afraid, entering retreat mode.

But instead she longed to open for him, unfold her petals like a flower starved for sun.

"I see you. I do see you." In his whisper lived sensitivity she'd long since deemed impossible for a man to possess. "Looking for someone to care for you."

But before she gave up and gave in, succumbed to the temptation to give her entire self to him, Helen closed her battered blossom. Too risky, too dangerous to bloom. Best to hold back, for even she didn't suffer complete awareness of the gangrenous ugliness haunting the depths of her soul. Not safe to flaunt her scars.

She shut her eyelids, snipping the tie of their communion and retreating from a fright he guided them toward. He led the dance with supreme skill, though, a fearlessness that coaxed her to melt into his arms and weep.

She owed him some attempt at honesty. "I have a really hard time being vulnerable. Being one-hundred percent *there* with another person."

A lifetime of residue shoved into her breastplate, pressurized and ready to burst as she spoke more. "So basically what I'm saying is that there are things I can't give to you. I'm not saying you want those things from me. I suppose I'm warning you is all. When you say you see me, I'm warning you that there is a lot of garbage you don't see."

"Nothing about you is garbage." In dim light approaching darkness, he spoke a lullaby, everything she hadn't known she needed. Or didn't want to need. "But if any part of you, physically or emotionally, isn't comfortable, we can stop. I promise I won't be upset or act sulky or passive-aggressive. If you've had enough, just say the words. Please don't feel like you owe me sex."

Helen opened her eyes, avoiding locking his for fear she'd cry. Instead of surfing a wavelength with Brian, travelling to a place where she might find herself raw, she fixed a hard stare on the tin-stamped Fleur de Lis tiles gridding the ceiling. Metal plates, arranged in neat rows and columns. Oh, to be as tidy and ordered as that stupid ceiling pattern.

But she was chaos, not order. This man, this wonderful person, she'd put him at risk with her reckless choice. If she ruined him, she would never forgive herself.

She refused to pull the plug on their impending intimacy, though, for a not-inconsequential part of her burned to follow him to the precipice of her abyss, her secrets. Helen couldn't give him much beyond the physical union of bodies tangled in bed, but lovemaking represented a small gift of care.

"I don't feel obligated in the slightest. I want to be here, with you. So much. But this has to be just sex. Nothing complicated or ambiguous, no caveats. Anything more could confuse the situation, confuse our goals." Translation: anything more than sex would scare her too much. The epiphany darted out before she could plug its escape hole.

"Well, then, allow me to show you great sex. If that's what you want." The soothing note in his timbre shifted to a randy, gruff burr. Still, the rich way he said the word "sex" rendered such a base concept inadequate to describe or do justice to their impending act.

Enough analysis. Helen reacquainted herself with her good old buddy snark. "You do realize you've asked for my clear consent a good three times. The only thing you're missing right now is a shirt that says 'Feminist' across the front."

"I'd wear it. What can I say? I'm in the 'consent is sexy' camp."

"Consider it given with the utmost enthusiasm." Steering their encounter back on the amorous track, she flashed her best seductress's grin.

He replied by dropping a quick kiss to the tip of her nose, a subtle gesture of affection tendered in nonverbal whimsy. "I'm glad."

With a swift physical transition, deft but not methodical, Brian moved his lips to Helen's. He brushed her mouth, savoring. Then, in a show of dominance that stole her breath, he molded his mouth to hers and took her with his tongue. The waltz began as he explored the inside of her and she replied in kind.

His cock thickened, growing back to full readiness while they kissed. Soon he was as stiff as a poker, pushing into the crease of her thigh in rhythmic hip thrusts. Sucking her lips while thrusting dry, Brian moaned into her mouth and closed his hand around hers, interlacing fingers, and squeezed their palms together.

She welcomed the closeness of his callused skin, warm and dry, foreshadowing the physical release of two people escaping to the joys of each other's bodies. This man was a gentleman and had sex like one, even if sex was all they were doing.

Wetness flowed from her center and dampened her panties, and she opened her legs farther in invitation. Brian's sensual kisses travelled a downward journey to her neck, a flurry landing on the pulse point behind her jaw. Nipples peaking and clit throbbing, she punched up her hips.

"Are you ready?" he murmured into her tingly skin, taking his oral attentions to her collarbone.

"Yes." She tugged the elastic hem of his boxers. A glimpse at the pattern on the fabric made her smile. Tiny Christmas trees dotted festive red cotton. The out-of-season underwear endeared her to Brian. They demystified him and represented his lack of pretention, rendering him accessible, human, real. "I'm so ready. Fuck me."

"Not before I taste how ready you are." His exploring hands pressed her breasts together, and he lapped and nipped each large swell. He sucked one pebbled tip, grazing her sensitive bead with gentle teeth. "Perfect."

She gasped, moaned, a tingle shooting from her chest to the hard bud between her legs. Brian took his lips to her opposite breast and licked the underside of her nipple, rubbing the other between a wetted thumb and forefinger. Her sex lit up, pounding, need growing to a near-painful burn.

Running her fingers through his hair, she stretched her legs wider. Just a brush of contact to her clit and she'd come, he'd worked her up so much.

"I love your beautiful body." Brian kissed her belly button, her hip bone as he made his way down. "I want to kiss each and every one of these precious freckles."

He kissed several of the small birthmarks dotting her body. She'd always been mildly self-conscious of them, as they evidenced a few summers' careless sunscreen lapses, but in the present moment she felt gorgeous. Inside *and* out.

"You're so good at this." Helen's throat tensed. "This" meant more than sex and, as much as she'd tried to kick her denial into overdrive, she knew the act wasn't just about fun. He was caring for her.

She willed herself to stay in her body and focus on the pleasure Brian gave her. Pleasure was okay, beauty and tenderness and caring were not. She couldn't fall for him. They could enjoy each other, sure, but nothing more serious. Because the truth was as stark and clear as an exit sign. Brian's life hung in the balance, and she was to blame.

If she fell for him, she would lose him. Such was Helen's fate, and if history was any indication, the grim decree had been prophesized.

"Are you still good to go, sweetheart?" His voice was rough now, raspy.

She could tell he was horny, impatient to slide his hard cock somewhere wet and stroke until he came. But he wouldn't do that unless he could rest assured that she was with him all of the way.

Why did Brian have to be so special? A lousy lay in the form of an arrogant, famous jerk making love to his own ego she could have detached from with no effort.

"I want you to keep going." She treated his neck to a little massage. "I haven't had sex in awhile is all. I suppose I got a little overwhelmed. But I want to, Brian, with you."

"I still get nervous sometimes, too." He took his hands from her chest and held hers for a moment, squeezed, and resumed his kisses.

She smiled at the thick hair on top of his head, not buying the claim for a single second. Everything about his approach so far was practiced, experienced, in control. Methodical, yet spontaneous. Suited him perfectly.

"If you say so," she said.

"Just relax and let me make you feel good, if you're sure." He glanced up to her.

"I'm sure." She was. And for the time being, despite how fleeting and illusory and sex-clouded the feeling might be, Helen lost herself to the scary-amazing emotion running through her.

The goodness might vanish when they parted ways in the Denver airport. Or get snatched away the second she got used to it, like all of those foster families did. But for now, she treasured something mysterious and precious. The word started with an L and she was not permitted to feel the stirrings anymore. Never again, and for sure not now.

Brian nuzzled her pelvis, filling his palms with the roundness of her hips. "Bet you turn heads so hard they whiplash."

With her ginormous boobs, round hips, and big ass, Helen affectionately thought of herself as an hourglass with a little extra sand, though at times she longed for a perfect beanpole yoga body like Lisa's. Now, though, under Brian's hands and mouth, she unequivocally loved her goddess curves.

Okay, okay, maybe she could feel the banned L-word about herself.

Brian took her panties down in a single firm tug, Helen assisting with hip wiggles. He found her swollen center, the work of his lips drawing a moan from her. He kissed her lower lips like he'd kissed her mouth, romantically. His nose brushed the neatly groomed hair above her seam. He kept the kiss up, languid and unhurried.

His tongue darted out, fast and surprising. Helen gasped and bucked off the bed, surged by a jolt of pleasure.

"You want me to lick you?" Brian grabbed her bottom and held on, the frank question a dirty, thrilling preview.

"Yes times a million." Her clit was so tender the spot hurt. Her bent knees shook. This wouldn't take but a minute.

He got to work, lapping her stiff, bulging bud with firm ministrations. Medium pressure, steady pace, long strokes up and down. He found her nub's underside, the hot spot, and massaged with his perfect and dedicated tongue. A handful of licks, and the buildup pulled in her lower abdomen. She panted, pressure focusing to a beam of tension.

"I'm close." Her tense voice mirrored the ratcheting tightness inside. Brian took her nerve bundle in his mouth and sucked. The wet suction propelled her to the edge.

Balling fists of sheet, she screamed, existing on the knife's point of release. He sent two curled fingers into her, found her pleasure on the first attempt, and stroked, coaxing a leveling earthquake from her core.

Climax ripped her open, erasing relief tearing from center to extremities. A waterfall gushed from her, and she writhed, groaning, lost to bliss, out of her mind.

Finally, the pulses slowed to aftershocks, and Helen fell limp on the bed, gasping and seeing stars. Brian let up on the sucking, withdrew his hand, and lapped her opening like her fluids were nectar of the gods.

"Thank you." She petted his hair.

"My pleasure." He rose, returned to kneel between her legs, and wiped his mouth. Winked. She gave him a big smile. So dirty-cute and naughty-nice. The man wielded his contradictions with adroit mastery.

Helen stole a look between Brian's legs. Her brows widened. His cock stood at proud alert, fully hard and curved, an impressive length reaching his belly button. A thick silver hoop pierced the head of his penis, looping through his urethra. She slid his adornment in a circle, finding the chunk of metal warm. "I like. Did getting pierced here hurt?"

"Oh, probably." He grunted, eyelids fluttering as she played with the intimate jewelry. "I wasn't exactly in a sound state of mind at the time."

Brian was an official secret badass. A milky bead of fluid bubbled from his opening, and she slicked the moisture across the smooth flesh of his crown.

Relief from her orgasm ebbed as she anticipated the feel of him inside of her, how the piercing would stimulate. Helen ran her hand up and down Brian's shaft.

"Did, *uh*." A broken, hoarse cry interrupted his speech. His cock jerked, the tip darkening. A blue vein pulsed on the side. "Did you bring a condom?"

Oops. She'd subconsciously assumed he had protection covered. Helen pumped her lightly curled hand up and down his length, keeping him primed. "No. I take it you didn't either?"

"No. Like I said, I'm not all that active sexually." He bit his lip, stomach muscles clenching. "I wouldn't last anyway...fuck. Don't stop touching me. Please. Ah, I'm sorry."

Dirty decadence made a fleeting vixen out of Helen. She'd brought Brian Shepherd close to unraveling with a few rubs. No point in pretending to deny the high of that drug. "You're almost there, huh?"

She jacked faster, studying his expression. Eyes hooded, mouth open, breath choppy—he without a doubt sailed to the precipice.

"Can I finish on your breasts?" His request rushed out in a hungry slew of gasping syllables.

Depended on whether he could still banter. "Can I give you a prostate massage?"

"Love, right now I'd agree to let you give me a root canal without anesthetic."

She chuckled. "Stellar comeback. Get on up here, the dentist is in."

Brian moved to kneel at Helen's chest. She did quick little up and down motions right beneath the ridge of his crown, drinking in the sight of his face drawn in a pained cast of pre-orgasmic desperation.

The tightness pinching his features crumbled into relief, dazed and awestruck, his gaze landing on her naked chest. "Oh my God."

Already rigid manhood swelled to impossible stiffness in her grip. A deep groan erupted from Brian, blissful and long to accompany the white streams shooting from him. Three thick ropes splashed her breasts with liquid warmth while he moaned through the finish, thighs and abs clenching and releasing.

When he was done, Brian hunched forward, catching his breath in big pants and rubbing his stomach.

"I hope you're still speaking to me after I embarrassed myself like I did." A trace of worry underpinned contentment. Smiling sheepishly, he stripped a pillow and wiped Helen clean with the case.

She patted his leg above the knee. "We don't have to put that narrative around it. Instead, how about we say that my dry hand jobs are the stuff of legends."

Brian threw the pillowcase to the floor and reclined to lay beside her, bringing them face to face. He brushed hair from her eyes and kissed her lips and cheek. Sweet and unhurried kisses, for lust had been sated. There was no hurry anymore. "No doubt about it."

A rumble sharper than thunder sliced silence beyond the window.

"Look." Brian pointed to the glass, pulling Helen to rest in the crook under his arm.

She laid a hand over his thudding heartbeat, her gaze skating across the rising and falling plateau of his tattooed chest as she snuggled into his warmth.

A light show of city buildings dusted ebony skies. In the elevated blackness, above domes and skyscrapers, red taillights blinked. She kissed his pectoral muscle, breathing in the rich scent of his post-coital satisfaction. "An airplane, yes. I'm literally from flyover country. I've seen them overhead."

"Ah, but have you flown in one complete with leather seats, your choice of drinks, and a private bedroom in the back?" He murmured the words into her hair, lazily palming the side of one nude breast. "Throw in a catered meal, and Fanny's your aunt."

She laughed, not with complete lightness as she retreated from his subtle advance. His question danced too close to fanciful ideas of a happy future. "What do you think?"

"I have a jet. Hardly ever use the plane, but I'd like to again. I could fly you out to visit me and then we could set off to, I don't know, Hawaii. Or Aspen, if you'd prefer to ski. And you, my dear, would look criminally cute in snow pants and big clunky goggles." He nibbled her earlobe.

Tight pain coiled through Helen's torso. He was teasing her into believing he had feelings for her. She could not let herself think a chance existed. They'd discussed this issue. Brian had no right to mess with her like this.

"You don't have to flaunt your wealth to impress me. And I couldn't accept a big gift like that." Her response came out snappier than she intended. The sharp tips of her words turned inward and scraped off old scabs. Damn him.

Brian drew back with a frown. "I apologize. Did I offend you? It was just a spontaneous idea—"

Three knocks pounded the door, an angry sound that fried Helen's nerves. Was a break-in underway?

"Get out here, Shepherd." Joe's distinctive, worked-up voice shouted beyond the wall. "You have got some serious explaining to do."

TWELVE

HOVERING IN THE HOTEL ROOM DOORWAY, JOE, RED-FACED WITH A vein popping near his temple, yelled at Brian about some social gaffe he'd allegedly committed.

Helen shrank in the wake of the manager's furious accusations. Screaming matches still rattled her, excavating memories of hiding in the closet of her volatile, toxic home. She wrapped herself in a hug, picking at the decal on her old sleeping T-shirt.

"I don't owe you so much as a hello. As the matter of fact, you're fired. Get out, bugger off, and leave me alone." At Helen's side, Brian shoved the door into Joe, pushing him into the hall.

Joe growled through a useless attempt to insist his way into Brian's suite. His sausage fingers appeared in the crack between door and jamb, knuckles white and tendons straining, but he retracted them before the force of Brian's weight trapped and smashed the digits.

"I'm sorry, mate. I tried to keep him away, but he was on a mission." This from a third man. He spoke in an English accent like Brian's but with a husky smoker's gravel.

"Don't do this, man," Joe bellowed, but a tremor of fear shook his voice. "I'm going to tell you one more time that you need to do the right thing and abide these guys. For your band. Your career. Your daughter."

Brian snarled, muscles feathering in his neck and jaw. His entire body tensed, and he emitted a scarlet, furious energy. In a big yank, he tugged the door wide.

Joe stumbled over the threshold, a feral look in his eyes. His shirt was inside-out and backwards, and he smelled fishy and foul. Dude came off like a complete shit show, which made his presence more worrisome. Desperation could act as a powerful drive, goading people into all sorts of abusive and hurtful acts.

With a hard shove, Brian pushed the manager back into the hallway. "If you ever, *ever*, threaten my daughter again, you are dead. Understood?"

The third man, handsome in a rugged way with brown waves grazing beefy shoulders, caught the manager before he collapsed. His hair and thick build rang bells, conjuring up memories of magazine covers. Thom James, the bassist whom Stacy had been with.

"I'm not sure he's the one threatening your girl," Thom said.

"The fuck you talking about?" Brian shot Thom a look of wounded confusion, then glowered at Joe.

"I'm warning you." Joe panted. "It isn't me. There are guys higher up than me, way higher. But I've made promises that I must honor. These guys have expectations."

Who were "these guys"? Music industry cult members like Elwell? Helen better figure out what this slimy little orc knew and how much skin he had in the whole fucked up game.

"Who are you talking about?" Helen took a step forward. "You need to be more forthright, because we could all be in danger."

Joe sneered at Helen. "You aren't part of our 'we,' *honey*."

"Leave her alone. You heard her. Start spilling," Brian said. "Details. Now."

Thom propped Joe upright and thrust a manila envelope at Brian. "He says someone slid these under his door. I was on my way to the ice machine when I saw him headed for your room. I said I needed to take a look."

Face pale, Brian accepted the tan folder and unfolded its metal clasp. He slipped out a stack of black and white, eight-by-ten photos and flipped through grainy pictures.

None of the four people present uttered a peep. Time hardened into amber, fossilizing everyone in mute paralysis. Down the hall, a vacuum cleaner buzzed.

The first shot showed a headshot of a gorgeous teenage girl with a cropped pixie haircut.

Glossy paper made a whisking sound as Brian flipped. Same girl, sitting on a couch with several other girls, drinking coffee. In the third, she leaned over to buckle one of her sandals. The pose and lighting created a striking, unsettling sense of intimacy. Stalker-ish.

The fourth shot was a close up of the girl's sleeping face.

The fifth, an empty cot in the middle of a dingy basement.

The sixth, a wormy pile in the center of a pentagram. Someone had knifed the word "*sacrificium*" in scratchy white streaks over the gruesome visual.

Nausea wrenched Helen's stomach as bile vaulted up her esophagus. But the pictures could be a scare tactic, a deliberate manipulation engineered to induce panic. Best to remain as calm as the bleak situation would allow. She clenched Brian's forearm. "We can't say for certain—"

"Where is she? What have you done?" Brian shouted at Joe, agony tearing ragged holes in his voice.

Joe put up his hands. "She's fine. This is a threat, a shot fired. But rest assured, they haven't done anything yet. They want you. But they will retaliate. Which is why I'm telling you, you can't back out now."

"Oh, you best believe I won't rest assured." Brian ran to the bedroom. He returned hopping into jeans. A wrinkled T-shirt haphazardly clung to his torso, hiked up enough to show a dot of dark blue bruise above his hip. A creepy sensation tightened her skin. She hadn't noticed the mark when he'd been naked minutes ago.

"What's going on?" Thom scratched his head of mussed hair.

"I'll explain later," Helen said to the bewildered bass player. Brian's bandmates could serve as allies, eyes and ears.

Cell phone pressed to the side of his head and pictures clutched in his free hand, Brian paced. "Tilly, thank God. Thank God. You're at your Beverly Hills flat right now? Good. Good. Stay there baby, okay? Lock all of the doors and windows and get out your pepper spray. Call nine-one-one if anything suspicious happens, and I'll be there in a couple of hours.

In the meantime, I'm sending over a security detail. What? No, you're not grounded. I'll explain soon. On my way right now. Don't move."

With a massive sigh, Brian hung up, shoved his phone in his pocket, and stabbed a finger into the entrails picture. "Don't you dare hide anything or lie. Who sent these?"

Joe fished a hankie from his back pocket and sopped a glistening brow. "I don't know. Like I said, ditching the Bronze Phase wasn't the right move. But the good news is the Silver Phase is next week, and when you go you can make amends."

"Fuck off," Brian yelled at Joe. Hurrying into his shoes, he turned to Helen. "I need to leave. Come to the airport with me. You're welcome to fly to Los Angeles, but if you need to head back home, I understand. I apologize, I'm..." His voice broke like he battled tears.

Helen's heart hurt for Brian, but at the same time a sense of duty and obligation crystalized inside of her. Literally, crystalized. She had an idea for how to use the crystals and bust out a Left Hand spell that could help them get to the bottom of this insanity.

The universe had already punished her for choosing the wrong magic, so no putting the genie back in the proverbial bottle. Might as well use the powerful Left Hand path to maximum advantage.

She'd better get bold, take control, and use her witch powers to put Joe in his place and protect Brian and his daughter from harm. This dire situation called for hardcore witchcraft.

"I'll stay. I have to wrap some things up here before I leave, but I'll be fine. I promise. You go take care of your daughter, and we'll be in touch soon."

Brian closed his eyes. "Are you sure? We have another few shows on the Western seaboard. I'm going to take Tilly along with us for the rest of the tour, never let her out of my sight. After the performances are over, I'll be free for a bit. The finale is in LA, eight days from now."

Joe made a nervous noise, like he struggled to suck in oxygen, a second after Brian mentioned the final show. Rubbing Brian's arm with comforting touches, Helen studied the manager. He picked a sore on his cheek and sent a darting gaze this way and that. Why had he reacted to Brian's comment about the finale? Did the final show relate to this Silver Phase?

"I'm fine. You focus on your family right now," she said.

Brian hugged Helen, pressing her to his body and encircling her with both arms in a gesture no doubt as much about his comfort as hers. "Thank you. I'll ring you as soon as I can."

She didn't feel right about letting him slip away, but no way would she stop Brian from taking care of his child. "Sounds good. Keep me updated."

"Bye for now." Brian broke the hold, kissed her lips, and joined Thom in the hallway.

"Bye for now." The words washed her tongue with poison. But this moment was not about Helen or her feelings.

Thom grabbed Joe above the elbow and dragged him behind as he followed Brian.

"My room's right over there. I'm staying on this floor." Joe writhed against Thom's hold.

"Not anymore you aren't. I texted the front desk and had them disable your key card. My mate Brian said you were fired. Meaning if you don't cooperate, I'll have someone much less pleasant than me escort you from the building."

The three men walked to the golden elevators, Joe bitching his protests.

Helen secured all three locks on the hotel room door. A heat-seeking missile on a mission, she dashed into the living room, shook the bag of crystals onto the carpet, and cracked the grimoire. Her intuition churned like a whirlpool under the sea, frantic and strong.

Chewing her lip as a hunch festered, she arranged the incomplete set of crystals, the sets of seven each missing their clear ones, into two lines. Different shapes and sizes, some shiny and others matte or waxy, they made a motely crew of rainbow nuggets.

Two paths, two groups of crystals.

Dark magic caused a lot of trouble, but she couldn't turn back now. At some point, perhaps she'd try the Right Hand method of drawing from her inner strengths, but now was not the time. She couldn't afford to sacrifice power to chance, not when she needed quick results for getting the drop on Joe and helping Brian and Tilly. She had to work harder than ever to protect relationships with those she cared about, and at least she had experience in that area.

Wait, why was she interpreting her actions that way? This situation was completely different from the times she'd labored to win the approval of foster families with her brains, moxie, humor, and adaptability. Right?

Helen made a blubbery noise with her lips and evicted herself from the funhouse of her spinning thoughts. Dipping into the past wasn't allowed. Time to act, to move, to fight for safety.

She picked up the yellow stone in the Left Hand sequence, its sunny hue bringing a bit of cheer. Yogis associated the color yellow with the manipura chakra, the energy wheel at the navel. And boy, did she have fond memories of finding her inner strength doing meditations associated with that one. Strength sounded useful right about now, too.

The feel of the stone in her palm, smooth and round, pleased her. Meditation centered around this color had helped Helen find conviction, self-confidence, and personal empowerment during a time when she'd lacked all three.

But again, no point in nostalgia. Helen opened the book to the approximate page of the spell she'd done in her apartment before an idea struck her. She could mix Right and Left magic and perhaps mitigate fallout from the darkness.

Speaking of Right Hand practice, astral travel could help crack the demonic sacrifice plot. She'd start by accosting Joe and scaring him into giving up the details, the location of the clear crystal, and a way for her to recover it. Immense personal satisfaction validated Helen. Being a witch was freaking awesome. Super empowering, and she couldn't wait to learn the extent of her powers.

After some flipping past random words and drawings, Helen paused on a page with a graphic. On the warped, stiff parchment, a staircase rendered in sumptuous black ink dipped down and soared up, the ends meeting in an infinity loop. Pretty cool, like an M.C. Escher drawing. Some text wasn't in English, but she could make out enough to apprehend meaning.

For the advanced practitioner of the spirit element, seamless merging into and out of the astral highway can become akin to teleportation. Once mastery of this travel method is achieved, practitioner may enjoy such abilities as limited corporeal levitation and telepathy. Proceed with caution, always using personal talismans to minimize byproducts and harmful aftereffects.

Helen snorted. The boat had already sailed on minimizing byproducts and harmful aftereffects, but she'd still involve her special crystals as much as possible. She laid the yellow stone on the top of the page, right above the staircase. With any luck and a little skill, she could use astral projection to find Joe, scare the crap out of him, and extract every drop of info.

She tapped her foot. Was she an advanced practitioner at this point? The book didn't clarify what distinguished one level from the next. Whatever. She had to be close. "Let's do this."

Seated crisscross on the floor, she fixed a soft gaze on the crystal and slowed her breathing to a meditative rhythm.

Helen fell into meditative bliss, toasty and perfectly spaced out. She'd done a memorable meditation like this years ago, at the beginning of yoga teacher training, and saved her life, her sanity, her health. Guided meditation taught her how to appreciate herself and purge a lifetime's sludgy backup of negativity.

Time passed, a hazy blue and pink tint soon lightening dark skies outside the hotel. Helen's perception looped and spun, fading in and out, merging dreams and wakeful impressions until she couldn't be sure if she was awake or asleep.

She jerked, an abrupt and involuntary twitch that shook off the stupor of her trance. Helen swung her legs in empty space, the movement propelling her upward. She bonked the crown of her head on something hard.

"Ow." Rubbing a swelling lump, she flailed for purchase, drifting like a man overboard in the ocean. But she wasn't in the ocean. Helen swum in the hotel living room, hovering near the ceiling. Excellent.

She flipped, planting palms and soles against smooth plaster. From its spot on the floor, the crystal shone with the muted glow of mellow sunlight. Recognizing the rock's sentient quality, a friend looking out for her, Helen nodded at the personal talisman.

Using hands and feet for traction, she crawled upside-down across the ceiling.

Cool, cool. Pretty witch-tastic. Her vision changed, apprehending in the murkiest of senses what lay beyond the walls and door of the hotel room. The confines had become semi-translucent, formed out of blocks resembling gray gelatin.

In other rooms, maids fluffed pillows, people channel-surfed. Jelly walls and hallways wobbled, coming into focus and revealing an expanding array of visuals. Empty wine bottles, beds, someone replacing a coffee filter.

As she swam through semi-solid space, muscles burning as she worked to push past barriers, a certain objectionable someone came into view. Apparently he'd slipped away from Thom.

Same sloppy clothes, bald head, frantic mannerisms, Joe shoved a credit card into the crack of space between a hotel room door and the jamb.

The card broke, falling to the floor in two halves. Joe doubled over, howling. Drifting closer, Helen sucked her teeth, embarrassment gunking up her insides.

She'd never met a worse train wreck of a person. And Joe's off-the-rails behavior made him pathetic, yet troublesome. He was the same as a junkie in the full bloom of addiction, willing to stab his mother for a fix. And by stab his mother, she meant cut open Brian. Which begged the question: what did Joe stand to gain from all of this crazy?

One way to find out. She shoved her way through gelatinous slabs until she broke out into the hall, golden ball of light spinning by her solar plexus acting as a beacon of strength. She could beat this guy. She was tough, smart, vital. Had this in the bag.

Stuck to the ceiling of Joe's hallway, Helen concentrated on drifting down until she floated to the floor. Her bare feet hit nubby industrial carpet designed to withstand repeated shoe traffic. Strange, the physical things one notices after spending a fair amount of time ungrounded.

"Hi," she said.

Joe shrieked like a little girl. His eyes blacked with hate. "Quit creeping up on me, you dumb bitch."

"What's your problem with me? Are you a generic misogynist, or do you have a personal grievance?"

"Lick my nuts." In a futile, impotent gesture, he slapped the closed door. He cussed, jiggling the handle.

"Are you frustrated that your magic isn't working, so you resent me because mine does?"

Joe slid Helen an apprehensive glance of interest, wrinkling his nose in a childish, pouty tell. "No." A juvenile whine fit his expression.

She laughed. "Liar. I get it now. But what's in that room you want so badly?"

"I'm not going to stand here and tolerate an interrogation by Brian Shepherd's groupie whore." He scratched his ass, and she scrunched her nose when a rank odor fouled the air.

Helen pinched her thumbs and forefingers together into mudras, closing her eyes and bending her head to the ceiling. "Okay, that's fair. Unfortunately for you, I have something you want, being the hex generator and all. But never mind. Whore, out. Beam me up, astral highway."

She chanted a long "om," pretending like she'd dematerialize any second. Hook, baited.

"Wait."

Helen tilted her chin down and opened one eye. Nibble, nibble, good little prey.

"Can you get in there? With your *magic*?" Contempt a slimy film on the word "magic," he nudged the door with his toe.

"Sure. What's in it for me?"

He scoffed. "I dunno. Money. Lots and lots of money. You won't even have to suck any more rock star cock—"

Helen took two big steps to Joe and clasped a hand around his throat, shutting him up as she pinned him to the door. Ugh, this guy. This fucking guy.

"What did I say back at the fair about slut shaming? Forget it, you blew it. Now. Unless you want me to crush your trachea with my superior witch strength, tell me everything you know about the plot against Brian. Where the clear crystals are, what they're being used for and how to end the scheme, and the deal with these parties. Go."

"Or else what? You'll choke me to death in this hallway? Good luck getting away with murdering a Hollywood executive, you white trash, cow-town tramp."

The slight slid off of her back. "No, I don't plan to kill you. Not here, not like this at least. Not when I could boil your flaccid little penis in my cauldron while keeping you alive, listening to your cries as you beg to die."

She tightened her grip. A cross between a croak and a whimper belched from his parted lips.

"Speak." She clenched harder. His pulse hammered against the pad of her thumb.

He pressed his mouth into a line, face turning a livid purple.

Acting on a hunch, Helen rolled her eyes, pointing them at a spot between her brows, site of the mystical third eye. A click sounded in her head.

Joe's mouth dropped.

They had to be pure white, like Nerissa's were in the house. Awesome.

"A vision of the white eyes is the first sign of my witchcraft curse against you coming into fruition. Next, I enter your dreams and steal your peace. After that, I enter your body and steal your health. Finally, I enter your thoughts and steal your mind."

A bunch of random references cobbled together from horror movies and enhanced with her imagination, but hey. Every player benefitted from keeping a good bluff handy.

Joe scoffed. "Nice try. I saw guys doing worse shit than that on my lunch break last Tuesday."

'Kay. Time to break out the big guns and try Nerissa's out-of-body move. Helen barreled her stare into Joe, concentrating until a pressure originating deep within his head tugged on the muscles behind her eyeballs. She dragged her gaze from his up to the ceiling, and the weight of his essence followed her up there and landed on a spot near a lighting fixture.

"*Wh*...why am I on the astral plane?" Joe whispered.

"Because I've taken control of you and sent you there. And unless you start yakking, I'll plop your eternal soul anywhere I please and draw from your worst nightmares for inspiration on where to put you. I'm thinking the bottom of a sewage tank. Or how about sharing a body with a torture victim while your meat sack lies comatose in a hospital bed feeling every cut and burn?"

"Okay, okay." Joe spoke in a raspy voice. "I'll tell you anything you want to know."

She loosened her hold, and he coughed and wheezed. "I'm listening."

"It's a cult, a fringe thing that takes elements from all kinds of places, from Satanism to European paganism to far-out, esoteric occult mysteries you've never heard of. They're into channeling, opening doors to other dimensions and welcoming through various entities and beings. Also enriching personal power by learning to remote view and levitate."

He massaged his neck. "The hot thing is still celebrities. Twenty years ago, the 'it' practice was turning them into vampires. Now the name of the game is possession."

"Getting demons to possess celebrities."

"They turn girls into sex slaves and have them do the most depraved shit you can imagine, but for the most part everyone wants in on possessing the celebs."

"Why?"

Joe's expression grew shrewd. "Control. The host has to agree to join forces with the parasitic visitor for the ritual to work. Once union is achieved, the host body can live for decades beyond the natural human life span, but without the side effects that come with being a vamp. And the drones appear normal on the surface, regular, no fangs or sun allergies. But on the inside they're compliant. Docile. Do as they're told, able to be programmed and controlled from afar by spells and shit. And we can keep eyes on them through remote viewing and astral travel and intervene in case they get out of line. Real convenient."

The agenda was to make Brian a pliable drone easy to pilot, a zombie to order around and send on stage, making money for other people without protest or a pesky mind of his own.

And those poor women. These dudes were some sick motherfuckers. "Where do you get your spells? How did you conjure this demon from the pit—yes, I know—and why are my crystals involved?"

"There's a book that gets passed around. Big, authentic-looking thing with a leather cover. I haven't seen the inside, but the guys at the top talk about the contents. It's the directions manual, I guess. I dunno. I just recruit the talent and take my cut."

Now she was getting somewhere. If she recovered the book, she might stand a chance at ending their ability to cast spells. "Where is the book? And my crystals?"

"The book, I don't know. Clear crystals are in one or more of the shrines. There are three total. One's in Wyoming, one's in Los Angeles, and I have no idea about the final location."

"So what's in the room?" She gestured at the hotel door.

"A few of Brian's guitar picks and some other stuff he asked me to hold for him awhile back. Notes, a book or two. The top brass wants some of his possessions before the Silver Phase to commence the next step of the ritual."

If she got her hands on one of Brian's possessions and used the item in the right way, perhaps she could slow down or stop the possession plan. And now she had two locations to search for the crystals. Ideas gelled into the start of a tangible plan.

Helen patted Joe on his shoulder. "Thanks. You've been a big help, champ. Now run along before I zap you to Mars. Sleep tight."

Joe dashed down the hallway, stopped at the elevators, and mashed a button. Stabbing his finger into the white circle, though he'd already pressed it, he cast a furtive, nervous glance over his shoulder.

Just to mess with him, she responded with a goofy grin and a princess wave.

He cut a high-pitched squawk of a fart while running into the elevator.

When he was gone, Helen dropped herself into the trance state and astral projected to the hotel room she'd shared with Brian. He'd left several items behind. She stuck a guitar pick, a business card, and a miniature tin of mints in her luggage and packed the rest of her belongings as fast as she could. Time to get home and kick Operation Witch into high gear.

THIRTEEN

MESSENGER AND YOGA BAGS BOUNCING AGAINST HER BACK, HELEN blazed her homing-pigeon path down the sidewalk to Light and Enlightened. Overcast skies and a crisp fall breeze made for dull weather, but inside she was a bundle of optimistic sunshine and sapphire heavens frosted with creamy white clouds.

The seaweed green, one story craftsman bungalow, stout lawn sign painted violet with the name written in blue cursive, made her smile. And with Brian's life on the line, she needed a mammoth dose of positivity.

L&E stood out against trendy restaurants and boutiques lining the busy Uptown Minneapolis street. The moment Helen had laid eyes on the house two years ago, she'd fallen in love. A sense of home overflowed from scuffed hardwood floors, built-in bookcases, and crown molding. A home of her own, to fill with the peace and love she'd never known.

But despite all of the goodness associated with L&E, an astronomical mortgage on an entire house in Minneapolis's hippest neighborhood worsened financial woes. Lisa advised holding out for a more sensible location in some suburbia strip mall, but Helen had been madly in love and eager, so eager, to build a nest.

Halting her trip down memory lane, she bounded up crumbling stone stairs. She had a class to teach, students to impress and, soon, a spell to cast.

She turned the key in the lock, taking a moment to appreciate the plant-filled, enclosed porch where she read and meditated. Her favorite lilac and jasmine incense soothed her senses as she unlocked the main door. Breezing across creaky floors, she stole a second to admire the practice room.

Clad in leggings the color of a fire engine and a white tank top that flattered her curves, she stood tall in the ceiling-high mirror covering the west wall. Helen had earned L&E shaking the only good things her mama gave her. Lisa's throwing her savings into the pot despite deep reservations was a tremendous leap of faith and a gesture of true friendship.

Since her magical practice was going so well, a money spell was in order to get cash flowing into L&E's coffers. But first she would lead an invigorating practice designed to keep the yogis renewing their memberships.

She pushed aside the rainbow-colored beaded curtain shielding the yoga space from the rest of the house and ducked inside. Paint the color of lime sherbet enhanced a calm, relaxing atmosphere. A bronze statue of Ganesh, the Hindu elephant God in charge of removing obstacles, sat tucked in a corner. She tossed the path-clearing pachyderm a nod, unzipped her long bag, and freed her pink yoga mat. Rubber unrolled onto wood with a determined slap.

Beads bumped each other in a succession of soft clacks.

"Hey, how was Denver?" Lisa poked her head through the curtain.

Unsure how to respond in a manner both truthful and coherent, Helen sat on her mat and finessed an answer. "Hectic. But I think I found some leads. I'm headed over to Nerissa's after this. I know, I know, I'm crazy and irrational. No lecture needed."

Lisa took a seat on the floor beside Helen. "I owe you an apology for being so mean at the fair."

Automatic self-deprecation was easier than thinking or feeling, so she chose the safest route to smooth over conflict. "It's all good. I realize that I deserve a medal for Kook of the Year—"

"No, you were right. You were looking out for us. Even if I didn't agree with your methods, I had no right to insult or patronize you like I did. At least you were taking proactive action. I could stand to be more open-minded. I was hurt and angry, which is no excuse. Our friendship and partnership means everything to me." Lisa touched Helen's upper arm, the gesture underscoring her words.

Right then, planets aligned. Dust specks glittered like fairy sprinkles in the air, sparse daylight filtering in to cast artistic shadows on chestnut flooring. The rekindled connection with Lisa, sisterly like it used to be, filled the building with safety.

Helen choked back happy tears. "Thank you."

"No, thank you."

Helen pushed into the outer corner of her eye and blinked, pretending to battle an irritant.

Maybe she should just let herself cry for once, fucking sob out all of the shit inside. Emotional catharsis would probably make her feel better. "Ugh, allergies. And thanks for what?"

"For the recruiting. The new students. They're talking us up all over town, and people keep coming in. So however you are wowing everyone, keep doing it. Because..." Lisa grinned, pressing steepled fingertips to her lips.

Helen's heart leapt. "Because what?"

"The mortgage is current, so the bank is off our back. And since we're way ahead of schedule, I've started to attack the bad credit card."

Did a balloon inside of Helen burst and spew confetti? 'Cause that's how elated she felt.

She threw her arms around Lisa and hugged the shit out of her. "Good news. The best news. Oh, my God, I'm so happy."

"Me too, me too. I wanted to catch you before you taught, but I need to run. Now that we can afford to fix things up, I've gotta get to the store and buy a new toilet. Have a fabulous class." Lisa stood.

"You bet." Helen flashed thumbs up.

Lisa left, the wind chimes on the front door tinkling goodbye.

Stare trained on her messenger bag, Helen did a little happy dance. Things were looking up at last, and she'd be remiss not to keep the positivity train chugging. And what better way to do so than to deploy some magic in the name of financial solvency. Helen was powerful now, and she could use that power to secure the stability she longed for.

Her exuberance sagged. Something about her thought about stability felt wrong and off, but she couldn't pinpoint why. A gross feeling, like she'd drunk dirty water, filled her stomach.

Whatever. Thirty minutes until class, perfect amount of time to get witchy. Anticipation rising to the juiced-up level of someone about to surf for porn, Helen popped the clasps of her messenger bag and tugged forth the grimoire and her crystals. Next up in the chakra sequence was green, color of the heart center. Apropos for saving something she loved. Helen picked up a piece of jade marbled with sable veins, kissed the stone, and placed her little green pal at the front of her mat.

In what had become a routine, a ritual anchored in intuition, she perused the grimoire until a particular page compelled her to stop and notice. One incantation hummed with auspicious meaning:

Abundant blessings, come to me.
Bestowing power, clarity.
What is one, make it double
And give me power to halt all trouble.

Additional directions accompanying the spell evoked the others she'd cast. Use personal talismans and charms to access a trance state. Immediate recognition boosted Helen's confidence. Spell craft was becoming her thing, a competent area of expertise. Boo-yah, baby.

"Let's do this." Her voice echoed off of the walls. She glanced around, the hairs on her neck and arms rising. Had there always been an echo?

Noticing the change in acoustics made her aware of an unseen presence looming in the room, like an invisible being peering at her. Odd. She'd been alone in L&E tons of times and never gotten the creeps.

Shaking off her willies, she followed the instructions. They said to recite the chant twice in quick succession, meditate on the personal talisman for at least thirty seconds, and repeat until a cosmic sign or serendipity announces the magic has worked.

Helen did her thing. Soon, she forgot where she ended and time began. Her body was fluid, a meaningless concept. The studio walls blurred, expanded, contracted. Boundaries crumbled. Veils dropped.

Muscles in Helen's head strained and stretched, her eyes clicking backward into her skull. She rose to her feet and wandered, drifting through the astral, dreamlike version of her studio. Corridors darkened, temperatures dropping to degrees that bit her skin through flimsy fabric. Something cool, rough, and leathery brushed her ankle.

She glanced to the ground, and a fizzle of chemicals sparked her nerves. At her feet sat a snake as long as her leg and thick as her arm. Brown spots patterned scales the color of jungle leaves. The reptile looked up at her with a sentient, aware expression in beady black eyes. Helen put up her hands but swallowed a shriek.

"Don't sneak up on a girl wandering the astral plane. It's worse than waking a sleepwalker. I made that up, but it sounds legit, yeah?" Humor failed to calm. The energy wasn't right. Had the temperature gotten colder still? She rubbed her arms, teeth chattering.

"I had to stop you here. What you've unleashed is getting stronger. Menacing forces are afoot in the universe." The serpent spoke in Nerissa's voice.

"The hex? No worries. I've got a plan in place to—"

"Not the original hex." Snake Nerissa tightened into a coil. "The auxiliary you summoned. Stop casting Left Hand spells. The universe has spoken. This path doesn't suit you, and you do *not* serve the sisterhood by dipping into the sixth circle."

"The universe didn't say to never cast another Left spell. I assumed the repercussions began and ended with the curse."

"And now you know the danger of such assumptions."

A wave of shame, thick and hot, crashed over Helen. She managed to stick heavy hands on her hips. "Seems like you gave me just enough rope to hang myself. Why? Do you want me to fail?"

Prickles hit the inside of her nose as a cynical thought surfaced. The old witch dangled something awesome in front on Helen's face, snatched the prize away, and reprimanded her for reaching for it. Typical, a person with power over Helen sabotaging her.

"This defensive attitude of yours, this persecution complex and chip on your shoulder, will be your undoing." A forked tongue shot from the serpent crone's mouth. "I'm trying to help, to talk some sense into you.

If you disregard everything else I say, please remember this: the double is getting stronger and more dangerous, and once it joins forces with the original hex? It's all over for you and your guitar hero."

Three rhythmic snaps, loud as gunfire, ricocheted in Helen's ears.

"What's wrong?" A concerned female voice spoke.

Helen dragged up heavy eyelids. Blurry color swam in her vision. Pins and needles stabbed her feet and toes with their sharp, tiny teeth. She waved at the person in front of her, movements slow and thick as bicycling through sand. "I'm fine. Got lost in a really deep meditation. Sorry about that."

"It's okay." A crouching Stacy came into focus, platinum hair with its black underside piled into a sloppy bun. "I wish my practice was as dedicated as yours. You're, like, a true guru."

"Oh, I don't know about that." The content of the astral vision seeped into Helen's consciousness, bringing frustration. But she couldn't obsess about her encounter with Nerissa. Not when a studio full of students sat before her, yoga mats arranged in a patchwork quilt of colors across the floor.

"I do. I know. Not sure if you've noticed, but I've been coming here every day lately. I'm called to this place. Can I be your apprentice? I've always wanted to find something I'm good at. Maybe I could learn to do some of the trippy stuff you do." Stacy waited, green eyes big and clear with expectant hope.

"That's not a good idea." No way would she inflict her disaster on Stacy or anyone else. No, the name of the game right now was cope with real life and undo the damage she'd already done. Damage which, if Nerissa told the truth, was snowballing.

Stacy's shoulders slumped. She slunk back to her mat.

Damn. Helen hadn't wanted to hurt or disappoint anyone. Why did she have to be such a screw up? Enough. Beating herself up wouldn't help. She couldn't do much now except lead a great class and create some compassion for herself and the students.

"I'd like to begin today by doing a meditation on our heart chakras. This is the seat of love, compassion, and understanding. So close your eyes, deepen your breath, and think about who in your life could use some healing. Visualize the color green. An emerald, a lush and healthy forest. Green is the color of abundance, so you can meditate on that as well."

She led the class through a calming and restorative practice, picturing leafy, vegetal hues exploding from the center of her chest. An intense, energizing practice followed, full of back bends and child's pose and other heart-opening postures. Along with her students, Helen rested in savasana, mind an unmarked canvas.

Lying still on her back, she unlocked a truth. The secret, the meaning of life. Stillness. The realization wasn't so much a thought, but a shimmering, sentient light glistening a path across her awareness before dancing into nothing. Brief and fleeting and glimpsed out of the corner of one eye.

Two streams of tears trickled from the outer edges of her eyes and streaked her cheeks. Those tributaries of warm water flowed into the cracks in her heart, filling them until tropical tides washed away years of debris. But she couldn't stay in her happy place forever. She had a job to do, a job she was hella good at if she did say so herself.

"Begin to deepen your breath. Everyone slowly return to your bodies, wiggling fingers and toes."

Rustling noises and sighs followed Helen's cue.

"Roll to one side and push up on your right arm, coming to a comfortable seated position." Helen obeyed her own words, stealing a peek at her class. Smiles and expressions of pure peace painted faces.

"Place your hands in prayer over your heart. The highest light in me recognizes the highest light in you. When we are in that place together, we are one. Namaste."

"Namaste." The class said in unison, a harmony of male and female voices.

She bowed to each and every one of the fifty students. After a few announcements about upcoming workshops and such, the people filtered out.

Stacy tiptoed to the front of the room, fidgeting with a corner of her rolled-up yoga mat. "I want to thank you again for this. I finally have a meaning in life, you know? A purpose. I'd really love to learn all of this from you. You sure you don't have any teacher training planned?"

Helen picked up the jade stone. Stacy was so real, so kind, and those traits combined with her dedication would help her become a great teacher one day. She'd have to keep practicing to build up her yoga skill level, but Stacy was capable of putting in the work.

For so long, L&E had been too deep in the red for Helen and Lisa to even begin to think about planning anything as big as yoga teacher training, but now she supposed she could at least consider the prospect.

"I've got a lot going on right now, but I'll think about it. I would love to have you in a class for aspiring teachers. Eventually."

"I realize that I need to practice for awhile first, but I want you to know that I have long-term goals. I'll see you in Vinyasa Flow tomorrow."

"You betcha." Helen unfolded her crossed legs, rising to a squat. She coiled her yoga mat into a column.

"Are you still seeing Brian?" Tucking her violet mat under one arm, Stacy lobbed Helen a glance keen with interest.

Mention of his name made her heart do a bunch of things at once. Flutter like it beat in the chest of an infatuated teenage girl. Clench as she remembered the mess with Joe, how Brian had run off to Los Angeles. Jump with anticipation, because she needed to call Brian. Or should she wait for him to call?

"I never told you I was seeing Brian."

"No, but I'm not dumb. When you brought him up in the elevator I had an idea, based on how your voice got all breathy and goofy. Then, the other day, Thom mentioned how Brian hooked up with someone in Denver, and how that was kind of a big deal for him. I figured the lady was you, since you'd been out of town, with Lisa subbing your classes."

"Things are still a little touch and go."

"Yeah. Dating a rocker requires titanium skin and a battle-hardened heart. But it sounds like Brian really likes you."

Helen perked up. "Oh yeah?"

Stacy laughed. "Yeah. Can you send some of those exclusivity vibes my way? Like, I'm hooking up with Thom again because I'm addicted and pathetic, but I'm pretty sure he'll never date a lowly groupie. He's holding out for a model or someone else in his league." She sighed and pouted.

"Hey." Helen laid a hand on the other woman's shoulder. In an instant, Stacy fixed her slouchy posture. "You aren't lowly. And if he doesn't see your value but keeps stringing you along so he can sleep with you, forget him. You deserve better."

"Nobody's ever told me that before." Stacy's eyes misted.

"Well, now someone has."

"Dang, I wish I'd had friends like you in high school, when the mean girls were peeing on my gym clothes and writing 'slut' in shit on my locker door. I gotta run, those drinks don't sling themselves. See ya tomorrow." Stacy hustled to the door.

Helen padded through the empty building, creaky hardwood floors the only sound as she turned off lights and set the thermostat. She whistled an upbeat tune, filling silence with cheery noises. Though things on the Brian front remained scary and unknown, at least she'd taught an awesome class. Even though her trance had gotten a bit strange at the end, the money spell had to be doing its thing.

Circumstances were improving, and Helen ought to honor and appreciate bursts of good energy when they erupted in her life. Express her gratitude to the universe and humbly ask for more bounty. Committing to operation count blessings and recognize positivity, Helen scooped her car keys out of a dish on an end table.

Chimes rung, the front door moaning. Who could that be? She'd just taught the last class of the day, and none of the studios in town offered yoga at the current hour.

But in the doorway stood Nerissa, jaw set in a clench. Balancing on a carved wooden cane capped with a porcelain bulb, she walked into L&E shaking her head. "Oh, child, it's worse than we thought."

"So now you show up, right on cue to reprimand me? How convenient. I get avoidance and phone tag until I'm due for my slap on the wrist." Helen blew out a candle, the force of her gust excessive for the task.

"Not that I owe you an explanation for my methods, but I'm busy. Many clients, duties. Obligations. My own craft requires regular and diligent practice. I'm not on call for baby witches." Nerissa walked into the vestibule and lowered onto a bench.

Helen sat beside the older witch. "Do your other clients include a shady as fuck music industry manager by the name of Joe, perchance?"

"No." Nerissa rested her chin on the tip of her cane. "But I'm aware of him, his coven. It's a bastardization of our practices. They've co-opted our lineage and line. Think Left Hand magic practiced with reckless abandon and zero training or skill, deployed in the service of absolute greed."

Helen stroked the tassel edge of the seat cushion. "Let me guess. Their connection to us allowed them to commandeer my crystals and fill the rocks with their own evil juju."

"More or less. Clear crystals are highly receptive, and our rival coven's powers are stronger and more concentrated than yours. My astral connection to this cabal isn't great, as their practices aren't pure, but I have seen. Oh, I have seen." Her voice rumbled, foreboding in its gravely, mannish timbre.

"I don't want to know what you saw, but I'm guessing I need to."

Nerissa nodded. She'd worn her hair loose, and a tangled riot of cobwebs rested against a T-shirt screen printed with discs of the moon phases arranged in semi-circle. "This music manager and his cohort wish to recruit the clone into their own agenda. And seeing that they have two of your crystals? They are already halfway there. Once they're able to wield both hex and clone? Good luck stopping them. Such a thing is so far out of my league it's an altogether different sport."

An acute sense of defeat scooped out every ounce of Helen's optimism. She hung her head. "I guess I'm destined to fail."

Nerissa grabbed Helen's hand, her touch papery and cool. "Enough. Enough of your bad attitude. Claim your strength. Find your true power and use it not only to beat these fools, but to become the best version of yourself."

"How? How do I do that? Because even though you sound like a best-selling self-help book right now, I'm not sure what your words mean."

"My words have been clear as those crystals. The Left Hand path does not suit you. Spells are boomeranging, becoming sentient beings in their own right as they run amok, seeking practitioners who can aid their agenda of destruction. Stop enabling, now."

Helen threw up her hands. "Okay. As of right now, I hereby declare that I will stop doing Left Hand spells and stop enabling. But I'll confess I'm clueless as to how to fix what I've done."

"No, no. You aren't clueless. You have more than a clue. What can you do with proficiency now that you couldn't achieve before you began your practice of the craft?"

"Astral travel. Remote viewing." Well shit, that answer came out in a spurt of confidence. Felt pretty damn stellar to wear accomplishment like a cute new outfit.

"Good girl. Now steer yourself onto the appropriate path. Reject the lures of the Left, leave such things to these buffoons you now must defeat."

"Again, this sounds great, but how? Do I just say my intention to switch trajectories out loud, and boom, done?"

A chuckle from the old witch. She laid two firm fingers below the dip of Helen's collarbone and tapped twice. "Your change of course comes from here, my darling coven daughter. It's already in there, albeit latent and unsung. So sing it."

"Could you please not speak in riddles and just tell me what to do?"

"I am telling you every single thing I know, so listen." With a grunt, Nerissa stood. "The clear stones are the ultimate tabula rasa, reflective of the practitioner's deepest truth. Once you are one with yourself, they will do your bidding. But that time hasn't come yet. You have much to learn, many obstacles to overcome. When you've recovered the stolen crystals, bring them to me, and I shall help you charge them for your final battle."

"How about a hint as to how I'll use them in this battle?"

"Once your course is set on the proper line, purpose will reveal itself through the workings of the universe." Nerissa ambled to the door. "I'm not omniscient."

"Thanks." A begrudging sense of appreciation saved Helen's reply from outright sarcasm status. At least Nerissa intervened. "This has been marginally helpful and quasi-enlightening."

"Helen." Nerissa turned over her shoulder, a spark of knowledge flashing across her face. "One more clue has come."

"Lay it on me."

"Recall what happened the day the hex began its work. What you did, where you went after you left my home. With whom you interacted and any emotions associated." With those parting words, the elderly witch left L&E, leaving the mirthful tinkle of wind chimes in her wake.

FOURTEEN

Tilly glanced up from one of the many fashion magazines fanned across the mattress of her canopy bed. Though she glared like only a mad teenager could, the childish dimensions of her—her bent and swinging legs, her fuzzy frog slippers—slew Brian.

The blue silk pajamas swallowing her gangly frame brought out the ferocity in her sapphire eyes, scalpel sharpness she'd inherited from her mother.

"What? Loom much?" Tilly said.

Brian stood in the doorway of his daughter's old bedroom, which fortunately he'd preserved even after she moved out to live with her stepmother, Kris.

Tilly's new bodyguard, Brutus, an ex-military man with python arms, texted from his seat on a pink couch. Relief and worry cascaded over Brian in competing intervals. Tilly threw a wobbly when he'd told her she was going on tour with him, an epic fit of inconsolable proportions. They'd compromised with the bodyguard. She was safe, that was all that mattered.

"Nothing," Brian replied.

"So why are you staring at me?" A blend of irritation and amusement strung her melodious syllables, bringing out the faintest flutter of an English accent.

He scratched the back of his neck. "I'm relieved."

She wrinkled her nose. "You never told me what's going on, and why I have to be held captive here like a baby when all of my friends are going to the rave."

"Someone threatened you in an effort to coerce me. It's just for a little while, until I can establish if the threat is legitimate. You saw the girl being cut at that ceremony, so you should understand the severity of my distress."

"Ugh, everyone who's anyone in Hollywood right now is fake Illuminati. I'm sure it was nothing but a branding ritual, a little tattoo on her tummy. I overreacted. You are such a helicopter parent. I'm seventeen, not seven."

She resumed reading, leafing through glossy images of emaciated models matching the ones cut out and taped to the walls. He needed to distance his daughter from the toxic modeling lifestyle Kris seduced her into, but that problem would have to fill up a future day.

"I need you to take this seriously, Matilda. I was gobsmacked by what I saw."

"Okay, okay, whatever. I won't accept candy from the clown who drives the white van."

"No sneaking out tonight. I mean it. If I find you gone, you really are grounded. Which means no more fashion shoots."

"Tyrant," Tilly grumbled. "Fine. Consider me your gulag prisoner."

Brian exhaled a burden of tension, laying a hand over his heart. "Dinner's at six. Or should I say, brinner. I'm making your favorite, chocolate chip pancakes."

"Those haven't been my favorite since I was ten. And quit trying to use modern expressions, it's cringe-worthy. Oh, before I forget, some woman was here to see you." She ripped out a page.

Startled, he ran through possibilities. A state-of-the art security system kept overzealous fans, stalkers, and other uninvited guests far away from his Los Angeles home nestled deep in the Hollywood Hills.

"When? What did she want?"

Tilly snipped, red scissors outlining a woman's picture. She popped out her paper doll and set the cutout on a growing stack. "Earlier this morning, while you were out running. It was weird. Like, really really weird."

"What do you mean, weird?"

"I dunno. Like she wasn't all there. I can't explain." Tilly rolled out of bed and walked to her dresser. She taped the latest photo to the wall, adding to a collage of scantily clad stick figures posing around the oval of glowing bulbs that circled her mirror.

"Well, can you try?"

"She was like...spacey. She blinked a lot. Then she was babbling, then she ran off before Brutus could deal with her. I assumed she was some nutty groupie or whatever."

That hadn't happened in years, not since one of Thom's jilted conquests turned up on Brian's property barefoot and screaming, wielding a gun and demanding Brian call his bassist.

He'd had the gate put in the next day, thirty feet of iron and spikes not even an Olympic pole vaulter could clear.

"What did she look like?"

"Cute. Pretty, in a regular person way. Dark eyes. Long brown hair with blonde highlights, freckles on her nose and cheeks. Big boobs, not super skinny. She was wearing a silver dress, like haute couture, and she talked with a funny accent. Like the people in that movie *Fargo*."

Confusion smacked Brian upside the head, knocking out reason and logic. Minnesota accent? Helen? No way. "She didn't say her name?"

Tilly kicked discarded clothing out of her path and made her way back to bed. She belly-flopped on her mattress. "Um yeah, she did. Ellen? Haley? Something like that."

If Helen was in town, she wouldn't have shown up unannounced, acting odd. But he hadn't spoken to her since leaving Denver a few days ago, and this incident was as good of an excuse as any to call.

"Alright. I'll figure it out. Don't sneak away from Brutus. You are not safe."

Tilly rolled her eyes.

Brian left his daughter and walked down the hallway to his room. He took his phone off the nightstand and went out on the patio, leaning over the glass balcony overlooking his infinity pool. Shimmering water merged with scruffy hills and the twinkling orange and yellow lights of the Sunset Strip below. The deck, terra cotta tiles, and padded lounge furniture in vibrant colors of aqua and cobalt, livened up his pool deck.

Though he got lonely in his castle on the hill, Brian's comfortable home did calm him. Nice to have a break from touring to spend some time appreciating the fruits of his labor.

Sure would be nice to have a certain someone around to share the luxury with, sip margaritas and watch a sunset after a swim. Drawing in a rich breath of decaying foliage tinged with the dusty bite of smog, he rang Helen.

"Hey, Brian. It's good to hear your voice. How is everything?"

Subdued waves rippled in an undulating pattern, the color-change lamps at the bottom of the tank infusing the liquid with an emerald glow, like an otherworldly aquarium. He sought centeredness in the water's lapping rhythm, how its hue changed from green to blue to purple in a slow, dreamlike cycle. How much trust he could invest in Helen was still up for debate, he hated to admit, and because of the uncertainty he ought not go to mush.

"Stabilized. Tilly's fine. The LA finale is in three days. Friday can't get here soon enough. How are you?"

"I'm also fine. The studio's doing well. Is there something else you want to say? You sound distressed."

She saw right through him. Aggravating and endearing at the same time, to find himself unable to hide from the workings of the woman's inquisitive mind.

"This is going to sound strange, but you aren't in town, are you?"

A puzzled laugh from Helen. "No, I would have told you."

In the extended silence that followed her denial, he plucked piece of errant debris off the steel bar capping the railing. "What?"

"Nothing, just thinking."

"About what?"

"This whole mess. How to clean it up."

"Well, perhaps we can clean it up together. We were making progress in Denver." His cheeks warmed. Anyone's guess whether they were, in fact, on their way to fixing the alleged supernatural debacle. But, despite lingering reservations, he felt better having Helen around.

And from the moment he'd walked away from that hotel room with Thom and Joe, a familiar ache returned to the middle of his chest. When he was with Helen, the hurt disappeared, replaced by the pleasures of holding her, kissing her, talking with her. Losing himself to the feel of her soft skin, her touch, the sensual pleasures they brought to each other.

He could not take for granted the straightforward yet brilliant joys of being around a person, a woman, he liked.

"Yeah. We were. Though I confess I've hit a bit of a standstill," she said.

"How so?"

"My mentor put hard brakes on the kind of magic spells I'm allowed to cast. Which sucks, because I don't know what else to do."

"Los Angeles is a hotbed for New Age practice. There's shops all along the boardwalk, psychics and palm readers, and all types of practitioners. Perhaps if you came out here you'd be inspired. Find someone or something who could lead you—us—in the right direction."

"That's a good idea. Maybe I could get away for a few more days, spend a little time out there. It might help to have me around during the finale. Keep my eyes open for suspicious activity."

He flicked a sliver of leaf off the guard rail. The slice of dead foliage swayed in a mellow back and forth dance down to the pool and made a silent landing, impact perceptible only by ripples.

There was that old saying about a butterfly flapping its wings somewhere and making an impact on an entirely different course of events elsewhere in the world. Perhaps Helen's presence would influence him in a positive way, soothe his agitated mind through the ripple effect made by her charm, her humor.

Her proximity improved his state of mind, a simple yet assuring truth. She could relate to what he was going through. She acted as a harbor in the storm of his life, despite the fact that she played no small role in stirring up that storm. Making their bond a shade dysfunctional, but still he missed her. Brian almost never followed his heart anywhere anymore, so the sheer concept of emotional abandon in and of itself made for an allure.

"What are you thinking about?" Her voice was low, smooth, and husky.

He laughed, the sound boyish and silly in his ears. "You. I miss you. Some random person came to my door today, and I let myself imagine she was you. How preposterous am I?"

In lieu of Helen's immediate response, a faint electronic whine of interference travelled through the line. Off in the distance of the rocky hills, a coyote let off chilling howl.

"Did she look like she could have been my twin?" When she spoke at last, not a trace of the former casual lilt remained. Helen's tone was as pressed and no-nonsense as a detective interrogating a murder suspect.

Nothing could be simple with Helen, never easy or light. Not for more than a few shoplifted moments. "I didn't see her, Tilly did. Why, do you have a twin?"

"I'm a fraternal triplet, so yes I have a sister who looks almost exactly like me. But we haven't spoken in years. There's someone impersonating me. A doppelganger from another dimension."

Wind sliced through in a cutting gust, making the hairs on Brian's arms stand. A cluster of brown leaves skated over the deck, some landing in the pool where they floated like dead birds. He squirmed. "The things you ask me to believe."

"I'm aware how outlandish it all sounds. Am I un-invited?"

He should say yes. Take Tilly and disappear. Get as far away from Helen and Joe and witchcraft and the occult and Los Angeles as he could. Go back to London. Start over.

But as bolloxed up as it was, his gut told him not to flee. Not to run from the first person in years who'd made him feel something other than ambition. The first person in forever to pull tenderness out of the forgotten chamber inside of him was complicated and challenging, a fact he didn't resent as much as he wanted to.

Perhaps fate wanted him to have some sloppiness in his life, some chaos. Some darkness to throw the order of his well-planned existence into disarray.

Perhaps to live his most complete self, to write and create and love again, he needed to court disorder, the temptations of the universe's secrets. Helen symbolized so much, yet at the end of the day was simply a woman he wished to be around. The universe worked its mechanisms in weird ways.

Desire coursed through him, hot as the singing wind. He could, he really could, toe the edge of some kind of crazy-beautiful abyss. Touch mysteries. Play at the border of magic, live vicariously through Helen, taste taboo along with her sex.

Wasn't attraction, chemistry between two people, ultimately witchy?

Wasn't he a fucking artist, a songwriter and musician suited to draw inspiration from the swamps of Dionysian murk?

"Can you get here in the morning? Ticket is on me, of course, and I could pick you up at the airport."

"Let me text Lisa and ask if she can sub for a few more days. But yes, I agree that I should be close by for this finale show. Can I text you in a second?"

Warmth spread through his chest, making its way down to tighten his balls. He glanced back at his bed, a California king dressed in hotel whites and navy pillows. He'd never brought a woman into this brand-new bed, the one he'd bought as a replacement after catching Kris screwing some photographer between their wedding sheets.

What a perfect opportunity to christen the new bed with Helen, lay out the luscious witch and slide into her body. Take her. Claim her, in all of her power and glory and beguiling enchantment. His cock plumped. Was this what the history books meant when they spoke of men being bewitched? If so, sign his name on the applicable line.

"Hurry up." His voice was bestial. He practically growled.

This horny, alpha-male side of himself came out around Helen. Whether the inner beast turned him on or frightened him or both, he couldn't say, but goddamn the novelty thrilled. He longed for Helen, body and soul.

"Or else what?" She popped off her taunt, her dare, without a moment's hesitation.

He smirked at the rocky slopes beyond his property. Brian Shepherd could play. He could peacock, strut, release the macho. Albeit a bit in jest, a self-aware experiment, but that didn't make it any less fun.

"Or else when you get here I'll punish you. Tie you to the bed and pleasure you until you scream my name. With a healthy dose of 'yes, maestro' mixed in."

"Not bad, not bad. You should write that down."

"Perhaps I will." He stood up straighter, thoughts bouncing between Helen in his bed and making music in his home studio.

He'd fuck her in the studio, if she was game. Bend her over the couch, shag her up against the wall of the sound booth. His skin tingled, excitement spurting through his veins. A groan slipped out before he could stuff it.

"Are you looking forward to seeing me? Cause I'm willing to bet there's a drumstick in your pocket."

God, she could be so shameless. He loved that about her. She was unrepentant where he was uptight. Helen gave him permission to release reins, to free the stallion and charge. "Nice Mae West reference. Suits you. And what do you think?"

"Yes. I think yes."

"So get your affairs in order and get your sexy self to California."

"Yes, maestro."

He sucked in a breath and adjusted his fly. "Quit teasing."

"Why would I do that? It's too much fun."

He moaned. Yes, she'd reduced him to a nonverbal shaft of male lust, a phallus, a caveman.

"I'm hanging up." His head swam, his swollen erection claiming all of the blood.

"Same. I'll talk to you soon. See you soon." Christ, her voice. Rough yet smooth, silk stockings ripped off of spread legs under red lights. The phone clicked. Brian stood there for a second, worked up and dazed. He hissed out a breath and fanned his forehead.

His phone blooped with notice of a text, the device vibrating in his hand. Helen sent a thumbs up. Pulse bumping, he went online, bought her a ticket, and texted her the flight details.

Sure, he had an assistant to take care of administrative matters, but this chore fell into the category of something so important he'd do it himself. She texted back with another thumbs up and a red lipstick kiss.

Gaze on those puckered red lips, Brian walked back into his bedroom and latched the sliding glass doors to the deck. Those lips, those lips. How would her lush pout feel wrapped around his knob, licking and sucking? God, he needed her so bad. Had to have her. Craved her, the heady sensation of losing himself in the wet heat between her legs. His tongue had been there, but not his manhood. A travesty.

Brian locked his bedroom door, grabbed a tube of hand lotion off of his dresser, and saw to his urge. He stroked himself at a fast pace, images of Helen's face and naked body in all sorts of sexual situations forming a dirty movie.

Right at the end, he used two simultaneous images to bring himself home. One, Helen bouncing on top of him. Two, Helen kneeling at his feet, disheveled and sweaty after a good fucking and multiple orgasms. Eyes closed, mouth open, and tongue out, she prepared to accept a face full of his offering with gratitude.

Yes, he had filthy, politically incorrect fantasies sometimes. So sue him. Fantasy number two delivered the payoff, and he erupted into splintering relief. Climax ebbed, leaving him hollow, because he had no Helen to cuddle and stroke and bask with in the mellow afterglow.

But piss off, sadness and moping. She'd be in California soon. He checked his phone, ensuring he hadn't imagined the text. Of course he hadn't. The little bubble with the thumbs up and lipstick kiss remained. He picked up the mobile and planted a lingering smooch on the screen. Laughing at his foolish heart, he threw the phone on the mattress, tugged his underwear and pants over his hips, and sauntered to his master bathroom.

As he cleaned off, he took stock of the space, chuffed as he admired his spoils. Elegant yet tasteful, all sleek lines and chrome accents. The shower was a modern glass box, large enough for two, though he'd never tested out the post-Kris remodeled space with a partner.

Home renovations proved efficient to heal from his ex-wife's cheating.

Brian fixated on the luxury surrounding him before he could spend too much time analyzing the state of his heart, the depth and extent of his feelings for Helen.

She would love the spa showerhead with the LED lights and seven different massage settings to pamper the scalp. After a decadent, steamy shower, he'd dry her off in one of his fluffy towels. Wrap her in a bathrobe and make her a fine cup of imported English tea.

Whistling a song he'd written after leaving Denver, Brian turned on the hot water and soaped his hands under the steaming jet. What was the most impressive thing he knew how to cook, for when he made her dinner? Shrimp scampi. He dried off. No, braised rabbit. Shite. Was she a vegetarian? There was still a lot to learn about the bewitching brunette from Minnesota.

A litany of stabbing pains, a thousand times sharper and more penetrating than any of the needles he'd allowed to breach his body, assaulted a spot above his groin. Brian doubled over, eyes watering, and gripped the lip of the sink so hard he feared he'd rip the basin from the wall.

"Ow. Fuck." Jamming a hand under his undone pants, he fumbled at the area, mind blanked by shredding agony. Though he expected to brush his trembling fingers against a scorpion or shard of glass picked up from God knows where, he groped at nothing but his own glimmering, throbbing skin.

Brian shoved his pants down, lips parting when he targeted the source of his grief.

A bruise, the size of a golf ball and mottled hideous shades of black and mustard yellow and livid magenta, marred the skin right under his waistband. Had he whacked his side on a hard surface? No. He would have noticed and remembered a wallop like that, considering he didn't drink to excess or do drugs and thus moved with balance and clarity.

Another disturbing detail came into focus as Brian gawked at his wound. He blinked. Two sets of red puncture sticks lined the top and bottom of the injury. He'd been bitten by some animal.

His mind spun. Hand shaking, he flung open the medicine cabinet and pawed through contents. A plastic jar of vitamins and a travel size container of shampoo clattered into the wash basin. He snatched a small tube of ointment, wracking his brain.

A stink washed over him, the unmistakable rot-sweet of decomposing flesh. Meaning a rat or similar had crawled into a crevice unseen and died.

The slow creak of a door. Out of the corner of his eye, he caught a shimmery, glittery flash. Beside himself, numb from the confusing barrage of sensory input he struggled to categorize, he glimpsed.

Helen, or a woman who could have been Helen's twin, stepped out of the shower wearing the slinky metallic gown Tilly described. This was not the woman he'd spent time with in Denver. The thought registered in an instant. Her eyes, though the right color, were dead. Too dark, dull as coal.

"Who are you?" he whispered.

"Oh, Brian, oh yes maestro. Fuck me. That feels so good. Come all over my face. You two idiots are making this so damn easy for me." Her laugh was ugly. She stepped closer.

The lights flickered. One bulb above his medicine cabinet blew out in a minor detonation of pop and fizz. Another light bulb sparked, the explosion's aftermath leaving a sooty stain on frosted glass.

"You're behind the vase and the live wire in the interview, aren't you? The knife in the garbage disposal, the hot crystal and pains in my palm?"

She shrugged one creamy shoulder, her hateful facial expression rendering Helen's breezy beauty malevolent and garish. "Primitive attempts from my pre-corporeal self, when I was merely some amorphous hitchhiker without form, following the path blazed by the hex. But now magic has fully lifted the veil, and I'm getting smarter every day. Looks like my boss has his hooks in you, so to speak."

Feminine fingers brushed the mark on his side, a hand identical to the one he'd held, yet alien in the most important ways. A chill iced his nerves following her invasion of his personal bubble, but the tactile element of her touch didn't register.

There was no opposing pressure, no protection offered by the boundary of his form. Her digits slipped right through his pelvis and slid out of an area near his pubic bone.

Brian backed away, skin crawling at this imposter's death touch, the impossible and violating penetration.

"Of course you know where the missing crystals are. Joe's messing with them, isn't he? And I'm going to guess that you're working for him and know the precise location of those stones."

"I serve a far mightier master than your sad little wannabe warlock. He's but our pawn, our puppet. Once we're through with him, we'll eat his flesh on a platter along with yours and your girlfriend's." She drawled the words in his ear, a breathy rumble bringing with it a rotten, diseased stench.

Brian coughed, turning his head and guarding his nose against another blast of bacteria breath. "You don't scare me. Helen will be here in the morning, and she's preparing a spell to send you and your so-called master straight back to hell where you belong."

No idea how true that was, but he damn sure better project toughness right now.

Indulging fear would cloud his thinking, pump him full of stress hormones, and compromise his ability to make good decisions.

"Unfortunately for you, we're a grab bag of surprises. You'll never see us coming. And that's a cute threat, but as we both know, your moronic novice witch couldn't divine an answer from a Magic Eight Ball without sowing utter discord in the force." She poked a finger into his bruise, setting off another spray of icicle bullets through his bloodstream.

"I don't need to see you. I can smell you across the room."

She furrowed her brow, tapping her chin and pushing out her lips in an exaggerated gesture of contemplation. "Good to know. Thanks for the feedback on how to improve my stealth factor. Next time I'll be less stinky. See you soon."

The clone backed away, disintegrating into flimsy clouds of translucent mist. She faded, leaving a faint whiff of death and the lingering apparition of her Cheshire Cat smirk.

FIFTEEN

I<small>F</small> J<small>OE</small> <small>WAS</small> <small>TO</small> <small>BE</small> <small>BELIEVED,</small> <small>ONE</small> <small>OR</small> <small>BOTH</small> <small>OF</small> <small>THE</small> <small>CLEAR</small> <small>CRYSTALS</small>
resided somewhere in the city. In a shrine. Helen shivered in the mild
Los Angeles night. This temple could be anywhere, even beneath the
ground of the LAX arrivals loading area where she stood.

Palm tree leaves fluttered in breezes that carried notes of cigarette
smoke and ripe garbage. Under saturated orange security lamps bathing
the evening in eerie tones, fellow passengers waiting for rides looked
suspicious, the cars idling on the curb suited to transport dark secrets.

Looping overpasses domed an unforgiving concrete jungle teeming
with wild vehicular rumbles. Motorcycles, helmeted drivers fused to
seats like futurist robots, whizzed down blacktop pavement, gassing
unnatural petroleum odors. An airport employee drove a beeping luggage
cart in front of Helen, shooting her a crusty, lizard-like look, though
she'd done nothing wrong and wasn't in the way.

Everything and everyone in her vicinity morphed into monstrous
strangeness.

Helen poked down jitters and anxiety and fought to snap out of the
twitchy fugue. She was piqued from jet lag, and in the context of her
agitation and relative nearness to the missing talisman and affiliated

scheme, her agitated psyche overloaded the world with spooky meaning. The mind had a tendency to speculate, fill in blanks with menace.

She inhaled and exhaled with mindful purpose, adjusting her messenger bag and rubbing the achy shoulder under its wide strap. The grimoire had become her constant companion. A weight in her purse, a monkey on her back. Other people felt naked without their day planners or main credit card. These days, Helen didn't leave home without a volume of witchcraft as fat as a phone book. Talk about added responsibility.

Yes, she had to follow strict orders to stay away from Left Hand craft, but she'd need the book for reference.

A sports car with California plates pulled into the loading zone, sleek as hell with paint like polished obsidian and tinted windows cloaking inhabitants in mystique.

The make and model escaped her, though she swore she'd seen the exact car in James Bond movies. Low to the ground, all curvy lines and rounded hood, the ride stood out as a love letter to international automotive sexiness amidst a sea of chunky SUVs and domestic sedans.

Her pulse quickened. She knew who owned the car. Woven in with anticipation of seeing Brian, though, was a vaguely icky trace of something related to jealousy or resentment. She didn't belong in that cool Hollywood car. She made sense in one of the generic, sensible vehicles. Or in Minneapolis, driving her Mini Cooper to the body shop to, at long last, repair an expensive fender dent.

As predicted, Brian got out of the driver's side, radiating fame and grandeur in tailored black jeans and an old Led Zeppelin shirt. He slammed the door and strode to her.

On cue, people swiveled, stared, broke out their phones and snapped pics. Though she moped in the glare of attention not meant for her, at least the peevish response triggered a good self-scolding. With a curse to lift, there was no spare energy to waste pouting that the cool factor of the famous guy she was visiting beat hers by a factor of infinity.

His hug, strong and confident, paused her sulky episode.

"You smell so good," Brian murmured into her hair. "I remember this fragrance from when I held you in Denver. Lilac and jasmine and vanilla and you. Pure you."

A disarming rawness shaped his admission. Romantic and intimate, sure, but tender with the distinct quiver of relief.

Helen closed her eyes and attempted to melt into his body, rubbing up and down his back in tender strokes. But their embrace failed to dissolve her tension, her aggravation. Something was wrong. Something always was. No rest for the wicked, no break from dancing on the tips of her toes.

"What happened?" she asked.

Passersby tittered, stealing candid photos with bursts of greedy clicks. A few of the gawkers had swapped phones for bulky cameras with neck straps and retractable lenses, upped stakes of intrusion that raised the scepter of paparazzi harassment.

Brian, who no doubt had a sixth sense for such things, flinched in Helen's arms. He kissed the shell of her ear and pulled away. "I'll explain in a minute. Let's get in the car before the hyenas start circling in earnest."

A flash went off with a squeal, a blast of light making her squint. A goateed man in plaid shorts advanced, panting as he snatched more shots. She got why people flipped out and punched these assholes, but at the moment they were mosquitos and she had a hydra to fight.

"Good call." She grabbed her wheeled suitcase.

He popped the trunk, which slid open in a graceful, futuristic motion making a spectacle of the car's fanciness. Hesitant to touch his criminally cool supercar, she handed over her luggage. With a friendly smile, Brian set her bag in the trunk and opened her door for her. "It won't bite."

Leather seats the color of whole milk welcomed her body with supreme comfort, and a cluster of black tree air fresheners hanging from the rear view mirror perfumed the interior with an edgy, masculine fragrance.

"How's your daughter?"

"Pouting like a child who hasn't got an ice cream, but otherwise fine. I couldn't convince her to go on the tour, but her bodyguard is doing his job."

She'd never met anyone with an on-call bodyguard. Money had a way of solving problems, and Brian was drowning in dough.

Taking advantage of plentiful legroom to stretch her sore calves,

Helen settled her eyes on a dashboard panel of buttons and dials expansive enough to pilot a UFO. She could never date a famous person. They were too wealthy, too different, too egotistical. And being around such a heightened level of excess and entitlement twenty-four-seven would have her irritation piqued at all times.

Brian hummed and fired up the ignition. The engine purred like a kitten; the cliché was true.

"You okay?" His considerate question made double the impact because he was the one in trouble and she should have asked first.

Though she hadn't eaten all day, the faint gnawing in her belly fled. She tried in vain to press a delete button and erase the thought about Brian being egotistical, but it wouldn't vanish.

What was wrong with her? He wasn't *that* egotistical, but the visual reminders of his fame and success threw her relative insignificance and litany of failures into relief. All of these logical points made sense, but intellectualizing didn't help. "I'm fine. Tired is all. Long flight."

"Well, relax and enjoy the ride in a custom-made One-Seven-Seven Aston Martin. While you're here, I'd love to take you for a cruise down the PCH and show you what she's made of. Rest assured, it's not to creep through the traffic we're about to hit."

Face boyish in its delight, he yanked the gearshift into drive. He owned the stick, a firm and confident grip. Pulling the wheel in a similarly deliberate tug, hands at the ten and six position, he zipped out of the loading zone and onto the exit ramp. The tune he hummed triggered a memory. He was singing one of his own band's songs.

Overcome by a low-grade stomachache, Helen resigned herself to emotional defeat as she sank into the swampy bile of her past.

A typical Midwestern girl growing up in the decade she had, she'd spent many a tweener night gazing up at the Fyre posters on her walls, coveting those hot-yet-nice British rockers, good boys playing at being bad who drove hormonal, star-struck girls to the brink of madness.

At thirteen, when she'd seen them live in some amphitheater in Bumblefuck, Minnesota, she'd sworn, as all female peers of her generation did, that Brian had looked right at her during that dumb "Deep Dark Woods" song.

Well, correction, it wasn't a dumb song. It was a chart topper, a masterpiece, the single that earned Fyre a Grammy and made them a household name.

Her feelings, the meaning she ascribed to Brian and the song, were dumb.

An intoxicating spate of teenage fever dreams followed that false magic moment, school days and lonely nights in un-homes spent fantasizing, at times in embarrassingly specific detail, that she'd make her way backstage at one of their concerts, connect on a soul-mate level, and find herself whisked away from her shitty life by a sensitive rocker white knight.

And now here she was, fifteen-plus years later, riding in Brian Shepherd's overpriced European car under outlandish paranormal circumstances. Ridiculous. Absurd.

Where was he when she was getting slapped around by that one drunk foster dad? Where the hell was he when she was showing her pussy and asshole for crumpled dollar bills? Probably getting his dick sucked in a car much like this one.

And now *she* had to save *his* life. But what happened to her glitzy, rock star savior fantasy? Where had that gone, why hadn't the universe offered that up when she'd would have chopped off a finger to have it?

In lieu of fulfilment of her youthful wish, she got bungled witchcraft, a curse, and the toxic adhesive resulting from it binding her and Brian together. Helen swore sometimes that she was the butt of a cosmic joke.

She bit down on her tongue and stared into the space in front of her, a fleet of red taillights like alligator eyes peeping out of black bayous. God, she had a shitload of unresolved issues, and the present instant managed to trigger every single one of them.

Brian addressed her silence with a patient murmur. "You aren't obligated to talk to me. It's not lost on me that you're putting yourself out on my behalf. This is stressful for you. I want you to know I care. And that if you want to talk, I'm here to listen."

She crunched a mint, its wintergreen sting burning away the funk. Unfair to lash out at Brian because, after all of these years, she still sorta low-grade hated herself and the idea of him swirled around the outer orbit of that hate field.

In fact, allowing such toxicity to run amok was super unfair and messed up. Because as easy at it was to resent Brian for his money and status and inability to save a younger version of her, he was innocent. A victim of her mistakes.

"I'm trying to be more emotionally intelligent, more measured in my reactions to things, but sometimes I melt down and get really angry. That's as best as I can explain it right now," she said.

"Did I do something wrong?" he asked as the car nudged forward.

In the slow-moving cell, there was nowhere to go. Nowhere to run and hide from the clusterfuck of her feelings, the decades of garbage floating up from her subconscious, the unbearable impulse to rapidly regress.

"No." She scratched the tops of her thighs, the repetitive motion making a series of comforting friction sounds. "It's hard for me to talk to people, to be vulnerable. Instead I get pissed off and retreat into this cyclic fixation on my grievances from the past. I swear I've had therapy. Probably not enough. Nothing is ever enough."

Brian stroked the steering wheel in those practiced and deliberate touches of his, as if he wanted to massage meaning out of the leather circle.

"I can relate to feeling like nothing is ever enough," he said.

Maybe if she eased up on the angst valve, a better version of herself could breathe in Brian's presence. He'd oxygenate her potential by recognizing it. He was genuine, integrated, generous. A bit cocky, sure. But his pride was commensurate with actual meteoric achievements— the man was no narcissist steeped in delusions of grandeur, no overcompensating Napoleonic nobody.

"How so?" she asked.

A comfortable silence expanded throughout their bubble, soft illumination from the dashboard contributing to the sense of personal, reserved bonding. The car made for a confession booth, with he and she alternating roles of priest and parishioner.

"When I feel overwhelmed, or afraid, I focus on success and money and material possessions. I still find myself looking to money and things when feeling certain emotions is just too bloody hard. I revel in consumption to fill the hole in my heart, I suppose, and of course no matter how much stuff I have, stuff will never suffice to bring me spiritual wholeness. Which means I'm not blameless in this. My involvement with Joe arose from greed."

"Fair." Her voice came out croaky. She cleared her throat, some of the hard and brittle dirt inside crumbling with a detoxing breath, a yogic lesson. Breathe in positivity, breathe out negativity. Unknot fury and heal the grief beneath it. "I have a hole in my heart, too. More like a rotten pit, but I digress."

He turned his head, cheek muscle twitching with a melancholy bend of the lips. "Seems we're a bit of a pair in that regard. It took me so long to even begin to figure out how to fill that void, that screaming gap threatening to suck up everything. When I was younger and the band was starting out, during our first stateside tour in particular, I sought fulfilment in every single cocked up way you can imagine. Drinking, drugs, surrounding myself with an entourage of flatterers and fake friends. Buying junk just to spend money. Sex with people I didn't care about—that one probably took the biggest pieces of my soul. And I wondered why I kept feeling worse and worse despite doing more and more of those things. Stupid of me, not to see the truth in front of my face. I'm still struggling with the materialistic mindset, chasing external validation and victory and such, but I'm trying to be better."

Brian deserved more credit. He'd figured a lot out, accrued a king's ransom of wisdom while navigating, as a young man, a career and lifestyle set up to reward and enable hedonism and excess.

"I am, too. Trying to be better. But I could try harder. And I admire you for everything you've done," she said.

"Not sure how admirable I am, but thank you. And I look up to you as well, to have achieved so much after everything you went through. So don't sell yourself short. We're both works in progress."

Her guard lowered enough for her to acknowledge that she liked, she really liked, the ongoing and consistent way that Brian rolled the two of them into a "we." A team, which they needed to be to solve the problem plaguing their lives. Fixing their broken pieces, together, might come later.

In the left lane, a Jaguar the color of earwax inched by. A hirsute, shirtless man hung out of the passenger seat, shaking a fist and hurling invective at Brian's rolled-up window.

Helen studied his tirade with a blend of discomfort, amusement, and empathy. She taught yoga for important reasons, and with conviction. To help others, and herself, let go of all of the crap and embrace the Zen.

"You think he has a hole in his heart, too?" she asked.

Brian threw his head back and let rip a peal of laughter, the roundness and timing blasting tension into smithereens. He cast a baleful glance at the provocateur. "Among other issues, I'd wager."

Glittery with spontaneity, she pulled her wallet from her satchel and slipped out one of the free class cards. Of course the random dude wouldn't come to Minneapolis, but the thought counted. She handed the card to Brian and bent her head at the commotion beyond his Aston Martin. Brian took her offering, shared a knowing look with her, and rolled down his widow.

Screaming Dude accepted, scowled at the paper rectangle in his hand, and threw the card onto the street. But at least he quit yelling and rolled up his window.

"Oh, well," Helen said.

"You had a good idea. Some people are inconsolable."

"Wonder what his problem is."

"That kind of thing happens all of the time here. He might have a gripe with me stemming from something in the past, some beef with one of my band members or ex-manager."

The invocation of Joe cast a pall over the car, Brian's indirection and censorship of the man's name worsening the discomfiture. A figurative specter now haunted them. The crisp fragrance of perfumed ornamental trees became a stifling miasma. So much for nixing tension. No better time than the present to yank off the sticky bandage.

"That reminds me, what did you want to talk about before we got in the car?" she asked.

"Ah, God."

And here they went, careening down the road to hell once again. While stalled on an actual road, going nowhere. There had to be some symbolism. Helen let out a sarcastic snicker.

At times like these, one really did have to make a choice between tears and laughter.

"Lay it on me." Hey, this was becoming her catchphrase. Boo-yah, and stuff.

"The clone we talked about showed up again, after I rang you. She stuck a hand through my body then vanished into nothing. She put marks on me, or took credit for an injury."

Helen rubbed her forehead. A nearby car's honking horn set off a flurry of successive bleats, their cacophony worsening the chaos in her head. "Are you okay? Hurt?"

"I'm fine. A bruise is all. I can't say for certain if she really caused the wound or was bluffing to try to scare or rattle me."

Sharp edges of the grimoire pressed into her flesh through her bag, the book making its presence known like a dead albatross. "Did she offer any clues, anything I might be able to work with? Hints as to the locations of the crystals, the next steps of their plan?"

"Vague threats. She said that Joe was a pawn in the scheme, that they would kill him after he'd served his purpose. And that she was confident you wouldn't be able to stop her."

A jab of indignation spurred Helen. "She has another thing coming."

There was the whole "ban on Left Hand spells" issue to navigate, but Helen wasn't about to swallow this doppelganger's slight like some pathetic loser. She needed a win, bad.

"There's my Helen." After saying her name, he trailed off.

"What?"

"Nothing, it's silly. I realized I didn't know your middle name."

"It's Britney. With one "t" and an "e.""

"Helen Britney Schrader. Brilliant."

"It's schlocky, but you're sweet. What's your middle name?"

He made a face like he'd eaten a lemon. "Not telling. It's too awful."

She pushed his arm, a gentle shove. He replied with a theatrical flop to one side, affectionate nonverbal play. "Middle names are supposed to suck. Tell me."

"Fine. It's Eugene."

"Aw, that's not so bad. Stately, in fact. Very English."

He rolled his eyes. "Stop."

"No way. I declare that we get to steal at least a few minutes here and there to pretend to be regular people who like each other. And that involves the usual get-to-know-you chit chat."

He took a hand off of the wheel and stroked the half-moon of one of her cuticle beds, a tiny touch so personal as to be huge. "We may not be regular people, but in no way am I pretending to like you."

She leaned in and rested her head against the firm muscle of his upper arm. "Ditto."

In the temporary silence of Helen's calm mind, a picture changed. The two of them weren't stalled in horrid traffic, they appreciated an opportunity to slow down and reflect. An opportunity to explore more of the odd ties connecting them.

Who knew she'd end up having so much in common with this person, someone so famous, so far away, so high above her.

But in the moment, awash in traffic and darkness and touches of local color in the form of highway-flanking palm trees and hilly slopes, Helen fell into serenity. She couldn't say which of the elements had that effect on her, or if it was the intangible woo-woo factor created by their gestalt, but the old higher power was a tease when it came to showing its enigmatic machinations.

"What are you thinking about?" Brian's question had a dreamlike aspect, as if he'd siphoned off a drink of her contemplative elixir.

"Right this second? The imperceptible, subtle nature of causality."

"Ah. Let me guess, you went to university and majored in philosophy."

"Yep. Good guess. I almost got a PhD, too." She tipped her head, looking up at the side of his face. She was baby birdlike in the exchange, smaller and younger and dwarfed by his star, and in some safe space way the power dynamic suited her.

"Why almost?" Their hands remained locked, fingers entwined in an interwoven grip.

The closeness of the hold evoked the intimacy of the sex they'd shared, yet surpassed those bedroom delights. Complexity and history thrived in the spaces between their laced fingers.

"Long story short, it was a difficult time in my life. I was working a degrading job and also reading tons of self-help books and doing yoga teacher training to try and fix my damage and better myself. Grad school fell between the cracks. Now tell me more about you."

"What do you want to know?" He kissed her hair, right on the part.

Beside him, in the force field of his current, Helen yielded. With his small moves, Brian attuned to her needs.

"When did the band form?" The car's atmosphere was a cozy sanctuary. No pentagrams or spells or insidious clones allowed.

"Ah, yes. We met in secondary school. A bunch of fourteen-year-old lads messing about. The school had a talent show, and a scout showed up. God, what an intense time. The New Wave of British heavy metal reigned. These executives were scouring the UK, Helen. They craved the next Iron Maiden, Zeppelin, Leppard. I could see dollar signs in the man's eyes."

"So you guys rang the right bells?"

"Oh, yes. The sound struck his fancy straight away. Our school uniforms triggered an AC/DC association. Bonus."

"And the name?"

"Jonas, our drummer, is spiritual. A bit like you, actually. He'd recently read this rather strange book, *Chariots of the Gods*. He had this whole concept. We would be the next big thing, these rock gods who would descend upon the world and take it by storm. In our teen arrogance, we loved it. The vehicle association thrilled us, too. The label wanted an alternative spelling to push the Zep/Lep button. That's what they called it. Sometimes I look back and it all seems preposterous."

"I knew it." She tugged Brian's shirt, high on the confirmation of decades-old hunch.

His crow's feet deepened, and laugh line parentheses popped with his dimples as a whole face smile took over.

"Knew what?" Brian urged her closer, maintaining his one-handed steering. They were like two teens in love in the car, canoodling as unstructured time flowed in circular loops.

The L-word she'd thought, though, didn't escape the loop. It sailed down the tubes in her brain and heart, a dense pinball ricocheting against the walls. The machine inside lit up, red signs. Danger, danger. If she didn't stomp the ball of feelings into submission, though, it got less scary. So, with managed expectations and on a trial basis, she let it be.

"I had a strong inkling you got your band name from von Daniken's interpretation of the Krishna story in *The Bhagavad Gita*, the whole idea that ancient aliens visited our world and taught us how to evolve. Cosmic astronauts. I would have gone with either the Z or the Y, not both, but I digress."

"Well, subtlety isn't exactly the record label's forte. I'm surprised they didn't make us slap an umlaut over one of vowels."

There was much to appreciate about Brian, a ton of stuff in the win column. His dry humor and versatile, sparkling mind. He was mordant, though not cynical, an entertainer with the comedian's gift of coloring his world. She nuzzled his arm with her cheek, holding his hand like he was the anchor preventing her from flying into outer space untethered.

"Would you sing me a song?"

"Of course. Any requests?"

"'Deep Dark Woods.'"

The opening refrain of the classic rock anthem, her generation's "Stairway to Heaven," prompted a divine series of chills, a rush of stirrings in her soul. Her eyelids fell as he treated her to the private serenade in his distinctive, tenor-baritone croon, a voice made to crush it in arena rock while remaining true to English blues-rock roots. Stuff of beauty, legends. Music touched sacred emotional places.

Brian sang, melodies rising and falling in weightless crests.

Scar tissue healed. Time dissolved. There was only his magical voice, the medicine of his song.

When she returned to consciousness, the car crawled up an incline. They twisted through narrow roads, past an assortment of Georgian mansions, futurist experimental structures, and ranch homes with orange trees out front.

"Welcome to the Hollywood Hills. You're beautiful when you sleep. Want to visit the sign?" Brian pointed out the window. Past his vector, legendary white letters in an uneven alphabet soup welcomed visitors to LaLa Land.

"Nah, I'm good. I just want to get home. To your home, I mean." Home. After all of these years, the word was tough to think, let alone say. She shook her head, the pinball re-activating in another round of frenzied banging. Stupid anxiety.

The mishmash variety of houses gave way to pervasive opulence, sprawling mansions and golden gates emblazoned with cursive initials. Bereft in the face of wealth on display, she gaped like a goldfish who'd leapt from its bowl and landed on the floor.

"Me, too." He hummed, steering the car into a driveway barricaded by a fortress of an iron gate fit to protect a medieval castle. Brian leaned out of his driver's side and punched a code into a box.

Double doors parted with an electronic groan, and he resumed the drive. A black ribbon of private road unspooled beyond the windshield.

Their path ended at a roundabout with a glittering fountain in the center. Cobblestones abutted the most elegant home Helen had ever seen in person. Three stories of blocky, geometric architecture, lots of glass and metal, piled upon each other in a haphazardly artsy arrangement.

A smattering of interior lights made the palace gleam like an alien king's castle. Mahogany double doors complete with gargoyle knockers offset the modernist design with a funky, vintage-goth feel.

A car was parked out front. A guard dog of a massive SUV sat in Brian's roundabout, golden hubcap rims shouting "behold my bling."

Brian mumbled a string of British curses, his hands tightening on the wheel like he wanted to strangle it.

SIXTEEN

"NOT EXPECTING COMPANY?" HELEN HAD ZERO IDEA HOW THE RICH operated, if Brian could anticipate members of an entourage hanging around his property whenever.

"It appears my daughter has manipulated her bodyguard into ringing her stepmother. Looks like you'll be meeting the ex-wife this evening."

"Ah." With any luck, the encounter would end quickly, and former supermodel Kris King would be on her way.

The forty-five-year-old stunner had traded appearances in top fashion magazines and sashaying down Paris runways for managing acts and making guest appearances on talent audition shows and other reality TV fare.

Yes, Helen had Google-stalked the woman to whom Brian had been married for two years. And she didn't measure up to Kris in looks, status, wealth, or anything else. Not a huge source of distress, given the magnitude of all of the other shit she had to deal with, but not pleasant, either.

Brian parked his car in front of Kris's. He looked over at Helen, features drawn in a blotto sort of resolution.

She got it. He didn't want to leave the cocoon they'd created in his car during their slow roll through Los Angeles. She didn't want to pop the bubble either.

"Sorry in advance," he said.

"She's that bad?"

"No, she knows how to act and be polite, but if I had my druthers she'd bugger off and I'd never see or speak to her again." The iciness with which Brian spoke, combined with the absolute, unwavering certainty undergirding the words, exposed a hidden side of his personality.

When he cut people off, she bet goodbye was forever. Respectable and intimidating.

"What did she do?"

Brian broke eye contact. A subtle bow of his spine and caving of his chest, like he wanted to protect his underbelly from attack, pinged her radar. "I caught her shagging someone else, walked right in on it. The worst part was her cynical justification, this line about how it meant nothing and she was only doing it to advance her career. To her credit, she was right. I served her the divorce papers the morning after I found her and the other man in our bed, but the following week, she's on the cover of the *Vogue* collector's edition. So she got what she wanted."

Twinned tendrils of embarrassment and petty vindication curled through Helen. On a lark, she'd purchased the fat anniversary commemorative, a glossy doorstop paying homage to one of her mythical namesakes.

The cover featured Kris, decked out in gossamer robes of virginal white silk and a golden tiara emphasizing rivulets of hay-colored curls, standing on a beach flanked by azure ocean.

The retreating ships were shown only by shadows, for even the thousand-vessel fleet launched on behalf of the planet's greatest beauty mustn't compete with the camera's close-up on her perfect face. Inside the pages, while the battle of the Iliad raged in a background diorama of toy soldiers, the camera made love to Kris's classic Scandinavian elegance, looks exceptional even by elite modeling standards.

The inwardly directed joke had been self-deprecating, yet another tired instance of trite and pathetic witnessing to Helen's low self-esteem. Helen of Troy, ha ha ha. Obvious who *really* deserved such a lofty comparison.

But now, it wasn't so obvious. Human ugliness skulked behind every unobtainable façade.

"I'm sorry, Brian. I've been cheated on, too. It sucks."

"Royally."

"Did you love her?"

He moved his head side-to-side. "In a way. She was gung-ho to get involved, and our managers thought we'd be a perfect power couple. So it was easy, you know? Like an arranged marriage. And it did feel more like an arrangement, a business partnership. Which was probably why the coupling appealed to me in the first place. I was still reeling from my first wife's death and terrified to feel again. What developed was more like a best friend kind of affection than passionate love, but yes I did love her, enough for her betrayal hurt so badly that I barely dated for a long time."

Helen fidgeted with her fingernails, picked the chipped burgundy polish she hadn't had the time or energy to update. "It's easy to push people away when we're hurt, to shut down. We may want to let someone in, but it's hard. There are barriers, and they don't go away on their own."

He caught her chin with the pads of two of his fingers and tilted her face upward, bringing her eye to eye with him. His gaze burned through the aforementioned barriers. "Are we talking about you and me right now? This thing between us?"

A sense of covering her eyes and backing away from a gory crime scene swooped in. Nothing to see here, do not register or engage. "Which thing between us do you mean? Because there are several. The curse? The clone?"

His stare didn't waver. "You're doing it again."

"What?" She knew what, but "it" didn't yet have form. Now and then, an impulse, swift and reactionary, swept through Helen and stole her center.

The thieving invasion replaced her integrity, some precious gem nestled in the deepest point in her core, with a corrupt blob of cynicism. An inhabitant fit for the rotten pit.

Said inhabitant had served a purpose in the past, a vicious attack snake poised to snap its fangs at anyone who dared to advance.

Helen dissociated, spaced out hardcore, and fell down the rabbit hole of the snake metaphor. She lost her mind to a wicked, heady version of déjà vu. Nerissa appeared as a snake, a symbolic serpent. Had this been the elder's motive, to plant a seed, to use the power of suggestion to prompt Helen to examine and analyze the deepest, nastiest aspects of her subconscious?

Brian spoke. "You retreat. Not all of the time, but it's enough of a pattern to where it's noticeable. I get close, and right as it seems like a breakthrough is coming, you go away. Then this other version of you comes out, the one that's prickly and quick with the comebacks."

Though two halves of Helen fought to join, she stayed detached and disintegrated, one part watching the other as if observing a play. In the crack between two selves, a eureka sprang.

"Oh, my God. This is it. This is why Nerissa thought I wasn't suited to the Left Hand path."

Disappointment registered in Brian's face, testimony given in deepening wrinkles, lips rubbed together. "I thought we were talking about us."

"We were, we are. But it's connected. It's all connected. The reason I haven't been able to do Left Hand work without blowback is because I'm split, fractured, not at peace with myself yet. So like you said, there are two versions of me, and they don't line up into a harmonious whole. When I try stuff like psyche splitting magic, it doesn't work right, the results come out weird, because I, myself, am fundamentally split." Her blood pounded. Pulse drummed. Mind raced, struggling to keep up with revelations.

She'd cracked a code, figured out something huge. Helen wasn't unsuited to Left Hand spells, but she hadn't been doing them in the optimal mindset.

"Sounds like you have all of the answers." He pulled his fingers away and tapped the gear shift twice, a terse gesture devoid of whimsy.

"Don't tell me you're upset at me. This is important. For the work we're doing."

"Of course." A false smile, half-formed and watery. Brian opened his door. "Ready?"

"Brian, come on. The stakes of this are massive. I didn't mean to shut you down. I do want to have heart-to-hearts, but in that exact instant it felt like I needed to work through an insight having to do with my magic. This affects you."

"I know, I know. It's your process. I honor and respect that, and I'm aware that the supernatural project needs to take priority. But there's something more, yes? Something between us that isn't strictly business?"

Seeking cheap safety, Helen built a wall between her and Brian. "Do you mean the sex?"

"In part, sure."

"Don't you do that kind of thing all of the time, though? Bang groupies in your hotel rooms? Be real." On the heels of the disingenuous question tailored to alienate came a burst of lava, incendiary secretions that cooled into an unpleasant, familiar plaque.

Brian scoffed. "I get it now. You construct a story in your head in which I'm a pig and a user, some caricature it's easy to judge and disdain, thereby absolving yourself of having to face your own struggles with intimacy."

Tears assailed her ducts in quick and savage stabs. She'd been exposed. "You have no right to analyze me."

"Why not? Because holding a mirror to you frightens you too much and reveals too many deep flaws? Forces you to confront the fact that you might need to do more work on yourself before you can be okay, forces you to accept that yoga didn't cure everything?"

Naked, she drew her cruelest weapons. "Good job. Bravo, Dr. Shepherd, what an enriching therapy session. Did you earn that psychology degree of yours while partying backstage after *opening* for Def Leppard approximately a hundred years ago?"

The arrow boomeranged, impaling Helen with a gut shot. What the fuck was wrong with her? Regret was immediate and stark. "Brian—"

He silenced her with a pointer finger in the air, swung his door wide, and leapt out of the car. The soft way in which he shut it was worse than the angriest slam.

She sat alone in the passenger seat, a one-inch-tall lump. Sick and scuzzy from drinking her own poison, Helen hauled herself out and followed Brian to the trunk, which yawned open in the sci-fi show.

He removed her bag and placed it on the ground. Next came a package, wrapped in matte paper the color of a violet and tied with a glossy blue bow. Brian handed the box to her without comment. The colors matched those on her L&E business card. Oh, no.

She accepted the gift, those few pounds of weight a boulder of shame in her hands. He'd bought her a present. She was officially awful, the worst.

"Brian, I'm sorry. You're right, one-hundred percent. I'm a Russian nesting doll of pathologies and maladaptive behaviors, and God help whoever finds whatever twisted gremlin lives in the little one. I don't open up or show myself easily, or at all really. I have one close friend. One, and I almost managed to sabotage that. And I have no family. But I've made gains. I'm capable of change and growth and getting close to people in my own way. My yoga training was not a cure-all, true. But if only you'd seen the freak show I was before I started yoga. I'm not asking you to take a chance on me, but just to hear whatever you can."

His eyelid twitched. "Apology accepted. I wish you wouldn't bite my head off, but I understand you're under extreme duress. I'm here for you. Try to remember that I care."

"I do. And I'm so sorry."

"I'll have you know I met heaps of interesting people on that tour, broadened my horizons and mind, talking to men and women from all walks of life and all over the world. I've learned volumes over the years from people. And what gives with the slam about me shagging groupies? I thought I redeemed crucial points from you when you saw that my bus wasn't a den of sex and drugs."

"I guess nobody's tried to figure me out before, not in the way you have. And you're doing A-OK with points from me. Not that points from me are valuable currency. I should be begging people for points, not doling them out."

"I started to view them as badges of honor once I realized how difficult they were to accrue."

"You're so competitive about everything. Admirable. But breaking through this..." she hoisted the package under one arm and waved a hand up and down the space in front of her body, "and finding the sweet and mushy goodness underneath the armor might be an insurmountable challenge."

Brian stepped in, closing a couple feet of distance between them.

Moonlight and ambient flickers from his mansion reflected in his eyes. "So you're challenging me to get close to you?"

"I don't want to set you up to fail. Nobody else has gotten in."

"Nobody else besides me can claim three separate, original, diamond-certified albums in the States. Not the band you cited. Not anyone's rock band but mine." His nostrils flared. He smelled male and cut a swaggering, I-own-the-town presence in the Hollywood night.

"Impressive stats, yes, but trust me. This is harder."

The upward jut of his chin paired well with a slow nod. "Okay. Challenge accepted, Helen Britney Schrader."

Brian strode to his front door and keyed in a string of numbers. A click issued from behind the grand entrance of dark wood.

Compelled by an ongoing respect for Brian that continued to build, Helen stepped to the threshold and laid a hand on the small of his back. "We've got this. And thank you for the gift. I can't wait to open it."

"We've got this," Brian said with confidence.

A sprinkle of fleeting peace rained over her, and she looked into Brian's eyes, speaking to him with that emotional cousin of telepathy they both understood.

"You're beautiful, Helen."

She permitted a little taste of the meaning to enter her system and let go of some crap. No need to deflect, deny, joke, or retaliate. The compulsion to guard, parry, attack, and defend eased. For one sweet moment, she wasn't bitter. Or split or wounded. Brian saw the best of her, and she let him. "Thank you."

He dropped a kiss to her temple and opened the front door. Monotonous club beats accompanied by Germanic vocals streamed through the foyer of his grand home. Their tender bit of synergy drained into whatever weird shit was going down. Never a dull moment.

"My daughter's acting out. One moment." Brian walked inside at a brisk clip, wheeling Helen's bag behind him. "Tilly, what's going on?"

Helen followed him into the mansion. Vaulted ceilings carried the eye high, tempting the guest to gawk upward like a first-timer in the Big Apple. The airy, open layout engulfed her, and gleaming bamboo floors, a sectional couch in white leather matching his car seats, and a baby grand piano presented spoils of fame. Platinum and gold records lined the walls. Several shoebox amplifiers and guitars in floor stands occupied a corner. A slim bookcase boasted a plethora of shiny awards. It was a *lot*.

The old cramp of being an interloper in someone else's sanctuary clenched her lower belly. At least they'd more or less acknowledged the impermanence of their situation, meaning she didn't need to feel bad that he would never invite her puny self to join, in any permanent way, the fabulous life he'd built for himself. Which was fine. She didn't belong in this prestige den, this pinnacle of architectural and interior design paying splendid homage to one of history's most famous, beloved, and renowned rock musicians.

The teen girl from the Denver pictures came bounding down a streamlined, angular metal staircase. A sloppy pile of clothes and shoes spilled from her arms, and she galloped like her bare feet couldn't move fast enough.

"Hi, Daddy." Following her chipper greeting, she breezed past, on route to the front door.

Brian caught her upper arm, causing a pair of hot pink jeans and a shoe with a heel shaped like the business end of a revolver to fall to the ground. The footwear looked to be made out of upcycled tin cans and maybe a real firearm.

"Where do you think you're going?" he demanded in a fatherly tone.

"Calm down. I'm just going to stay with Mom for a few days. And watch out. These are designer pieces." Tilly stooped and retrieved the gun shoe.

"You absolutely are not going to stay with *Kris* for a few days. It's too dangerous." He set Helen's bag down by the foot of the stairs.

"Quit babying me," Tilly screeched. "I'm not a little girl. I'm nearly grown. And I can't stay cooped up like this. How would you feel if I locked you in a tower and told you you could never practice with your stupid band ever again? I got called back for a second audition shoot with *Vanity Fair*, and if I miss it my life is over. I'm as good as dead."

"Tilly, you're being melodramatic—"

"What is the source of this awful squabbling?" A feminine voice, sanded to fit the mold of a blasé trill drained of personality, drifted down the staircase. Kris descended on stilts of tanned legs. Black bootie shorts wrapped her straight hips, and a matching tank top clung to a midriff as flat as a cutting board. She carried a silver clutch no larger than a pack of cigarettes in an alarmingly white-knuckled grip.

"Are you attempting to manipulate her into moving out again, Kris? Because your dodgy tricks won't work. And right now it isn't safe. I mean it."

"Tilly, sweetheart, go put those in the car. I'll send some people over in the morning for the rest of your things." The supermodel came into full view, an impeccable chignon knot the color of champagne atop her head and facial features frozen into permanent, plasticized pseudo-youth.

Brian held on to Tilly, who pouted and stomped a bare foot. He said, "Kris, listen. There's something going on right now, something awful, and I need you to take it seriously. There's been a threat on her life."

Kris sashayed over in a long-limbed, runway glide, stopping a couple of feet from Brian and Tilly. "Brian, honey, you're so predictable, You've gone and offended someone significant in the Order of the Priory of Knife and Phoenix, haven't you?"

Helen set her present on an end table, fished her journal and a pen from her purse, and wrote down that fucking ludicrous name. "Someone? Anyone in particular you know there who would make death threats if offended?"

Kris made a huffy noise and slid Helen the hairy eyeball. "Are you going to introduce me to your new friend, Brian?"

"Not until you tell me what you're doing in my home and what your designs are on my daughter. And the Priory of Knife and Phoenix? Talk, Kris."

"Of course you don't know of them. You can take the boy out of the English midlands farm, but you can't take the *hick* out of the boy. It's an elite organization. They make threats all of the time, but it's all bluster. They don't want people leaving the organization and yammering to the media, spoiling their reputation. Come on, Matilda. Let's go."

Tilly wiggled. "Let go of me. I'm late."

"Like hell." Brian held on tight.

Helen stashed her journal. "So it's a cult, yeah?"

Kris's frown morphed to a bemused look. "I'm sorry, you are?"

"My name's Helen. And it would really help if you tell me everything you know about this Order of the Priory of Knife and Phoenix."

The supermodel's pale blue eyes gleamed with interest. "I can take you to a meeting. Are you relocating to Los Angeles permanently?"

"I don't want to be recruited. I want you to tell me whatever you can about this group. Their practices, anything illegal or ritualistic you may have observed. Have you seen anything that's scared you? Activities with religious overtones, like a black mass?"

Kris blinked. "I don't know anything about that." She glanced in both directions, her speech and movements eerie and robotic.

The creeps crawled under Helens' clothes. Kris was gone. She'd disappeared, leaving Helen with the distinct sense that she no longer spoke to a person. The cult had activated one of the drones that Joe brought up in the hotel hallway.

"You know their name, and that they had Brian in their sights. Meaning you know something. And we're quite possibly all in danger here, so if you have facts please share."

"I don't know anything about that." Kris stared vacantly.

She turned on a sneakered heel and swayed to the door, exiting and closing it behind her.

An engine rumbled and petered out as Drone Kris drove off.

Tilly dropped her pile and blasted a shrill scream. "I hate you. You suck. You ruined my life." Wailing, she raced up the stairs.

Brian touched his nose and lips. "At least she's safe. This'll blow over."

"You realize the implications." Helen chewed the end of her pen.

"I think I sense the vicinity. Kris is one of them. She's close to it all, near the center even. At least we have a name."

"True. And you better put Tilly on lockdown from here on out and watch yourself, too. Because I can't say for certain they won't kidnap her as bait to lure you."

SEVENTEEN

THE DAMN THING WOULDN'T TUNE. BRIAN TWISTED LADY S'S TUNING pegs and strummed. Tinny whines grated against him. Nope. Off-key, sour.

He tuned and played a chord, adjusted a dial and played a chord. Nope, nope, nope. One of Brian's heroes, a guitar great, had gifted Brian Lady S while the two had toured the man's English estate years ago. And in the present moment she tuned about about as properly as a pawn shop cast off.

Brian slung the strap over his torso and propped Lady S against his overstuffed chair. He walked to the mini fridge, got out a beer, and twisted off the cap. A long pull of his frothy, wheaty Bavarian brew cooled him down, blotting the chatter in his head with sensory pleasure.

Despite everything else happening in his life, he had a tour finale to practice for, and the show had to go on. Meaning he'd better get into the zone. Brian shoved thoughts of rituals, witchcraft, and clandestine organizations out of his head and appraised his home studio.

The mixing board with its panel of dials and buttons was pro grade. News clippings, awards, and photos lined walls with proof of Fyre's accomplishments. Two computers sat on the office desk, twin high-tech soldiers tasked with editing tracks.

Amidst the reminders of his band, his art, his career and dearest friends, he got a grip.

Sequestered in the glass of the sound-proof booth, Jonas sang, practicing his vocal range as he swayed with hands over headphones.

Brian grooved in time. His drummer wasn't half bad. Higher octave, equally melodious but a bit less romantic than Brian. Reminiscent of Robert Plant.

One of the few Black men in contemporary rock, Fyre's drummer had carved out a niche for himself as one of their main songwriters and the band member most talented at arranging lyrics, riffs and melodies into whole songs.

In addition to keeping egos in check and fights over women and money to a minimum, finding and accepting defined roles proved crucial for the band to remain intact and successful for multiple decades. The four of them were a team down to their marrow. A brotherhood.

"You look pensive. Something on your mind, mate?" Jonnie, sunk into a tan leather couch and strumming a yellow Fender, chanced Brian a knowing, brown-eyed glance.

He accepted the other guitarist's gentle call-out with a grumble. "Yes. Something by the name of Order of the Priory of Knife and Phoenix."

"'Scuse me?" Jonnie's long fingers bent over his fretboard as he turned out an upbeat rock and roll riff.

"That's the name of the cult that's cutting people, the one with ties to Joe. Kris was here earlier, and she named them." Acting brainwashed, a whole other matter.

"I take it this development links up with the bird who's staying with you now, the woman you met in Minneapolis and brought to Denver?"

"Yeah." It sickened him to admit the tie. "You met her when you came round for practice, I take it?"

Jonnie tucked hair behind his ears. "Uh-huh. Ran into her on my way in today. She'd been out to the farmer's market and was bringing in grocery bags. Look, I don't want to make any waves, but I want you to know that I hear the uncertainty in your voice, and I think it's valid."

His stomach closed around the liquid he'd drank. "Why do you say that?"

"I mean, like I said, mate, I don't want to make any waves. You deserve to be happy, and if you like Helen and want to date her, then I like her too. And I support your choice."

Please. If Jonnie meant that, he wouldn't have spoken in the careful tone of a diplomat or hostage negotiator.

Brian finished his beer, though now it tasted skunky. "But?"

With an apologetic shrug, Jonnie fiddled with the knobs on his guitar neck. "If it were me, I'd steer clear from anyone even tangentially connected to Joe or cults or magic."

Doubt shrank Brian's world into suspicion. Cautious cowardice, he told himself, was smart and necessary. "Well, as we both know you're even more apprehensive about relationships than I am."

Jonnie groaned. "What's my love life got to do with yours? Look, if you like her, keep seeing her. I never advised you not to. All I'm pointing out is that I register and agree with your tacit, unstated acknowledgment that something is very strange here."

"You think I'm making a mistake with her."

"I didn't say that."

"That's what you meant."

"I'd proceed with caution and be mindful of how much emotional investment might or might not be clouding your judgment. That's all I'll say."

Brian peeled off his bottle label in one satisfying sheet. He wasn't sure what he wanted from Jonnie. Permission to surrender his misgivings and fall in love with Helen, or confirmation that it didn't make him an arsehole to retreat from her. Her internal struggles, the insecurities and such that made bonding with her a challenge, also caused concerns.

At the end of the day, she dragged frightening baggage. Black magic. A clone. Occult sacrifices, secret societies. Helen wasn't innocent. A heavy feeling weighed on Brian. His horizons contracted.

Thom burst in, two equipment cases in tow, sunglasses and cowboy hat shielding his face. "Awful quiet in here. Is this a world famous rock band's studio or a retirement home?"

The bassist unfolded a metal chair and sat at a card table. He snapped open a plastic rectangle and popped a luxurious, bronze-hued Rickenbacker from its foam protector.

Methodical, Thom unpacked an amp, hooked it up, and chorded.

"You're late." Brian caught whiffs of feminine perfume blended with a far more personal tang, and thus didn't bother to ask about the reason for Thom's tardiness. Everyone knew what the confirmed bachelor got up to when not making music.

"Sure am." Satisfied smirk on his weathered face, Thom worked through his warmup. "Porn stars never cease to amaze me. We're talking genius talent when it comes to stimulating the male pleasure centers."

Brian ignored the suggestive bit and focused on Thom's music, easing his worried mind as he left interpersonal mode and ventured into his musician headspace. Thom, who took the strongest affinity to the blues aspect of Fyre's sound, plucked out a rich number. He tapped a cowboy boot-clad foot to the beat.

Thom slid a brass tube over his pinky and moved it up and down the strings, creating a loopy, warbling effect. Despite Thom's amorality and predilection for debauchery, the man wielded commendable skill. He was a true artist, his emotional connection to harmony the most profound of the quartet. Thom channeled intangible and ethereal mysteries when he played.

Brian grabbed Lady S by the neck and joined the bassist at the square table. She tuned up right and proper this time. He layered in his own riffs. Their sounds mingled, danced, merged in the hypnotic way unique to English blues-rock. He nodded at Thom, switched his tuning to Drop D, and played in A minor, a modification which took his sound darker, more brooding.

Jonnie threaded in a dreamy, mythological experimentation.

The door to the sound booth shut, and soon a deep bass groove trembled in Brian's bones.

Lost to the instrumental communication, he glanced over to see Jonas seated on the couch, dreadlocks hanging in front of his eyes while he played a bass guitar.

Brian moved his fingers through chords, his most cherished possession doing his bidding yet again. This new song had a heaviness to it, a gravity, a weight.

Architects of moral panic decried rock and roll as the devil's music. Though Brian mostly laughed at such fear mongering, at times he felt it.

At the very least, something Dionysian and wild, the essence of a snarl or a cocky sneer and a phallic and thrusting guitar, lived forever in the soul of rock.

Fuck, he loved his band. His music. The lighthouse in his storms, always and forever.

With or without Helen, he'd always have his bandmates, his calling. Even if their affair broke his heart, he'd never be without purpose.

"Yeah," Thom said, deep voice smoky as he broke into song.

Unrepentant and sexual lyrics of troubadours and carousing, roaming and prowling, conquered the room. The restless nomad's tune challenged Brian's romantic reverie.

"Our sensitive singer is having lady troubles again," Jonnie said dryly.

Brian's mates got on him for falling for every bird he touched. It wasn't quite *that* bad; he knew when to exercise discretion and reject female charms, but perhaps the boys were on to something with their ongoing advice that he needed to get better at protecting his heart from the wrong women. Kris King was proof.

"I'm telling you, you don't need some relationship to find inspiration. The muse comes from in here." Thom slapped his chest. "And here." He grabbed his balls.

Fighting a grin, Brian continued to play. His bassist loved who he was without regret or apology. A leering imp, a randy jester, a decadent rocker to his marrow. Still, he couldn't miss a chance to take the piss. "Before you know it, you'll be the eighty-year-old with a nineteen-year-old girl on your arm. Which isn't cool. It's pathetic."

"Tell that to my eighty-year-old cock when it's getting sucked by said nineteen-year-old." Thom fetched a beer and used end of the table to crack off the cap.

Tilly's smiling face flashed into Brian's mind, and he irrationally squirmed with an urge to sock Thom's jaw. As twisted as it sounded, part of him was grateful that Janet's untimely death had left him to the task of raising their young daughter by himself. Stumbling into single fatherhood and figuring out how to parent a girl from age six onward had taught him sobering lessons on why the world needed feminism.

"By that time, let's hope no young woman feels compelled to service you for any reason. And I'd rather not entertain a conversation with your knob, no thank you," Brian said.

Thom slid mirrored sunglasses down his nose, light brown eyes aglitter. "Lemme get some girls over here. We'll find some inspiration the true rock star way. For old time's sake."

Brian worked through his solo. "That isn't me, and you know it. You're a sad old man grasping at the scraps of his lost youth, not some sly devil dangling temptation. Better I tell you than someone else."

Thom laughed a robust laugh, shaking his head and sending long hair flying. His song reached a denouement.

Supplying rhythm and backbeat, Jonas and Jonnie kept up their parts.

"We've gotten boring. Look at us, a pack of geriatric men sipping beer. We used to pass girls around and pull trains in studios much like this one. Remember?" Thom's jackal smile revealed the fistfight-chipped tooth he hadn't bothered to fix.

Most of the wilder exploits from decades ago were bound up with so-called partying, otherwise known as alcohol and drug abuse, and Brian had no desire to relive them.

He'd long since come to terms with the excesses he'd indulged in around the time of their first tour, learned lessons, and moved on. Sex with groupies had been just another drug. No intimacy, no shared humanity, no affection or true spark of desire. A manifestation of addictive behavior, an attempt to relieve boredom and fill a deeper emotional and spiritual void with a momentary rush, a fleeting high.

And, of course, such behavior involved treating the women not as people with their own feelings and needs, but as consumables laid out on the rock star's endless buffet of party favors, toys to be used and discarded.

"Nah. I don't think moving past sharing women with your bandmates means getting old and boring. I think it's a sign of personal growth. Maturity. Insight. And I'm grateful I figured that out quickly, so such behavior represents a misspent year of my youth, not a permanent marker of my character." Brian wadded up a piece of notebook paper and threw it at Thom.

"The man's got a point," Jonas said from the couch. "You know many of those girls didn't have their heads on right. And how we took advantage...not good for the soul. I couldn't get to sleep at night if I was still on the shag."

Thom put a thumb over his bottle and shook it up. Fizz left glass with a hissing pop. "I hereby consecrate, beatify, and declare you Saint Brian. That's what you want, right? Or do you need to trudge to Jerusalem with a crucifix on your back and have someone nail you up?" The bassist pressed his damp pad between Brian's brows and moved it to his chest and each shoulder, making the sign of the cross. He flipped Jonas the bird. "Why don't you come over here and suck him off, Mr. Yes-Man Drummer? I sleep fine, thanks."

Jonas swapped his bass for a mahogany Fender and wailed out a solo. The drummer had a brutally calm way of ignoring attempts to lure him into conflict.

"Enough," Brian said through an appreciative chuckle, wiping wetness from his forehead. "I, too, sleep fine at night. I'm happy with who I am and who I've become."

Perhaps he ought to look in a mirror and reconnect with the good man he was when he started to feel jumpy about his personal life. His conscience would guide him to the right decisions.

A series of knocks struck the door in a jaunty rhythm, cutting short the camaraderie.

Brian opened the studio to Helen. She wore a goofy grin and a T-shirt with a graphic of a kitten riding through outer space atop a slice of pizza. "Hey. I recognize that guitar from Minneapolis."

Puzzled by the random intrusion and clumsy, forced comment, he stroked Lady S's glossy finish. "Right, well, she's my special instrument. What's going on?"

Helen waved jazz hands in the air. "I know, I know, I'm totally pulling a Yoko right now, crashing your practice. But I have big news."

The excitement in her voice perked him up. "Do tell."

She bit down on her bottom lip, drawing out a dramatic pause. "Two words: Soul Krush."

Many of his acquaintances in the entertainment industry took spin classes and practiced yoga in the elite studio, though he found it odd that she chose this exact moment to mention the gym. "What about it?"

"They've invited me to guest teach a couple of classes while I'm here as long as I give a good audition. This could really open doors for me back in Minneapolis. Be a huge opportunity to enrich my brand and gain some name recognition."

"Congratulations." He stepped forward and wrapped Helen into an embrace.

The way she returned his hug, with two pats on the back and her bottom stuck out so their pelvises didn't touch, confused him. But Helen was a bit awkward, so maybe this stiffness came with her feeling nervous about auditioning.

"Thank you. Can I ask a favor?"

"Of course."

"I was hoping to go over there this afternoon and scope out the space. Would you mind coming along and watching me practice my sequence? Give feedback?"

Thick jumbles of questions about her request floated around his mind.

"I don't know how much help I'd be, seeing as I've never done yoga. I'd snap these old bones in half." He bent his head at a comical angle, an attempt at humor mismatched to his state of mind.

"I value your opinion, though."

Helen didn't know anyone in Los Angeles and therefore didn't have anybody else to ask for help. She was reaching out to him, and he wouldn't push her away. Not when she was trusting him to weigh in on an important part of her identity. Helen's request represented an effort to bring them closer after she'd pushed him away in the car. So what if she hadn't nailed the delivery.

"Sure. Give me fifteen to wrap up."

"You got it." She shut the door behind her.

Brian returned to the jam session, though a nagging feeling as bothersome as a rock in the shoe irritated the back of his mind.

"That was off the wall," Jonnie said.

"She's so hot. Let me know if you two split up." Thom pumped a suggestive fist up and down the neck of his bass, coaxing a moan from his instrument.

Jonas slugged Thom's arm. "How does it feel, being a stereotype of the oversexed rocker?"

"Feels like a wet dick and an empty set of balls."

"Off the wall how?" Brian asked Jonnie, unfocused anxiety rushing over his skin.

"Never mind. Forget it." Jonnie fiddled with the volume on his amp.

"Tell me."

"I thought her voice sounded a tad fake," he muttered.

"Fake in what way?"

"Don't get pissed. You asked for my honest opinion, and I gave it. Helen gives me pause. She made a questionable first impression. I get a strange sense from her, like she's hiding things. There, I said it. But you're a grown man, and I don't purport to tell you how you ought to live your life."

"Yet you just did."

"Can we please not bicker?" Jonas said. "I'd love it if we could get through this finale show without bungling songs we've been playing for thirty years due to you two fighting about a woman. After the finale we have six months before we're back in the studio, and then you can do whatever you wish."

"He's right." Thom played an early Fyre song. "Focus."

The remainder of band practice transpired with a marked, uncharacteristic lack of socializing, and when all concerned were confident they'd shaken off the rust, Brian hung Lady S on her wall-mounted hook. "You three sticking around?"

"Yeah, figure we'll do a bit of experimenting." Thom rested his instrument against a chair and made his way to the sound booth in a carefree gait.

"Alright. Take care. Jon, you remember the new security code for the house, yeah?" Brian asked.

"Of course." Jonnie grabbed Brian's arm, his eyes darkening.

"What? You look like you have something you want to say." Brian tensed against his best friend's hold. The last thing he wanted was to suspect Jonnie of secrets.

Jonnie drew in a loud breath and hissed it out. "No. I don't." He let go.

Fighting a destabilizing, flummoxed feeling, Brian left his studio and ambled up the carpeted steps. He popped out of the door adjacent to the kitchen.

Helen stood at the island chopping produce. The sight of his chef's blade in her hands, ten inches of sharpened Japanese steel gleaming in the remains of sunlight, caused the willies to slip down his spine. Ugh, what was wrong with him?

"Glad to see you've made yourself at home." He kissed the top of her head, seeking comfort in her distinct aroma but finding little. Her hair smelled like roses and coffee. "New shampoo?"

"Huh?" She sliced a carrot, polished blade sliding through the root vegetable like it would a stick of butter.

"Nothing. Ready?"

"You bet." She leaned on her tiptoes and planted a kiss on his cheek, her lips cool and dry. He'd remembered the feel of Helen's mouth as warmer, juicier, though perhaps the change in climate or smog affected her body chemistry.

Helen hummed a tune and crouched, pulled a tube of plastic wrap from under the island, and covered her mixing bowl. Whistling, she stuck the container of veggies in the fridge.

He recognized the tune and brightened. "'A Thousand Suns.' That's when I knew I liked you, when you told me how you connected with it."

"Yeah, totally." She donned her messenger bag and breezed past him. "Let's roll. The Uber's here."

"Off we go." He followed, though some invisible force pulled him back. Her tone was weird. Glib, superficial. Lacking awareness.

But there wasn't really anything for him to say short of interrogating her about some passing comment she'd made in Minnesota, which would make him look and feel like a paranoid sod. He blamed Jonnie for planting unfounded suspicions and buggering up his thought process.

She left the house, he behind her. A cheap foreign car the color of cat vomit sat in the roundabout. Pulse spiking in a succession of erratic, irrational bursts, Brian walked around to the back window. No logo advertising the ride service.

"What?" Helen chuckled. Setting sun streaked through her hair in luminous shards, imbuing her with an angelic glow. She climbed into the backseat.

He was being an idiot. Tilly was safe with her bodyguard and tutor.

His bandmates would intervene in the event of any problems. Brian shook his head, got in beside her, and shut his door.

Mundane details, from the car's stench of air freshener to the driver's mounted cell phone showing GPS directions to their destination, failed to ease his duress.

"Are you nervous?" he asked Helen, buckling his seatbelt.

"Nah." Her smile was a closed-mouthed wisp of a thing fit for housing a trapped canary.

The driver steered his car down the driveway, punched in the code that Brian supplied, and curved through the hills and onto an Interstate.

"Are you sure? You're awfully quiet."

She shrugged. "Just thinking."

"About your audition?"

Every pause, every lull, was painful. The sobering, sinking feeling that something was not right settled into the cabin like a looming fourth rider.

"No."

Cool, processed air teemed with solid awfulness. The car pulled off on an exit ramp and hung a quick right turn, bouncing over potholes as it passed a junkyard filled with piles of decaying car skeletons, a neon-yellow sign advertising a pest control place, and a bail bond establishment with bars protecting windows already shattered with spiderweb cracks.

Their driver turned into the parking lot of a storage locker facility. No other vehicles in sight.

"Helen." Brian gritted his teeth. "Where is Soul Krush?" He held on to a morsel of stupid hope.

The car turned a corner, and the open metal door of one of the lockers came in to view. Inside the square of space there was no old furniture or paintings, no worthless items of sentimental value the owners couldn't stand to part with.

No, in the center of the barren concrete floor, someone had etched a pentagram in red paint. Or at least he hoped it was red paint. Three robed figures flanked the five-pointed star, laying what looked to be trinkets in various parts of the painting. Slabs the color of stainless steel covered their faces. His heart sank. This was not Helen beside him. He should have gathered that.

He was a fucking numpty, fooled by this. His pulse slammed, and sweat dampened his underarms. With a shaking hand, Brian reached for the mobile phone in his pocket.

The imposter posing as Helen opened her bag, pulled out the knife, and pointed the tip right under his chin. "Soul Krush? It's somewhere on Venice Beach I think. But that doesn't concern you. Your job right now is to prepare yourself for the Silver Phase."

EIGHTEEN

HELEN UNLOCKED BRIAN'S FRONT DOOR WITH THE SPARE KEY, pensiveness weighing on her thoughts. She'd busied herself with quite the productive outing while he practiced in his home studio.

Her trip to the Venice beach magic shop ended with two bags full of pamphlets, various spell craft tools, and advice from the crone in charge. The woman confirmed Helen's suspicion about the problems with her Left Hand magic and state of mind.

The front door gave way to a din of male voices engaged in subdued chat. Though tempted to forge ahead with the suggestions of the Venice witch, Helen would be remiss not to first explain to her mentor her reluctance to abandon the Left Hand path. She did some nail polish picking as she walked inside. Nerissa might balk, but she at least needed to hear Helen out. Consider her reasoning.

Jonnie Tollens approached her from across the living room, focused and serious.

"How was the audition?" he asked crisply, dark eyes assessing her with unmitigated skepticism.

Helen cocked her head. Brian's friend's palpable distrust swirled all around him, and his mention of this audition topic confounded her in a gruesome way.

"What audition?"

Jonnie crossed his arms over his chest and drew back as if recoiling from her physical presence. "The one you mentioned when you stopped by the studio. Where's Brian?"

"When I stopped by the—" Her stomach iced. A dread cloud eclipsed confusion. The clone was afoot, and had escalated her meddling by duping Brian into going somewhere with her. "Oh, shit."

"Look, Helen, I don't know what your endgame is, but I'll admit I don't like you."

"And that's fair. I don't blame you. But if you'll excuse me, I need to try to help."

He scowled. "You aren't making sense. Is Brian safe?"

She looked Jonnie square in the eye. "No. He isn't."

Two more men walked up and assumed posts at Jonnie's sides. Thom from Denver and a guy wearing a warmup suit. She put two and two together, placing the third man as Fyre's drummer, Jonas.

"How did you get back here so fast?" Thom furrowed his brow.

"She's dodgy as hell and full of lies." Jonnie spoke through clenched teeth.

"Look, I get your apprehension, I really do. But I need you all to listen to me right now. I have work to do, and I need the house to myself for awhile. Can I trust someone to take Tilly for the rest of the afternoon?"

Jonas nodded. "I'm taking my kids to the movies. She's welcome to tag along and stay the night at our place if you need more time." Though his posh voice betrayed worry, his kind, helpful energy assured her he was good people.

"Perfect." Helen blew out a big breath.

"No, not perfect. I demand answers. Where's Brian? You're mixed up in that cult, aren't you? Friends with Joe?" Under a tight white T-shirt, Jonnie's chest rose and fell in confrontational swells.

"You know Joe?" Thom scowled at Helen.

"Just hang tight, okay? I'll explain soon, I swear."

Tilly joined the fray, wearing baggy sweatpants and munching potato chips from a can.

A middle-aged woman trotted behind her, huffing while schlepping a pile of textbooks.

Alongside the lady walked a tank in camouflage khakis with a gun holstered to the belt.

"What's all this drama? This is my tutor, Karen, and my bodyguard, Brutus, by the way."

Karen smiled thinly and adjusted the stack in her short arms.

Brutus grunted.

"Nice to meet you, Karen. Class is dismissed for the day. Tilly, go with Jonas. He's in charge. Brutus, stick close and don't let her out of your sight."

"You are not the boss of me." The teen spoke in a slow, deliberate tone. She probably imagined dropping a microphone.

Helen got in the girl's face. "If you want to stay alive, then yes, yes I am."

"Sounds like a threat," Jonnie said.

Helen whipped her head in his direction. "I sympathize with your reservations, but I need you to back off. I won't hurt anyone, but unless I can do my thing, we're all in grave danger. Do I make myself clear?"

The bandmates exchanged looks of surprise.

Karen cringed.

Brutus issued a grunt lower in pitch than his earlier vocalization. Helen interpreted the noise as an affirmation.

Tilly rolled her eyes. "Whatever."

Jonas elbowed Jonnie.

"Yes. Fine," Jonnie said.

"Good. See you all soon, and I promise I'll have things to say in defense of myself." Helen's heartbeat kicked in to a higher gear. She had her grimoire, various magical accessories on hand, and no time to lose.

Everyone left, with Tilly whining about how the various activities that Jonas proposed were "baby stuff."

Helen unleashed a gust of relief, arms and legs loosening as cars started and drove off.

The minute engine sounds trailed into silence, she dashed up the staircase, dumped bags of arcane wares onto the floor of Brian's bedroom, and cracked her magic book.

No point in panicking. No time to check in with Nerissa either, unfortunately. The clone was perpetrating something awful, and Helen best act with decisiveness and resolve if she wanted to even bother to hope for a fleeting chance at stopping the double's sinister machinations.

"Okay, okay." Her pulse rate went ape, urgency fueling her as she zipped through pages.

Acting on a combination of hunch and limited experience, she opened to the section of the book she'd landed on prior to undertaking previous trips down the astral highway. One part of the book applied to her and her unique powers, no doubt about it.

Drums thumping in her ears, Helen raked through crinkling pages until one commanded her attention. Her world collapsed to script and drawings. Into solutions.

Doppelgangers often arise when inexperienced practitioners fail in their efforts to execute psyche splitting spells.

Helen scraped a thumbnail bare, tightness cinching her midsection. On the charge of failing to execute a psyche splitting spell due to lack of experience, the defendant had been found guilty. She kicked guilt to the curb and read on. This moment was about solving a problem, not wallowing in its effects.

These inter-dimensional travelers are extraordinarily difficult to manage and overcome, as they are cunning, intelligent, and adaptable. Frequently working in service of more powerful evil energies, doppelgangers, like their masters, seek permanent residence and power on our material plane. Every human life they extinguish serves this end.

Shit.

To rid oneself of a malignant clone, practitioner must travel to and confront it, force it onto the astral highway, and seal the gap between worlds that allowed it to pass through. Using the graph below, design a circle mapping your personal element against its opposite and recite the incantation at the bottom of the page.

Helen glanced below the text. Sure enough, a detailed graphic cluttered with symbols, text, and six interlocking circles. She found her opposition element and pointed a hard gaze past the sliding doors. The blue-tinted water of Brian's infinity pool undulated with tiny waves.

Game on, baby.

* * *

BLACK CHALK SCRAPED ACROSS BRIAN'S TERRA COTTA DECK TILE AS
Helen drew the sixth circle, making a chain link of interlocking hoops.
Why six, when there were only four elements plus the fifth for spirit?
Now, though, was not the time to contemplate esoteric questions.

She popped a tiny glass jar's cork and sprinkled salt water in one
circle to represent the element water. Next came the salt jar. Helen
opened it and emptied white grains in circle two, representing Earth. She
lit Frankincense, jammed the stick it in a wad of clay, and set it in circle
three. Cool winds carried away filmy grey smoke. Air.

Shielding a teardrop flame from breezes, she placed a candle in the
middle of the fire circle. Into the spirit circle went her personal talisman,
a shimmery sapphire stone bursting with iridescence.

This part of her circle construction, use of the stone symbolizing the
next highest chakra in the line, was improvising. But hey, Helen had been
flying by the seat of her pants since the start. And calling upon the
power of the chakra representing voice seemed like an apt strategy when
she had to tell a doppelganger, in no uncertain terms, to fuck off into
the sun.

She stood, backed up, and eyed her handiwork. Even in dusky
twilight, the blue stone glimmered like a Christmas bulb. The pool
loomed large, its design creating the illusion of a sheet of water
stretching to the horizon.

Helen undressed, the cool of dusk clipping her bare skin. Before she
could second-guess herself, she walked to the water's edge and, as per the
spell's instruction, slid into an amniotic embrace of heated liquid.
Floating on her back, her hair a fan of tentacles, she looked at a random
point in the sky.

Submerging oneself in water, according to the grimoire, facilitated
and directed a spirit witch's movement into the astral realm, aiding her
ability to arrive at a specific location quickly.

No more wading through gray aspic. Helen would now do the
teleportation the book mentioned earlier. If she got lucky. If she got
*un*lucky, well...

She swallowed a big gulp. Cowboy up, Hell-ster.

"Hail to the four corners and the sentinels of the watchtowers."
Goddamn, saying that aloud make it sound extra hardcore. Far off in the
distance, a faint rumble shook the air. Helen flinched. Probably just a car
motor. Yeah.

"Sister Water, I, a spirit born, humbly call upon your powers. Please
expedite my passage into the astral farther and send me to fight an
imposter who loves me not."

A fork of lighting slashed the sky, lighting gray electric purple. Helen
clenched fists. She couldn't wimp out due to a little rough weather.

"Sister Water, I, a supplicant, bow to you and request your assistance.
I must accost a malicious doppelganger and transport its victim to
safety." Allegedly, the spell, if executed right, would empower Helen to
pull someone else onto to astral road and teleport them right along with
her. In other words, this was her shot to get her nude ass to the
doppelganger, collect Brian, and bring him home.

A complex plan with a lot of moving parts, but she did not have a
plethora of options.

Thunder rolled through the air in an unmistakable bowling pin crack.
Okay, okay, this had to be Sister Water jazzing up the whole ordeal. No
sweat. She couldn't freak. No way would the elemental goddess she
begged for help allow her to die by electrocution.

Right?

A foreshadowing note of ozone joined the airborne palate of
pollution and autumnal ripeness. Drops of water struck Helen's nose and
forehead in a tepid trio of pats. She had to stay cool. For Brian. Fear
raced through her in chaotic spurts but, nevertheless, she persisted.

"Sister Water, please deliver me now. Allow this physical coil to serve
as my anchor as I detach and travel to my impostor."

The sky parted in a godlike roar, a barrage of streams hurdling toward
Helen's upturned face as the storm launched an assault.

* * *

CONCRETE PRESSED HARD AGAINST HELEN'S SKIN. HER EYES BURNED.
She lay in the fetal position on the floor of some kind of shed or storage
room that smelled of mold.

The space held no packed boxes or crates, but it wasn't empty. In front of her, hems of black robes grazed bare feet. A pentagram, the inside peppered with items, marked the floor in red. Inside the star sat a business card, a guitar pick, and a miniature tin of mints. The objects she'd taken from Brian's hotel room.

Kris must've somehow pilfered Brian's items from Helen's suitcase during the fight with Tilly. Stuck them in her clutch.

Positioned in the center of the sinister drawing, something glasslike caught limited light—one of the clear crystals.

Act fast. Helen clawed her way over on her hands and knees and scooped up the assortment of objects. She leapt to her feet, an attempt to shout Brian's name, stymied by a burning sensation in her lungs. A violent cough tore up her esophagus, bringing with it a stinging surge of water that she spat.

"Hey, what the fuck?" a man shouted, speech muffled as though an object covered his face.

"Brian." Her word was a scraped croak. She sized up the scene. Three people in robes and silver masks. One clutched a tome to their chest.

The doppelganger held a knife to Brian's neck.

"Drop the knife or I swallow this." Helen hoisted the crystal in the air.

The clone released Brian and stalked toward Helen with the blade pointed. "I'll cut you open and take it back."

"You better not, because if you kill the hex generator this ends right here."

"She's right, we need her involvement." One of the robed figures spoke in a tense male voice, putting his hands in the air. Great. She had the motherfuckers on the run.

"Drop the knife," Helen said.

Snarling, the clone continued her menacing march.

"Jesus Christ." Brian drew out every hushed syllable.

As if mocking his prayer, a guttural, screeching roar filled the small space, so loud and horrid the air shook in primordial trembles. The clone froze in her tracks. Helen's bowels quaked with liquid doom.

A funnel of white mist poured from her transparent stone in a continuous, billowing plume. The cloud shot to the ceiling, where it coalesced into something with a sloppy form, but a form nonetheless. Beady eyes, two rows of jagged teeth filling a gaping maw, noodles of endless arms ending in bestial claws that flapped about as if hunting for flesh to tear. The longer she looked, the more the inchoate blob developed into a figure.

The clone dropped to her knees. She set the knife down with a soft tap and folded her hands in front of her chest. "Master."

The masked men bent their faces skyward and gawked at the floating fiend.

Helen and Brian exchanged glances loaded with meanings. Fright, but not shock. Anticipation. The intellectual part-assembly feeling of hatching an unspoken plan.

Creeping on her tiptoes, Helen snuck up on the clone and snatched the knife.

Deep in reverence, the clone didn't notice.

The three enraptured men in costume didn't budge either.

The entity on the ceiling growled again, lowering itself and coiling around Brian. Puffs the color of engine exhaust wafted off the body, twisting around him as the thing raked cloud-claws on a spot above his hip.

"Do you forsake all other masters, both worldly and beyond, giving yourself in joy and supplication to the joining?" Joe spoke, upswing and shakiness in his voice.

"No," Brian said.

The monster howled as if enraged by Brian's calm demeanor. A smoky face and hands pressed, poked, and rooted around the same area on Brian's body while he stood there as poised as a Buckingham Palace guard.

Helen squeezed the handle of her knife. Blood whooshed in her ears. Smells of dusty paper and rodent musk darkened the already dim space.

When her moment to act came, she would seize it. That moment was not now, though. The occultists outnumbered her and Brian, and she lacked a read on how the monster and clone would react if she charged their handlers.

"I order you to forsake all other masters, both worldly and beyond, giving yourself in joy and supplication to the joining," Joe yelled in a tantrum-screech.

"It's no use," one of the other robed participants said. "He won't comply. Our best bet is to attempt to control the hex generator and leverage her magic."

"Hold up. I found something." Masked Man Number Three waved his open book, brought it back in front of his face, and exhaled. "Hail to the four corners and the sentinels of the watchtowers. Sister Folly, I, chaos born, humbly call upon your powers. Please use your dark magic on this devil doll to give her the power to possess bodies. Muddle her essence with that of the hex generator and bend them both to our will."

"What's chaos born?" Joe asked.

"Shut up, I'm working. Sister Folly, I, a supplicant, bow to you and request your assistance. Meld the devil doll with the hex generator and make her porous and receptive."

The monster raged and flew around the room in a frenzy. The clone sprang to her feet, eyes white and arms outstretched. A zombie, she lumbered toward Helen muttering in the ancient language used in the pit ceremony.

"What are you doing?" the non-Joe man without the book shouted.

"If we can bind the hex generator's essence to the doll's, we can get Master's essence to possess her. Then with any luck, Master will be well-fed and strong enough to enter the target without his consent."

"I don't know." Joe cowered as the smoke fiend blew past him.

"I bind you, hex generator. May our doll's essence infiltrate your psyche and eat your soul," Masked Man Number Three bellowed like a wizard.

"Nah, you can eat shit instead." Clutching a death grip on the trinkets, Helen dropped the knife and grabbed the clone by the arm.

She ran to Brian, dragging the zoned-out double behind her, and pressed her body to his.

In a loud and assured tone, she recited verbatim the incantation that landed her in the storage locker.

* * *

Air rushed into Helen's lungs as she broke through the surface of turbulent wetness. Waves crashed into her mouth in relentless, chlorinated assaults. She slurped air, blubbering out invading liquid. More water rained from the sky in merciless sheets. Electricity coursing in her veins, she swung legs in a bottomless well, flailing and panicked. Where was she? Lost at sea, floating in stormy, open ocean?

"It's okay." Brian's voice was as strong as his arm, looped around her midsection. "I've got you. Float."

Hacking and spitting, she allowed herself to lean into his body. They drifted until she braced her feet on the rungs of a metal ladder. Right. She bobbed in his infinity pool. And he was here, meaning she'd rescued him from the clone. Speaking of the C word...

A cushion drifted on the water's surface. Deck furniture lay upturned. But no clone swam with her and Brian or stood amidst visual reminders of the storm's destruction.

Brian climbed out of the pool and hoisted Helen out behind him, her body a soaked rag doll in his arms. They sat on the concrete and hugged each other for a moment, each both a life raft and a drowning person. Rain drilled, gathering warm beneath their molded bodies.

"Quite a monumental end to the California drought." Brian forced a chuckle and flung water from his face.

"It's not over." The masked men cast a spell. During her journey back to the pool with Brian and the clone, the double vanished. But Helen hadn't sent her anywhere intentionally. Not good.

"It is for now." He spoke with hope. "You saved me, Helen, saved my life. Thank you. I was a bloody fool not to see that it wasn't you who approached me in the studio and led me to that locker."

"No, the problem wasn't foolishness. She's adapting faster than we can keep up, and she'll continue to learn. I need to work. I need to make sure she's permanently banished." Her circles and talismans were crucial, but the rain had washed them away. Shit, shit, shit. Upon feeling a lump in her balled fist, she calmed some. At least she'd recovered one of the clear crystals.

Brian stood and pulled her free hand, bringing her upright. "Where's Tilly?"

"She's with Jonas and his family, staying the night until I get this sorted out. Brutus is with her. I have to work. There are six circles, and something about chaos born. It's significant. Meaningful."

"No. Rest for the night. As of right this minute, the clone is dormant. Tilly is safe, and we're safe together. After you get a good night's sleep you can try some new things, but for now you've done enough." He cupped her face in both hands, the look in his eyes a haven.

"It's not enough, Brian. I can't slow down. I can't rest. Not until it's over. Not until you're saved." Her voice broke, and tears wobbled in her vision.

The onslaught of rain continued, stinging her exposed skin as needling drops landed in a rapid blaze.

"Enough for now, love." He pressed a kiss to her forehead, the tenderness cracking what remained of her defenses. "Good enough."

Those last words he spoke penetrated to her core. There, they went to work detonating years of residue and demolishing hurtful buildup. Brian spoke those words with a sincerity that ruined her. A cry broke from her throat, deepening into a sob to accompany the warm streams sliding down her cold cheeks.

"I'm sorry. I'm so, so, sorry. If I could, I would go back in time to that day at Nerissa's house and do everything differently."

"Don't apologize," he whispered into the skin between her brows, like a deity delivering intuition into her mystical third eye. "It's going to be okay. We're okay. I'm okay."

Tears fell, rivulets sluicing from her ducts. Had she ever cried like this, therapeutic sobs in the arms of someone she trusted? No. No, she had not. "I should apologize a thousand times, because all of this is my fault."

With the pads of his thumbs, Brian massaged the straps of muscle running up her neck, kneading her like malleable clay.

"I don't accept that. You're just like any of us, doing your best. And don't forget, don't you ever forget, that the reason this is happening is because you saw something wrong and intervened to help me. You didn't have to. You could have left me to my own devices, and I'd be dead already. Yes, it is spiraling out of control now, but all that means is that whatever we're up against is mighty and intent on not giving up. But what's important is that you took action. And you continue to take action to solve a huge, complex problem. I admire you, and I respect you. I'm grateful to you, grateful for your presence in my life. You're a good person, Helen."

Amidst the detritus of her disrupted magical circle, her sapphire stone gleamed in the halogen glare of Brian's deck lamps. Except its hue had changed to a radiant amethyst that dazzled the night in blinks of iridescence.

Interesting, how the color of voice had morphed to the color of insight and intuitive awakening. She'd moved up the chakra line to the third eye wheel. Without a spell, no less. Upward progression in the absence of Left Hand magic renewed her faith in herself.

As she watched the luminescent twinkles of the stone symbolizing the third-eye chakra and its powers of intuition, Helen let go. Let go of her defensiveness, her anger. Let go of her sorrow, grief, and loss. Let go of a lifetime of fury and the suffering behind it.

And as she let go, the scabs that had grown over that third eye broke off and dissolved.

With that cruddy material gone, she was able to see Brian in his entirety. He was a person, as flawed and messy as any other, with a multitude of traits sometimes in harmony and sometimes at odds. He was meticulous and exacting, but wielding a wry sense of humor and a love of life that kept him from being stiff, boring, or unapproachable.

Artistically gifted and devoted to his craft, he didn't mess around when it came to excelling in his musical talent.

Fantastically lucky, yet at the same time testimony to the power of a stalwart work ethic and unflappable determination to never surrender dreams, Brian served as inspiration to strive for goals no matter how lofty.

She saw how he loved his friends and daughter with fierce loyalty and gave others the benefit of the doubt until they squandered his goodwill. Then, watch out. He knew what he wanted and went after it. The man was honest to his core, a sound person who conducted his life from a place of integrity.

Brian complemented Helen, and he challenged her. He was a man she could look up to, and someone who motivated her to be better. Though she didn't envy or crave his money or fame, they nonetheless symbolized commendable parts of him. Drive, determination. Dedication. Passion and conviction.

The crystal glimmering in the corner of her eye, she pulled back to match his stare.

Granted, there were many small to medium things she didn't know about Brian. Factoids such as his favorite foods, pet peeves, general array of likes and dislikes.

Huge stuff was also missing from her repertoire of Brian knowledge, like how he felt about his early years. And stupid little bits of first date trivia like the one movie he'd watch a hundred times if trapped on a deserted island with that file and nothing else.

Yes, she had quite a bit further to go when it came to getting to know Brian. But in the depths of her heart, a place that could, if she let it, expand beyond its shrunken state, she knew something big.

I love you, Brian.

Yet she could not push the words out of her mouth. Because if she did, if she allowed herself to not only feel but to *express that feeling* from the most authentic space inside of her, would cruel forces snatch him away? Would the threat escalate?

Instead of confessing her truth, Helen fumbled out, "I'm glad you're safe, right here in this moment. We're together. That counts."

His facial expression softened as he parted his lips then shut his mouth. Brian clearly picked up something in her voice, her holding back. But being the respectful man he was, he didn't storm the gate of her one remaining fortress.

It wasn't that she didn't want him to, but at the same time she loved him even more for refraining.

"It counts for everything," he said.

In the unspoken moment that followed, a look communicated what words still were not permitted clearance to articulate.

Their lips crashed in a collision of damaged hearts yearning for unbridled release. More license, more permission, more possibility. More chances to heal festering sores from buried years. In the freak rainstorm, two cursed souls trying to save each other, they kissed like their fates depended on it.

NINETEEN

B<small>RIAN WALKED OUT OF THE MASTER BATHROOM SHROUDED IN A WHITE</small>
terrycloth robe matching the one subsuming Helen. But, at her behest,
their meaningful breakthrough moments ago gave way to the demands of
the mission. Curled up on his bed with the grimoire, she ran her finger
down a page.

Everything about the ominous reading material vibrated with malice,
from paper warped to the stiffness of preserved hide to the stains and
drawings crowding out white space with the magnitude of their
strangeness.

Her stomach seized every time she turned a page as she crawled to
the finality of the entire massive tome, enduring the chunk of writing
devoted to dark arts. The sixth circle of craft hid near the back, writhing
in a twisted mass of scary.

"The sixth symbol matches the one you saw on that woman's
abdomen, and the element is Folly. Whatever that is. Children of Folly
are chaos born. If I can grasp more of the concepts here, I might be able
to head the black robe and mask brigade off at the pass."

The bed springs squeaked, the spot beside her sinking into a slight
depression. Brian stroked her wet hair, finger-combing out tangles in

perfect pulls that tugged her scalp in all the right places. "Helen. It can wait until the morning."

"I don't know." Runes and drawings crammed rough-looking end pages stained with old splatters of dark mystery fluid. Like some gnostic bastard of the Book of Revelations. She looked past the sliding doors to where the storm had slowed to a drizzle. The pool lolled, a slab of water rendered uncanny by fantastical underwater lights and an insidious undercurrent. "I just feel a weight in my bones. Like they're plotting as we speak, that she's stalking us right now."

And she did feel heavy, stiff like she'd been sitting in a crappy plastic chair all day.

Granted, she hadn't been practicing magic long, but it hadn't impacted her body before. She stretched her folded legs, wincing when a sharp pain tweaked a tendon in her knee.

"Not that I know what I'm talking about, but it does concern me that I see it has taken a toll on you. Which is why I think it would help if you took a night off. I don't see what use you are to anyone if you're knackered and stretched too thin. Hazarding a guess, but it can't be good if your concentration is compromised."

Helen snuggled into Brian, closing the tome in favor of soaking in the scents of his freshly showered skin. Ignoring him wasn't cool, and relaxing sounded a helluva lot better than driving herself nuts staring at weird shit that made no sense. "I should snark at you for mansplaining witchcraft to me."

"Consider me corrected. Unless you need to turn me into a frog to set things right." He completed the banter circuit, like always. The fact that the two of them had become an "always" didn't even freak her out anymore.

Her temple resting against his chest, she allowed the picture of their two pairs of feet side by side to mellow her with a snapshot of mundane domestic ease.

"I suppose it wouldn't be a bad thing to take a few hours to recharge. And it's after eleven in Minneapolis, too late to call Nerissa. I'll hit this hard in the morning."

"I meant what I said outside."

Silence brought her focus to the low hum of their shared breathing, the intimacy of bodies together in bed.

She pushed the magic book off of her lap, Sisyphus shirking her burden onto the floor. "Which part?"

"The important part. All of it."

"Me too." And she existed in a maddening sort of stasis, a purgatory where she was both imprisoned and free. Free of the chains of her past, the internalized jailers who stopped her from being able to love.

But at the same time, an unguarded flank quivered. Unknown and unresolved, a threat desecrated the otherwise sanctified bedroom. Helen dropped a baleful glance to the grimoire. The book was her ally, albeit a cursed sort of comrade, and one she could not shake. Magic shackled her heart.

"Clue me in on the brilliant workings of your mind?" His breath heated the shell of her ear, the sensation swirling with the coldness of wet hair licking her flesh.

Sensitive nerves registered every caress, the delightful dampness on her tender skin. A promise of bliss teased her with whispers of a short vacation to heaven through tactile pleasures.

"I'm thinking..." Helen closed her eyes, stress and release fighting for purchase inside of her. "How good it feels to be with you. But that I'm also afraid. And worried, and uncertain about the future. You're right. I should shut it off for the night, but it's like I can't. My mind is racing."

"I have an idea." Speech near her ear transitioned into slow kisses, a trail of sensual brushes down her neck.

Troubles melted into the intimacy she hungered for. "I'm sure it's a good one."

"Yeah." The way his word edged toward a growl, gruff and excited, sparked awareness between her legs.

Eager to lose herself, to forget, Helen angled her body so she lay flush with Brian and kissed him. Her hands got busy opening the soft fabric of his robe. His tattoo came into splendid view, the secret badassery of him rendered in body art.

Brian moaned when she stroked his ink, her greedy touch traveling the maze. Too impatient to tease or hold back, she undid his robe's knot. Pliant fabric flopped open, revealing the delights of his flat stomach and fit chest. The prize between his legs was stiff and at proud alert, plump crown engorged and decorated with that naughty piercing.

She went down with a line of kisses, sloughing off her troubles like the dead leaves that fell to the ground outside. She nibbled his torso, licked his happy trail, dipped a playful tongue in his belly button.

His hands dove in her hair, pants and moans tensing as they grew faster, clipped.

Brian's firm thighs flexed, widening to accommodate her as she settled between them and curled her hand around his shaft.

He pushed her robe over her shoulders, licking his lips when the covering slid past her breasts. He stared, eyes hooded, while she took him in her mouth. The first flavors of him, salty musk mixed with shower fresh clean, tantalized her taste buds.

She cupped his full, tight balls, playing with the ribbed skin and seam while she bobbed on him. He punched up his hips in rhythmic thrusts, driving his erection into her throat.

Licking and sucking, she attended to him, his pleasure becoming her own. She'd found a steady pace when he urged her off his erection. "Come up here, beautiful." The sound of his excited voice ignited both her body and heart.

Helen knelt between his spread legs and threw her robe over the side of the bed.

He traced her curves, squeezing her breasts then her hips on a path down the hourglass. "I bought condoms."

"So you assumed we'd end up like this? How presumptuous." Their rapport had gotten so easy, so fun. A bond formed through stolen joy. He was hers, and she was his.

"Call it optimism." He treated her to a full-watt grin, the charm of it made dirty-hot by the spark in his eyes.

She liked Brian so much. He embodied his contradictions with panache, excelled at being himself. And he was weird, like her, yet so different. Yang to her yin.

"Checks out. So suit up."

Wasting nary a second, he opened a nightstand drawer and pulled out a foil packet. Keeping up the no-nonsense approach, he ripped it open and slid the tan circle down his shaft, stretching the film to the root and pinching off the reservoir tip.

With an attention to detail and meticulous methodology that characterized even the smallest of Brian's actions, he made the mundane act of safe sex prep hot as sin.

Their eye contact was fierce, unbroken. She climbed him like a tree, planted her hands on his shoulders, and lowered herself onto him.

His gaze slipped to the spot where their bodies joined, and he clamped firm hands below her waist. "You're gorgeous."

"I'm up here." She pointed at her face as she ground back and forth, filled up by the unique, tingling invasion of penetration. Filled by the man she loved, and by love itself.

"I'm looking at your gorgeous pussy right now, love. How you're swallowing me up. So slick and hot."

She quickened her pace, gasping when the metal hoop at the tip of his dick rubbed her G-spot at the most perfect angle. Tension gathered inside, building at a startling pace. "Is that thing made to please a woman?"

He winked at her. "My big cock, you mean?"

Okay, a second to unpack *por favor*. The statement should have registered as obnoxious or insufferable, or at most a charming-ish performance of alpha-cocky cliché begging to be excoriated.

But on Brian, the wackiest experiment in bad good boy-slash-good bad boy ever concocted, it was hilarious in the best way possible. Because he asked the question in a way no one else could.

She busted out laughing. "Yeah. That. At first I thought nature intended it as a means to scare off rival elephants. My bad."

Her giggles didn't subside, and he added a chuckle to the mix. Playfulness shone through his eyes, and the corners of them crinkled like they had at the fair. Nostalgia, awareness of of the history of the two of them, sweetened lust and turned sex into making love.

Brian leaned up and wrapped his arms around her, the warm friction of their chests pressed together rich with import. She kissed his cheek, squealing as he flipped her onto her back without disengaging. Talk about skilled maneuvering.

He situated himself on top of her and propped up on his elbows.

"You're a goddess, all spread out before me." He pumped, gaze roving over her face like he wanted to memorize the sight of her for all eternity.

"You never answered my question." She squeezed his biceps, widening to provide him optimal access. Her body language gave consent to go harder, deeper, and the intensity of his eye contact accepted her gift of license.

"About what?" He slipped a hand between sweaty bodies, the pads of his fingers targeting her clit.

His mid-tempo strokes coaxed pleasure from her, bringing her higher with each circular motion. She built to a crescendo inside, too. The delicious feeling against her internal nub evoked her earlier inquiry.

"Your piercing. Did you get it to please women or for you?"

"Both. It's supposed to feel good for both people during sex. You getting the contact where you need it, love?" Plunges quickened in time with his hand. A sharp grunt left his lips.

"Yeah." Most mental faculties fled her as the bulk of her awareness gathered between her legs, into ratcheting hunger, heat, and tightness. Pleasure intensified, propelling her to an apex.

"God, you're hot. And wet. The most beautiful woman I've ever had."

The last part begged for a snarky, self-deprecating comeback, but Helen would be remiss to spoil their moment.

"You feel so good inside of me." Did he ever. Long and hard as steel, he hammered away, faster and faster as he chased his payoff. Judging by the quickening speed of his fingers, he sought to bring her along for a mutually orgasmic ride.

"Oh, Helen Britney." Two drops of sweat fell from his brow and struck her shoulder. His motions were relentless, needy, cries and groans quick and desperate.

She faded into him, his eyes and flesh. Sacred oneness with her lover.

"Yeah, that's it." Her own craving notched higher, twin tops swiveling on a couple of dense nerve bundles.

Amazing, how two little spots held the capacity for so much feeling.

Amazing, how her wrecked heart held the capacity for so much feeling. For being in synch with a partner like this.

She flung her legs in the air, giving them a few more decadent inches of penetration. The headboard thunked, banging into the wall.

Mattress springs squeaked, a fog of sweat and sex making for an earthy intimacy.

"You make my dick so hard." Wet skin slapping underscored his shameless, perfect words.

She cracked, splintering into shards and spinning off her axis. Helen was gone, no mind or thoughts, just the unbelievable, pulsating relief of climax. She'd never come this hard. She moaned and wailed her way through.

Brian read her body and face, zipping quick fingers over her clit until he'd milked her dry, then caught her legs at the ankles, yanked her feet as far apart as they'd stretch, and pounded.

He locked eye contact with her like the strength of their connection was the only thing that mattered. Everything that needed to be said traveled the passage between their eyes. Yes. That's good. Don't stop. Harder, faster, more.

I love you.

A light flickered across his gaze the instant she felt the sentiment.

Brian shoved with a gusto she would not have guessed he had in him, cursing and shouting and crying her name.

A second orgasm barreled in, originating from deep inside and tearing her asunder. Pleasure, but a destructive and rampaging sort, raged.

"Brian, I'm coming again." Her voice was a pathetic plea, or a confession, chasing the heels of such profound disbelief she couldn't help but tell him. He needed to know what was happening to her.

He yelled his triumph, uninhibited in his frenzy. Thrusts grew sloppy, lost their steady rhythm. His gaze never wavered, though the humanity behind his eyes gave way to maniac sex ecstasy.

She shuddered, her explosions tapering to fluttery aftershocks though he was ramping up in earnest, racing to his finale. Worked out well, for now she could enjoy him, his broken noises as he came undone and fell apart.

Such a thrill and a treat, to witness a composed man like Brian reduced. An aphrodisiac and a feminine sort of power.

He froze, every muscle in his body locking up. With one more big push, he surged forward, folding her in two and pushing the bottoms of her feet into the board as he buried himself balls-deep and shot. His lips parted, and out poured a series of sharp noises.

The spectacle of her lover's ruin might have satisfied her more than her own orgasms. Wrecking a man by way of abandon was the best kind of magic.

Sexed-up madness dribbled off, awareness of the present returning to showcase the embodiment of post-coital humanity.

He let go of her ankles, and she collapsed on crumpled sheets, nude and spread eagle, catching choppy breath.

Sweat glued bellies together. The smash of damp bodies separated with suction pops.

He, a riot of akimbo limbs and a robe hanging on for dear life, sighed and kissed her jaw. His heartbeat thumped against her breastbone, her own pulse complementing the percussion.

Brian rolled off of Helen and onto his back, splaying a hand over her tummy in a gesture that sweetened the afterglow with claiming and affection. He was letting her know that he wouldn't retreat after the deed was done.

She didn't need the aftercare, but she honored the good place from which his effort came.

Speedy and discreet, he peeled off the loaded condom and lobbed it into a wastebasket. "I knew it would be good with you, but damn. That was..."

Though the vocabulary word escaped him, she got the gist of the sentiment. Some silly cliché like "mind-blowing" would not suffice to describe their passion.

Helen shifted to her side. His face in profile, celebrity at rest in the backlight of the pool, was surreal. "I agree. I'm not sure what goes in that blank, but it's awesome."

Brian turned to face her, wearing the disheveled bathrobe and a grin. "Your dirty talk is white hot. I banked up all of the things you said for future solo use. Though I hope that I won't have to fly solo as much anymore." He wiggled his eyebrows, tracing the outline of her curves with one lazy finger.

But Helen's couldn't participate in the jest. Not when she saw the mark marring Brian's body. Though his robe must have concealed the bruise during their lovemaking, his repositioning jostled a corner of the cloth behind his hip.

A ghastly shiner rimmed with puncture marks darkened a golf ball-sized area where his leg met his lower belly.

Despair burned dirty tributaries into her vein networks. The splotch showed up in Denver, but she'd thought little of it. She pushed white fabric aside, attaining the closer look she didn't want.

"What happened?" Her voice shook, but she wasn't shocked. Nothing shocked her these days, which made her so fucking tired.

"Oh, it's what I told you about in the car, how the double put marks on me. Ugly, but I hardly notice it anymore."

But Helen noticed, because the colors changed before her eyes. Broken blood vessels crawled outward from the impact sight, squiggly inchworms dipped in blood. The stain spread like red wine spilled on a carpet. Regret slammed. Pieces clicked.

"We shouldn't have had sex," she said.

He sat upright and pulled his garment together, cloaking his injury and nude body. "Did I do something wrong?"

"It's not you, it's the curse. I should have known. Fuck. I knew some feeling inside of me generated the hex, but I haven't understood until now. It wasn't my desire for money or to save my studio that emboldened it, allowed it to latch. It was my desire for you. In no way was your involvement a random occurrence." She knocked the back of her head into the wall a couple of times like she could whack their mistake into a harmless torpor.

"We can't be sure."

She jumped out of bed and paced, tearing at a nail.

"No, we can. It adds up. You were the target because I wanted you to be. On some subconscious level I pinned this thing on you. I sought you out. You connect to my past, and the idea of you was all knotted up in this messed up savior fantasy I had, so when the curse needed to latch, all it had to do was reach in and root out the trace recollection of someone I desired, but desired in a way mixed up in resentment and desperation and other unhealthy shit. That's a curse, a hex. That's all it is. Toxic mental sludge, bad energy we attach to other people, the ways that we make others responsible for our own garbage and pin our trash on them. So the setup's in place before I even start screwing with the supernatural, with the Left Hand path. Then I find you at the fair, and bam. It's too easy. I delivered you right into this thing's clutches."

"Hold on." Brian put a hand in the air. "All of that may have been true the day we met, but you aren't doing either of us any favors by blaming yourself. And you know what? I have a radical idea."

She ceased treading a track in his floor and halted the gross practice of mauling her finger. "I'm listening."

"This whole time, you've been casting me as an innocent. Oh, poor Brian, skipping along, minding his own when some senseless hex stabs hooks into him. But what if that's wrong? What if my own karma brought this about? I've lived a blessed life, Helen. I've gotten so lucky that it's kept me up at night wondering when I'll have to pay the piper. Wondering when it will all come crashing down, when I'll owe some cosmic debt for enjoying a life that most men could never even dream of. Maybe this is it. My penance."

She pressed fingertips to her skull, battling a headache born of equal measures denial and the wisdom bomb Brian dropped. "But you're a good person. You don't objectify women or abuse drugs or hurt people. You aren't self-absorbed or greedy. You're kind and funny and talented—"

"I'm not good, though, not compared to the people we don't see, the people who fight in obscurity to make the world better. Me? I'm rich and famous, and I've made a ridiculous amount of money singing and playing guitar. Success and fame on my scale, we're talking one in ten-million odds. If that. And I'm not bragging. I think about these existential things. I live in a palace on a hill while people on the other side of the world die of preventable diseases because they don't have clean water. Do you want to know how my first wife died?"

No, but the doozy of a pivot seemed relevant. "Alright."

He scooted to the edge of the bed, knuckles pale against his knees. "She was a fashion designer, at the top of her field. Janet was her name, and she got her start working as the wardrobe woman on one of our American tours. That's where we met and fell in love. She was ambitious and talented. Fast forward to when she's a powerhouse. An activist journalist reaches out to her, invites her on an investigative trip to Bangladesh. So she can tour one of the factories where her pieces were made. The third night, she calls home sobbing. Just broken. She's describing girls who were Tilly's age at the time, six, working the assembly lines from sunup to sundown. Crying for their mothers, wetting their pants because they weren't allowed bathroom breaks. Some had stumps where their little fingers used to be."

Tears stung Helen's ducts, though she didn't yet see the point of the tragic story. "That's so sad."

"The next day the sweatshop exploded. She was inside."

Gauzy, crushing images of tears and fire and black smoke flooded Helen's addled mind. "She died in there," Helen concluded.

Brian nodded grimly. "Her and hundreds of others."

"I'm sorry for your loss, Brian. I can tell that you loved her. To lose the mother of your child, too, and when Tilly was so young. I can't imagine. It must have been hell."

"Thank you. It was rough, though we managed. I went through my grief, my stages, did the therapy and support groups. In the midst of mourning my dead wife, shouting at God for taking her from me in this meaningless accident—and right after she's had a revelation about the abuses inherent in her industry no less—I wondered if it was a cruel kind of design." His tone was flat though severe, his face a mask of funeral stoicism.

Dismay spread from her middle, motor oil soiling her edges. If that's how the hex was working on the macro level, humming along in a clockwork evil until a ticking hand decided it was time for someone to pay the fee on their fortune and balance some kind of mystical scale with blood, she had no clue how to win at such a cruel game of chance.

Brian cradled his head in both hands. "Maybe I deserve what's coming to me. Perhaps my time is up."

"Don't say that." Lame reply. But she lacked the tools to argue, for in this arena, the tidiness of the scientific method did not apply.

She sat down beside him and touched his thigh, for assurance of touch was all she could offer. Human closeness alone made for a paltry sum, but care counted.

His sigh was a portend. "I don't think it's bad to say it, though. I think it's honest. And if it gets you to stop blaming yourself, I'm all for putting these dark thoughts out in the open. Consider it more information for us to work with. But I stand by my claim. I reject this idea that you're the nasty, reckless witch and I'm the pure and clean male with a heart of gold who found himself ensnared in your treachery by no fault of his own. I reject this nonsense, this misogynistic notion that the original sin sticks to the woman."

In a halfhearted return to humor and play, she tugged the collar of his robe. "Time to take this off and put on your 'Feminist' shirt. Or better yet, one that says 'Eve was Framed.'"

He took her hand. "She was framed, no doubt about it. And I'm nowhere near perfect, but I try to be evolved and enlightened. But back to the serious note, let's keep on being a team, okay? No more guilt dragging you down. Accept that I play some part in this. And hell, if magic is real, which it clearly is, there's a reason I ended up caught in this curse. Maybe we're meant to be together, and this just so happens to be the force in the universe that's set on aligning our paths."

She blew a loose piece of hair off her forehead. "I like the idea. Still, we shouldn't have had sex."

He pressed his forehead against her temple. "But it was so fucking good."

Her laugh brought healing rain, rare respite. "Truth."

"We'll clean up this mess together, Helen. I swear. But first we need to rest."

Nighttime rituals followed, routine made special by being undertaken with Brian.

They brushed teeth in his opulent bathroom, and she stroked the shiny finish of his sink when he wasn't looking, allowing herself a giddy half-second to appreciate his fancy home.

But as they settled in, bodies entwined in their lover's hold, Helen's system kicked into an agitated gear. She felt it all around them.

Felt it in the shadows on the walls, in every little whimper and whine the mansion uttered.

Though Brian snoozed like a man who'd exerted himself sexually, she lay piqued and restless. Flat on the bed in a sarcophagus pose with folded arms, she bore witness to a nighttime theatre surrounding her with its shifty, furtive performance of movement and sound.

This went on for awhile, though she refused to glance at the hell-red numbers on Brian's digital clock.

"It's okay. You're allowed to sleep. Nothing bad will happen if you sleep for a few hours." She'd almost convinced herself with the pep talk when the deck doors slid open on their own volition.

She bolted upright. But nothing would budge. Her arms were dead logs. Legs tubes of wet sand. She was trapped in paralysis, as rigid as a corpse. To the soundtrack of her choppy breathing, she tracked an undulating rope the hue and consistency of skim milk as it floated through the air.

It reared back and shot straight toward her.

Helen was smart enough not to scream and grant the phantom access to her mouth, but her precaution didn't matter. The mist burrowed in to her ears and nostrils while she lay in the dark, trapped in her useless body.

"*Sacrificium*." It repeated the word in her head until syllables ran together.

TWENTY

BRIAN WOKE FROM A DEAD MAN'S SLEEP, GUIDED BACK TO consciousness by a triangle of late morning sunlight that spilled through the patio doors and glazed his hardwood flooring in buttery tones.

For once, he had someone to spend such a graceful morning with. He reached for Helen, but his hand brushed against an empty spot. Confused, he sat up in bed.

"Helen?" Brian swung his legs over the side of the mattress and tugged on discarded boxer shorts. A wrinkle of tan latex hanging over the edge of the waste bin reminded him of their passionate sex. Surely she hadn't pulled the dreaded morning-after disappearing act.

A check of the bathroom came up empty, and he was about to call her when he noticed the patio door ajar and went out on the deck. Helen sat poolside in her bra and underwear, messy hair flowing down her back, head hung as she stirred the water into froth with slow kicks.

Brian gathered a blanket off the bed and went to her, goose flesh flaring on his skin. The climate was brass monkeys for Los Angeles, and she must've had some heavy things on her mind to not be distracted by the cold.

"You must be freezing." He draped her in the comforter.

She didn't so much as twitch, didn't speak a word. The cool feel of her skin leeched into him, bringing a deep sense of doubt. After the bathroom and storage locker incidents, he couldn't assume he was talking to Helen and not her imposter. What a hideous feeling.

But when she turned to him, he connected with a texture in her eyes. The precise nature of the humanity inside Helen, an ineffable quality that the clone lacked, pulsed like a flame.

Human life had a sheen, a depth, but also a limit. Vacancy lurked in the clone's stare, a retreating endpoint fading into an infinite horizon. Real Helen bore the sentient glimmer inherent in the look of a thinking, feeling, mortal person. He sure was learning a thing or two about metaphysical matters from their ordeal.

"The cold keeps me awake."

As soon as she spoke the words in a resigned monotone, he noticed the dark rings under her eyes. He sat beside her, concrete nipping the backs of his legs in icy-hot pricks. Brian dipped a foot into the water in a halfhearted attempt at camaraderie.

"Why do you want to stay awake?"

"It came to me." Her voice quaked.

"What did?" His heart plummeted. Why did he ask? He knew.

"The curse, the cloud of smoke. And it, and it, it... God, it was the worst thing ever." Her face contorted in a grimace. She shook her head like she wanted to purge whatever she was remembering and flopped into his side.

He pulled her swaddled form close, taunted by the futility of his hug. He could alleviate her physical chill, but not the cold inside.

"Oh, Helen. What did it do to you? I'm sorry. I'm so sorry." A thousand half-formed scenarios, each more depraved than the next, played a sinister compilation reel in his brain.

"Don't apologize. Don't you dare. It possessed me. Spoke in my head, ordering me to do things. It tried to move my body around, puppet me, but thankfully it couldn't pull that off. Not yet."

They were alone in his castle, so alone. Spiritually alone. The fortress walls at their backs closed in, as did the rocky hills beyond his property, shrinking his world to a goddamn fiasco. "What did it order you to do?"

She buried her face in his chest and let out a keening wail. "It's too awful, too awful."

"It's okay, Helen." Brian was rocking her now, though it was he who felt as helpless as an abandoned baby. "We'll figure it out and fix it together. We've come this far."

She broke away, her face pale and thin-lipped. The fear in her eyes flayed him raw.

"No. I don't think we will. I don't think we can."

"What are you talking about?"

She stared into the pool like answers would erupt from water. Or perhaps she couldn't face him.

"Helen, tell me. No secrets. I can handle it."

Her chin quivered. "It ordered me to kill you. And with so much detail, directions. It told me to get a belt from your closet and kneel on your back while I strangled you. It was awful, so awful. Oh God, it's voice. It was all raspy, like exactly how you'd imagine a demon would sound. I'll never forget that voice. It eats through my brain like battery acid." Her speech came in a whisper punctuated by jolts of unregulated breathing.

"But you didn't hurt me. You didn't even try."

"Not this time, but it's tried to possess me before, and the first thing it did to announce itself after I drank the potion was speak in my head. It repeated the word it spoke that day, too, 'sacrifice' in Latin. So it hasn't forgotten its mission. Things are intensifying, speeding up. And I have a hunch that whatever those masked guys were saying in the storage locker, all of that shit about Sister Folly and chaos born, has helped it make gains."

"You have your spell book—"

Helen jumped to her feet. He followed suit, though the distancing autonomy of her motion didn't miss him.

"Spells make it worse, which I already knew. Or they make it better at first, but then it gets worse later. Some kind of boomerang effect. I'm screwing up, over and over," she said.

He held her arms, pinning her in place. "Wait. You can't be sure of what you're saying."

Robust winds made whirling dervishes of her hair. Unspoken sadness passed between them. "Let me go, Brian."

Brian released his grip, keeping his hands in the air. Her point emerged into focus, a finality whose sharp edges sliced. Boundaries weren't fuzzy. She'd thought this over and made a decision. Didn't make it hurt any less.

Still, he said, "Come on now. Let's take today to think about our options and make a plan."

She brushed past him, up the ladder to the deck and into the house. Brian walked a few steps behind her, details unfolding in harsh clarity. Her fast hands, snatching clothes from her suitcase. A mole on her leg as she hurried into jeans. All of the wasted opportunities, the things he still had not told her. The things he didn't know about her. Their special ease with each other had been cancelled by evil.

With a tug so big it ripped a seam, Helen pulled a T-shirt over her head. Traces of her vanished from his life, bit by bit in a disappearing act of eccentricities. Spell book shoved in a messenger bag. Then her phone. Laminated buttons adorning the front of her bag slipped from view when she slid it around her back.

Though they'd spent only a single night together, already the lack of her opened a familiar abyss. He looked into that howling chasm, stared into the hole in his heart.

"I'm not leaving because I don't care. I'm leaving because I do. I'm not a safe person, Brian."

"You are safe." He reached for her in one final, desperate effort. "You're safe here, with me."

"Stop." Her voice cracked, those soulful brown eyes he could gaze into every morning for the rest of his life moistening. "You know what I mean."

"The finale show is tomorrow. I need you by my side. In case something happens."

"Something happening is what I'm worried about." Hopping on one foot, she wrestled with hiking sandals, the crunch of Velcro gunfire in his ears.

Brian's wound opened, a festering boil erupting on the surface. One by one and in their own unique way, they all eventually did this. His beloved mum, hustling his thirteen-year-old self on a train to London.

Grandmother, withdrawing her warmth for reasons he'd never figured out.

Kris.

Even Janet, leaving him and Tilly alone.

The thoughts were selfish, unfair, and indicative of problems with women. But self-awareness didn't heal the sore.

Even the word that sprang up from his poisoned bog was lonely and sick, a child shaking in an orphanage. Abandoned.

His heart tore in two. Aftershocks reverberated through the depths of him. He turned his back on Helen before he cried. "Fine. Leave. Run away instead of facing this thing with the strength I know you have. You're weaker than I thought."

Her hand, soft like she bathed in coconut oil, caressed the arm he folded over a chest crushed by pain. "Someday you'll understand."

Streams rolled down his cheeks. Someday would never come. Yeah, he was cursed alright. This time an actual entity orchestrated the maleficence, but the hex had been around for years. About time the monster came to collect.

"Don't pander to me. Just leave."

"Brian, stop. You think I'm not going through hell? What we had was special, and I've never felt anything like it before. It's killing me to do this, because I lo—"

"Don't say it." His voice wobbled wetly, but he didn't care. Some stupid societal mandate to uphold the lie of hard, unfeeling masculinity was the least of his concerns. Something beautiful inside of him, something precious he'd thought he'd lost years ago, had been nurtured back to good health only to be stomped and murdered.

"I mean it. I've never said it to anyone, and you need to hear it. I love—"

"I said be quiet," he shouted at her, yelled at her, making him a bona fide heel. A real git. Shame for lashing out assailed him in a fresh assault of stabs. He bit down on his tongue and shirked off her touch.

The feel of her skin went away, leaving a sucking emptiness and the ghost of her contact. Numbness washed over him, a hateful and familiar sedative. He looked outside without seeing anything but formless shapes and drab scenery.

His bedroom door opened and closed. The snick of the tab engaging brought closure to her unceremonious exit from his life.

Robotic and numb in lieu of going to pieces, Brian dried his tears and put on clothes. He ought to do something, undertake a pursuit in service of his career. His ambition had kept him alive through the years, cushioned his landing from devastations such as the one moments ago.

The taste of heartbreak salty in his mouth, he went downstairs, the belly of his cavernous home swallowing him.

Tilly sat at the kitchen island, hunched over a laptop as her bugged eyes darted over a screen.

An army of credit cards lay strewn about. Brutus sat beside her, watching videos on his phone.

Brian opened the fridge and took out a jug of orange juice, averting his eyes from the salad False Helen had mixed. Needed to get rid of that. Needed to show up for his daughter as a stable adult. "Morning, princess. What are you doing?"

Tilly jumped and yelped. "Ugh, you startled me." She knotted her face into a concerned wince. "What's wrong?"

"That obvious?" His voice was hoarse. He poured juice. Supposed he ought to heed his usual pre-show routine, rest his vocal chords for awhile then do some warmups. Head over to the venue tomorrow afternoon for meet and greet, sound check, and the rest of the rigmarole. Lock step, march through the motions, good toy solider. Joe would have been pleased.

"Yeah, you look like you got hit by a truck."

"Helen left for good." There, he said it. Spoke the truth. Didn't make him feel any better. He drank, seeking to drown his feelings in citrus sweetness. Didn't work. Perhaps he ought to drink a bottle of vodka. Who cared?

His daughter closed the laptop lid. "Bummer. I was starting to like her."

"Same. Well, correction. I already liked her. A lot."

"Sorry, Daddy. You wanna cancel your concert? We could binge on ice cream and watch sad movies."

"No. The show must go on. But I was thinking after this finale, perhaps we could make a change. Start over."

"What do you mean?"

He finished his juice and set the glass down. "You ever want to move back to the UK? Head up north, live on a farm like your grandparents do? Nothing but sheep and chickens and rolling green hills?"

Tilly scrunched her nose. "Hard pass. All of my friends are here, and no way am I leaving the country in the middle of senior year. You aren't selling that plan well at all."

He conjured a sad laugh. "I suppose not. I think I just need a dust-up."

She donned a mischievous smirk. "I *suppose* I'll allow you to chaperone the senior trip to Cancun if you want."

"Senior trip to Cancun. Is that why all of my cards are here?"

Her sheepish glance slid from the assortment of plastic rectangles to him. "Yeah. Can I go on the senior trip to Cancun?" Tilly fluttered thick false eyelashes.

Perhaps a vacation with his daughter would calm his spirit with familial bonding. He hadn't a clue how he'd keep a herd of teenagers out of trouble, though such a challenge might offer a learning experience and welcome distraction. Plus, Tilly had been so good overall, coping with recent madness. He owed her a nice present.

"Sure."

"Yay." She clapped. "Thank you. Which card has the highest limit?"

He pointed to the black one he'd planned to use for his and Helen's trip to the slopes or beach and tried to ignore the churn of his guts.

Tilly scooped it up and re-opened her computer, doing a little dance as she keyed in numbers. "Your girlfriend is the real deal, by the way. At first I thought she was annoying, but I think she's actually a superhero missing her cape."

He forced himself not to picture Helen. It was all still too soon, even as he transitioned into the zone of categorizing her as a person from his past. "How so?"

"Yesterday, she took charge. It was cool. I think she knows what she's doing, what she's talking about. It was just neat to watch was all. I dunno. I can't explain it, exactly."

A smile made of memories graced his lips. "Can you try?"

"It's like she doesn't take any shit. She took control of the situation even when everyone was resisting her, was all assertive without being bitchy. Just strong. It was cool. I never got to apologize for being bratty to her, either. Speaking of apologies, I'm sorry that I said that I hated you and that you suck and ruined my life. I didn't mean those things."

"A real boss lady," Brutus said.

Assertive and strong, competent and decisive. A real boss lady. That was his Helen. Sorrow amassed in Brian, dense and indigestible. He needed to exorcize this "his Helen" nonsense. "All is forgiven, darling. And Helen is something alright. One of a kind."

"So why did you let her get away?" Tilly's question forged a spike, with Brian a bubble headed to the point.

"I didn't let her get away. She decided she needed to leave, and she did."

"But you didn't tell her all of your feelings. All of the reasons you wanted her to stay."

He bristled, though his wise child was right. "I did. I tried."

"Not hard enough. You didn't *make* her stay."

"Well, I'm not in the habit of coercing women, and I wasn't about to beg."

"Nah, but what you did was worse. You pulled into your shell, didn't you? Let everything with Mom and Kris and all the rest get to you."

"I don't want to have this personal conversation with my teenage daughter. Besides, what's done is done."

Victory glimmered in her eyes. "Ah. So I am hands-down correct."

"I didn't say that."

"Sure you did, in your own words."

He grumbled. "Okay, out of the mouths of babes it is, I suppose. So what am I to do, sage little one?"

Tilly put her hand over her chest and affected a theatrical swoon. "Duh. You execute a grand gesture to win her back. Prove and profess your love in a sweeping declaration of performativity. Like John Cusack with his stereo thingy in that ancient movie. Or a romance novel."

He drummed his fingers on marbled granite. She made a solid case, and what was he if not a performance artist? Still, though, he had practical facts to grapple with. "It sounds good on paper, but it wouldn't work in practice."

Silence followed. He circled a hand, urging Tilly to counter his claim.

Instead, she keyed in the numbers of a different one of Brian's credit cards.

He narrowed his eyes at her.

With an innocent expression on her face, she said, "I need to collect my fee for counseling services rendered before offering more advice."

"Fine."

She clapped and clicked the track pad, completing some purchase. "Yay. And to your point, that's a total cop-out. You're afraid is all, afraid to fight for the person you love."

He flinched as Tilly skated near a tough truth, but fortunately she was so absorbed in online shopping she didn't catch the reaction on his face. "I'm not afraid. I'm wary."

She shrugged. "Same thing."

"It is not. Acting with caution is smart, self-protective. Acting out of fear, on the other hand, is a way of mitigating risks by shrinking one's world."

"And you don't see how the thought processes you described reflect the exact same sort of cowardice?"

He slid his juice glass back and forth.

"Look, all I'm saying is that we humans have two baseline motivations that drive our choices." She flipped open a palm. "One, fear. Fear is shrinking, as you said. Small, contracted, all about limits and boundaries and avoidance. Avoiding harm, risk, feeling."

Tilly presented her opposite, upturned hand. Two fans of long fingers hung in the air like balanced scales. "The other driving force is love. In stark contrast to fear, love is expansive. Opening, welcoming of possibilities. Heart, a big tent, accepting."

His daughter never ceased to surprise or amaze him. "Where did you learn all of this parlance?"

"We live in Los Angeles, Daddy, otherwise known as woo-woo central. So I dunno, I think a psychic on the Santa Monica boardwalk said it to me once. But it's insight, you know? It stuck with me. And speaking of woo-woo insights, I would have thought that Moonbeam Starchild, the crystal witch, would have imparted all of this hippie yoga wisdom to you already."

She had, in her own way, imparted spiritual wisdom to him. By showing him that he had the courage to love again.

"It's complicated." It wasn't. He was still in hiding, secreted away in self-created emotional witness protection. But it was time to leave.

Helen tried to tell him her feelings. Albeit in a terribly inopportune moment when he'd been hurting too badly to allow himself to absorb the message. But that didn't make his conduct right.

She'd been ready to open up, and he'd lacked the capacity to see past his own pain and meet her in a place of emotional honesty. If he could take back that moment, backtrack and allow himself to feel the entire array of things that surged through him before she'd left, their goodbye would have happened differently. She might have still left, but they would have parted with hearts unburdened.

"Tell her how you feel," Tilly said.

Brian never once faced a task so herculean. Especially now, since, thanks to his reactive behavior, he'd gone and broken what they'd shared. "I doubt she's still speaking to me."

"You're making this harder on yourself than it has to be. Get her to come to your show, and do something awesome onstage that sends a poignant message. Do you know how many of your fangirls would kill for attention like that? And since it will be authentic, we're talking high-impact wow factor. It's your area of expertise, and I'm certain you'll think of a better gesture than I will. But don't give up. I haven't seen you as happy as you were with your weird new girlfriend in a long, long time."

"She isn't weird. She's quirky and interesting and intelligent and—"

"My point, proven."

"You win." Brian hugged his daughter. The boniness of her bothered him, but he'd keep working on her health. At least she was home and safe, consumed by excitement about her senior trip.

She still smelled a bit like her baby blanket, and always would carry that residual aroma of scalp and powder, but he wasn't about to bring up her infancy like some sentimental slob. "You've gotten to be quite the sharp young woman."

Wiggling out of his embrace, she shrugged. "School is going better. I like my tutor."

Zero mention of modeling, a blessing he didn't dare jinx. "Wonderful news."

She slid him a sidelong glance. "I'm not going anywhere rural, ever, but maybe I'll reconsider college. Tour some places around the country. New York, Colorado, Minnesota."

Mention of the last location, though she spoke the state name casually, sent a jumpy sensation skittering over his torso.

Time to connect with Helen and grovel before he lost her for good. Screw this stupid curse. So what if she'd cursed him with witchcraft, so what if some demon she conjured was sharpening fangs at this very moment, eager to drag him to hell.

They'd manage. As a team, they'd not only manage. They'd prevail.

Brian kissed his daughter on the cheek and returned to his bedroom. He grabbed his mobile and was preparing his mea culpa when the sight of a staggering number of missed calls stunned him.

The number eighty-seven sat in the upper-right hand corner of the green phone icon.

He staggered backward, reeling from despair. Something awful had happened to someone, his mum or dad or brother Alan, or to Grandmother or one of the boys in the band.

Upon clicking on the square, cooling relief and a vortex of concern competed. Most of the calls were from Jonnie, with a smattering of others showing Thom's and Jonas's phone numbers.

Okay. An industry matter. He could cope. Mini-crises exploded in his professional world on a semi-regular basis. Such was expected in a field stocked with massive egos, bigger money, and hot-blooded artists with megawatt dreams.

He sat on his bed and rang his best mate.

Jonnie answered after one ring. "Are you sitting down?"

"Yes, why?"

"Joe Clyde died last night. They're listing the official cause of death as suicide, but I'm not buying it."

Vertigo contracted and expanded Brian's perception. Had the termination driven Fyre's former manager to suicide? "Why not?"

"The circumstances had ritualistic overtones."

TWENTY-ONE

HELEN'S TEENAGE YEARS THUNDERED IN, BATHED IN HORMONES AND wearing nihilism like cheap stilettos.

Her wardrobe of facile insights on life and love resulted from the embarrassingly immature error of mistaking depression for depth of intellect. During that bleak period, she'd cauterized her spiritual and psychic wounds with the mean tools of negativity and cynicism.

The concept of soul mates had been collateral damage, dismissed and derided as a prime example of the stupid nonsense concocted by the patriarchy to make women into docile sex objects. More capitalist malfeasance, an ideological arm of the wedding-industrial complex deploying flowery rhetoric to dupe needy girls into embracing their own submission and buying shit they didn't need.

See? Look at that profound socio-critical analysis.

But this was before she'd met someone who *got* her, who saw a truth so real yet so atrophied she'd succeeded in neglecting its existence. Before meeting Brian, Helen would have never entertained the notion that she had a male counterpart. Someone with whom she shared a rapport that testified to synergy being an actual thing. Someone with whom she could simply be, drop any and all pretenses, airs, and general fake bullshit.

Stretched on her couch while an inane reality show played on the television, she pulled a fleece blanket over her head and tried for another half-hour snatch of sleep. Soon beaten, she stood on stiff legs, scuzzy and piqued from insomnia and anxiety.

Brian's gifts to her—a bejeweled dream journal and a black gown complete with witchy bell sleeves—peeked out from a nest of white tissue paper in their opened box. She couldn't look at the present or she'd start crying.

She should not have gone back to Minneapolis like a spineless coward. The chiding criticism knocked around her brain on repeat.

But what was she supposed to do? She went to her kitchen and prepped the coffee maker. Wait around and chance it that she would kill Brian while under the possession of the hex-cloud? Hell no.

An oppressive blast of white sunlight spilled through her window as the pot belched and hissed. The time on her microwave read eight-fifty-six. Not too early to call Nerissa.

She and Brian might be broken up, but she hadn't *given* up on saving his life. Helen called the old witch.

"My poor child."

Helen rubbed morning crud out of her eyes and sent a silent prayer of thanks to the universe that, at least, she didn't need to endure Nerissa yelling at her about the spell. "I'm glad you aren't angry."

"Why would I be?"

"Because I didn't listen to you and I cast another Left Hand spell. And, lo and behold, it caused huge problems."

"You've learned, though."

Helen sloshed coffee into her travel mug and topped it with almond milk. "Too late, though."

"No, not too late. Come by my house. Bring everything relevant."

Was that hope she heard in Nerissa's voice? One way to find out. She gathered up the crystals and book, shoved them into her bag, and hustled out the door.

Clinging to the words "not too late," thin as dental floss but nonetheless material, she ran a red light on her way to the witch's home.

* * *

A CAT, SCRAGGLY WITH MISMATCHED EYES, JUMPED INTO HELEN'S LAP. As she petted its matted coat, it occurred to her that she and Nerissa sat in the exact same spots as they had during their first meeting. Though now, with Helen on the saggy sofa and Nerissa in the recliner across the coffee table, Helen was overcome with an acute sense of how she faced the witch as a different person.

She was humbled before magic, stripped bare. She'd done fantastical things, sure, proven her might to herself.

Helen fought for her home and won it—L&E was solvent. But the sacrifice had been mighty and come at a price.

She fell in love. Not desperation, grasping, clinging, or begging. Not what she'd felt when wheedling foster families. No, she'd felt true love. A bond with another person that touched the goodness she spoke of in her closing class meditation, the best of her seeing the best of him and vice versa. She'd felt it and lost it.

Not too late. Not too late. Helen fiddled with a stubby dreadlock on the cat's coat, a hard stump of hair rolling between her thumb and forefinger. "I'm sorry, Nerissa."

The elder looked on with gentle eyes. "For?"

"For not listening to you. For getting carried away."

A knowing grunt slipped from Nerissa's closed lips. "Lay all of your supplies between us."

Helen eased the cat off her and hauled her bag up from the floor. She set the grimoire on the surface of Nerissa's coffee table, followed by her stones. Crystals clattered onto scuffed wood stained a dramatic shade of ebony.

Chanting and muttering, Nerissa waved her hands over the assortment. "It's here."

Helen flinched and gulped a swig of java. Caffeine was required to deal with curses.

The old witch laughed. "Not that. Look at your talismans."

She scanned the cluttered table top, mouth opening as she spotted both clear crystals side by side. "Someone returned the other one to me on the sly."

"No, no. It made its way back to you."

Flush with a strange sense of gratitude, Helen picked up the see-through hunk and looked at it like an old friend. The crystal seemed to wink at her, self-aware and jaunty. "Why?"

Nerissa leaned back in her recliner, a faraway look crossing her lined face. "Crystals are sentient, dear. You know this. You've been in communication since the very beginning. So don't ask me. Tune in and query the stone yourself."

Helen clutched the piece of mineral in her palm, warming it with her body heat. Subtle vibrations traveled from the rock and into the creases underneath her knuckles. And yes, it communicated with her, through a subtle language that registered as imperceptible emotional adjustments in her body.

Like a slow, chill counterpoint to a wake-up call, the crystal talked in an intuitive pre-language a bit like telepathy. Not wanting to live in Joe's shrine, the stone came back to her in a series of tiny motions, drops and rolls and slips from a pocket.

"I'm thankful, but I'm not sure I understand."

"You understand your chakras, how they move up from the lowest levels to the seat of enlightenment. You've mastered the first six, so the seventh is ready for you."

"Thanks, but—"

"Is your beau safe? Yes, I saw him in my visions." Nerissa licked her lips. "Quite the looker."

"No, he isn't safe."

"Are you permitted to cast any more Left Hand spells?"

Helen stared at her lap. "No. No I am not."

"So you have your answers. Go." Nerissa made a shooing motion at the door.

"I don't think I have answers, actually. What am I supposed to do?"

A wistful expression from Nerissa. She stroked her braid. "Congratulations, you have just about mastered the craft of color magic, and the clear crystals are prepared to work in your service and do your bidding for the remainder of your days. I'm proud of you, coven daughter."

Helen managed a confused laugh. "I haven't done jack."

Nerissa shrugged. "Not while you sit here stalling."

"Message received." Helen scooped up her stuff. She had one more shot, and she'd take it. Sure, she might fail, but nothing beat a fail like a try. And while she was at it, she would try to convince Brian to give her one more chance.

Scratch try. Do or do not. Time to nix that "try" crap once and for all.

"Good girl. Before you go, know this. These morons will use every trick in the book, literally. They are messing with the sixth circle when they know not its caprice. But their hubris shall mold your advantage. None can harness the power of Sister Folly, and their appeal to chaos will spell their undoing. Especially when you counter with your Right Hand power. Show up and face them from a place of authenticity. Bring your purest self."

"Thank you. And speaking of, what's up with all of that? Folly and the sixth circle and all of the stuff they were saying about chaos born?"

Nerissa's eyes hardened. Helen shuddered. The mage in front of her had *seen* some shit.

"Never you mind, spirit born. And you must make me one final promise. Never, ever touch the energies of the sixth circle again. You are never to etch one or to utter the name of Folly or to evoke the chaos born. Never, ever."

Helen swallowed a dose of guilt along with the excess saliva in her mouth. "That why all of this happened to me and Brian in the first place, isn't it? Because I brought this Fo—you know who and her chaos into the mix without realizing it."

"Yes. I wish I could have told you more to warn you, but I didn't realize the extent of the Left Hand's fickleness and greed, how it operates even in the shadow realm of hexes. Your complete and total ineptitude with the Left Hand path wreaked havoc. In all of my days, I have never seen a witch more incompetent with the ways of the Left. But fortunately for you, though the elemental sister in question is quick to unleash her wrath, her impulsivity makes her weak and beatable with the proper tools. But we must never speak of this ever again. This talk ends here and now. Do I make myself clear?"

Complete and total ineptitude. Ouch, but fair enough. "Yes."

"That's 'yes, Mother Spirit' to you. While the elements are all of our cosmic sisters, those of us who master them are the coven mothers. We act as mentors to the next generation. To our daughters."

Helen stood up straighter, an invisible rope on the crown of her head pulling her confidence and self-esteem skyward. For the first time ever, the word mother sounded loving and right, like a big hug. "Yes, Mother Spirit."

"Good luck, child."

"I'll need luck?"

"All witches need luck. It's a force deserving of our reverence as much as any other. Twice as much for us spirit born."

"Gotcha. Gotcha Mother Spirit, I mean." Reunited with her full set of stones, Helen expedited her plan the second she landed on Nerissa's front stoop and the lock clicked behind her.

Clutching one of the clear crystals, she put herself into the trance state and pictured Brian's home, the bed where they'd made love. "Hold on tight, just for a little longer. I'm on my way, Brian."

* * *

THE RIDE SERVICE CAR PULLED UP ON THE LOS ANGELES CURB AND idled behind a chain of vehicles depositing concert-goers in front of the venue. Sure she could have teleported from Brian's mansion to the arena, but Helen bet an Uber would work out better than floating through the astral plane in search of the precise location and optimal entrance of a massive downtown LA performance center. Drivers had GPS, and traffic had been bearable.

Hey, sometimes luck and technology worked like magic.

"Thanks." Helen jumped out.

Throngs of people milled about, taking selfies and gathering into a line lengthening from an origin point at the doors. Cigarette smoke and perfume layered in with food and exhaust smells thickened balmy night breezes.

Guitar-heavy, recorded Fyre music blasted from a tent, mixing with ambient chatter from a crowd of fans. Electric blue lighting poured from the stadium interior, casting moving bodies in an upbeat glow apropos to the anticipatory pump of a sold-out event.

Pixelated images of the four band members standing below the band name, the day's date, and energy drink ads cycled across the front of a gigantic screen near the building's roof.

She held her hand to her forehead like a visor and scanned for her contact.

No ticket, no problem. Provided a certain rocker chick showed up at the rendezvous point. Yes, Helen could have called Brian, but she lacked the valuable commodity of time, and time would have been crucial to explain and apologize and otherwise have a meaningful phone conversation.

A young woman in a cheetah-print tube dress as tight as paint slipped through the crowd, turning heads as she sashayed in Helen's direction. The liquid nymph wore thigh-high black boots fit for a dominatrix, and purple streaks highlighted platinum hair sailing over bare shoulders.

Awesome. Stacy delivered on her promise. She said a silent prayer of thanks that Stacy's issues with Thom hadn't ruined the super fan's hobby of following Fyre around the country.

Helen stuck a hand in the air and waved, not caring how silly she looked. Go time.

Stacy broke into a trot and joined Helen on the sidewalk, narrowing eyes lined with a copious amount of kohl. "Okay, what is up with you? How did you get here so fast? Lisa texted that you stopped by the studio to pick up some stuff in the afternoon, and not even a direct flight to LAX is this efficient."

"It's a new airline. I'll explain later. How do we get backstage?"

Stacy laughed. "Someone's ready and raring to see Brian." She drew out her pronunciation of his name in a teasing, girly sing-song.

"You could say that."

Stacy grabbed Helen's hand and led her around the side of a building, stopping at a yawning entrance to an underground parking garage. A trio of bored-looking people in Fyre T-shirts and laminate passes stood around smoking.

"What up, Stace?" A man with tattoos on his face offered a friendly nod.

"Hey, Steve. This is my friend Helen. Who's working security tonight?"

Steve scratched his shaved head. "Uh, Ken, Misty, and Skeeter."

"Awesome. Catch you guys at the party later." Stacy pulled a fist down like a lever and guided Helen into the bowels of the concrete pit.

A limo, a semi trailer, and a black bus similar to the one Brian had exited from at the fair occupied parking spaces. A heavyset man unloaded the big rig, carrying a guitar the color of mint.

"Hey, Ken," Stacy called. "Can you hook up my friend and I?"

Without a word, Ken rummaged in a fanny pack and produced two stickers with the band name, date, and words "all access special guest" printed on them. He handed them over.

Helen followed Stacy's lead and stuck her pass on the front of her shirt. "Dang, girl, you have superpowers."

Stacy shrugged, her heels clattering like gunfire as the pair followed Ken through a door and into a cinderblock-walled corridor with dirty linoleum flooring. Pass-bearing staffers sprinted about, hauling equipment and pushing carts.

"I've got mad groupie skills at least."

Walking beside Stacy down the hall, Helen cringed before she could stop herself. Ugh. She needed to play it cool. Stacy was assisting her, big time.

Stacy slid Helen a sly look. "I mean, I know everyone on the tour and can get where I need to go with ease, perv. And besides, you'd be proud of me."

The women zigged and zagged, soon advancing upon a wide doorway. Beyond the entrance, a spotlight flickered across a punch bowl of stadium seating. Red chairs filled up with chattering people. Recorded music streamed over speakers. Helen's internal butterflies got more agitated with each step closer to the floor. Showtime, the moment of truth in more ways than one, awaited.

"I'm proud of your yoga practice, but I have a feeling that's not what you mean." At least talking to someone she knew provided welcome distraction and saved her from feeling alone and overwhelmed.

"Nah, I mean I'm taking a break from hookups with bands and roadies on their tours. I'm sick of being a freaking human sacrifice, offering my heart and body to the horny men of the music scene who couldn't give a wet fart about me or my feelings. So no more sex. From here on out, I'm only going to shows to hang with my girls, rock out, and have a good time."

Ooof. Human sacrifice. If only Stacy knew the gory extent.

Leaning against a wall, a buxom blonde in a red leather miniskirt chatted with a small group of scantily clad young women. She stuck a hand in the air. "Stacy."

Helen caught Stacy's fingers before she drifted off to join her people. "I am proud of you. For everything. I'll see you back at Light and Enlightened, okay? I'll talk with you about possible teacher training if I...*as soon as* I get home. I'm glad we've gotten to know each other over these few weeks."

Stacy squinted. "Are you okay?"

"Yeah." Helen blinked back tears. "Wish me luck."

Stacy pounced on Helen and squashed her in a massive hug fragrant with various products. "You've got this. Brian adores you, and he's a great guy. Really great. You wanna know a secret?"

"Sure."

Stacy broke away and backed up a few inches. Body glitter on her chest caught the light, giving her the aura of a coquettish fairy.

"About six months ago, a bunch of us were partying in a hotel suite. Thom ditched me to hang with these two new girls from Chicago, fake-ass groupies who weren't even fans of the music but wanted to star fuck their way to hotter Instagram followers. Whatever. Anyway. I was mad, so I went after Brian to get back at Thom. Brian was playing poker, and I sat on his lap and murmured all sexy in his ear that I'd suck his dick if he won the game. For incentive. You want to know what he did in return?"

"I suppose?"

"He had a roadie pull up a chair, and then he dealt me in. I sat next to him like an equal. Then we just talked, you know? And he asked me questions about myself and everything, got to know me. So I'm sitting there next to Brian Shepherd, the big kahuna himself, just stunned. Because he didn't want to use me for a blowjob. He didn't want the free sex. Didn't even talk down to me or make fun of me or mess with my head. He's one of the good ones. And we still talk now and then. He sent me an email with a link to an accounting school, cause he said it seemed like I was good with numbers. I never made a move on him after that, because I knew he deserved someone really great and special, a chick who could challenge him, who he could admire."

Stacy took Helen's hands. "He deserves you."

The final bit of assurance gave Helen the incentive to see the mission to the finish and reunite with her man. "Thank you, Stacy. Have an awesome night."

"I never told you the secret."

"Oh. Lay it on me."

Stacy leaned in and whispered, "This brainless groupie whore trounced all of those fuckers in Texas Hold 'Em. I walked away with over five thousand bucks."

She turned on her spike of a heel and strutted to her friends, leaving a cloud of candy-scented perfume in her wake.

In a sudden, monumental shift of atmosphere, background noise exploded into cheers.

The lights of the stage area fell to blackness, dark pierced only by a show of multicolor lasers as they flicked across whooping fan faces.

Screams tore through the air as the frenetic drum opening to a beloved Fyre hit from a few years ago blew down the hall like sonorous thunder across the ocean.

Helen ran to the action. She still wasn't quite sure she was doing, but she sure as hell wouldn't quit.

TWENTY-TWO

PANDEMONIUM, INSANITY. HELEN WAS IN COLLEGE THE LAST TIME she'd been to an arena concert and had forgotten about the sensory overload. From her front-row post on the floor, amplified guitars pumped through her blood.

Thom's bass beats trembled low in her belly as he swaggered back and forth across the stage, hair hanging over his eyes and cowboy hat topping his head. Fans pressed into her back, angling to get closer. Warm beer splashed her ankle, the space's palate a swirl of petroleum-tinged electronic smoke and all manner of human smells.

Alertness was key. A high-tech lighting grid hung from the ceiling. Jonas's wild hair swung, the drummer and his kit elevated on a riser while he thrashed out beats.

Fyre's legendary set prop, a gothic black carriage pulled by two maniacal carousel horses as large as elephants, hung suspended over the performers by webs of fat clear cables. The piece was massive. A death trap.

The longer she looked at it, the worse her willies got.

One horse, an orange stallion with a gaping mouth and a mane the color of flames, pulled the carriage toward hell.

The other, silvery and white, flew on seraphic Pegasus wings and tugged the operation to heaven.

She jerked her head around, aware in an acute sense of how packed and crowded the arena was. It wouldn't be hard to get people panicked and scurrying.

Her thoughts ping-ponged back to the horse and carriage. Were they made of fiberglass? Steel? Haunted by maddening intuition, dread without a referent, Helen squeezed her clear crystal from its pouch and stuck the charm in her pocket. Perhaps the sentient travelling mineral would offer direction in crunch time.

Music stopped. Fans went berserk. Lights blinked off, and darkness swallowed all.

Dread emerged from the far corners of her consciousness. Evil was coming for her. All she could do now was look for signs and trust her abilities.

A new light show, a color wheel of pastels hued pink and cerulean and sea foam, danced through the space in streaks as enchanting as the aurora borealis.

Darkness dropped again. Music ceased. People shouted and cheered, stomped feet, the pitch rising and rising. Helen went at her nails as her underarms sweated.

A spotlight blinked on, highlighting Brian. Wearing his stage uniform and the red guitar, he looked right at her, into her eyes, facing a crowd but seeing nobody but her.

Man, on any other occasion she would have mainlined that shit like heroin, the whole cliché of the rock star crush singling you out. But something was wrong, and it would not serve the mission to surrender to swooning.

"It's been a long and wild ride, and I want to thank each and every one of you for your unfailing support and loyalty on this tour. The fans are our lifeblood, our backbone, and none of this would have ever been possible without you," Brian boomed into a microphone mounted on a stand.

The crowd erupted.

A lace bra flew on stage and landed at Brian's feet. Two more followed. Fans whistled.

Brian read off the sizes and brand names on the tags and tossed the undergarments back once he'd identified their owners. "You might miss having these."

She swooned a tad at the sight of his consideration. So humble, so appreciative, light years more evolved than the stereotype of the blasé, egotistical rock star regarding his admirers with disdain as he granted them the privilege of bearing witness to his talent.

Nope, he appreciated his fans and cared about them. Right down to women like Stacy, who were used to being treated like trash. On high alert, Helen combed for suspicious people, shady activity.

Brian leaned into his mic. Noise lulled, and obedient silence fell. "Sometimes when you meet someone, you see into their soul. Their body symbolizes their spirit in a certain auspicious synecdoche—part to whole, whole to part. And when you see into that soul, you see expanse. Infinity. The essence of the universe distilled but not diluted."

He tuned his guitar and played opening notes, an aching melody that echoed off of stadium seats in sensual, enchanting beats. Some low notes, some high, made up long dreamy riffs. The tune had a coaxing feel, circular and drifting. Very much the core Fyre sound.

People hoisted phones, their flashlight apps turning the arena into a planetarium dome of electronic starlight.

"This one's for you, Helen Britney, my constellation of stars. I'm sorry. Forgive me."

"Aww," the crowd cooed.

"Forgive him, Helen Britney," a man several rows behind her yelled.

Helen mangled a hangnail until it bled. She'd never felt so helpless, so small, yet at the same time so cherished. Brian was the man for her. Every single cell in her body absorbed this absolute, unflappable truth.

To the tune of his instrument, Brian launched into lyrics, "Star in the night, webwork of heaven, your love it seduces the sky. Goddess incarnate, the way where you see me, your magic it takes me. Bewitched and beguiled, I turn to a child, no choice now but to comply." He sang a few versus, played a solo, and sang more.

"Now repeat," Brian told the crowd.

Everyone swayed in a back and forth rhythm, singing the chorus in their vocal hodgepodge.

He finished the song to a standing ovation, gaze trained on Helen. She laid a hand on her heart, vowing to fix their nightmare. She was close. She had to be.

Jonnie transitioned away from the ballad with an upbeat, gritty riff. They moved through a set of hits and radio anthems. High-energy vibes returned, clapping and cheers filled the seats.

Rock music rollicked, the guys giving it their all as they strutted one-by-one down a column extending into the crowd.

After two hours of music, Fyre played their biggest hit. A big-time song signaled the onset of the denouement, Helen's nerves frying in time. Her pulse became a war drum. Her senses sharpened, cataloguing as much as possible. A pink Harley Davidson shirt. Reporters aiming black cameras as big as old-fashioned boom boxes, recording the action. Asymmetrical golden zippers slashing the legs of Jonnie's tight leather pants.

A flash of movement offstage. Golden head. But when she blinked and looked again, the figure was gone.

Guitars and drums reached a frenetic pitch, grinding as the musical number raced to a crazed climax. A spray of pyrotechnic jets as blue as the flames on a gas stove erupted near the front of the stage, warming Helen's face. Fellow front row spectators squealed and jumped back.

Brian attacked his red instrument, shredding away. He toggled the whammy bar, drawing out the notes. His pinky, sheathed in a brass tube, slid over the strings. Blues-y, quavering tunes dominated.

Near the back of the stage, the flames of six tangerine geysers burst. While the band played, more went off, forming a ring surrounding the performers. Sweat slipped down Helen's back.

"Fyre! Fyre! Fyre!" The chant filled the crowded arena, pagan and crazed, like something from *Wicker Man*. Helen's perception trembled, loopy from the surreal madness.

She floated out of her body, split, a buzz of flies assailing her ears. The clear crystal was hard in her pocket, pressing a pointed corner into the top of her thigh.

Amidst the pyrotechnic frenzy and bowled over by a sharp awareness as dour as it was stark, she locked eyes with the orange carousel horse and dropped into her trance state.

It's happening. She couldn't quite say yet what "it" was, but she needed to work with what she had. So, Icarus seeking the sun, she became a guided missile and propelled herself toward a crimson burn. She entered the flames, her lashes singeing. She focused every ounce of her energy on the feeling she wanted to bring to Brian. Safe. Protected.

But then she gasped, struggling for air in sucking breaths as she rejoined with her body as fast as she'd left it.

The stage was a structure fire of controlled arson. Explosions boomed into bonfires. A gigantic, thundering flame erupted, giving Brian a fiery wingspan spanning the stage floor.

Pyrotechnic fire shot from the horses' eye sockets. Red flames spewed out of the demon horse, and white blasted from the Pegasus.

Then came a massive snap.

A single scream set off a domino effect of vocal panic. The smoking set prop sagged toward the ground in stretching slow-motion, the upended bulk garish and out of place, a violating disarray.

Performers scrambled offstage as the disaster hit the ground with a biblical crash. Alarms blared, emergency siren howls mixing with shouts and cries in a cacophony so brutal she had to cover her ears to think.

Bodies darted in every direction, uncoordinated roaches scattering.

Red lights lit up the perimeter, blinking. Whistles blasted. Security guards performed crowd control. The stench of burning plastic rotted her lungs, seared her eyes.

Sprinklers released, dampening her face with mist.

And then she saw it. Out of the vacant socket of the crushed set prop, the demolished and broken horses crackling with residual sparks as they lay caved in to the elevated ground, slithered the phantom. The murky color of air pollution, her nemesis crawled from the dead eye like a tapeworm and slipped to the side, vanishing offstage.

Helen dashed in the direction of a barricade cordoning off the backstage area.

A guard grabbed her arm. "Evacuate to the nearest emergency exit," he shouted, echoing robotic instructions blasting out of loudspeakers.

She linked in with the crystal, blanked her mind, and teleported to the other side of the metal gate. "No can do."

He gaped, rubbing his eyes. "How did you do that?"

Amidst the onslaught of alarms and indoor rain, Helen raced down the corridor, tracking the fog monster. Better not call Brian's name and risk drawing attention to herself or him. But she didn't have time to waste on a blind hunt, either.

Helen ducked into a supply closet and, standing in the middle of piled speakers and amplifiers, visualized her target and tranced out.

In five seconds, she was astral and floating. She flew through the air, wiggling through jelly walls as she swam through the backstage bowels.

Nobody was around, they'd all evacuated. Classic distraction, basic bitch of a ruse.

An almost-noise as subtle as the musical hallucination of a remembered song sneaked in below the blasting screech tearing through the arena. No mistaking chanting. She followed it until it got louder, weaving through corridors and hallways and down staircases until she hovered at the threshold of a door the color of rust.

Ancient pipes bellied the ceiling, and water-stained concrete the color of old meat covered the floor. The alarm was muted down in this secret place, overtaken by the clunk and gurgle of some sort of boiler. Louder, though, was the chanting beyond the door. Choral, ritualistic, hauntingly familiar.

Steeling her resolve, Helen pushed herself through the barrier and confronted a horrible sight. Pentagram chalked in red on the dirt floor. Guts in the middle, trinkets positioned in the tapered corners of the star.

A man, face hidden by a gold mirror-mask, read from the same fat tome as the one from the storage locker. The weird language tumbled from his mouth. Two others chanted in unison.

Brian lay on a cot, tied down and unconscious. He was clothed, but his pants were disrupted enough to reveal the bruise on his hip. The monster hovered in the air above him, hissing.

Helen zapped herself into physical form and pointed at the innards on the floor. "Greetings, assholes. Stepping things up a notch with a little good old fashioned human sacrifice?"

The phantom snarled, revealing two ghastly rows of crooked fangs.

"I knew Clyde would be more use to us dead than alive," a masked man said. He gestured to the guy with the book. "Dispatch this stupid cunt once and for all, boss."

Gone was the incompetence, the bumbling idiocy. These guys *had* stepped it up a notch. They knew what they were doing now.

Book Man read. The others chanted, those same gurgling demon-sounds, the mystery and power behind it all frightening and awful.

The reader broke into English. "Sister Folly, send this enemy to suffer in the realm of the shadow ones and return our devil doll in her place. We command you to overtake this man so he may do our bidding."

Capillary networks of red webbing spread over the smoke being, stitching its amorphous shape into a body with contours and edges, form. Humanoid, but a few feet taller than the tallest man. Skin as red and glistening as a newborn mouse coated spindly arms and legs. Head bald, ears pointed, eyes pits of ink. The demonic, demented creature from her apartment vision descended upon Brian and knelt on his chest. It aimed knifelike claws at his mark.

"No!" Helen's scream was impotent, too late. She snapped into nothing.

Singing cicadas and croaking frogs woke her up from dreamless unconsciousness. She opened her eyes to gunmetal dusk. The soles of her shoes sank into sucking mud.

To her left, willow trees' drooping foliage wept into glinting, placid water, thick roots carving cubbyholes in the dirt. Helen walked along a soggy, untrodden path, bayou night air rich with brackish odors. A Chinese lantern of a yellow moon, full and bright and presenting its leaping rabbit, hung high in the sky.

Several feet ahead, faint rustling sounds fluttered.

"Welcome to your new home. It's awful, but you sort of get used to it. Not me, though. That's why we're gonna trade places." Helen's own voice spoke, and she turned in the sound's direction. The double leaned against a hefty tree trunk, a slinky evening gown the color of spun gold twinkling in the moonlight. Of course. The Golden Phase was underway. Not for long, though.

Helen pulled the clear crystal out of her pocket and pointed it at the clone. Energy poured from it, a glitter cloud made up of winking shades of honey and amber and vanilla ice cream laved in caramel. The heavenly light, humming and pleasant, oozed from the stone and hung in the air.

The double stepped closer. She poked the crystal with the tip of a finger, and the beautiful energy turned gray and fell to the dank ground as particles of ash. "My realm, my rules. I caught the song dedicated to you. Your boyfriend was quite the poet."

Helen's eyes watered at the stench of death breath. "Is."

"Nah. He's done. And so are you." A mean hand grabbed Helen's hair and bashed her head into the nearby tree.

Dazed and hurting, she blinked, fighting for consciousness.

The other woman dragged her a few feet and trudged into the swamp, pulling Helen behind by the hair. She fought in vain, cold water seeping up to her knees, her thighs. Something taut swam past, brushing her hip. She screamed.

"Atta girl. Get scared. This place is scary as fuck." The clone shoved her down.

Helen's head plunged under water. She rebelled against its fetid flavor, gagging and struggling until her lungs hurt. The double pulled her up, and she gasped, her world an upside-down of misery.

"It's always nighttime and always wet. There are venomous snakes and alligators and giant leeches and nowhere warm and dry to sleep."

"I can help you," Helen stammered, spitting out silt and algae. This miserable place was some self-created hell born of negative energy, she bet, and if granted a moment to concentrate she had an idea for how to transform it.

Changing base elements into refined ones was the essence of alchemy, and she could do it. Heal her own energy as she switched from Left to Right for good and elevate the clone's in the process. She clutched the crystal as tight as she could.

"God, you're dense. You're helping me by taking my place so I can go up and party with the dime store Satanists as they execute their Golden Phase."

Helen went back under and up again, dead leaves and soaked hair sticking to her face, her scalp in agony from the hard pull.

In the dark pit of despair, Helen felt the crystal, pure and good and tingling, in her palm. She knew its love, in her, along with Brian's. Helen focused everything she had, every ounce of her being, on the love in her heart.

A column of energy, soft white and shot through with golden slivers, charged through her body and burst from the crown of her head. In her, with her, and all around her. Pure love, expansive love, love for people and animals and everything that ever was or could be. She visualized a habitat of kindness, a place where intentions were kind and happiness reigned and no living thing had to suffer ever again. "I've got your Golden Phase right here."

The clone morphed into the monster up in the secret room, all claws and teeth, leathery red skin. "Don't you fucking dare! You will not interfere with the sacrifice. You will *not*."

An image from childhood registered in Helen's brain. The monster before her resembled the one Little Helen had imagined lived in her closet.

The thing about monsters. Helen's mother's voice spoke in her head, kind and clear and soothing. She pictured the woman, savored one of the few good memories of her from the time before she'd snapped.

Helen was four, perhaps, trembling under the covers and terrified of the dark.

Dolores sat on the bed, maternal and loving, looming large as a giantess and projecting comfort. In that rare moment, her unreliable and unstable mother was a goddess.

Monsters can only hurt us if we let them. If we choose to see the good, then that's what we will see. Don't notice the monsters. Choose not to see them, and concentrate on something beautiful instead. Like how much your mama loves you.

The bedtime monster never bothered Little Helen again, and a lesson from decades ago rang true at last. There was always—*always*—love to be found.

Even in the most hopeless places. Even in the butchered depths of her heart, in the wounds her mother and the foster families had inflicted, love could grow.

Forgive. All of it. "You're cancelled," Helen said.

Helen's skull cracked open without pain. Light spilled out of the cavity, overtaking the fiend with its glittering bronzes and sparkling snows and luscious hues the color of baked, spiced apples. Sparkly vines, golden ribbons of love, engulfed every inch of the monster's scarlet flesh.

The thing faded, magic encircling its red arms and legs. For a second she swore she caught an expression of peace on its hideous face.

The nasty swamp transformed to a resplendent tropical beach. As the force radiating from her crown chakra tapered to a trickle, a pod of pink dolphins broke the water's surface and romped.

She and her sister Maya spied dolphins during a Disneyland side trip to the Pacific Ocean the summer before their world crumbled. They'd huddled together on the sand, squealing, each looking through one lens of their shared binoculars. The dolphins, she figured, represented an auspicious sign of closure with the past. All was right in the world now. A wound had healed.

Well, almost all was right in her world. Time to get home to Brian.

"Don't forget about me." The doppelganger spoke.

Helen turned around.

On the frothy, lapping shoreline sat the clone. Aquamarine and mint green waves sailed past her bare shoulders, and hardened plaques of seaweed served as a tube top. Silver and blue scales dusted her skin, beginning mid-waist and increasing, ending in a fishtail. Two rows of gills pulsed on her neck. The doppelganger slapped her shiny fin into wet sand, grinning at it.

The women's eyes met.

"Dude. You turned me into a mermaid."

"Looks like it."

"We always wanted to be a mermaid."

"Yeah." Helen's intuition spoke. She'd lifted the hex, and Brian was alive. "We did."

Something beautiful came from the ugly and transmuted base energies into gold. Her shitty past afforded her magic and forgiveness grander than she'd ever dreamed. A phoenix rose from the ashes of Helen's defeats. Alchemy for the win.

The mermaid said, "I'll do my own thing here, you do yours back home. If we cross paths again, are we good?"

Now that the doppelganger was comfortable in her home environment, she wouldn't get up to mischief. "Yeah. We're good."

"Alright, well, I'm off to go search for a shipwreck or something." The mermaid turned around and floated into the ocean on her back.

"I better get going, too." Understatement of the century.

"'Kay. Happy witching."

"Happy mermaiding."

The other woman darted off and swam deep into rolling water until her shimmery tail blended in with the waves. A bit of an awkward goodbye, but as far as paranormal encounters went, she'd take awkward over some of the other alternatives any day of the week.

Time to haul ass back to Earth, save Brian, and resume living her best witch life. She squeezed her crystal and leapt into an oncoming wave. "Sister Water, please grant me safe passage through the astral farther."

TWENTY-THREE

HELEN'S WORLD SPUN AS SHE STRUGGLED TO FIND HER FOOTING. THE soles of her feet were on the floor, and her stomach turned in roiling nausea. She blinked until dizziness ceased whirling and her surroundings came into clear focus.

The pungent, sour stench of the sacrificial entrails grounded her with an overpowering blast. A new clamp of sickness gripped her belly, but she defeated the urge to puke.

Brian still lay bound on the cot but had worked his hands underneath it, where they moved in subtle yet sustained back and forth motions. He caught her gaze and nodded, and she nodded back. A few feet away from him, the three masked men stood hunched over their book, grumbling the ancient language in a tense, rushed tone while flipping pages.

"Hey!" One of the masked occultists shouted and charged Helen. "Where is he? What did you do with Master?"

Think fast. Helen pulled the clear crystal out of her pocket. "He's in here. Trapped forever."

As if tendering an acknowledgement, the stone pulsed with three phosphorescent bursts that reflected off of the cultist's golden mask in starburst shimmers. Cool. Silent, begrudging props to Master for the confirmation.

"Give that to me right now." The man grabbed Helen's wrist, his hold hard and mean.

A theory forming in her head, Helen ventured, "It won't do you any good. I'm the only one who can free him. I'm your little mist demon's *master* now."

The stone illuminated with the phosphorescent glow. Boo-yah. Her genie-type theory had to be right.

"Let Master out, or you will regret it." He wrenched her arm, causing a sharp pain to surge from elbow to fingertips, and pried at her fist. But Helen clenched the stone.

In her peripheral vision, something fell soft and slack to the floor. She slid a sidelong glance in the direction of the movement and swallowed a gasp. The top part of Brian's ropes lay beside the leg of the bed. He sat up and worked on the cords binding his ankles.

The other two captors remained engrossed in their book and didn't notice. Meaning Helen needed to keep distracting the third man until Brian broke free. She might even have a plan.

"Take off your mask." Helen spoke into the mirrored shield, addressing the reflection of her own face twisted in pain. Though hurting, she held control over her powers.

"Why?"

"Because I fucking said so. You want to see your master again? Do it."

He slid the mask to the top of his head. Hello, Elwell from the Denver research.

"Ah, shit," one of the others barked with a mixture of anger and frustration. "Bad move, buddy."

The other two must have noticed Brian breaking free, because they sprinted to him. Brian jumped off the gurney and kicked a length of rope to the floor as he got on his feet.

A sickening crunch of bone, flesh and plastic colliding assaulted Helen's ears. One of the occultists fell to the ground. A scuffle ensued, marked by a blend of male grunts and shouts in two distinct voices.

Brian had his captor in a headlock when Elwell put both hands around her neck and squeezed. "Release. Master. Now."

Instead, she locked in with his pale eyes and clicked hers to white. Relying on the same technique she'd used to subdue Joe, she pushed his essence from his body and stuck it on the ceiling. He let go of her neck and dropped his hands to his sides. She sucked down a cool, relieving breath.

Brian's struggle continued in thumps and thwacks, groans and snarls. Her head throbbed, eyelids begging to blink. She slipped and allowed her lids to fall for a second, and when they did Elwell's consciousness drifted down and hovered halfway between the ceiling and his body.

"Brian, how's it going? I'm losing him." She squinted and pressed her fingertips to her temples, massaging the site of burning tension.

Brian let go, and the man in his grasp sank to his knees, muttered gibberish, and flopped unconscious beside his pal.

In Brian's hand, a thin point of silver glimmered in the dark room. He ran to Helen and jabbed a needle into Elwell's arm. Elwell's mouth gaped, and he hit the floor with a satisfying thud. Helen released his essence and rubbed her aching eyes.

The needle fell from Brian's grasp and landed on concrete with a clatter. He swept Helen into his arms, and she melted into him.

A phantom muscle made of stress and worry unclenched deep in her body. She clutched his life, his physicality. "You're okay."

They embraced in silence for a bit, breath and heartbeats. They had survived. Survived together.

"I love you, Helen." Brian caressed her scalp, his body against hers an anchor of home and stability and caring. His touch augmented every syllable of his admission.

"I love you, Brian." She poured the words, the sentiment, from an unlocked space deep within. Alignment emerged where things had once been skewed.

She didn't have to fight anymore. She could go with the flow, chill, float down that elusive lazy river of peace. Love Brian, and love herself. Love life.

Because, with Brian, she had found love in a hopeless place.

She kissed his chin and stepped back. He cradled her face in both hands.

"You," he whispered into her hair in a voice low and reverent. "You saved my life. Again. And you came back to me. I thought you were gone."

"No way. Not gonna let the bastards get me down. How did they get you in here?"

"Someone came up from behind me and stuck me with some drug during the evacuation. I blacked out, then I woke up in here, tied down. The crap they injected me with sure came in handy."

"What do you want to do about them?" Helen glanced askance at the passed-out cultists.

"Call the authorities. I'm guessing this trio is only the beginning, and that their group has plenty of secrets ready to be exposed."

"Let's get out of here."

"You don't have to tell me twice."

They bolted from the chamber and down a hall. Outside, a sea of evacuees stood on the sidewalks and in the parking lot, some with phones pressed to ears.

Stacy and a few other women hung around by a pickup, talking with some security guards and the crew people who'd been smoking by the garage. Fyre music played through the truck's rolled-down window, radio tunes livening up the night with a makeshift show.

Sirens wailed emergency whoops as police cars and fire trucks arrived. In short order, cops and firefighters hopped out of their vehicles and jogged into the arena, several of them retracing the steps Brian and Helen crossed on their route to the exit.

In a flurry of calls and texts, Brian checked in with his bandmates and Tilly. Everyone was okay. From the looks of things, they didn't need to tip anyone off about what awaited them in the secret room. The first responders would find the aftermath of the thwarted ritual and go from there.

"I'm fine. Going to leave town for a bit, mate," Brian told someone on the other line. "Gather up Tilly and take a break. A vacation. I'll see the three of you in a few months."

After he hung up, Helen took his hand. "Where are you going?"

He met her gaze, wrapping her with tenderness. Red and blue lights from the cruisers skittered over his face, heightening dramatic effect. "If it's alright, I'd like to spend some time in Minneapolis with you. Get to know your home."

"Brian?"

"Yes, my love?"

"Wherever we go, wherever we are, will be my home. As long as you're with me."

"Likewise. Now how about we head to my place, gather up what we need, and go stay in a fancy hotel for the night before we set off to Minneapolis?"

"Make it so."

"Your wish is my command." He pushed a button on his phone, and in a minute a white Lexus pulled up. Brian ushered her inside with a hand on the small of her back, the chivalrous yet territorial gesture absolute perfection.

She snuggled into him, losing herself in the essence of her great love. Though she'd saved him, he'd saved her. And he would continue to protect her, and she him.

They were a unit, their bond forged in battle-tested steel. They'd gone to war together, fought for each other and for their love, and emerged from the trenches.

"You're granting wishes now? Don't give me any ideas." Helen nibbled his neck, enjoying his body but in no hurry to expedite the progression of their play. They had the rest of their lives ahead for sexy time.

"We still have some catching up to do," Brian said. He directed the car to his home, and the Lexus got rolling.

"True. Should I start, or do you want to?"

"You. Tell me some Helen Britney trivia."

"Let's see. Okay. I've tried to go vegan a few times, but I love cheese too much. My favorite move is *Young Adult*, I'm not a pet person, and I won't watch spectator sports because it makes me too antsy. Oh, and I can't cook for squat, but I have found some success with those meal kit services."

Brian played with her hair. "Why does watching sports make you antsy?"

They travelled down a stretch of Interstate. A muted, mellow song played on the car stereo, complementing the cabin's tasteful powder scent and enhancing the effects of hard-fought relaxation.

"I guess I feel self-conscious about sitting there on my butt, often eating something unhealthy like nachos, while watching others work out. Makes me feel guilty, like I should get off the couch and go play tennis."

He laughed, understated and toasty. "Fair."

"Your turn."

"I run six miles every morning, cook a mean green curry, and read every night before bed. And I can get behind *Young Adult*. It's rather brilliant, actually."

"Whoa. I thought everyone but me hated that movie. No love for the female anti-hero, yet people fell all over themselves for *Dexter* and *House*."

Brian plucked a fallen strand of her hair from her jeans, an endearing mammalian gesture of care. "I suppose I related to a theme of what I interpreted as writer's block. Though I'm glad to say I don't have that issue anymore. Thanks to you."

"You're sweet."

"I'm being honest."

"Stop it before I cry. Now give me a wacky anecdote about life on the road."

His good-natured murmur held decades of memories and stories, a treasure trove of Brian-related things she looked forward to learning bit by bit. "I have some choice cuts. What do you want to know?"

"Tell me the story of the weirdest person you've ever met on tour."

"I have it at my fingertips. You're in luck. So a bunch of us are playing poker in a hotel room one night, and this man strolls in like he's a crime boss. A real rough character, about seven feet tall with a black beard and size-fourteen motorcycle boots. He stank like an ashtray and had scars on his face. He sits down at the card table and starts talking himself up. Says he works in the black market as a mafia fixer, and that his main job is making guns disappear. Then he's on about about how he lived in Israel and trained in Krav Maga and has killed dozens of men. Etcetera."

"I call bullshit. An authentic mob goon wouldn't blab about it to strangers at the first opportunity."

"You'd think," Brian whispered in a theatrical voice. "But his eyes, Helen. They were as dead as doll eyes."

"So you let him win?"

"Hell no. I cleaned him out. He was rather daft, but terrifying at the same time. I made my bodyguard sleep in front of my door that night. In case What's-His-Name tried to break into my hotel room and kill me with his Krav Maga."

"If that was for real, wouldn't he have killed everyone at the card table with his Krav Maga and taken all of your money?"

"She's too smart. Yet another reason I love her."

Chit-chat and banter went on for awhile like this, and the more they talked, enjoyed an easy and looping rapport in the car, the deeper she fell in love with Brian. She learned about his early life on a rural farm in the English Midlands, how destabilizing it was for him to move to London at thirteen. He talked about his cold, unloving grandmother and his struggles to fit in at the elite school he attended to refine his musical talents. The story of how he met the other Fyre guys, and how the ragtag bunch of outsiders found themselves through friendship and music.

Brian started out on the violin and showed great academic promise, but to the disappointment of his teachers and grandmother, he dropped out of Cambridge after a year to focus on Fyre. He admitted to some regrets, but emphasized that he would not go back and live his life any other way if given the choice. He'd been shy and clumsy with girls ever since puberty and never quite took to the hedonistic groupie scene throbbing at the sweaty core of rock and roll. Sure, he tried to get into the parties because everyone was doing it, but figured out quickly that shallow sex and excess weren't his preference.

Helen told him her life story while he listened, attentive, reassuring her with nonverbal cues and touches.

The conversation reached a comfortable lull, at which point Brian broke into a delicious rendition of Fleetwood Mac's "Dreams." Every word in his rich, deep voice was heartfelt and trippy, the stuff of transcendental dreams.

While he sang of crystal visions, loneliness, and thunder happening only during the rain, Helen knew that she was exactly where she needed to be. Her dreams had come true.

She looked up at Brian. Though he was above her, height-wise, he looked up at her as well.

In that moment, tiny yet massive, the cosmos showered blessings upon Helen, and she allowed herself to receive them with gratitude.

She'd found not only her forever person on her crazy magical journey, she'd found her purpose. Her passion. Her place. She'd conquered her demons—figuratively *and* literally.

With her man beside her, it was time to get back to Minneapolis and run a rockin' business. Expand. Teach workshops. Be the best guide and mentor she could be.

For the first time in years, maybe ever, Helen looked forward to the future. Her world stretched before her, a meadow to skip through instead of a graveyard full of zombies ready to rip her flesh.

She didn't have to run from one unstable domicile to the next in search of that elusive home. She was there.

As if reading her, Brian leaned in and claimed her in the softest, sweetest, most swoon-worthy kiss.

Lost in a cloud of love and positivity and endless possibility, Helen gave thanks. To everyone and everything as she embraced her inner beauty.

Talk about awesome magic.

THE END

Thank you for reading! Did you enjoy?

Please Add Your Review! You can sign up for the City Owl Press newsletter to receive notice of all book releases!

And don't miss more paranormal romance like FORGOTTEN MAGIC by City Owl Author, Eden Butler. Turn the page for a sneak peek!

SNEAK PEEK OF FORGOTTEN MAGIC

Magic is elemental. It's a full-bodied thread in all that we are. To me, to all my folk—witches and wizards of every make and the other supernatural creatures that co-exist in our ley line-loving world—magic simply *is*.

It was magic that lived deep inside me, hidden beneath the wretch of who I'd been, of what I'd done ten years ago at age eighteen. My father would call me a hypocrite— if we were still talking. He'd tell me that keeping myself from the covens in New York and from my family back in Crimson Cove, keeping myself from the life he taught me to be proud of, was a coward's way.

I was a witch only when it served my purposes.

Like now, slipping inside the dreams of such a talented writer. My client, Ivanna Ride (pseudonym, of course), was the hottest thing in erotic romance. She outsold and out published even the most popular authors and she did it on her own. There was no major house working behind her. Just Ivanna, her clever English-nerd husband, and me, Janiver Benoit, graphic artist extraordinaire. Well, that might be pushing it. It was magic that made me extraordinary and it was my gifts that helped me slip inside Ivanna's mind and discover the theme, the vibe, the truly disturbing imagery she saw when she dreamt of her characters.

This time around it was Kjel, the 1050 A.D. Viking warrior in love with an enemy clan leader's daughter. Blood and war and lots of sex. That's what I had to make come to life on the cover of her book.

Walking inside Ivanna's mind was like taking a stroll through a Renaissance Fair—on acid. The mist around me as I stepped into her dream was thick, a clotting smell that stuck in the back of my throat and choked me with the heavy scent of lavender. It hung in my sinuses, made my dry mouth collect with saliva. But on the back of that scent was something I recognized only vaguely as sweat. In Ivanna's dreams, there was sex. It became apparent that's what she had in mind, literally, when her REM cycle kicked into high gear.

Kjel—or who I took for Kjel—stood barefoot atop a bear skin rug in a rugged stone hut, glaring down at some whimpering, silly girl who looked more turned on than frightened. She was the enemy's daughter knocking on the door of womanhood, looking at Kjel like she wanted him to guide her way through it.

With a shudder of sound and the shift of light, the scene changed and the small room with its dirt floor became a boudoir with fine, cerise linens and a massive four-poster bed. The girl's face transformed to mimic something like Ivanna's. At least, how she'd looked this afternoon when I listened to her babble on and on about the pending Kjel series and her vision for the rest of her books, her promo graphics, and the blog tours she wanted to organize.

I'd listened to her politely, nodding where appropriate as this mid-forties woman tucked strands of curly brown hair behind her ear. Damn. Was it petty of me to notice that there was gray flirting in those strands near her temples? She guzzled on an iced coffee as she talked, never once asking for my opinion or curious about what ideas might have come to me when I'd read the manuscript. That didn't bother me, though, not really. My clients typically didn't want to know what I thought. They just wanted to make sure I made magic happen on their covers and their promo materials.

Funny how close that was to the truth.

I'd listened to Ivanna for nearly an hour, sipping my own Venti English Breakfast Tea, more interested in the chipping black paint on my fingernails and the wadded napkin Ivanna had used to wipe her mouth. That would be the souvenir I'd take to give me access to her dreams.

Magic, no matter what fantasy authors or Renaissance vendors tell you, is just an old school name for the things mortals want proof of to believe. Everything we do has to be logical, must have an explanation.

It is true that there has to be basis for every spell or hex. There has to be something elemental that connects our target or, in my case, client, to the magic we twist. It isn't simply supernatural. It's dependent on the natural. Magic elevates it. That's why I needed Ivanna's napkin. It was something she'd held, something that she'd left a bit of herself behind on, and it was the element I needed to slip into her dreams.

But I didn't like doing it—dreamwalking. Not like this. It was an invasion that made me feel cheap and simple. Intruding into someone else's private dreams? Seeing the things they'd never freely admit to desiring? I was like some kind of perv trying to make my clients happy by copying their own imaginations.

Still, it paid the bills. So I stalked in the shadows in my client's dreamworld. Kjel and dream Ivanna were starting to go at it. Bleaching my eyeballs was the first order of business when I woke up, which needed to happen right now. I had work to do.

I started that slow awakening, the controlled transition that would bring me out of Ivanna's mind and back to the "real" world. It was a simple enough process—a little focus on my breathing, on the things around me. I drew upon a picture in my mind's eye of my tiny apartment, of myself lying in only a black tank and red boy shorts, my dark hair covering my face, tattoos and runes dotting around my ankles, thighs, up the side of one bicep. The black ink was shaped in ancient languages, looping around my arm, connected to a black and gray rose on my left shoulder.

Things were calm, my mind working effortlessly to bring me back safely, away from Ivanna's Viking wet dream and her saccharine world. I was nearly there, watching myself sleep, turn beneath my white sheets, knocking over an empty tumbler on my bedside table—not the bourbon, thank God—and then, the alert of a video chat on my laptop blasted across the room.

Jani! Jani! The alarming scream of my brother's voice shot through the slow retreat my mind made. Sam's voice became a grating, loud yelp that made my chest constrict as my heart sped.

Jani! Jani, for the gods' sake, wake up!

And I did, jerking from my sheets, sending my pillows shooting onto the floor and the thick gasp of air in my lungs coming out like a yelp.

"Shit!"

The bell alert from my laptop lying on the floor next to my bed kept ringing, that low, constant loop that announced an incoming video call. Sam hadn't actually spoken to me, but still had a way of scaring the hell out me, nineteen hundred miles away. My brother could call to me, unannounced, whenever he wanted, but especially when I was unconscious. The annoying sibling connection was a nuisance I'd never be rid of.

"Stupid, intrusive..." My laptop flopped against the mattress when I picked it up and jammed my finger on the surface to accept the call. I didn't bother letting my big brother explain a damn thing. "You asshole, I was in someone's dream."

"Well hey to you too, little sister."

A quick glance at my cell phone to cut off the insistent text I knew Sam had sent me and I caught the time. Shit, someone was probably dead.

"Who died?" My brother's small chuckle was the only thing that made me relax enough to leave the bed and tug on my jeans.

"No one yet, though I'm pretty close to killing your brother-in-law." My brother always blamed me when shit hit the fan, and from his tone, I'd guessed that this time the shit had slammed into the proverbial fan in buckets.

Still, that wasn't my fault. "Ronan is your brother-in-law too, Samedi."

"Yeah." The frustration was heavy in his voice at my using his full name. "Well Mai is your twin, *Janiver,* and since it's her husband that started all this shit, it should be you that gets us out of it."

Mai was younger than me by only four minutes, but somehow we were years apart. I always picked up the pieces when she let her world fall apart—like it was now, with her in the middle of a bad breakup with her lazy, perpetually cheating husband. Still, it wasn't my fight.

"You've got the wrong twin."

I cut Sam off from whatever excuse I knew he was going to use when he cleared his throat by shaking my head and reaching out to grab the bottle of bourbon that had been sitting on the table beside my bed. I took a deep pull on the bottle, despite the glare my brother gave me. "Ask Mai to work out this mess."

"She can't. She's gone off the rails."

That meant trouble. It was habit, something my twin did when she couldn't handle the messes she'd made for herself.

"What..." A small exhale and I readied for the bad news I suspected was coming. "What do you mean?"

"She's back at Papa's and won't come out of her room."

"*Circe help us.*"

The bourbon didn't burn when it went down, despite the long swig I took. My throat had grown numb to the sting of liquor a long damn time ago, and the small little noise of judgment Sam made got completely ignored. When you numb yourself in order to forget, something that had become one of my more practiced habits, you tend to get used to both the bite and the judgment, no matter where they come from.

Mai's hiding away—my twin's way of forgetting—wasn't the worst of the situation. Not by a long damn shot.

"She caught him with that same stripper from last year."

"The one with the pixie cut?"

"Yeah, whatever, but this time he didn't bother begging Mai not to kick him out." Sam leaned on his arm, rubbing the back of his neck. His complexion was darker than mine or Mai's, taking on more of our mother's Haitian creole features than our blue-eyed father's French, but like both me and Mai, Sam had full lips and hazel eyes. We were all a good mix of both our parents. "Papa thought giving Ronan a job would maybe keep that asshole from running off for weeks at a time." Sam looked tired, like he hadn't bothered with sleep in days. My stomach tightened at the thought, and I couldn't quite ignore the weight in my chest that settled there. My brother had enough to deal with. He didn't need Mai's jackass of a husband doubling up his anxiety.

"Bet that was pointless."

"You got no idea." Sam released one long exhale and scrubbed a hand against his fade at the back of his head. He'd abandoned the short afro he'd grown out the last time I saw him and looked more like himself. "He totally fucked us over."

"What do you mean? What happened?"

"If Papa hadn't let Ronan take care of so many clients when they came calling, none of this would have happened. He just botched up too many jobs, was too sloppy, and I was too busy to notice that his haplessness had become a serious problem."

The whole time he had been talking to me, Sam had kept looking at his cell phone. It wasn't like him to let a text distract him. The string of beeps coming from his phone was odd, but the expression on his face was almost funny. *Almost.*

"The whole damn town is talking about it. Papa says if we can't pull in a big client, our name will be ruined." Another heavy sigh and Sam threw down his cell. "Not to mention all the damn attention we've been getting from the mortals."

Watching Sam, seeing the tension bunching up his features, I suddenly realized that this conversation was the longest we'd had in a year. In the past, we simply fought all the time. Even after our mother died five years ago, we hadn't managed a civil conversation. But then last summer, his wife, Adele, and their unborn child died in a car crash. The kid that killed them had been confused, barely legal, and since their deaths Sam and my conversations had simply become short and to the point. But this was different.

"Has Ivy or his men been snooping around?" I'd held my breath after asking that question. Ivy Beckerman was Crimson Cove's chief of police. We all suspected he wouldn't blink twice if he caught any weres shifting into their animal forms or spirits haunting the edge of the cemetery, never mind any chance encounters with a wizard doing something beyond human comprehension. There was something about the man that made him different from the other mortals. They only saw what they wanted. But Ivy was smart, observant; he saw things that the others didn't. So far, though, he'd kept his questions to himself.

"No, not so much," Sam said, once again focusing on his phone when it beeped, offering only a glance my way when he spoke, "but he did come by asking who busted in the store window." Sam waited for that to make an impact.

"What the hell happened to the store window?"

"Some asshole pissed off that we hadn't done our best to hide whatever bullshit they didn't want the mortals to see, we think. Thanks to Ronan, we got a sledgehammer through the front window."

That was unnerving. My father had managed to keep up the façade of running a respectable antiques store for decades. It was a decent way to front his real business—making sure the mortals never caught wind that a good majority of the Cove's residents weren't mortal at all; Papa was what the supernatural community called a "fixer."

"How bad is it really, Sam?" That question came in front of a small, silent prayer that I could help my family from the comfort of my fifth-floor walkup in Brooklyn.

I should have known better.

Another of Sam's exhales came out slow, this one with a labored drag of frustration, maybe the small hint of defeat. "Carter Grant has pulled his coven's contract with us. He doesn't want to be involved in any accidents we can't quite cover up."

"Shit." That revelation warranted another swig and another disapproving shake of my brother's head. If the Grants, a founding family and one of the oldest covens—and the one family our ancestors had pledged fealty to generations before—cut ties with us, then things were about as bad as they could get.

"We've asked a couple of the other Finders to help out, Jani, but none are as good as you. Papa says you're our last resort."

Whatever I was ten years ago—Finder of Lost Things, twin of a mighty healer, daughter to a man who swept our lives away from mortal eyes—I'd packed up in a steamer trunk my father swindled from a Tulsa antiques dealer and hopped a bus to New York. I'd been eighteen and thought Crimson Cove had seen the back of me. I hated being wrong.

It probably was tearing Papa up to know Sam was going to ask me to come home. He'd always maintained that once you left, that was it. No need to drag up the past with a trip down memory lane. Besides, he'd always told me "nothing but heartache for you here, Janiver." But after the bomb my brother dropped, I had little choice.

"I'll take the red eye."

"About that, Jani..." Another alert. This time Sam read the message then immediately snapped his gaze back up to the screen. "You don't need to worry about getting a ticket." My brother swallowed, shifting his attention away from the camera like he'd rather do anything than explain himself.

Damn it. This definitely required more bourbon.

"Thing is, someone is coming for you."

"Who?"

"In a few minutes, actually."

"Samedi, who?"

"Should be there. Now."

"Son of a bitch."

Please don't let it be him, I prayed.

I wanted to handle this issue my family had and be done with it. I had no intention of *reconnecting*.

Please, please, don't let it be him.

"He was already in the city."

"What are you talking about, Sam?"

"Look, Jani, something happened, with the Elam."

The Elam? The talisman through which all the magic in Crimson Cove converged, which kept us hidden from mortal eyes and in check?

"Someone attacked and took it..." Someone had *stolen* it?

"You don't lead with *that?* My God, Sam..."

"I know...it's just... Look...we really, well, we tried finding anyone else to help find it, but shit, sis, you're the best and there is so little time and he was there in New York and..."

"Balls..." I said, already knowing what point my brother was skirting around.

This was bad. Very bad. No wonder my family was on the edge of panic. I emptied the bottle but kept it between my legs as Sam tried and failed to explain himself.

"I just hope you don't—"

Three loud drums of a knock on my door had me almost jumping out of my skin. The temperature in the room suddenly shifted, and on the other side of the door I picked up two signatures: elemental magic that identifies a witch or wizard like a thumbprint. Unbidden, my pulse started racing, and I found it hard to breathe.

"Jani..." Sam's warning was too little and way too late. Nothing would save him from the shit storm I'd level at him as soon as I landed back home.

"Not another damn word, big brother."

One of the bodies out in the hallway radiated heat and a familiar spicy, rich smell that made my mouth water.

"Jani...let me explain."

Sam's voice was rushed, muddled as I left the bed and stood in front of my door, my hand hovering over the handle. I didn't need to look through the peep hole to know who stood out in the hallway.

"Whoever stole the Elam used old magic. They needed an old bloodline to make the hex work." I squinted, looking over my shoulder toward the laptop as I twisted the handle, then didn't blink or breathe at all as my gaze lifted to see Bane Iles. He stood on the other side of the open door.

"Yeah," he said, as if he had been listening to our conversation. Just as shocking as his appearance at my door was the fact that his face was bruised, and there was a cut along his bottom lip —injuries that shouldn't be there at all. "And that blood was mine."

* * *

Don't stop now. Keep reading with your copy of FORGOTTEN MAGIC available now.

And visit www.amberkbryant.com to keep up with the latest news where you can subscribe to the newsletter for contests, giveaways, new releases, and more.

Don't miss more of the Coven Daughters series coming soon, and find more from Kat Turner at katturnerauthor.com

Until then, try FORGOTTEN MAGIC by City Owl Author, Eden Butler.

* * *

Bane Illes never smiled. He never spoke.

But each day, that brooding wizard gave Janiver Benoit a glance. And when she could not take another quiet stare, or the warmth that look sent over her skin, she took from Bane something he'd never give freely —a lingering, soul knocking kiss.

Ten years later, someone has stolen the one thing that keeps magic hidden from the mortals in Crimson Cove and only Janiver can recover it. But returning to her hometown means she'll have to face the past and all the secrets she left buried there, including the one person she promised herself she'd never see again.

The dangerous wizard that might make leaving Crimson Cove the last thing she wants to do.

* * *

Please sign up for the City Owl Press newsletter for chances to win special subscriber-only contests and giveaways as well as receiving information on upcoming releases and special excerpts.

All reviews are **welcome** and **appreciated**. Please consider leaving one on your favorite social media and book buying sites.

For books in the world of romance and speculative fiction that embody

Innovation, Creativity, and Affordability, check out City Owl Press at www.cityowlpress.com.

ACKNOWLEDGMENTS

It takes a village to write a novel, and I've been blessed with an outstanding community. This project would have never become a real book without all of the special people who have graced my orbit.

To my earliest readers, Eliza, Karyn, Marteeka, Vanessa, Ashley W., and Lena: Thank you for offering both encouragement and thoughtful and kind, yet honest, critique. I had so much work to do back in the days of Magical Thinking 1.0, and all of you helped me figure out the path forward.

A shout out to the Yahoo critique group, especially Margot, Nancy, and Ainsley. Your close reading and thoughtful input on chapters of early drafts helped me learn the fine art of revision and rewriting, and also the best practices for incorporating feedback.

Keith, Lorna, and Danielle, thank you for reading early drafts and talking through ideas with me. Renee Leigh, you were my first "real life" fiction writer friend, and our page swaps and chats over Mexican food gave me hope and encouragement when I dearly needed both.

I truly believe that there are special people who come to us in quite auspicious circumstances, magical synchronicity even. When I was feeling down, an email from Katie B. would arrive at the perfect moment to lift me up. Love you bunches, author sister, and I'll always hold that jade stone close!

I met numerous awesome authors during Pitch Wars whom I now consider to be dear friends. First and foremost, lots of love to Nadia. From tough love to support to brainstorming sessions in endless Twitter DMs, you are truly a rock star critique partner. I'm so thankful that we've gotten to hang out in real life, and I hope that we can attend another writing conference and stroll though an art museum again in the near future.

Huge thanks to Felicia for reading an early version of this during Pitch Wars and making me smile. You instilled in me a robust appreciation for the MST3000 style of critique! Lora, thank you for catching some zingers before I embarrassed myself, and thanks also to Brighton and Mary Ann. Jeni Chapelle saw directly into this manuscript's soul and walked me through a major fix up. Thank you, Jeni!

Thank you Luna for reading this manuscript (and the other one!). I can't wait to see our book beauties side-by-side! Renee, Reina, and Celia: your steadfast support has been a precious gift, and I'm so glad that we connected through the CP match. Michelle (and Felicia again!), thank you for reading over the series proposal and for your cheerleading. Speaking of awesome cheerleaders, thank you Evie, Lily, and Katrina.

To Tee Tate, my brilliant editor: you are amazing. I'm delighted that you love Brian like I do.

Lots of love to Barb for reading a later version of this book. Jaqueline, thank you for helping me out with that last-minute request, and for validating my decision to keep those darlings alive. I also owe a debt of gratitude to the 2020 Debuts and All the Kissing groups, as well as the City Owl Press team, for their steadfast support. Last but certainly not least, thank you to Mark for supporting my writing in countless, invaluable ways. Bricolage was the coolest name ever for a pop culture-themed bar, and I'll manage to slip that into another manuscript somewhere down the line. Love you!

ABOUT THE AUTHOR

Kat Turner writes urban fantasy, paranormal and contemporary romance, and domestic suspense. When not reading or writing, Kat works for a university, teaches yoga, and lives the mom life. She has two pet rats and too many plants, guards her gym time with her life, and is quite adept at picking up objects with her toes.

katturnerauthor.com

ABOUT THE PUBLISHER

City Owl Press is a cutting edge indie publishing company, bringing the world of romance and speculative fiction to discerning readers.

www.cityowlpress.com